The Legend of Dave the Villager

Villager

BOOKS 6–10

by Dave Villager

First Paperback Edition (October 2021)

Website: davethevillager.com
Email: davevillagerauthor@gmail.com

CONTENTS

Dave the Villager

BOOK 6

The Robot King

Dave the Villager

CHAPTER ONE
Future Dave

"Tell me about the future," said Carl. "Do I become rich? Do I get a mansion with a heated swimming pool?"

"No," said Future Dave. "You die."

"Oh," said Carl.

"You get torn apart by robot ocelots," said Future Dave. "I can still remember your screams."

"I wish I hadn't asked," said Carl.

"Hang on a second," said Dave, standing up, "this is ridiculous. How can you be me from the future? This doesn't make any sense. How did you go back in time?"

"With this," said Future Dave, taking out a purple orb from his pocket.

"That's the teleportation ender pearl thing," said Carl. "The one we took from Robo-Steve's chest."

"My team of scientists modified it so that it could teleport me through time," said Future Dave. "But it only had enough energy for one jump. I can't go back."

"Wait, I have a team of scientists in the future?" said Dave. "That's pretty cool."

"That's because you become the leader of the resistance," said Future Dave. "The resistance against the Robot King."

"Who's the Robot King?" asked Dave.

"You've met him before," said Future Dave. "Although when you first met him he went by a different name."

"Let me guess," said Carl. "Robo-Steve?"

"Yes," said Future Dave, sounding surprised. "How did you know?"

"Well we don't know that many robots," said Carl. "So it was pretty obvious."

Dave stood up and started to pace the room. All this time travel talk was hurting his head.

"So," said Dave, "what you're saying is that in the future, Robo-Steve changes his name and takes over the world?"

"Not in the future," said Future Dave. "It's already happening now. I wanted to arrive earlier in the past, but it would have put too much strain on the pearl. In your time—right now—the Robot King has already taken over Robotropolis. Or, as you probably know it, Villagertropolis."

"Wait," said Dave, "what about Herobrine? I thought if anyone was going to take over the world, it would be him."

"Oh he tried," said Future Dave. "There was a great war between Herobrine and the Robot King. The land was ravaged and many fell, but in the end the Robot King was victorious. In my time the world is a ruin, which is why I've come back to the past, to stop the Robot King before it's too late."

"So what can we do?" asked Dave.

"In three days time, the Robot King unleashes his robot army," said Future Dave. "They go forth from Robotropolis and march from village to town, taking over. We need to stop the invasion before it starts. We need to sneak into Robotropolis and assassinate the Robot King, before it's too late."

"Wow," said Carl, rolling his eyes, "when you say it like that you make it sound so easy."

CHAPTER TWO
Saving the Future

"Er, Sally," said Dave, "do you mind looking after Porkins for a few days? Carl and I just have an errand to run in Villagertropolis."

Future Dave had insisted that they tell as few people as possible about their mission, to stop word reaching Robo-Steve. Dave hated lying to Sally, but Future Dave was very insistent.

"Of course," said Sally, smiling. She was in the kitchen, making stew. "After what you three did for Greenleaf, it's the least I can do. Er, who's that by the way?"

Dave looked round and saw Future Dave standing in the doorway of the kitchen.

"Um, that's my uncle," said Dave. "My uncle... Dave."

"Pleased to meet you," said Sally to Future Dave. "So you're called Dave too? That must get a bit confusing."

"Sometimes," said Future Dave. "My lady, do you know where we can find horses?"

"We only have pigs in Greenleaf," said Sally, "but Little Block has horse stables. That's a village about half a day north from here. It's on the way to Villagertropolis."

"Thank you kindly," said Future Dave.

Before they left, Dave and Carl went to say goodbye to Porkins. The pigman was still fast asleep, healing up from when he'd lost his arm in the Nether.

"We'll see you soon, Porkins, I promise," said Dave. "Sally will look after you."

"Sorry again about your arm," said Carl. "But if it makes you feel any better, I've got no arms—so you still have one more than me."

Dave turned to Future Dave.

"Is he going to be alright?" Dave asked. "In the future, I mean."

"Oh yes," said Future Dave. "In the future Porkins becomes a great general in the war against the Robot King. His troops call him the One-Armed Pig."

"That's not a very nice nickname," said Carl.

"Porkins doesn't mind it," said Future Dave. "My Porkins, I mean. War makes men change, and no-one changes more than Porkins does. After the Robot King slays the last of the pigmen, the ones in Little Bacon, Porkins loses all hope. He becomes a fierce leader who shows the enemy no mercy."

Dave looked at Porkins as he slept. He couldn't imagine Porkins, the pink-faced pigman who always saw the good in everyone, becoming such a ruthless leader.

"What am I like in the future?" Carl asked. "You know, before the ocelots and the ripping apart."

Future Dave smiled.

"You and I remain good friends," he told Carl. "You're the number one fighter in my army, taking on scores of robots at a time, all by yourself. The men call you the Iron Creep."

"Don't you mean Iron *Creeper*?" asked Carl.

"No," said Future Dave.

"Iron Creep doesn't sound very nice," muttered Carl. "It makes me sound like a creep."

"But we can change all this, right?" Dave asked. "If we stop Robo-Steve now, the future will change."

"I hope so," said Future Dave. "It's the only hope we have. In my time, twenty years from now, the world is on the brink of ruin. Only a handful of mobs still exist; most have been turned into robots."

"So how did you end up time traveling back here?" Carl asked.

"The Robot King's forces had found our base," said Future

Dave. "They launched a final attack, sending a huge army against us. My scientists had been trying to make a time-travel device for years. The time pearl wasn't ready yet, but we had no choice. As the robots broke in and stormed the base, I used the time pearl to come here. Since it was unfinished, it couldn't survive the trip."

He held out the purple pearl again. Dave noticed that it was covered in cracks.

"So I'm stuck here, and I only get one chance to change the future," said Future Dave.

"Wait," said Dave rummaging in his pocket. He pulled out his own purple pearl, this one un-cracked and still glowing faintly. "I still have a working teleportation pearl. Can't you turn that into another time-travely thing?"

"I wouldn't know how," said Future Dave. "The scientists did the modifications to my pearl. I don't know exactly what they did."

"That's a shame," said Carl. "I always wanted to travel in time. I could go back to when I was six and my cousin stole my baked potato, and I could punch him in the nose."

Future Dave scowled.

"Carl, this is no time for jokes."

"I wasn't joking," said Carl.

"Come on," said Dave. "If we've only got three days, we ought to get a move on."

He put his hand on Porkins's forehead.

"See you soon," Dave said. "We'll be back before you know it."

"Unless we get killed by robots," said Carl.

"Yes," said Dave. "Thank you Carl. Unless we get killed by robots..."

CHAPTER THREE
Cool Weapons

Dave kitted himself out in a full set of diamond armor and Carl got back inside his iron golem suit. Dave offered to make Future Dave some armor, but he refused.

"I have something better than diamond," he said, opening his leather coat to reveal dark purple armor underneath. "Obsidian. The toughest armor there is. My scientists invented it."

"That is pretty cool," said Carl.

They had just left the village and were walking across a plains biome, and in the morning light Dave finally got a proper look at his future self.

Future Dave was twenty years older than Dave, but he looked even older than that. He had a thick gray beard covering most of his face, and lots of scars on his cheeks, from the many battles he'd fought in. A black eye patch covered his right eye.

He wore a brown leather coat that was so long that it almost dragged along the floor as he walked, and underneath the coat was his obsidian armor. He had a strange-looking sword stored in a scabbard on his back, as well as a bow and a quiver full of arrows. He had a trident as well, which looked like it was made of emerald.

"Come on then, Future Dave," said Carl. "Show us some of those cool future weapons you've got."

"I'm sure you'll see them in good time," said Future Dave. "If we get caught by the Robot King's forces we'll have plenty of fighting to do."

"Come ooooon," said Carl. "If you're gonna drag us along for this stupid quest, the least you can do is show us your cool weapons."

Future Dave grinned.

"I'd almost forgotten how annoying you could be, Carl," he said. "Ok, have a look at this."

He swung the green trident from his back, holding it out in front of him with both hands.

"The Trident of Emeros," said Future Dave. "An ancient weapon created by an ancient civilization of villagers. My troops found it while they were stationed at a desert pyramid."

"Come on," said Carl, "what can it do?"

"This," said Future Dave. He aimed the trident at a tree and a blast of green energy shot out of it, exploding the tree to bits.

"Wow!" said Carl.

"That was awesome!" said Dave.

Future Dave smiled.

"It's so nice to see happy faces for once," he said. "In the future, no-one has much to smile about."

Dave could see that Future Dave was starting to get sad, so he said:

"What about that bow?"

"Ah yes!" said Future Dave. He put the trident back in the sheath on his back, then pulled out the bow. It was twice as large as any bow Dave had ever seen, and was made of obsidian. Future Dave pulled an arrow from his quiver and notched it on the bow. The arrow head began to glow blue.

"Electro arrows," said Future Dave. "They have three times the range of a normal arrow and five times the power. Plus they can fire as both normal arrows..."

He fired the glowing blue arrow. It sped forward at super speed and went *thunk*, embedding itself into a tree.

"... or explosive arrows," Future Dave continued.

He pressed a button on the side of a second arrow, and the arrow head changed from glowing blue to glowing red. He fired the arrow at the tree and *BOOM*, it blew the tree to bits.

"Ok, that is really cool," said Carl. Dave had never seen the creeper so excited.

"And finally the sword," said Future Dave. He pulled it out from the scabbard. The sword was longer than a normal blade and needed to be held in two hands, but to Dave it just looked like a normal iron sword.

"Why did you save the boring one til last?" asked Carl.

"Sword... ACTIVATE!" said Future Dave. Suddenly the blade glowed a deep red color. It was hot too—Dave could feel the heat from where he was standing.

"Wooooow," said Carl.

"A redstone-powered inferno blade," said Future Dave. "The heat from the blade can cut through robots like butter."

"I don't suppose you brought spare weapons for us?" said Carl.

"Afraid not," grinned Future Dave.

"I wish I came from the future," said Carl miserably. "The weapons are so much cooler."

"I wish you could have seen what the scientists did to your iron suit," said Future Dave. "Over the years they kept making adjustments to it. By the end you could destroy an obsidian block with one punch, and you had blaster cannons attached to each arm."

"Wow," said Carl.

"Anyway," said Future Dave, "that's enough showing off. Let's get to Little Block and buy some horses. This road still exists in the future—after it goes through Little Block it should bring us directly to Robotropolis."

They continued to walk across the plains biome. The sun was shining brightly, and Future Dave kept grinning and holding his face up to soak up the sun.

"In the future the air is so thick with pollution that you rarely see the sun," he told them. "The Robot King's factories are always pumping out gas into the atmosphere. Plus, the war between Herobrine and the Robot King caused so much destruction that there isn't much plant life left."

"The future sounds a bit rubbish," said Carl.

"Oh it is," said Future Dave. "But we're going to change all that."

"What will happen to you after we change the future?" Dave asked.

"Well," said Future Dave, "if we stop the Robot King, there'll be no war, so I won't end up being sent back in time, so I should just disappear from your timeline. I'll reappear in my own timeline, twenty years from now, with no memory of any of this. At least, that's what my scientists thought."

"Man," said Carl, "time travel is complicated."

"Yes," said Future Dave. "That's why it's important to keep it simple and just remember the important bits. We defeat the Robot King, the war never happens, we save the future."

"Can I ask you some questions about the future?" said Dave. "I know that we're trying to change it, so things won't be exactly the same, but there might be some information you have that will be useful to us."

"Let me guess," said Future Dave, "you want to know how to defeat Herobrine?"

"Uh, yes," said Dave.

"Afraid I can't help you," said Future Dave. "I wasn't there when it happened. All I know is that there was a big battle outside the walls of Diamond City. The Robot King's army fought Herobrine's army, and eventually the two of them ended up fighting each other. The Robot King won, slaying Herobrine and winning the war."

Dave was disappointed. He had hoped that Future Dave might know what it would take to defeat Herobrine once and for all. From all that Dave had seen, it didn't look like Herobrine could be killed by any normal methods.

"I've got another question as well," said Dave, "but this one's a bit silly..."

"Go on," said Future Dave. "If I can help in any way, I'll be glad to. Your future is my future too, remember."

"Do I... I mean, do *you*... do we ever slay the ender dragon?"

For a moment Future Dave looked confused. And then he laughed, a big, booming laugh.

"The ender dragon!" he said. "I almost forgot! My gosh, that was why we set out on our adventure in the first place, wasn't it? That all seems so long ago now."

"So that's a no?" said Dave.

"Afraid not," said Future Dave. "Once the war with the robots broke out, I forgot all about the dragon. There were more important things to worry about."

"Oh," said Dave, "I guess that makes sense."

It seemed impossible to Dave that he could ever forget about his ender dragon quest. It was all he'd thought about for so long.

I'll never give up on my quest, he vowed to himself. *No matter what else happens, eventually I'll find my way to the ender dragon.*

"I've got a question about the future too," said Carl. "Do they still have baked potatoes? Because if they don't, I might as well give up right now."

CHAPTER FOUR
On the Road

It was early afternoon when they reached Little Block. Like Greenleaf, it was a small villager town with just a few wooden houses. But when they got there, Dave was surprised to see that the villagers there recognized him.

"Dave and Carl!" said a female villager in a red gown, who turned out to be the mayor. "It's an honor to see you again!"

Dave soon realized that the reason the villagers knew them was that they'd been down the pit in the Nether when Dave and the others had defeated Herobrine's forces. The mayor explained that she and the other villagers had been captured by zombie pigmen the night before they were due to join Dave's rebellion, and they had been taken by force to the pit.

"If it weren't for you, we'd all be zombies," said the mayor. "Is there anything we can do to repay you?"

"Er, you could lend us three horses," said Dave.

"No," said the mayor. "We won't lend you three horses, you can *have* three horses. The best horses in our stables."

The villagers brought out the horses. Unfortunately when Carl tried to mount his horse in his iron golem suit, he was so heavy that he almost broke the horse's back, so they decided to take two horses instead, and Carl would run alongside them.

"I don't get tired when using the suit," said Carl, "so I can run as much as I want. Still, it would have been nice to ride a horse."

So they set off: Dave and Future Dave riding on horses and Carl running in his iron golem suit. They must have looked quite a sight, Dave thought to himself: a villager, a future version of the same villager and a creeper wearing the body of an iron golem.

There were mountains in the distance, but the road they were following was taking them around the edge of the mountains instead of through them, Dave was pleased to see.

They rode until the sun went down, and then Dave built a small house out of the blocks in his bag, with enough room for three beds and a pen for the horses.

"Get some sleep," said Future Dave, climbing into his own bed. "We need to leave early tomorrow, as we've only got two days left."

"We could always ride through the night?" suggested Dave.

"No," said Future Dave. "As much as we might like to, we can't stay awake for three days straight. And besides, we're going to need all our strength to defeat the Robot King."

"How hard will he be to defeat?" Dave asked. "The last time we fought him, in the Cool Dude Battle Royale, he claimed his power levels were at one-thousand percent."

"Although then he went all weird and that pigman defeated him with a single arrow," said Carl.

"I don't know how powerful he'll be," said Future Dave. "In my time, twenty years from now, the Robot King has the power of a god. But that's because he's been updating his systems and making improvements to his body for so long. I think he'll be powerful now, but we should be able to defeat him. Especially with my advanced weapons."

"There's one more thing," said Dave. "the last time we met Robo-Steve... the Robot King... whatever you want to call him... he said he'd changed. He said the electricity had changed him and he begged us to save him."

Future Dave gave Dave a fierce stare.

"Dave, I know you mean well," he said, "but I need you to remember something important: we *must* destroy the Robot King. You have no idea how much destruction and misery his actions will cause if he's left alive. I've lost so many friends. You should have seen what those robot ocelots did to Carl. It makes me shudder to even think about it."

"Ok ok, we get the picture," said Carl, miserably. "Can you please stop talking about my horrific death?"

"Please," said Future Dave, "just remember how important this mission is. If we destroy the Robot King, his entire army will be defeated. They get their orders from him: once he's gone, the threat will be gone. And you can live out the rest of your life in peace and do whatever you want after that. You can go and find the ender dragon, just like you always dreamed."

"Ok," said Dave. "I understand."

But as he lay in bed that night his mind kept going back to Robo-Steve, and how helpless he'd looked.

"Please," Robo-Steve had begged them. *"Take me with you."*

If we'd taken him with us, maybe none of this would have happened, Dave thought. *Maybe we should have shown him mercy.*

But Dave knew better than most that it was useless to think about roads not traveled. What was done was done, and there was nothing he could do to change that.

CHAPTER FIVE
The Mountains

As soon as the sun began to rise, they set off again, following the path as it wound its way round the foot of the mountains.

They came round a corner and Future Dave suddenly thrust his hand up, signaling them to stop.

Dave and Carl came in closer.

"Robot soldiers up ahead," whispered Future Dave.

"Oh yeah," said Carl, squinting. The creeper had good eyes from living in dark caves for most of his life. "What shall we do, go and beat them up?"

"No," said Future Dave. "All the robots are connected to the Robot King. If even one of them sees us, he'll know we're here. We need to keep our approach a secret, or he'll send all his forces after us."

"How big an army does he have?" asked Dave. "He can't have that many troops. It's not that long since we last saw him."

"The Robot King has converted all the factories in the city to build his army," said Future Dave. "By the time he launches his attack, in two days time, he'll have over ten thousand soldiers."

"Ten *thousand?*" gasped Dave. "How can we ever defeat him?"

"I told you," said Future Dave. "You cut off the head of the creeper and the body dies."

"Hey!" said Carl.

"Sorry," said Future Dave. "I meant, if you slay the Robot King, his army will power down. That's why we must keep our presence a secret from him for as long as possible."

"So how do we get to Robo-Villagertropolis, or whatever it's called?" said Carl.

Future Dave looked up.

"We'll have to go through the mountains," he said.

Future Dave pulled out a compass from his pocket.

"I have this set up to point to north," he said. "If we follow it, we'll get to Robotropolis."

"I'll take your word for that," said Carl.

They began climbing up the mountain. The going was slow, finding a way up the blocks, and they soon realized that their horses were slowing them down rather than helping them.

"We'll have to release them, unfortunately," said Future Dave.

"Will they be ok?" asked Dave.

"There'll be fine," said Future Dave. "They'll find their way back home to Little Block easily."

So they said goodbye to the horses and let them go. As Future Dave had said, the horses ran off in the direction of Little Block, back down the road.

"Those horses are the sensible ones," said Carl. "They know to escape while they still can."

As they walked up the mountain the going got slower. There was snow up on the peaks, and it was starting to get cold.

"There are some llamas over there," said Dave, spotting a herd in the distance. He'd never seen a llama before, but he'd read about them. "We could tame them and ride them."

"It would take too long," said Future Dave.

"Climbing this mountain is taking too long," said Carl. "Even with my big iron legs."

"We need to find a route through the mountain," said Future Dave. "Keep your eye out for a cave entrance."

Soon they were so high up that when Dave looked round he could see for miles below them. He could see Little Block and Greenleaf in the distance, and the ocean beyond that: the same ocean that he, Carl and Porkins had crossed after the Cool Dude Battle Royale. It seemed so long ago now.

"I can see a cave," said Carl, "it's just up ahead."

Carl was right: up ahead there was a small gap in the mountain that led into darkness.

"Does anyone have any torches?" asked Carl.

"No need," said Future Dave. He pulled out his sword and said "sword activate!" and the blade lit up with red light.

CHAPTER SIX
The Cave

They entered the cave, with Future Dave's red sword lighting their way. The walls were dull and gray, but it was warmer in here than outside on the mountainside.

"You realize that sword's going to attract every mob for miles around," said Carl.

"Let them come," said Future Dave. "They don't stand a chance against all three of us."

Dave had to admit that his future self had a point. They had futuristic weapons and an iron golem suit on their side. What could go wrong?

As they got deeper into the cave, Dave saw deposits of various ores—gold, diamond, redstone and lapis lazuli—but he knew that now wasn't the time for mining. They were in too much of a rush.

On the way back to Greenleaf I'll do some mining, he thought. His resources were running a bit low, especially after creating so many weapons and pieces of armor for the battle against the zombie pigmen. Also it would be nice to just do some resource gathering, he thought. He, Carl and Porkins had got involved in so many big adventures recently that he needed a break. *I just want to punch a few trees and dig up some ore,* he thought to himself. *Is that too much to ask?*

"BUUUUURRR!!!!"

Dave was shaken from his thoughts by the sound of a zombie. The three of them turned around to see around ten zombies stumbling slowly towards them. Once that sight would have terrified Dave, but not now. Ten zombies was nothing to him, after fighting whole armies of zombie pigmen in the Nether.

"Stay back," Dave said to the zombies. "We don't want to fight you, but if you attack us we'll have no choice."

"Stupid villager," said a zombie. "We eat you now."

"No you won't," said Future Dave. Moving his hands as quick as lightning he pulled out his bow, strung a glowing arrow, pressed the button on the side of the arrow so the glowing light changed from blue to red, then fired it. The arrow exploded in the middle of the zombies, destroying them all and leaving only bits of rotted flesh behind.

"Nice," said Carl. "Can I borrow that sometime?"

"We could have convinced them to leave," Dave said to Future Dave.

"Dave, you need to stop thinking like that," said Future Dave. "The world is full of bad guys out to get you. You can show them mercy if you want, but they won't show you any back. It's kill or be killed."

"Or blow up or be blowed up," said Carl.

Future Dave laughed. "Carl gets it. Trust me, Dave, I was you once, remember? I know how you think. But being merciful only leads to trouble."

Dave said nothing, but he didn't feel comfortable with what his future self was saying. He didn't feel too bad about slaying zombies, but he would have at least liked to have given them a chance before slaying them all. Carl was proof that bad mobs could change their ways, just as Dave was proof that villagers could be more than just traders and farmers.

They walked onwards, past underground rivers and lakes of lava, going deeper and deeper into the caves, the ground sloping gradually downwards.

"Are we definitely going the right way?" asked Carl.

"Yes" said Future Dave, checking his compass. "We're still heading north. If we keep going, we'll eventually get to Robotropolis."

They were walking through a large cavern when suddenly they heard the clattering of bones. Coming out of the darkness was a skeleton.

"Skeletons, I hate these guys," said Carl. "Are you ok with us slaying skeletons, Dave? You're not worried about their feelings?"

"Ha ha," said Dave, rolling his eyes. "No, I have nothing against slaying skeletons."

"Good," said Future Dave. He fired a glowing blue arrow at the skeleton, hitting it right in the skull. The skeleton collapsed, and then *poof*, it was gone.

"You're not feeling too sad for the skeleton, are you Dave?" said Carl.

"No," snapped Dave. "Look, the difference with zombies is that they can talk."

"You didn't mind slaying drowned," said Carl.

"As far as I know, they don't talk," said Dave. "And even if they did, they were attacking us. I'll defend myself if I need to, but I'm not going to just slay every bad mob that I see. How would you feel if we just went around slaying every creeper we saw?"

"I... good point," said Carl.

"An enemy is an enemy," said Future Dave. "Better to strike first, in my experience. If there's even a chance that a mob is a threat, I don't hesitate to act. I don't care if it's a zombie, a creeper or even a villager."

"You've slain *villagers?*" said Dave.

"Only bad ones," said Future Dave. "In the war, some villagers and pillagers went over to the Robot King's side. When I fought them in battle, I didn't hesitate. If you're going to be a *true* hero, Dave, you have to put your doubts aside. A warrior must rid himself of doubt and turn himself into a weapon."

"Are you talking about being a warrior or being a hero?" asked Dave.

"There's no difference," said Future Dave. "If a warrior fights for what he believes in, he's a hero."

"Wait, what's that sound?" said Carl.

From all around the cavern came the sound of clattering and cracking bones.

"Sword, max brightness!" said Future Dave.

His red blade glowed even brighter, illuminating the whole cavern.

All around them were hundreds of skeletons, all holding bows. A few of the skeletons were riding skeleton horses and wearing iron helmets.

"Ok," said Future Dave, with a grin. "Now *this* is a proper fight."

CHAPTER SEVEN
Skeletons

Arrows came at them from all directions. Dave raised his shield, Carl tucked his head into his iron suit and Future Dave pulled out a small disk that lit up, creating a shield made of glowing red light. The three of them stood back to back, to block the storm of arrows.

"What are we going to do?" said Dave.

"Fight," said Future Dave. He threw his glowing shield; it span through the air, slicing through a group of the skeletons, cutting them in two before burying itself in the wall of the cave.

And so the battle began. Future Dave pulled out his trident and started firing blasts of green energy at the skeletons, each green explosion sending bits of broken bone scattering across the cavern; Carl charged into the skeletons, sending them flying, then started swinging at them with his iron arms, all while keeping his head safely tucked away to avoid the arrows; and Dave charged into the skeletons with his shield raised, shield in one hand and diamond sword in the other, swinging the blade at all the skeletons he could hit.

It was a new experience for Dave, fighting foes who could fire projectile weapons. He had to make sure that he was facing the skeletons at all times, never showing them his back. It was difficult though, as the skeletons were all round the room, firing at them from every angle.

Suddenly something struck Dave, plunging into his shoulder.

"Arrrgh!!!" he yelled. He almost fell to the floor, but somehow managed to stay on his feet.

If I fall over I'll be done for, he thought. *The skeletons will fill me full of so many arrows that I'll look like a pin cushion.*

So even though he had an arrow sticking out of his shoulder, Dave fought on. Every time he swung his sword a jolt of pain ran down his arm, but he kept going; pushing through the pain and continuing to fight.

There seemed to be an endless supply of skeletons, more and more of them appearing for every one that was slain, but eventually their numbers started thinning out. Future Dave finished the last of them off with a blast from his trident, blowing the skeletons to bits.

"Wow," said Carl. "Those bony idiots don't know when to give up."

"You both fought well," said Future Dave. "But we must keep moving."

"Can one of you help?" Dave asked. "I think I've got an arrow in my back."

"Ouch," said Carl. "That looks painful. You probably shouldn't pull it straight out."

Future Dave reached into his coat pocket, then handed Dave a bottle of red liquid.

"Potion of healing," he said. "Drink it all."

Dave took a swig from the bottle. It tasted disgusting.

"Keep drinking," said Future Dave.

Dave did as he was told. At first it felt like nothing was happening, but then his shoulder began to tingle. He looked round and saw the arrow being pushed out of his skin. Eventually it came out, landing on the floor. He ran his hand over the wound, but it had completely healed.

"Wow," said Dave. "Is that a potion from the future?"

"No," said Future Dave, "it's a pretty standard potion. You just know nothing about brewing. I should know—I used to be you."

Dave made a mental note to learn about brewing as soon as he could.

"Wait," said Carl, "did you both see that?"

"See what?" said Dave. Carl was looking down a passageway that looked, to Dave, like it was full of nothing but darkness.

"It was a creeper," said Carl. "It looked at us, then scampered off."

"Well if it's a creeper, can't you just ask it to leave us alone?" said Dave.

"You don't understand," said Carl. "It was a *blue* creeper."

Future Dave's face went pale.

"Oh no," he said.

"I don't understand," said Dave. "Are blue creepers different to green creepers?"

"Blue and green creepers are about as different as zombie villagers and villagers," said Carl. "Blue creepers are vicious animals. They can't talk, they move twice as fast as normal creepers and their explosions are much bigger."

"Plus, they hunt in packs," said Future Dave. "Keep your weapons ready, boys. You're going to need them."

CHAPTER EIGHT
Sneaking Through the Caves

Future Dave had decided that using his sword to light the way was too dangerous from now on.

"We don't want to advertise our presence to the blue creepers," he told them. "So from now on we'll have to trust in Carl's eyesight."

What that meant, Dave soon found out, was that they were going to be walking through the pitch black cave with no light. Since Carl could see in the dark he was at the front, leading them, but Dave and Future Dave could see nothing at all.

"Are you sure this is a good idea?" Dave whispered, as he stumbled through the darkness, his arms stretched out ahead of him to stop him bumping into anything.

"It's the only choice we have," Future Dave whispered back. "Trust me, we don't want to have to deal with blue creepers."

The blue creepers must be pretty dangerous if Future Dave didn't want to deal with them, Dave thought. Future Dave was one of the most powerful warriors Dave had ever seen, maybe up there with Steve, so if he was scared of something, it must be pretty scary.

"Where are you Carl?" Dave whispered. "Am I going the right way?"

"I'm here," said Carl. "Come on."

Dave had always hated the dark as a child, so this was all his worst fears come to life: wandering through a pitch black cave where monsters could jump out at him at any moment. He knew that Carl's eyes would see any mobs before they attacked, but Carl was only one creeper: he could only look one way at a time. What if a monster sneaked up on them from behind?

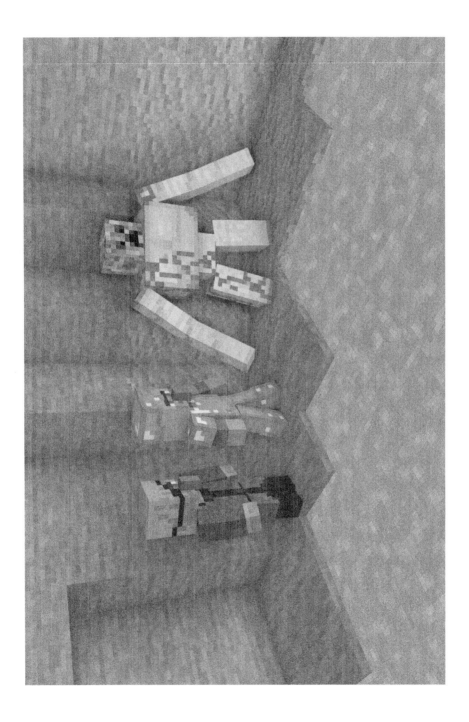

Suddenly Dave heard something: a deep, rumbling sound echoing around the walls of the cave. His blood went cold.

"W-what was that?" he said.

"Oh sorry," said Carl, "that was my belly. I'm dying for a baked potato."

To Dave's relief, the cave eventually began to get brighter.

"It must be daylight up ahead," he whispered.

"I don't think so," said Future Dave.

Future Dave was right. As they walked nearer to the light, Dave could see that it was coming from lava. They found themselves in a cavern with a lava lake in the middle. It reminded Dave of the cavern where he'd first met Porkins, and that made him sad.

I hope you're ok, Porkins, he thought to himself.

They stuck to the walls of the cavern, making their way carefully round the edge of the lake. There wasn't much room so they had to walk in single file. The lava was so close that Dave was sweating.

Dave prayed that none of the blue creepers turned up now. With lava on one side of them and the solid stone walls of the cavern on the other, they'd have nowhere to run to.

Thankfully, no blue creepers did turn up. They made it past the lava lake in one piece, without a mob in sight.

Future Dave checked his compass.

"We're still heading north," he said, "so it can't be much longer. I wish we knew how much time had passed, though. I've no idea if it's day or night."

"Then let's keep moving," said Dave. "We can't afford to risk losing any more time."

"Run!" Carl yelled.

Dave turned around just in time to see two blue creepers rushing towards them.

"Oh dear," he thought.

And then the creepers exploded.

CHAPTER NINE
Creepers!

Somehow, Dave was still alive.

He opened his eyes and saw that he, Carl and Future Dave were all inside a dome of red light. The exploding creepers had created a huge crater, but the explosions hadn't got through the red light force field.

"My holo-shield," said Future Dave. Dave noticed that he was holding the small disk that earlier had turned into the red shield. "It's strong, but I don't think it can take another hit like that."

"*HISSSSSSSS!!!!*"

Dave turned to see three more blue creepers running towards them.

Future Dave turned off the force field then, moving quicker than Dave would have thought possible, he took his bow from his quiver and fired a glowing blue arrow at one of the creepers.

KABOOM!!!!!

The creeper exploded in a blast of blue light, the explosion taking the other two creepers out as well.

Dave, Carl and Future Dave were alive, but the cavern was full of huge craters. The banks of the lava lake had been broken, and the lava was flowing across the room.

"More blue creepers!" Carl yelled.

He was right. Blue creepers were rushing at them from every side, hissing loudly. They seemed to care nothing for their own lives, some of them falling into the lava lake and exploding.

Dave took out his wooden bow, and he and Future Dave fired arrow after arrow at the creepers, each one exploding in a blast of blue light and tearing the cavern to shreds.

The tiny piece of ground they were standing on was almost surrounded by lava now, with nowhere to run to.

"This is just typical," said Carl. "Just when I start to think I could maybe become a hero, reality comes along and slaps me in the face."

"Well," said Dave, firing another arrow at a blue creeper. "At least it can't get any worse."

Suddenly they heard a terrible shriek from somewhere deep inside the caves.

"Oh no," said Carl.

"What is it?" said Dave.

"That's a queen," said Carl. "A blue creeper queen."

The cavern began to shake. *DOOM! DOOM! DOOM! DOOM!*

"Is that an earthquake?" said Dave.

"No," said Future Dave. "Those are footsteps."

The blue creepers continued to run at them, and Dave and Future Dave continued to shoot arrows at them, but behind the explosions Dave could hear the huge footsteps getting closer and closer.

"This isn't good," said Carl. "Not good at all!"

"Have you ever fought a blue creeper queen before?" Dave asked Future Dave.

"No," said Future Dave. "A squadron of my men ran into one

once though."

"What happened to them?" asked Dave.

"Nothing good," said Future Dave. "Let's just say, when they left the base they were a squadron of two-hundred, and when they came back home they were a squadron of two."

"What are we going to do?" whimpered Carl.

"We'll fight to the end," said Future Dave. "I'm not afraid to die in battle."

"Well I am," said Carl. "I always wanted to die doing what I loved best—eating baked potatoes and complaining about things."

This can't be how it ends, Dave thought desperately. Future Dave had fought so many battles for so many years that it seemed that he didn't know how to do anything but fight, and Carl was panicking so much that he wasn't going to be of any help.

Then it's up to me, thought Dave. *I have to get us out of this mess.*

He took a look at their surroundings, taking it all in. They were in a room full of lava, with blue creepers rushing at them from every angle, and some sort of huge creeper queen on the way. It didn't look good.

If they tried to escape into one of the tunnels that led out of the cavern, they'd either get blown to bits by the blue creepers, or they might bump into the creeper queen. If they dug down, they'd end up deeper inside the mountain, and might end up bumping into more blue creepers or falling into more lava. So, Dave reasoned, the only thing they could do was go up.

"Here," he said, reaching into his bag and handing Carl and Future Dave a handful of tiny blocks. "We need to go up."

"Go up?" said Future Dave. "What are you talking about? We need to fight!"

"No," said Dave. "We need to escape. Come on."

Dave jumped in the air, quickly placing a dirt block under his feet. Then he jumped in the air again, placing a wood block on top of the dirt one. Then he jumped in the air a third time, placing a cobblestone block on top of the wood one.

Dave looked down at Future Dave and Carl.

"Come on," he said. "Let's get out of here!"

Future Dave and Carl looked at each other, then started quickly building towers of their own. The three of them built their towers up and up, getting nearer and nearer to the roof of the cavern.

Below them the blue creepers rushed at the towers, exploding into them, but Dave, Carl and Future Dave were so high up now that the explosions couldn't reach them.

The three of them finally reached the roof of the ceiling.

"Do you two have pickaxes?" Dave asked them.

"No," said Carl. "I've only recently had arms, so this is all new to me."

Dave threw Carl a spare diamond pickaxe he had in his bag, and Carl caught it in his iron hand.

"I suppose you have some sort of super obsidian pickaxe?" Dave said to Future Dave.

"Actually," Future Dave grinned, "it's diamond. But it is a redstone-powered, automatic one."

He pulled out a diamond pickaxe, pressed a button on the side and the head of the pickaxe began to vibrate.

"Show off," smiled Dave.

The three of them were just about to start digging through the ceiling when *KRADOOOOOM*—one of the walls of the cavern blasted open below them, and a huge blue creature crawled out.

Dave looked down in horror as the biggest creeper he'd ever seen crawled across the cavern, its huge, tree-trunk sized legs splashing through the lava. As well as being much, much bigger than a normal blue creeper, it had four long legs that allowed it to move around like a crab, scuttling from side to side.

The creeper queen raised its head, looking up at Dave and the others, then it let out a terrible scream.

"*EIYYEEEEEE!!!!*"

It opened its mouth and a blast of blue fire blasted out. Future Dave quickly raised his shield, creating another red light barrier around them, but it kept flickering, the shield unable to to take the strain.

"Keep digging up!" Future Dave yelled. "I'll hold it off as long as I can!"

"What about you?" said Dave.

"If you defeat the Robot King, it won't matter about me," said Future Dave. "My past will change and I won't even be here. So go!"

Dave and Carl began digging upwards. Every time they broke a block above them they would jump up, placing another block underneath their feet. Carl's iron body was so big that he had to break two blocks above him each time.

Dave jumped up, placed another block underneath his feet and suddenly he was in complete darkness. The block below him had sealed him away from the cavern, so he couldn't see what was going on down there anymore. He could hear the faint sounds of the creeper queen screaming, but that was about it.

Don't worry Future Dave, Dave thought to himself. *We'll change the future, just like you wanted.*

Dave kept digging straight up, but then he began to get worried that he might dig up into another lava lake and would end up with lava pouring down on his head, so he started digging diagonally instead, his logic being that if lava started pouring down the slope towards him, he'd have time to put down a block and stop it.

Dave dug and dug until, finally, he broke a block and saw daylight shining down on him. It was so bright that he had to shield his eyes.

He climbed out of the tunnel and saw he was on the side of the mountain. Far below him a huge city stretched out into the distance. It was so big that it made Cool City look like a village.

"Wow," he said.

"Pretty impressive, huh?"

It was Carl. He was sitting on the side of the mountain in his iron golem suit.

"Carl, I'm so glad you're ok," said Dave happily.

"You know me, my life is nothing but a series of happy events," said Carl. "It's a shame about Future Dave though."

"Yeah," said Dave.

"I hope he gave that creeper queen a good fight," said Carl.

"I'm sure he did," said Dave. "I'm sure he did."

The sun was starting to go down, Dave noticed.

"Come on," he said to Carl, "let's build a shelter and get some sleep. We've got one day left. One day to stop Robo-Steve before he starts his war."

CHAPTER TEN
Bad Dreams

Porkins was dreaming of mushroom stew.

In his dream he was swimming in a huge lake of stew, drinking as much of it as he liked. His family were there and all of his old pigman friends.

"You know, sir," Porkins said to his father. "I had a terrible dream that you were all turned into zombies. Can you believe that? What a laugh!"

"That was no dream, dear boy," his father replied. Then Porkins noticed, to his horror, that his father's face had become green and rotten, the gray skull showing underneath. He turned round and all the other pigmen were rotting away too.

"Why didn't you save us, Porkins?" they were saying, as they started swimming after him. "Why did you let this happen to us?"

Porkins tried to swim away, but one of his arms was missing, and he kept going round in circles.

"Help!" he yelled, as he began to sink into the stew, "someone help me!"

Porkins sat up in bed in a dark room, his whole body dripping with sweat.

"What a nightmare," he gasped.

The door opened and Sally ran in, holding a torch.

"Porkins, you're awake!" she said. "Are you ok? I heard screaming."

"I... I had a horrible dream," he said. "I dreamed I lost my arm."

"Um, that wasn't a dream," said Sally nervously. "I'm sorry Porkins, but... you did lose an arm."

Porkins looked down and saw that she was telling the truth:

his right arm was gone, cut off at the shoulder.

"Oh gosh," he said sadly.

"I'll go and make you some stew," said Sally.

"No!" said Porkins. "Sorry… just anything but stew. Please."

After Sally had left the room, Porkins sat on the side of the bed, looking at the space where his arm had used to be. It all came back to him: the battle with the zombie pigman; a drop of the zombie potion landing on his arm; Dave cutting off his arm to stop him turning fully into a zombie.

The skin where his arm had been had healed up so perfectly that it almost looked like he'd never had an arm at all. *Sally must have used a healing potion,* Porkins thought. Back in the Nether, before Herobrine, Porkins's tribe had been great users of potion. Porkins couldn't brew much himself, but his mother had been a master potion maker. In the harsh world of the Nether, with ghasts and lava at every turn, there was always a need for more healing potion.

Sally came back in with some pumpkin pie. Porkins eagerly wolfed it down.

"How long has it been since the battle?" he asked Sally, his mouth full of pie.

"Two days," said Sally. "Most of the Greenleaf villagers are in the Nether now, helping to dismantle Herobrine's iron structures."

"Are the nether portals still active?" Porkins asked. He was thinking of the portal to Little Bacon.

"For now," said Sally. "Some of the villagers from other settlements are helping to dismantle Herobrine's buildings, so it helps if they all have an easy way to get to the Nether. But the plan is to eventually shut down the portals as well. It's just too easy for Herobrine, or another villain like him, to take over again if the portals are left standing."

"Then I must go," said Porkins. "I can't risk getting cut off from my fellow pigman. The only way I know how to get to Little Bacon is through the portals. Once the iron corridors are destroyed I'll have no way of knowing how to get there."

"You need rest," said Sally. "Why not wait until Dave and Carl get back?"

"Wait," said Porkins, "where are Dave and Carl?"

CHAPTER ELEVEN
The Neuro-Helmet

Dave and Carl were nearing the walls of Villagertropolis. They'd woken up at a first light, making their way down the mountain as quickly as they could, and now they were making their way through the fields and farms that surrounded the city.

There were huge fields of wheat and other crops, as well as fields of sheep, cows and pigs, all separated from each other by fences.

They were walking through a field of cows when Dave spotted something in the distance.

"Look," he whispered to Carl, "there's a farmhouse over there. And a farmer. We can ask him about the situation inside the city. He might even know a way we can sneak inside."

So they walked over to the farmhouse. The farmer was loading crates of carrots into a cart attached to the back of a horse, but there was something wrong, Dave thought.

"What's that stupid thing on his head?" Carl whispered.

The farmer was wearing an iron helmet, but there were two metal poles sticking out the top of it. On top of the metal poles were two red light bulbs that kept flashing.

There was something off about the farmer as well. As he packed the carrots into the cart, his face was completely expressionless, his eyes staring blankly into the distance.

"He looks like a weirdo," whispered Carl. "Let's keep going."

"Maybe that's how they dress in Villagertropolis," Dave whispered back. "That helmet could be a fashion item."

"Fashion is for losers," said Carl. "That's why creepers prefer to go around naked. Because we're cool."

Dave stepped forward.

"Hello there," he said to the villager. "A lovely day we're having, isn't it?"

The villager stopped packing the crates, and turned his head to look at Dave.

"Light levels are satisfactory for crop growth," said the villager, in a bored voice. "If rain levels continue to be as frequent as they have been in recent months, the harvest will continue to yield sufficient food to feed the population."

"Riiiight," said Dave.

Carl sidled up next to Dave.

"I think he might be a robot," Carl whispered,

"Negative," said the farmer. "My mob ID is villager."

"Then why are you speaking in that dumb way?" asked Carl.

"My cognitive functions are being improved by my neuro-helmet," The farmer said, pointing to his iron helmet. "It allows me to think logically, bypassing emotions and allowing me to live a more efficient life. Since wearing the helmet I have become fifty-three percent more efficient at farming."

"Did you put that helmet on of your own choice?" said Dave.

"Or was that Robo-Steve's doing?"

"If by Robo-Steve you are referring to the Robot King, then yes," said the villager. "The Robot King's soldiers forced me to wear the neuro-helmet, but since wearing it I have become more efficient and I no longer worry or feel sad, so these are all positives improvements."

"So this is how Robo-Steve takes over the world," said Dave to Carl. "He forced everyone to wear these helmets so he can control their brain."

"Negative," said the farmer. "My brain is not under direct control by the Robot King. The neuro-helmet simply allows me to think in a perfectly logical way. And using logic I have determined that the Robot King is the only leader who can make this world run at one-hundred percent efficiency."

"Ok, I've heard enough," said Carl, stepping forward in his iron golem suit. "Let's get that stupid thing off of his head."

"Wait," said Dave. "What if removing it scrambles his brain?"

"Come on," said Carl, "you've heard the way he talks. How much more scrambled can his brain get?"

Carl reached down and began to pull off the helmet. It was stuck onto the farmer's head tightly, but the farmer just stood there and let Carl try and remove it.

"What are you doing?" the farmer asked Carl in a bored voice. "Are you attempting to remove my neuro-helmet?"

Then *POP*, the helmet came off.

Suddenly the farmer's face began to change. His bored expression was gone, replaced by a look of horror.

"Oh thank goodness!" he said, running forward and hugging Carl's iron leg. Tears were running down his face. "Thank you, thank you, thank you!"

"Get off," said Carl. "I think I preferred you when you were all robotic."

"Can you tell us what happened?" Dave said to the farmer. "Can you tell us how Robo-Steve took over your city?"

"The Robot King, you mean?" said the farmer, wiping the tears from his eyes. "Aye, I will. But first I need a drink."

CHAPTER TWELVE
Tom the Farmer

The farmer poured Dave and Carl both a cup of warm milk.

"I'm Tom, by the way," said the farmer, sitting down opposite them at the table in the kitchen.

"Dave," said Dave.

"Carl," said Carl.

"Can you tell us about Robo-Steve's invasion?" asked Dave.

"Well, at first it was no invasion," said Tom. "The Robot King saved us. We'd been attacked by those undead pig people things. One day one of those purple portals appeared outside of our wall, and all the pig people poured out. They attacked our wall, and we attacked them back. We're only villagers, so we didn't know much about fighting, but some of our blacksmiths had built weapons for Steve before, so they knew how to make swords and armor.

"We fought back against the pigs as best we could, but we

were losing terribly. Then, from nowhere, an army of robots appeared. They all looked like robot Steves, with glowing red eyes. They defeated the pigs and saved the day.

"The trouble started later, when the leader of the robots, the Robot King, declared that he was in charge of the city now, and commanded everyone to wear one of his electronic helmet thingies. Anyone who refused was captured, and a helmet forced onto their head.

"I tried to run, but the robots caught me. They put the helmet on my head, and suddenly I didn't feel like running anymore. All my emotion—my anger at the robots, my love for my farm—it all disappeared. All I could think about was logic. I suddenly knew the most logical way to grow my crops, what to do to make sure my chickens produced the most eggs, all that stuff. Everyone else in the city is the same. They're all still working, but doing their jobs in the most logical way, without emotion."

"Like robots," said Carl.

"Aye, like robots," agreed Tom.

"It's too complicated to explain, but we need to get inside the city today," said Dave. "The Robot King is going to launch his invasion this afternoon. He's planning on taking over the whole world."

"Basically, do you know a secret way into Villagertropolis?" said Carl.

"Could we just dig underneath the wall and dig our way up when we're underneath the city?" said Dave.

"I'm afraid not," said Tom. "From what I hear, the Robot King has sensors underneath the whole city. If you try and dig through them you'll set off an alarm, and every robot in the place will be after you."

"There must be another way," said Dave.

"There is," said Tom. "But it's not pretty."

"Don't worry," said Carl. "Neither is Dave."

"In fact," said Tom, "it's downright ugly."

"So is Dave," said Carl.

"Ok," said Tom, "I'll show you."

CHAPTER THIRTEEN
The One-Armed Pig

"Where are you going?" Sally said, running after Porkins. He was walking down the road that led away from Greenleaf village, his rucksack slung over his shoulder.

"I need to make sure the chaps are ok," said Porkins. "If they're going to Villagertropolis they could be in danger. When I was in the Nether, spying on the witches in their cobblestone castle, I overheard that a robot army had taken over the city."

"Porkins," said Sally, "you've only got one arm!"

"I only need the one to hold a sword," said Porkins, with a grin.

"Ok," she said, "but I'm coming with you."

So Sally and Porkins set off for Little Block, planning to buy some horses to help them get to Villagertropolis.

"Are you sad about your arm?" Sally asked.

"I... I am a bit," said Porkins. "Mostly I'm sad that I'll never be able to fire a bow and arrow again. I was always better with a bow than I was with a sword, so I'm going to have to practice my sword technique."

"So you're still going to travel with Dave and Carl, doing hero stuff?" asked Sally.

"I don't know," said Porkins sadly. "I promised Dave that I'd stay with him to the end, to slay the ender dragon alongside him, but now that I know that there are more pigmen in the world, I don't know what to do. Should I join the chaps at Little Bacon, or stay with Dave and Carl?

"Anyway," he said, "I've been blabbing away about myself this whole time. How are you feeling? About Adam and all that?"

Sally sighed.

"If Adam came back now I wouldn't know whether to hug him or punch him in the face," she said. "I know he was only doing what he thought was best for me and him, but he betrayed the village. People were slain because of him. I don't think I can ever forgive him."

"Where do you think he went?" asked Porkins.

"I've no idea," said Sally. "He doesn't have any family elsewhere. I don't think he's even left the village before. I just hope he's ok, wherever he is."

"I'm sure he is," said Porkins. He didn't know what else to say.

CHAPTER FOURTEEN
Brown Water

Tom brought them to a nearby river. At first Dave couldn't figure out why, as the river wasn't flowing anywhere near the city, let alone through it, but then he saw an iron pipe sticking out of the side of the river, pumping brown sludge into it.

"Oh no," said Carl, "that's not what I think it is, is it?"

"It's the sewer," said Tom, with a grin. "It pumps all the waste from the city into the river. The river then carries it all the way to the sea."

"Why's the sewer water brown?" Carl asked, looking horrified.

"Sometimes it's best not to ask too many questions," said Tom.

So Dave and Carl went over to the sewer pipe. The entrance was covered in iron bars. They would be easy to break with an iron pickaxe, but to get the right angle, they'd have to get in the water, Dave realized.

"You go first," said Carl. "I'll stay with Tom and keep him company."

The water stank like crazy, but Dave knew they couldn't afford to waste any more time. He lowered himself gently into the river, making sure to keep his head above the water, then swam over to the pipe. The water coming out of the pipe was thick and disgusting, and it was all he could do not to throw up, but somehow Dave managed to hack away at the iron bars with his pickaxe and break them.

"Right," he called up at Carl, who was watching him from the riverbank. "You're gonna have to get in too now."

"Can't I just stay here with Tom?" said Carl. "I think I'd make a good farmer. I can milk the sheep, sheer the cows..."

"Carl!" said Dave.

"Ok, ok," moaned Carl. He lowered himself slowly into the river.

"Wait," said Tom, "will you be able to swim in that there iron suit?"

"Oh," said Carl, "I never thought of that."

Suddenly Carl lost his grip on the side of the riverbank, and went *SPLOOSH* into the water.

"Help!" he yelled, "I'm sinking!"

Carl disappeared below the water.

"Carl!" yelled Dave.

Suddenly Carl burst up from the water, grabbing onto the bottom of the sewer pipe.

"Bluurrrghh!!!" he spluttered. "It went in my mouth."

"Well, at least we've learned that iron golems can't float," said Dave, laughing.

"I wish you'd learn to shut up," said Carl.

Carl clambered into the sewer pipe, then pulled Dave up after him.

"Thank you for all your help," Dave said to Tom, who was watching them from the river bank.

"Yes, thank you for guiding us to this disgusting sewer," said Carl.

"Good luck, you two," said Tom. "Make sure to give that Robot King what for!"

"We will," promised Dave.

"Only... don't be too harsh on him."

Dave was surprised.

"How come?" he asked Tom.

"Well, the Robot King is bad, don't get me wrong," said Tom, "but he did defeat the pigmen. And he didn't actually slay anyone when he took over."

"He took over without killing anyone?" said Dave, amazed.

"I think so," said Tom. "Although taking over a city and putting all of its citizens under mind control is still pretty bad, I suppose."

"Well... we'll see what we can do," said Dave. "Goodbye Tom."

Dave and Carl began walking through the sewer. The smell was so bad that it made Dave's eyes water.

At first they had to wade through the disgusting brown water, but after a while the tunnel got wider and there was a walkway along the side, much to Dave and Carl's relief.

"You know, no matter what that farmer says, we need to destroy the Robot King," said Carl. "You heard what Future Dave said; All those terrible things that will happen if the Robot King takes over. I'll be honest with you, I don't really want to be torn apart by robot ocelots."

"I know," said Dave. "Don't worry. When the time comes, I'll do what I have to do."

CHAPTER FIFTEEN
Villagertropolis

"Look," said Dave. "There's a ladder up ahead."

"Thank goodness," said Carl. "I don't think I can stand being in this disgusting sewer a moment longer."

They'd been walking through the sewer for what seemed like hours. It was pitch black, so Dave had kept laying down torches, exhausting his coal supply.

Dave climbed up the ladder, Carl following behind him. The ladder led up a narrow vertical tunnel, and Dave could see a tiny square of daylight at the top.

"It's not easy climbing a ladder in an iron golem suit," Carl complained. "I can barely fit through this tunnel."

"Well it would be even harder if you weren't wearing it," said Dave. "You don't have any arms, remember."

"Oh yeah," said Carl.

They kept climbing, up and up and up, until Dave reached an iron trapdoor, with daylight shining down through it. He gave it a push, but it wouldn't budge.

"What's wrong?" Carl asked. "Why have you stopped?"

"This trap door... I can't get it to open," said Dave.

"Is there a switch nearby?" said Carl.

Dave felt around in the shadows. The walls of the tunnel were disgusting and slimy, and it made Dave feel sick to touch them, but eventually he found what he was looking for: a rectangular switch. He pressed it and the trapdoor swung open.

Dave peered out of the top of the trapdoor and saw that they were in the middle of a street, surrounded by huge iron skyscrapers. The buildings were huge: even taller than the ones in Cool City had been.

"I think the coast is clear," Dave whispered to Carl. It looked like there was no-one about.

The two of them clambered out of the trapdoor, then they stood in awe, looking up at the huge buildings.

"Where is everyone?" said Carl.

The streets were completely empty. And so *clean* as well. There was no rubbish, and all the buildings were spotless, their iron surfaces glistening in the sun.

But then Dave noticed that there *were* villagers walking around, but they were walking so silently that he hadn't even noticed them.

A villager in an apron was standing next to a food cart full of cooked chicken. Another villager came up to him, handed him a couple of emeralds and took a chicken—all without saying a word.

"They're all wearing those stupid helmets," said Carl.

He was right, Dave saw. Each villager was wearing a neuro helmet, the red lights on the top flashing occasionally.

It was really eerie, Dave thought, seeing so many people but hearing so little sound. He and Carl went up to one of the windows of a building and looked inside. It seemed to be a department store: store clerks were serving and customers were buying, but no-one was saying anything.

"Let's go and ask someone the way to Robo-Steve," said Carl. "Maybe he's got a palace or something."

"We're meant to be sneaking in," Dave reminded him.

"You heard what Tom the farmer said," said Carl. "The villagers aren't spying for Robo-Steve or connected to his mind, the helmets are just suppressing their emotions, making them all weird and logical. It's the robots we've got to watch out for, and I can't see any around here."

"Ok," said Dave. "Let's try it."

They walked up to the villager in the apron. He looked at them blankly.

"Um, hello," said Dave.

"Hello," said the villager.

"Do you know which way we should go to get to the Robot

King?" said Dave.

"Yes," said the villager.

"Well, can you tell us?" said Carl, sounding annoyed.

"I can tell you," said the villager.

"Well?!" said Carl.

"Well what?" replied the villager.

"I think I'm going to explode," muttered Carl. "Faulty fuse or not."

"Um... please tell us how to get to the Robot King," said Dave.

"Certainly," said the villager. "Go two blocks north, three blocks west and you will reach Hero's Square. There is a high probability that the Robot King will be there, as he is preparing his army for war."

"Thanks," said Dave.

"You're welcome," said the villager.

"Come on," Dave said to Carl, "it sounds like we've got no time to lose."

"Ok," said Carl, grinning, "there's something I've been waiting to try."

CHAPTER SIXTEEN
Robots!

CLANG! CLANG! CLANG!

Carl's heavy iron feet clanged across the cobblestone as he ran along the street, Dave riding on his shoulders.

"Are you sure this is a good idea?" said Dave. "I feel like I'm going to fall off!"

"You'll be fine," said Carl, "I can run faster than you, so this is the easiest way."

Carl was right, Dave had to admit. In his iron golem suit he could run as fast as a horse, and they were making speedy progress across the city. Dave was constantly amazed at the buildings in Villagertropolis: there were lots of huge skyscrapers, but also older-looking buildings made of brick and stone. There were parks and gardens and so many beautiful places, but it was still so *quiet*. All the villagers walking back and forth barely said a word to each other, all of them staring blankly as they went about their day-to-day business.

"We're nearly there I think," said Carl. "He said three blocks west, didn't he?"

"I think so," said Dave.

Then Dave saw something up ahead that made his heart jump.

"Stop!" he whispered to Carl.

Carl came to a stop.

"What is it?" he asked.

"Look, up ahead," said Dave. Ahead of them, on a street corner, was one of the midnight-blue robots they'd seen on the road. Even from a distance they could see its eyes glowing red.

"So what?" said Carl. "It's one robot. Let's go smash it."

"No," said Dave, "remember what future me said—the robots

are all connected to Robo-Steve. If one of them sees us, he'll know we're here."

Just then, the Robot turned its head and looked right at them. Its red eyes began to flash rapidly and it opened its mouth wide, the sound of a siren coming out of it.

"I think it's spotted us," said Dave.

"Really?" said Carl. "How can you tell?"

The robot started running towards them, its feet moving so quickly that they were a blur.

Suddenly other robots appeared too, coming out from alleyways and around street corners, all running at super speed. They all surrounded Dave and Carl, their eyes flashing. They all looked like robot versions of Steve, but made of shiny blue metal.

"INTRUDERS!" said the robot who'd first spotted them. "COME WITH US FOR NEURO-HELMET FITTING."

"I think we'll pass," said Carl. "Wearing a helmet would mess up my hair."

"ERROR DETECTED," said a robot. "YOU HAVE NO HAIR."

"Oh yeah," said Carl. "You're right."

And then WHAM, he slammed his huge iron arm into the robots, sending a group of them flying.

Dave jumped off of Carl's shoulders, pulling out his diamond sword. The robots ran at them and he slashed at them, cutting two of them in half.

The robots kept coming, and Dave and Carl kept fighting them off, Dave swinging at them with his sword and Carl with his iron golem arms. But for every robot they destroyed, more came to replace them. Dave could see hordes of robots appearing from every street and side street, all of them rushing towards him and Carl.

"There's too many of them," said Dave.

"Thank you, Captain Obvious," said Carl. "I can see that."

Dave tried to swing his sword hand but a robot grabbed his arm. Other robots were grabbing his legs, stopping him from moving. He could see Carl struggling as well, robots clinging onto his iron limbs, weighing him down.

Dave fell to the ground, dropping his diamond sword, lots of robot hands pinning him down.

"INTRUDERS CAPTURED," said one of the robots.

CHAPTER SEVENTEEN
Captured

Dave and Carl were marched through the city, surrounded by an army of blue robots.

"Where are you taking us?" he kept asking, even though he had already guessed the answer.

They're taking us to Robo-Steve, he thought miserably. He and Carl had let Future Dave down.

"Stupid robots," muttered Carl, as one of the robots gave him a push. "I'm going as fast as I can."

The robots had removed Carl from his iron golem suit, so now he was just a creeper again, with tiny legs. As far as Dave knew, they'd just left the suit behind in the street.

They came round a corner and in front of them was a huge plaza, surrounded by old buildings. In the middle of the plaza was a statue of Steve made of prismarine. It looked very old.

"Great, that's all I need," said Dave. "To be reminded of Steve. I bet he never gets captured like this."

"Probably not," said Carl. "We could sure do with his help right now, though."

They were marched across the plaza, to a huge building on the other side. It was made of polished granite, with a prismarine dome on the top. It looked like some sort of palace or government building, and Dave guessed that it must be where Robo-Steve was ruling from.

The robots brought them through the grand front entrance of the building, and they found themselves in a huge lobby with plush carpets and walls made of dark wooden planks. They were marched up some stairs, then some more stairs, until they found themselves in a grand room with a high ceiling and paintings all over the walls.

On a prismarine throne sat a golden Steve robot. He was wearing a diamond crown and had glowing purple eyes.

"Come on then, golden boy," Carl said to the robot. "Let's get this over with. Take us to your leader. Take us to Robo-Steve."

The gold robot stood up.

"I am Robo-Steve," he said. "Or at least I was—I call myself the *Robot King* now. Welcome villager, welcome creeper, I have been looking forward to seeing you again."

CHAPTER EIGHTEEN
How to Build a Ladder

Porkins and Sally were riding their horses through the mountains.

The two of them had gone to Little Block to buy the horses, but when they got there the villagers had recognized them from the battle in the Nether and given them the horses for free.

They'd ridden down the road to Villagertropolis, but as they'd got closer they had spotted some robot guards up ahead.

"Which way now?" Porkins had asked. "Will we have to go over the mountains?"

"No," Sally had replied. "I know another road, an old road. Hopefully the robots won't know about it."

Sally's "road" was a tiny track that wound its way through the mountains. It was an ancient road, according to Sally. The Old People has used it, many years ago, but now it had been neglected and left to ruin.

It was quicker than climbing across the mountains though, and Porkins and Sally had made good time. Before long they'd come out the other side of the mountains, and could see Villagertropolis.

Even though it was nearby, Sally had never seen Villagertropolis before, and had been amazed at how big it was.

So now Porkins and Sally were riding their horses through the fields towards the city walls.

"How are we going to get inside?" Sally asked Porkins. "It looks like the gates are shut."

"We'll find a quiet bit, one with no guards, and we'll build a ladder," said Porkins.

"Will you be alright climbing a ladder?" Sally asked. "You know, with your... arm."

Porkins hadn't even thought of that. He kept forgetting that he was now one arm short, but then he'd try and pull on the horse's reign or scratch his nose and he'd be reminded all over again.

This will take some getting used to, he thought sadly.

After passing several farmhouses and riding through fields of animals and fields of crops, they finally reached the city wall and climbed off of their horses.

Porkins put down a crafting table and pulled out some wood from his backpack.

"A ladder... a ladder," he muttered to himself. "It's been so long since I've made one that I've jolly well forgotten the recipe."

"Three sticks on either side and one in the middle row," said Sally.

"Ah yes, thank you!" said Porkins excitedly. He put a wood block down on the table, turning it into planks, then he put two planks blocks on the table, one on top of the other, and they turned to sticks. Then he placed the sticks down as Sally had suggested—three in the left column, one in the middle and three in the right column—and some ladders appeared.

"What-ho!" said Porkins. "Right, let's take a look inside the city, shall we?"

He placed a ladder block against the stone wall.

Immediately an alarm went off, blue lights flashing on the top of the wall.

"*INTRUDER ALERT!*" a robotic voice declared from some speakers on the wall. "*INTRUDER ALERT!*"

"Oh crumbs," said Porkins.

CHAPTER NINETEEN
The Robot King

"You're not Robo-Steve," said Carl. "Robo-Steve is all metal-looking. You're all gold-looking."

"When we last met my outer shell was badly damaged," said Robo-Steve. "So I decided to build myself a new body. From my research I have discovered that throughout history the colors gold and purple have often been associated with royalty, so when I declared myself king, I changed my outer casing to gold and changed the color of my eye bulbs to purple."

"You seem different," said Dave. "Last time we saw you, you said you'd changed. The electricity from the gas on Cool Island… did it do something to your brain?"

"That's correct," said Robo-Steve. "In my short life I have experienced many changes in my directives and personality. Recently I have been facing what you would call a personality crisis. I have been questioning who I am and what I want."

"So you've decided you want to put a crown on your head and take over the world," said Carl. "Very original."

"It was not a decision I came to easily," said Robo-Steve. "But after much thought, I decided that this is the most logical course of action."

"How can taking over the world be logical?" said Dave.

"I will explain," said Robo-Steve. "But first let me show you something."

He stood up and walked over to a door. Dave and Carl were forced to follow by the blue robot guards surrounding them.

"One thing first," said Robo-Steve, turning round, "even though we've met twice, I'm afraid I don't know your names."

"Dave," said Dave.

"Carl," said Carl.

"Thank you," said Robo-Steve.

Dave couldn't get over how different Robo-Steve was. The first time he'd met him, back in Snow Town, Robo-Steve had been a mindless machine who just did whatever Ripley, his creator, commanded. On Cool Island Robo-Steve had been a warrior without mercy, fighting for his life. But now he was polite and softly spoken. The difference was remarkable.

Robo-Steve led them into a huge room. It had obviously been used for important things in the past—the walls were covered in wood panels, there were fancy paintings on the walls and there was a huge fireplace—but now it was full of animals in pens.

He brought them over to a pen full of cows.

"Robot cows," said Robo-Steve. "They look just like the real thing."

He was right, thought Dave. If he hadn't been told they were robots, he would have had no idea. The cows were even eating grass—the floor inside their pen had been dug up and replaced with grass blocks.

"Well if they're just like real cows, what's the point?" asked Carl.

"They're seventy-five percent more efficient than normal cows," said Robo-Steve. "They produce milk at a faster rate than normal cows, and they produce more milk per amount of grass eaten. They're better than normal cows in every way."

Robo-Steve opened the fence, walked into the pen, then milked one of the cows over a bucket. When the bucket was full, he held it down to Carl.

"Here," said Robo-Steve. "Taste it."

"Um, no thanks," said Carl.

"I insist," said Robo-Steve. "You'll enjoy it, I promise."

Carl leaned forward and took a sip of milk.

"Hmm, doesn't taste too bad," he said. "I'd better take another sip, just to make sure.

He took another sip.

"Not bad," he said, licking his lips. "I guess I'll try another sip."

He took another, then another, then grabbed the bucket in his mouth and poured it all down his throat.

"WOW!" said Carl, milk all over his face.

"Did you like it?" Robo-Steve asked.

"I guess it was alright," muttered Carl. "Got any more?"

Robo-Steve got Carl another bucket of milk, then showed them around the room. According to Robo-Steve his robot horses were faster than regular horses, his robot sheep produced more wool than regular sheep and his robot wolves were twice as powerful and ten times more loyal than regular wolves.

"With robotics I can make improved versions of every mob," said Robo-Steve. "I'm even thinking of creating some robot ocelots."

"No!" said Carl. "I mean, er, no... that's not a good idea."

"Robot animals are one thing," said Dave. "But you've turned all the villagers into slaves."

"They're not slaves," said Robo-Steve, "they've just had the logical sections of their brains enhanced. I've made them *better*. They're more productive, more intelligent and their sadness levels keep going down. Villagertropolis is a much better city now than before I arrived, and soon I'll start improving the rest of the world."

Robo-Steve pressed a button on the back of his hand and one of his fingertips opened up, revealing a tiny microphone.

"Assemble the army in the plaza," he said into the microphone.

"Look," said Dave, "this is going to sound weird, but we... we met someone from the future."

"A time traveler?" said Robo-Steve. "How interesting. My research has shown me that most scientists believe time travel is impossible, so I would very much like to speak to this person."

"Well you can't," said Dave, "because he's... he's dead. But he came back from the future to warn us about you. This invasion you're about to start will cause twenty years of war. Many people will suffer. This perfect world you want to create, it's not going to happen."

Robo-Steve thought for a moment.

"That does not compute," he said. "I've run the calculations in my head thousands of times. Within a year, the whole world will be under my control, and every villager will wear a neuro-helmet."

"Look," said Dave, "I've learned that things rarely work out the way you plan. Look at the villager who created you, Ripley. He was a smart guy, but his plan to frame Steve went wrong. Ripley ended up dead and his village got destroyed."

"My father was indeed smart," said Robo-Steve, "although he didn't have the advantage of having a robot brain, like I do."

It felt weird to Dave to hear Robo-Steve call Ripley *father*, but he guessed it was true: Ripley had created Robo-Steve, so he was, in some sense, his dad.

Robo-Steve brought them to a small room full of sofas with a roaring fireplace.

"Sit," he told them. Dave and Carl sat. Four of the blue robot guards came in and stood in the corners of the room.

"This palace was where the mayor lived," said Robo-Steve. "After scanning her brain I found she was quite unsuited to being a mayor, so I've sent her to work in a bakery instead. Her brain function is perfectly suited for the skills needed to be a baker."

Robo-Steve sat down in an armchair.

"I was brought to Villagertropolis by a kind captain and his crew," said Robo-Steve, looking into the fire. "I was badly injured after our fight in the arena, and I wanted to get off of Cool Island."

Dave felt a pang of guilt. He, Carl and Porkins had left Robo-Steve in the arena, teleporting out as the electric gas had crept towards them, leaving the robot to his fate.

"As grateful as I was to the captain," continued Robo-Steve, "I couldn't help but notice how inefficient his crew were. The way they sailed the ship needed much improvement, in my opinion.

"Then when we arrived at Villagertropolis, the city was under attack by zombie pigmen. The villagers and their iron golems were doing a terrible job at fighting the pigmen, and instantly I could see hundreds of ways that they could be more efficient at fighting.

"I went to a factory near the docks and using my superior IQ I started assembling troops of my own, using whatever materials I could find. They were inferior to the robots I have now, but they did the job. My small army managed to defeat the much larger pigman army. The pigmen retreated back to the Nether.

"The villagers were overjoyed. It was a new experience for me, to have people look at me with admiration, rather than fear. I wanted to do something to help them. To improve their lives. So I invented the neuro-helmet. It would allow every one of them to maximize their productivity. As well as making them more logical, it would scan their brain and find out what they were best at, making sure that everyone did the job that they were most suited to.

"The people of Villagertropolis trusted me so much that they eagerly accepted the helmets. Overnight the city was transformed—the people were more productive and less unhappy. A few villagers resisted the helmets, but I made my robots force them to put one on. I knew it was for their own good.

"In a matter of hours my robots had rebuilt the damage the pigmen had done to the city. I closed the city gates, in case another attack came, and concentrated on making Villagertropolis the most efficient city in history. We would produce exactly the right amount of food, none of it going to waste, and everyone would have a job which best suited their talents. It was a paradise."

"Your idea of paradise sounds a lot different than mine," muttered Carl.

"However, I knew this perfect system couldn't last," continued Robo-Steve. "I knew that one day others would come. Maybe villagers from other settlements would feel that the villagers of Villagertropolis were being controlled, and would try to free them. I decided that the only logical course of action was to take over the world, turning every village, town and city into a paradise of logic and reason. There will be no more struggle, no more war, no-one going hungry. It will be an end to suffering."

"But there'll be no more fun, no love, no emotions," said Dave.

"You're turning everyone into mindless robots!"

"From what I have seen of emotions, they only lead to illogical decisions," said Robo-Steve.

Suddenly the door burst open and a robot came in. Like the others,this one looked like Steve, but he was made of red metal instead of blue.

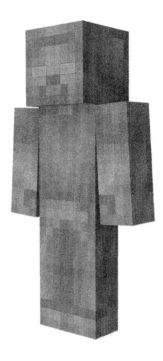

"Your majesty," said the robot, "we have caught two more intruders. We found them trying to build a ladder over the wall. I don't think they're very intelligent, if I'm being honest."

"Thank you, Charles," said Robo-Steve. "Bring them in."

"Bring in the idiots," said the red robot, Charles.

One of the blue robots pushed two prisoners into the room.

"Porkins!" said Dave. "Sally!"

"Hello, Dave old chap," said Porkins sadly. "I'm afraid I'm in a jolly pickle again. I came to save you and Carl and... well, I didn't do a very good job of it."

"No you didn't," said Carl. "Although we got captured too, so I guess we can't talk."

"Of course you got captured, idiot," said the red robot with a sneer. "None of you have the intelligence of a robot. Your brains are so inferior to ours that you never stood a chance."

"That's enough, Charles," said Robo-Steve. "Please show our four guests to the balcony. The troops should all have gathered in the plaza by now."

"Look," said Carl, "you've won. Well done. Now why don't you just put those stupid helmets on us and get it over with? I don't know if I can stand much more of your talking."

"You will all receive neuro-helmets in time," said Robo-Steve, "but first I want to prove to you that my logical methods of ruling work. I don't want to force you to wear a neuro-helmet if you don't want to. I'm hoping that, in time, you'll see that my way is right, and that you'll actually *ask* to wear a helmet."

"I can't see that happening," said Carl.

"Well, we'll see," said Robo-Steve. "Now please, let's go to the balcony. It's time for my invasion to begin."

CHAPTER TWENTY
The Robot Army

Robo-Steve and his robot guards led them onto a balcony that overlooked the plaza below. When Dave saw the plaza, it made him gasp.

Hundreds—maybe *thousands*—of blue robots had gathered together, all stood in perfectly neat rows. And they weren't just gathered in the plaza, they were lined up in the streets too. The city was full of them.

There's so many of them, Dave thought in disbelief. He'd thought Herobrine's zombie pigman army had been big, but that was nothing compared to this.

Villagers in neuro-helmets were looking out of every window and balcony at the robots. They all had bored expressions on their faces.

"Today is a great day, my soldiers," Robo-Steve shouted down at the robots. "Today we spread logic and reason throughout the world. You will march from village to town, ensuring every villager has a neuro-helmet of their own. A new, better world begins today."

"*EIYYEEEEEEEEEEEE!!!!*"

A terrible scream echoed across the city.

"What the blazes was that?" said Porkins.

But Dave knew what it was.

"Uh oh," said Carl.

BOOOM!!!

From far across the city, Dave saw a portion of the city wall get blown to bits by a blast of blue fire.

"What is that?" said Robo-Steve. "Charles, go and find out what that is."

But they didn't have to wait to find out. A huge blue creature was charging down one of the wide streets that led to the plaza, sending robots flying as it crashed into them.

"It's coming this way!" said Charles, the red robot. "Your majesty, we must evacuate!"

The creature burst into the plaza, trampling robots as it came to a stop. The remaining robots just stood still, still standing to attention as if nothing had happened.

As Dave had suspected, it was the blue creeper queen. But what he had *not* expected was to see a villager riding on the creeper queen's back.

"It's Future Dave!" gasped Carl. "He's alive!"

Future Dave has tied some rope around the queen's neck, using it as reigns like one would on a horse. He had his bow and arrow aimed at the balcony; the arrow glowing red.

"Get away from the Robot King," he yelled to Dave and the others. "He must be destroyed!"

Dave the Villager

CHAPTER TWENTY-ONE
Changing the Future

Future Dave let go of the exploding arrow, and it sped through the air towards the balcony.

Carl, Porkins and Sally all jumped out of the way. Robo-Steve just stood in place, too surprised to move. Without thinking, Dave pushed Robo-Steve out of the path of the arrow. The arrow whizzed past them, through the balcony doors, through the big room with the animals then into the room with the sofas, blowing it to bits.

Robo-Steve lay on the floor, looking up at Dave with confusion.

"Why did you save me?" he asked. "If your goal is to stop my invasion, that was a most illogical decision."

"I saved you because... because I don't think you're really a bad guy," said Dave. "I just think you're a bit confused."

"Incorrect," said Robo-Steve. "My programming makes it impossible for me to be confused."

"Really?" said Dave. "Because to me you look confused. You were programmed to be a mindless machine who obeyed every word of your creator, then you went against your creator, then you begged us to save you at the Cool Dude Battle Royale, and now you're planning to take over the world. It seems to me that you *are* confused: you don't know what you want, or what you want to do with your life, and that's fine."

Dave turned to look at his friends.

"Carl was a moody creeper whose only goal in life was to blow himself up," said Dave. "Now he's a slightly-less moody creeper who's joined me on my stupid quest to find a dragon. Also, he used to hate fighting, and now he loves it."

He turned to Porkins.

"Porkins has had to adapt to leaving his home and losing everyone he ever loved," said Dave. "He lost his family, but he found a new one with me and Carl."

"I see him as a sort-of annoying younger brother," said Carl. "The kind of one who wets the bed and always steals your toys."

"You don't have to be who you were programmed to be," said Dave to Robo-Steve. "Look at me—I'm a villager. I'm not supposed to do anything but trade and farm, but I've chosen to try and become a hero."

Robo-Steve thought for a moment.

"You make some interesting points, Dave," he said. "Perhaps a purely logical outlook has given me a limited view of the world. Maybe it would be best if I broaden my horizons, and see what the world has to offer before deciding to conquer it."

"NO!"

It was Future Dave. He had a glowing red arrow strung on his bow, aiming right at Robo-Steve.

"You don't get to start again, not after what you've done," Future Dave said to Robo-Steve. "I've lost too many good people to let you off the hook!"

Dave stepped in front of Robo-Steve, protecting him from Future Dave.

"Out of my way!" shouted Future Dave.

"No," said Dave. "He can change, I know he can."

"If he's going to change, then why am I still here?" said Future Dave. "If the war isn't going to happen, then I would never be sent back in time. So the fact that I'm still here means that the war *does* happen. The Robot King is going to destroy everything you've ever loved. I know because I've watched it happen to me."

Robo-Steve got to his feet.

"I assume this is the time traveler that you mentioned earlier," he said to Dave. "He makes a valid point. If I am going to change my ways and stop my invasion, as you hope, why would he not be erased from this timeline?"

"I... I don't know," said Dave.

"Perhaps it would be best if you let him destroy me," said Robo-Steve. "If I'm going to cause so much pain, it may be best."

"No," said Dave. "I... I can't."

"Listen to me, you stupid robot," said Sally. Dave was surprised to see that she was crying.

"I have to believe that bad people can change," Sally continued. "My husband did... he did some terrible things. But I still love him, and I need to believe that he can turn good again. If anyone can help you change your ways, it's Dave. He turned my village of farmers into warriors in a matter of days. If you went along with him, and joined him on his quest, who knows how much you'd change."

"Wait, what?" said Carl. "No way is this crazy robot joining us!"

"That sounds like a spiffing idea," said Porkins. "It'll be lovely to have another companion on the road."

Carl rolled his eyes. "Porkins you loony," he said.

Robo-Steve turned to Dave.

"Your female friend makes a valid point," he said, looking at Sally. "I know your feelings towards me are probably extremely negative, but, if you'll have me, I would like to join you on your travels. Perhaps along the way I will learn to look at the world in a different way."

Dave grinned. "Of course," he said. "Of course you're welcome to join us."

"Oh great," said Carl, "another weirdo."

Robo-Steve stepped forward, looking over the balcony at his robot army.

"What are you doing?" Future Dave said. "If you try anything..."

"Emergency code five one seven nine two," Robo-Steve said, his voice booming loudly across the city. "Initiate self destruct."

"AFFIRMATIVE!" all the robots said together. Then *BOOM BOOM BOOM BOOM BOOM* they all started to explode. Within a few seconds they were all destroyed, leaving nothing but bits of blue metal on the ground.

"Wow," said Carl.

The only robot left was Charles.

"W-What are you doing, your majesty?" he asked.

"Emergency code three three two," said Robo-Steve. "Deactivate all neuro-helmets."

This was less spectacular. Instead of lots of explosions, the red lights on the helmets of the villagers all began to turn off, and the villagers started removing their helmets, looking around like they were waking from a dream.

Suddenly, for the first time since Dave had arrived there, the city was full of people talking. It was like a completely different city.

"What... what's happening to me?"

It was Future Dave. He was starting to disappear.

"It's working!" he said happily. "You changed the future! Thank you, all of y—"

And then he was gone.

CHAPTER TWENTY-TWO
A New Companion

After a lot of debate, the villagers of Villagertropolis decided to let Robo-Steve go free.

"He did save us from the pigmen," said the mayor, a stern-looking woman in a sharp suit. "But if he tries anything like this again, he's gonna be in big trouble."

"Thank you Mrs Mayor," said Robo-Steve. "And I apologize once again for the trouble my actions have caused."

She also let Charles stay on in the city, keeping him on as her assistant.

The other question was, what were they going to do with the giant blue creeper queen? Future Dave seemed to have tamed it, and as it walked around the city plaza it didn't seem to be hurting anyone, but they all agreed that it couldn't stay.

"If it explodes it'll destroy the whole city!" said the mayor.

"You know, Dave old chap," said Porkins, "since the blighter was tamed by future-you, maybe it'll obey present-you as well?"

So as much as it terrified him, Dave had to climb onto the creeper queen's back, grab onto her reins and ride her carefully out of the city; Carl, Porkins, Robo-Steve and Sally following at a safe distance behind.

Dave brought the creeper queen to the foot of the mountains, then climbed off.

"Um, you're free now," he told her. "Off you go."

"*SKIIIIIE!!!*" the creeper queen said, leaning down and nuzzling her blue face against Dave.

"I think she likes you," grinned Carl.

"I think I've never been so terrified," said Dave.

Next, Dave, Carl, Porkins, Robo-Steve and Sally made their way back to Greenleaf. They didn't have horses, but the main road was clear of robots now, so it was much easier going than crossing the mountains or going along the old road.

When they reached the village, a couple of days later, Dave asked Sally if she wanted to join them on their journey.

"Thank you, but no," she said, smiling. "I know it's silly, but I want to stay here. In case Adam comes home."

So they said their goodbyes, then Dave, Porkins, Carl and their new companion, Robo-Steve, went on their way.

"What is our destination?" asked Robo-Steve. "How do you know which direction to go to get to this ender dragon?"

"Well," said Dave, "first let's go to Little Block and get some horses, and then I'll show you."

"Affirmative," said Robo-Steve.

"*Affirmative*," said Carl, rolling his eyes. "I never thought I'd say this, Porkins, but you're no longer the biggest idiot in our group."

"Thanks very much," said Porkins, smiling.

Carl just shook his head.

"Oh how I wish I could just blow myself up," he said. "If only for a bit of peace and quiet."

EPILOGUE

It had been a long week on the road and Porkins was feeling worn out. Not only had it been raining all week, but his remaining arm was aching. It was no easy thing to control a horse with one hand, and he was really feeling the strain.

Porkins could hear Dave and Carl snoring in their beds, but as tired as he was, he just couldn't get to sleep. He got up and went outside.

Robo-Steve was leaning against the wall of the house, looking up at the stars.

"It's strange," said Robo-Steve. "Even though I have an IQ of over 3,000, I have no idea what stars are. I have theories, of course, but even with all my knowledge I don't know everything. I don't how the world began. I don't know where life came from. There are so many mysteries that logic alone can't solve."

"I guess that's true," said Porkins. "Sometimes it's hard to know what the answer to even the simplest question is. I'm still not sure if I've made the right decision staying with Dave and Carl, or whether I should have joined my people in Little Bacon. It's a real pickle."

"I have noticed you've been struggling mentally," said Robo-Steve. "I'm beginning to become more attuned to emotions. I've also noticed that you've been operating at less than one-hundred percent thanks to your missing arm."

"Yes, it has been difficult," said Porkins, clutching the bare skin where his arm had once been. "But I guess it's just something I'll have to jolly well get used to."

"Perhaps not," said Robo-Steve. "I made you this."

He handed Porkins a strange metal object. For a moment Porkins had no clue what it was, and then he realized: it was a robot arm!

"I'm eighty-nine per cent sure it will work," said Robo-Steve. "Just place it on your shoulder, and it should attach magnetically.

Porkins took the robot arm and pushed it against his shoulder. Amazingly, it did seem to stick, as if by magic. For a moment the arm hung limp, like it was just a bit of metal attached to his body, but then Porkins could *feel* it. He tried to move the arm, and found out that he could.

"Good gravy!" said Porkins.

"It may take some getting used to," said Robo-Steve. "I estimate between three and five weeks."

Porkins leaped forward and gave Robo-Steve a hug. His body was cold and hard, but Porkins didn't mind.

"This is an unusual show of gratitude," said Robo-Steve. "What is it called?"

"A hug," said Porkins, grinning.

"A hug..." said Robo-Steve. "An interesting word. I will add it to my data banks."

*

Dave wiped the sleep from his eyes. The morning light was coming through the windows, and Carl and Porkins's beds were empty. He went outside. Carl was sitting against the wall of the house, watching Porkins and Robo-Steve practice sword fighting in the distance.

It took Dave a moment to realize what was so odd about this scene. But then it came to him.

"Porkins... has two arms!" he said to Carl.

"Yeah, apparently Robo-Steve built him a new one," said Carl. "Maybe that robot isn't so bad after all."

"Yeah," said Dave, grinning. "Maybe not."

"Listen," said Carl, "I know you like to believe that everyone can change, that we should give everyone a second chance, and that's fine. I'm big enough to admit I was wrong about Robo-Steve. But you need to realize that when it comes to Herobrine, it's not gonna work like that."

Dave felt a familiar cold tingle down his spine as Carl said the word *Herobrine*.

"I know that," said Dave.

"I hope so," said Carl. "Because you're not going to be able to say nice words to Herobrine to make him see the error of his ways. He's not going to become your new best friend and join you on your quest."

Dave watched Robo-Steve and Porkins play-fighting with their swords. Yes, Robo-Steve had changed his ways, but Carl was right—Herobrine *was* different. He wasn't misguided like Robo-Steve, bitter like Ripley, cowardly like Adam or stupid like Derek Cool. Of all the villains they'd met on their travels, Herobrine was the only one Dave would call *evil*.

"Don't worry," Dave said to Carl. "If we do ever meet Herobrine again, and it comes down to it, I'll do the right thing..."

Dave the Villager

BOOK 7

The Cult of Spidroth

Dave the Villager

PROLOGUE

"Charles!" shouted the mayor. "Where's my warm milk?"

"Just coming," Charles replied. He quickly lit the stove in the kitchen and started heating up a bucket of milk.

At first Charles the robot had been more than happy to be the mayor's assistant. Robo-Steve had programmed Charles to be an assistant, so it came naturally to him. But recently he'd been getting frustrated: the mayor had started treating him more like a servant, making him fetch her food and bring her warm milk in bed. She'd even started asking him to clean her living quarters.

"Here you go, Mrs Mayor," Charles said, handing the mayor a glass of milk. She was all tucked up in bed, next to her husband. Recently she'd insisted Charles stay with her and her husband in their living quarters. Officially it was so that Charles could be there to offer her advice if there was an emergency, but in reality Charles had just been bringing her and her husband food in bed and looking after their pet cat.

"Actually Charles," said the mayor's husband, putting down the book he was reading, "I wouldn't mind some pumpkin pie, if we have some."

Charles was annoyed. *I have a brain one-hundred times more powerful than this fool,* he thought to himself. *Why do I have to bring him pie?*

"Why are you looking at me like that?" the mayor's husband said. "Charles, buddy, you're freaking me out a bit."

"My apologies," said Charles, forcing himself to smile. "I'll go and get you some pie."

He left the mayor's bedroom, walking off down the hallway towards the kitchen. The mayor's living quarters were inside the huge prismarine-domed government building in the center of Villagertropolis. Charles thought wistfully about when the Robot

King had been in charge of this building, back when he'd ruled the city.

You should never have given up your throne, my king, thought Charles. *These illogical fools need a strong ruler like you.*

He walked past the kitchen and kept going, lost in his thoughts. Eventually he found himself standing on the big balcony that overlooked the plaza. He remembered how excited he'd been when the Robot King's troops had been gathered in the plaza, ready to begin their conquest. But then a villager named Dave had convinced the Robot King that he shouldn't launch an invasion after all. Charles had been convinced that the Robot King would laugh in Dave's face, but instead he'd listened to him.

Then the Robot King—calling himself *Robo-Steve* now—had left the city, leaving Charles behind. Now, after starting out as an assistant to a king, he was little more than a servant.

Charles headed back to his quarters, a small box room with a single window and a bed. He opened up the chest next to his bed and pulled out a diamond crown—his most treasured possession.

This crown had belonged to the Robot King, before he'd given up his title and gone off on a fool's quest to go and slay a dragon with the villager Dave. As Charles held the crown in his hands he couldn't help but wonder how different things could have been: if only the Robot King hadn't listened to Dave.

"CHARLES!" the mayor's husband yelled from down the corridor. "Where's my pie?"

Charles gritted his teeth. He was fed up with being ordered around like a servant, just because he was a robot. From now on, no-one would tell him what to do. In his window he could see his own reflection: he looked just like the Robot King, apart from his metal casing was red instead of gold.

Maybe it's time for a new king, he thought to himself. *If the Robot King no longer wants his title, then maybe I'll take it for myself.*

He placed the diamond crown upon his head, studying his reflection as he did so. The crown looked good on him; much better than it ever had on the Robot King.

"Long live the King," he whispered to himself, with a grin.

He sneaked out of the city that night, disguised in a cloak so that no-one would spot his metallic red body. The people of Villagertropolis had already proved that they were unworthy of being ruled by a monarch with a superior brain, so he would go elsewhere—to somewhere where they *wanted* a strong ruler. But first, he had to prove that he was the rightful heir to the title of Robot King. He had to find Robo-Steve... and defeat him.

CHAPTER ONE
Trouble Brewing

"So," said Dave, "we add the nether wart to the water, and cool it on the brewing stand?"

"Almost," said Porkins. "But that's just the base potion. The awkward potion. Once you have that, you need to combine it with another ingredient to turn it into a proper potion."

"So the awkward potion doesn't do anything on its own?" said Dave.

"No," said Porkins.

"Don't worry, Dave, you'll get it eventually," yawned Carl. "We'll just stay here for another thousand years."

Robo-Steve gave Carl a confused look.

"I don't understand," he said, "after one-thousand years your organic bodies would have rotted away to dust."

Carl rolled his eyes.

"I was only joking," he said.

"Ah, I see," said Robo-Steve. "I'm still getting used to jokes. I will add that joke to my memory banks for further analysis."

The four of them were by the shore of a big lake in a plains biome. The sun was shining, and even Carl was in a good mood. For the past couple of weeks they'd been traveling through rain and snow, so now they were making the most of the good weather.

Porkins was teaching Dave to make potions with a brewing stand while Carl and Robo-Steve sat on the grass. Dave had made a vow to himself that he'd learn how to brew. He'd seen how useful potions could be first-hand, and he wanted to be able to make them.

They'd met a wandering trader villager two days earlier and Dave had bought a book of potion recipes, but he was keen to learn some key recipes by heart, just in case he ever lost the book or had to make a potion quickly.

"Watching you make potions is booooring," said Carl. "Can't you make baked potatoes instead?"

"One of these potions might save your life one day," Dave told him. "And besides, we're out of potatoes—because you keep eating them!"

"It's not my fault they taste so nice," said Carl. "I can't help myself."

"Ok," said Porkins, taking the bottle from the stand. It was full of blue liquid. "Now we need to give it a second brewing, and add the glistering melon slice."

Dave pulled out a piece of melon. Its seeds were made of gold.

"I still think it's ridiculous we had to use all that gold to make this," said Dave. "And that wandering trader definitely overpriced me for that melon."

Dave went to take the bottle from Porkins, but suddenly it shattered to pieces in Porkins's hand.

"Oh dear," said Porkins, his cheeks glowing red. "I'm still getting used to this robot arm. Sorry."

"No worries," said Dave. "We've got plenty of other bottles."

Robo-Steve stood up and walked over to them.

"Don't worry, Porkins," said Robo-Steve, "you'll get used to the arm in time."

"Really?" said Porkins sadly.

"There is an eighty-six percent probability of it," said Robo-Steve.

"Um, thanks," said Porkins.

Carl came over to Dave.

"When's the last time you threw one of those ender eyes into the air?" the creeper asked. "Are we still going the right way?"

"Yesterday," said Dave. "I try to only use one every other day. I don't want to waste them. The last thing we need is another trip to the Nether."

"I agree with you there," said Carl. "I've had enough of that lava-filled hellhole to last a lifetime."

He quickly checked around his shoulder to see if Porkins had heard him, but thankfully the pigman was chatting away to Robo-Steve.

After some lunch (Dave, Carl and Porkins had some cooked rabbit—Robo-Steve didn't need to eat) they set off again, Dave, Porkins and Robo-Steve on horses and Carl running alongside in his golem suit.

"It's a shame I didn't bring any of my horses from Villagertropolis," said Robo-Steve, "they were much faster and more efficient than these organic ones."

"I'm sure they were," said Carl, "but at least these ones won't short-circuit and go on a killing rampage."

It seemed like Carl was starting to trust Robo-Steve more, but Dave knew that Carl hadn't forgotten about what Future Dave had told them. In an alternate timeline, where Robo-Steve had taken over the world, Future Carl had been slain by robot ocelots.

They rode on until it got dark, then Dave built them a temporary house. Robo-Steve had been trying recently to see if he could work out how to sleep, so Dave built four beds.

Before they settled down for the night, Dave and Porkins set up the brewing stand outside and got to work brewing some potions, Dave using both the instructions from his new book and advice from Porkins.

The next night they did the same, and the same on the night after that. Dave was quickly getting through a lot of the expensive ingredients he'd bought from the wandering trader and from a town they'd passed through, but he was learning. He even had a few potion recipes memorized.

They were going through a mountains biome when Carl spotted a large round hole that led down into the ground.

"I believe that type of cave is called a giant entrance," said Robo-Steve. "It spirals down into the earth, often cutting through coal and iron deposits."

"Well," said Dave, "it's been a while since we've done any mining. I don't know about the rest of you, but I'm running a bit low on supplies."

So the four of them headed down into the giant entrance of the cave, laying torches as they went. They made a small house underground out of cobblestone—so they'd have somewhere to rest, eat and sleep—and then they started to mine.

Robo-Steve had never mined before, so Dave and the others

taught him.

"I have plenty of information about mining in my data banks," he told them, "but sometimes reading about something can be very different from actually doing it."

They dug and dug, the four of them easily fighting off any monsters that dared to try and attack them. By the end of their third day underground they had so much iron, coal, diamond, emerald, redstone and obsidian that they couldn't carry any more in their backpacks. Robo-Steve had made himself a backpack out of leather from a field of nearby cows, and even that was full.

"Good gravy," said Porkins. "I don't think we'll be running out of materials for a while! And we've got plenty of dosh to spend at the next town. A jolly good haul indeed!"

CHAPTER TWO
Into the Forest

Dave was dreaming of dragons again. A huge black dragon was flying towards him through the darkness, its eyes glowing purple.

Then the dragon was gone and all that was left was an egg: a large black egg with purple spots. It began to break, light pouring from the cracks.

But then, from nowhere, a huge tidal wave appeared—water crashing towards him...

"Waaaa!" Dave yelled.

He sat up in bed, soaked with water. Carl was standing by the side of the bed, holding an empty bucket.

"Did you throw a bucket of water over me?" Dave demanded.

"Yep," grinned Carl. "You were having a nightmare. I thought I'd wake you up."

"Couldn't you just have shook my shoulder?" said Dave.

"Nah," said Carl. "That wouldn't have been as much fun."

When they were all up, Dave destroyed the temporary house they'd been staying in and the four of them set off again across the mountains. Soon the mountains started to flatten out, and they entered some woods.

"Come on Dave," said Carl, "can you check we're going in the right direction? I don't want to do all this walking for nothing."

Dave threw an ender eye into the air. It hovered for a moment, then sped off into the distance in the direction they were walking.

"You see?" said Dave.

"Fine," said Carl.

They started walking again.

"Those eyes of ender are fascinating," said Robo-Steve, studying one that Dave had given him. "There is no mention of them at all in my memory banks, or in any of the books in the Villagertropolis library."

"Yeah, but you didn't read *every* book," said Carl.

"I did," said Robo-Steve.

"That's impossible," said Carl.

"I have an average reading speed of ten thousand words per minute," said Robo-Steve.

"Show off," grunted Carl.

Robo-Steve held the ender eye he was holding up to the light.

"The people who lived in this world before villagers had technology that far surpasses our own," said Robo-Steve. "Even with my enhanced robot brain I cannot comprehend how this device works."

"Just don't go writing any books about it, or whatever," said Carl. "If Herobrine finds out about the eyes, there'll be big trouble. I'm not sure what kind of trouble, but I'm reliably informed there will be trouble."

"That's another fascinating thing," said Robo-Steve. "From the records and history books I've read, it seems Herobrine is one of the oldest beings alive. Perhaps *the* oldest. There are accounts of him in even the most ancient of tales. And still he doesn't know about the eyes of ender, or how to manufacture them."

"Well, let's keep it that way," said Carl.

"And none of you know why Herobrine wants to get to the End so badly?" Robo-Steve asked.

"We've no clue," said Dave.

"I reckon he wants to grab himself a dragon," said Porkins. "Imagine that scoundrel on the back of a dragon. No-one would be safe!"

Dave disagreed, but he kept his thoughts to himself. He knew there must be something more that Herobrine wanted in the End than just the ender dragon. Dave had seen Herobrine turn himself into a huge lava monster, so he didn't think Herobrine really needed a dragon.

The woods around them began to get thicker and darker; so dark that they could barely see the sky above, and it was almost like it was night.

"There's some sort of red building up ahead," said Carl, squinting. Having lived underground most of his life, the creeper had very sharp eyes.

"Let's keep quiet," whispered Dave. "We don't know if the people who live there are friendly."

But when they got closer it turned out that it wasn't a building at all, but a huge red mushroom.

"Good golly gosh!" said Porkins. "I haven't seen a mushroom this big since we dropped the princess off at Mushroom Town."

"And that was a mushroom biome," said Dave. "I didn't know you could get big mushrooms like this anywhere else."

"Well, at least that's lunch sorted," said Carl. He punched one of the red mushroom blocks with his iron fist and it exploded into a couple of smaller mushrooms. He destroyed a few more mushroom blocks, then Dave cooked them all some mushroom stew.

"Won't that damage your circuits or something?" Carl asked Robo-Steve, when he saw Robo-Steve drinking a bowl of stew.

"Negative," said Robo-Steve. "I don't need to eat, but my father made my body capable of consuming food so I could more easily pretend to be the real Steve."

"If you don't need to eat, why are you eating?" said Carl.

"I am hoping to get a better understanding of organic life by trying to emulate common behavior patterns," said Robo-Steve.

"So, pretending to eat and sleep?" said Carl.

"Precisely," said Robo-Steve.

After lunch they began walking again, and came across more huge mushrooms in the forest, red ones and brown ones. The forest got darker too.

"Did you hear something?" Porkins whispered, as they were walking through a particularly dark patch of trees.

HIIIIIISSSSS!!!!

Suddenly a spider jumped out of the trees, landing on Carl's head.

"Arrrrrgggh!!!" yelled Carl. "Get it off! Get it off!"

He was flailing about, smashing into trees with his huge iron body. Dave had to jump out of the way to avoid getting trampled.

"Carl, hit it with your arms!" shouted Dave.

Carl reached up and smacked the spider with his iron arms. It went flying into a tree, and then *poof* it was gone.

"I... I don't like spiders," gasped Carl, getting his breath back.

"They shouldn't even be generating in the daytime," said Dave. "I don't understand it."

"The light levels are so limited in this forest that perhaps mobs are generating as if it's night," said Robo-Steve. "We must proceed with caution."

Suddenly, from the trees all around them, came more hissing noises.

HIIIISSS HIIISSS HIIIIIIIISSSS!!!!

"More of the blighters!" yelled Porkins, pulling out his bow.

At first Dave thought the trees themselves were coming to life, but then he realized it was countless spiders, all looking down at them, their fangs dripping with venom.

"Weapons ready!" Dave yelled. He just had time to pull out his diamond sword as the spiders began jumping at them.

"Get away, get away!" screamed Carl, punching and kicking the spiders with his iron limbs.

Robo-Steve was effortlessly slashing at the spiders with his own diamond sword, moving so quickly and gracefully that the spiders didn't know where to turn.

"Take this, you bounders!" cried Porkins, firing arrow after arrow at the spiders.

Dave was hacking and slashing away at the spiders as best he could, but they kept running up behind him or jumping down at him from the trees. He had to keep jumping out of the way to avoid getting bitten.

The ground and the trees were so full of spiders that it was like the whole world was one wriggling, hissing mass of black limbs and red eyes. Carl was really starting to panic, Dave saw. He'd never seen the creeper like this: yelling and screaming like a little kid as he flailed his iron limbs around.

By the time the battle was won, and the last of the spiders disappeared with a *poof*, Carl was a nervous wreck.

"Are there more of them?" he gasped, his eyes frantically darting around. "Can you see any more?"

"They're all gone for now," said Dave. "It's ok, Carl."

"Sorry," said Carl. "When I was was little I got bitten by a spider. I've been afraid of them ever since."

Dave, Porkins and Robo-Steve picked up the loot the spiders had left—string and spider eyes—then the four of them started walking again, their weapons at the ready in case there was another attack.

BUUUUURRRR!!!!

Suddenly a crowd of zombies burst from the trees to the right of them.

"Stop right there," Dave said, pointing his sword at them.

But the zombies either chose not to talk or didn't know how, and kept staggering towards them.

"Ok, we warned you," said Dave. "Take them out, Porkins!"

Porkins fired a barrage of arrows at the zombies, quickly slaying them all.

"This is gonna take a long time if we have to keep stopping like this to fight monsters," said Carl. "Maybe we should just burn the woods to the ground. Look how close the trees are—the fire would easily spread. Then we could just walk through the ruins without anyone bothering us."

"We're not doing that," said Dave. "There might be good mobs living in these woods. There might be villagers."

"Why would they live here?" said Carl.

"I don't know," said Dave, "but we can't take that chance."

So they kept walking. Every so often zombies or spiders would jump out at them; they were easy to defeat, but it was tiring having to fight all the time.

"We don't even know if it's night or day," moaned Carl, looking up at the thick canopy of trees above them. "Maybe we should build a house and get some sleep?"

But Dave didn't want to stop the night here if they could help it. He couldn't explain it, but he knew that there was something not quite right about these woods. There was something sinister about them.

All of a sudden their way was blocked. There was some sort of wooden structure in front of them.

"What is it?" asked Porkins.

They walked around the wooden building and soon came across some windows. Inside they could see wide high-ceiling corridors lit by torches, with fancy red carpets on the floor.

"It's a house," said Carl. "A pretty gigantic house."

"I would class it more as a mansion," said Robo-Steve.

The woods were so thick that it was impossible to tell how big the mansion was. It seemed to be very big though: they couldn't see the top of it, and there was no sign of the sides either.

"You see?" Dave said to Carl. "If we'd burnt the woods we would have destroyed this mansion—and the people who live inside."

"Yeah, yeah," said Carl. "Come on, let's see if they've got any baked potatoes."

Dave was about to tell Carl to wait—that they should try and see who lived in the mansion first, in case they were dangerous—but Carl was already banging on the windows.

"Heeeellooo!" Carl shouted. "We're friendly adventurers, can you let us in?"

A villager appeared, coming out of a room. His face was

hidden in shadow.

"Hey you!" Carl yelled at the villager through the window. "Do you have potatoes?"

The villager turned to face them. As the light hit its face Dave saw that it wasn't a villager at all.

It was an illager.

And it looked *furious*.

"You shouldn't have come here!" the illager yelled, pulling out an axe. "You shouldn't have come here!!"

And then it charged towards them.

CHAPTER THREE
The Mansion

SMASH!

The illager jumped through the window, swinging his axe around like a crazy person. Dave blocked one of the blows with his sword.

"We're sorry," said Dave, "we'll leave your house alone!"

"You shouldn't have come!" the illager screamed at Dave, as he swung his axe at him again and again. "You don't belong here!"

"You want me to poke some holes in this chap?" Porkins asked Dave. The pigman had his bow aimed at the illager's head.

"No," said Dave. "Robo-Steve, can you knock him out or something?"

"Yes," said Robo-Steve. He reached forward and grabbed the illager by the shoulder, squeezing it tightly. The illager dropped his axe then collapsed on the floor.

"Is he dead?" Carl asked.

"No," said Robo-Steve. "Merely unconscious."

Dave had expected Robo-Steve to punch the illager in the face or biff him on the back of the head, but whatever Robo-Steve had done was a lot easier and cleaner. The illager was on the floor unconscious, eyes closed and breathing softly.

"Good work," said Dave. "Come on, let's go around the side of the mansion. We don't want to come across any of this guy's buddies."

"I think he was one lone nutter," said Carl. "Look inside—the place is abandoned."

Dave had a look through the broken window. Down the far end of the huge corridor he could see a couple of zombies and a skeleton wandering about.

"Maybe you're right," said Dave.

"Of course I am," said Carl. "I'm always right. There's probably loads of treasure inside."

So, reluctantly, Dave climbed into the mansion through the smashed window, the others following behind him.

"Y-you don't reckon this mansion is haunted, do you old bean?" Porkins asked nervously.

"Ha," said Carl, with a sly grin. "Are you scared of ghosts, Porkins?"

Suddenly a spider jumped out from the shadows, landing next to Carl.

"ARRRRRGGGGHH!!!!" screamed Carl.

Thunk! Thunk! Porkins fired two arrows at the spider and it exploded with a *poof.*

"I think you're the one who's scared, old chap," laughed Porkins.

"Hmmph," said Carl, crossing his iron arms across his chest.

Carl's screaming had attracted the attention of the zombies and the skeleton down the hall. Porkins raised his bow, ready to fire at them.

"Wait," said Dave, "let's give the zombie a chance to walk away."

He stepped forward.

"Excuse me," said Dave, "we don't mean you any harm."

"BUUUURRR!!!" said the zombie, and it kept stumbling towards them.

"It looks like another brainless one," said Carl. "Not all zombies can speak. In fact, I think most of them can't. It's the same with creepers—some of us, who live in wild places like this—are no smarter than animals."

"I didn't know that," said Dave.

Suddenly an arrow landed next to his feet. The skeleton and the zombies were almost on them now.

"Ok Porkins, take them out," said Dave.

Thunk thunk thunk thunk thunk!

Porkins fired his shots and the mobs fell down dead.

"I'm glad to see the replacement limb is working efficiently," said Robo-Steve.

"Yes, it seems to be," smiled Porkins. "I think I'm actually a quicker shot than I was before."

"Maybe you should chop the other arm off too," said Carl. "Then you'll be even quicker."

"That's actually quite a rum idea," said Porkins, completely missing Carl's sarcasm. "What do you reckon, Dave old chap?"

"No," said Dave, rolling his eyes. "No-one's getting any more limbs chopped off. Come on, let's explore this mansion—I want to be out of here before nightfall."

Dave led them down the huge hallway. The building looked old—the wooden walls had rotted in places and the carpet was well-worn—but the mansion didn't feel abandoned to Dave, even if there were monsters living inside it. For one thing, there were lit torches all down the hallway. Dave knew from his crafting book that torches would burn forever if left alone, but it still seemed strange that none of them had fallen off the wall or been extinguished, if the building really had been abandoned.

"CREEPER!" Porkins yelled.

A creeper had come out of a nearby room and was slithering towards them.

"Talk to it, Carl!" said Dave.

"Er, hi," said Carl. "We don't mean you any harm."

"*HIIIIISSSS!!!*" said the creeper.

"Yep, I think it's a brainless one," said Carl. "Heads down!"

The creeper glowed white as it prepared to explode. Carl ran forward and smacked it with an iron fist, and the creeper flew backwards and exploded against one of the wooden walls.

"There's a room here," Robo-Steve said, looking into the hole the creeper had just created. "But there's no door. How did people get in and out? And why are they storing lava like that?"

Dave had a look inside the room. It was one of the strangest rooms he'd ever seen: in the middle was a big cube of glass that was filled with lava.

"Maybe we should break the glass," said Porkins. "There might be treasure inside."

"Yeah, you go ahead and do that," said Carl. "Just don't complain to us when you get covered in lava."

"Come on," said Dave, "let's keep moving."

They continued down the hallway, passing strange room after strange room, each one with something different inside. There were normal-looking rooms, such as a room with cobblestone tables that looked like an office, and bizarre rooms, such as rooms that were full of wool blocks, piled up high.

Every so often they'd come across a zombie, a skeleton, a creeper or a spider. All of them seemed to be mindless monsters.

One of the weirdest rooms was one with a giant statue of a chicken made from wool.

"Who built all this crazy stuff?" said Carl.

Another room had a stage in the middle, with dark oak fences around it. On the stage was a solitary zombie. It tried to walk towards them but it couldn't get past the fences.

"I have information you may be interested in," said Robo-Steve, knocking on a wooden block. "From the acoustics, it seems there is a secret room behind this wall."

"Well go on, break through it," said Carl.

"Affirmative," said Robo-Steve. He punched the wall with his gold fists and the block broke instantly. Then he punched the other blocks until he'd created a passage big enough for them to walk through.

As Dave followed Robo-Steve into the room he saw something that took his breath away.

I've found it! he thought happily. *I've finally found it!*

"What is that thing?" asked Porkins.

"It's... it's an end portal!" said Dave.

CHAPTER FOUR
The End?

Dave ran up the cobblestone stairs that led to the portal, more excited that he could ever remember being. His long quest was finally at an end: all he had to do now was activate the portal with eyes of ender then go through and fight the dragon!

But when he reached the top of the stairs he became very confused.

The 'portal' was made from green wool blocks, and the 'lava' underneath it was orange wool.

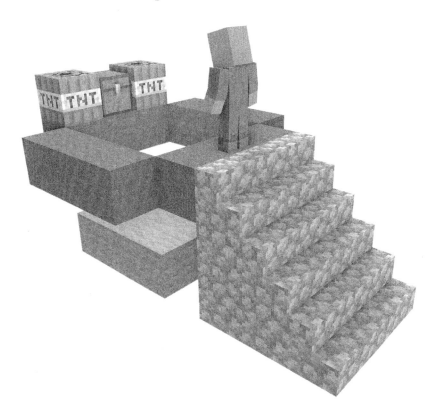

"I... I don't understand," said Dave.

"I have to say, I never thought an end portal would be made of wool," said Carl. "Life is full of surprises."

"Shut up, Carl!" Dave snapped, feeling anger rising inside of him. "Shut up with your stupid jokes!"

Dave turned around. Carl, Porkins and Robo-Steve were looking at him with shocked expressions.

"I'm sorry," said Dave, feeling embarrassed. "I shouldn't have snapped at you like that, Carl. It's just... I thought we were finally here."

He turned round and looked at the 'portal' again.

"It looks *just* like an end portal," he said sadly.

"What kind of chaps would build such a thing?" said Porkins.

"It does raise several intriguing questions," said Robo-Steve. "Throughout history the illagers have often been associated with cults. Perhaps this mansion was built by the illagers to worship the End, or endermen or the ender dragon."

"Or chickens," said Carl.

"Or chickens," agreed Robo-Steve.

"What makes you think the illagers built it?" said Dave. "The illager we saw didn't seem capable of building anything."

"He seemed like a nutter," agreed Carl.

"Agreed," said Robo-Steve. "The illager who tried to attack us did seem... I don't know what the polite phrase is."

"Like a nutter," said Carl.

"I'm unable to find anything in my databanks about the word 'nutter'," said Robo-Steve. "Is it a creeper word?"

"Come on," said Dave, "let's keep looking around the mansion. Maybe we can find some more fake portals."

"I say," said Porkins, "what about that treasure chest? Are you going to open it?"

Dave had been so concerned with the fake end portal that he'd barely noticed the treasure chest on the other side of it. Weirdly, it was between two TNT blocks.

"I wouldn't open that chest if I were you," said Robo-Steve. "Judging by its placement between that TNT, I predict there is a high certainty that it's a trap."

"Agreed," said Dave. "Let's keep moving."

They carried on down the hallway, finding lots more weird rooms. There were glass windows to the outside world, but all they could see through them was thick forest. The trees were growing right next to the mansion.

"Why would they put windows in if the view's so rubbish?" wondered Carl.

"Perhaps when the mansion was built the forest was not quite so near," said Robo-Steve. "The mansion could have been surrounded by gardens, and the forest crept nearer after years of neglect."

They came around a corner and saw a cobblestone staircase in the distance, leading up to the mansion's second floor.

"Do we really want to go upstairs?" Dave asked.

"Come on," said Carl. "Upstairs is where the treasure's more likely to be."

"You don't even know there *is* going to be treasure!" said Dave.

But Carl was already stomping down the corridor towards the staircase.

Dave was about to follow, when he heard a whisper from behind him.

"You shouldn't have come here," the voice whispered. "This place isn't for you."

Dave turned around. An illager had come out of a room behind him, Porkins and Robo-Steve. The illager was clutching an axe and rocking back and forth on his heels; madness in his eyes.

"This place isn't for you," the villager repeated. "This place belongs to the Void. This is the realm of the Sleeper, and you are trespassers."

"Look, we don't want to hurt you," Dave said to the illager. But then he heard footsteps behind him. He turned round and saw other illagers coming out of other rooms, all holding axes.

"Oh crumbs," said Porkins.

"Trespassers," said one of the illagers.

"Enemies of the Void," said another, "you shouldn't have come here. This is not your place."

Dave looked down the hallway and saw that Carl was surrounded by illagers as well.

"Look," Dave said to the illagers, "we thought this place was abandoned. Just let us go safely and we'll leave you in peace."

"You cannot leave," said an illager, walking slowly towards them with his axe raised. "You must come with us to the sanctum. You belong to the Sleeper now."

"You belong to the Sleeper," the other illagers repeated in unison. "We all belong to the Sleeper."

"What's the plan, old bean?" Porkins asked him. "Do we fight our way out?"

"What do you reckon, Robo-Steve?" Dave asked. "Do we stand a chance?"

Robo-Steve's purple eyes flickered as he looked round the room.

"Approximate chance of success in battle is... seventy three percent," he said.

"That's good enough for me," said Dave. "ATTACK!"

CHAPTER FIVE
Illagers

Dave and Robo-Steve rushed forward with their swords as Porkins started firing arrows. Nearby Dave could hear the sound of metal slamming against flesh, as Carl let loose on the illagers in his iron suit.

The illagers' iron axes were no match for Dave's diamond sword, but there were so many illagers that it was hard to avoid getting hit. He'd block one axe with his sword, then two other illagers would sneak up behind him. Thankfully Porkins's arrows helped keep them at bay, but it was a tough fight.

As ever, Robo-Steve was fighting so smoothly and gracefully that it was almost like he was dancing. It took all Dave's willpower not to just stop fighting and watch him.

Even though they were vastly outnumbered, Dave and his friends were holding their own against the illagers. But then Dave saw a different type of illager walking up behind the axe-wielding illagers; this illager was wearing a long black cloak with yellow lining down the front.

The new illager raised his hands and suddenly a row of what looked like huge *fangs* rose up from the floor. Dave had to dive out of the way to avoid getting hit. Little gray-blue flying creatures began flying through the air towards Dave as well, and for every one he slew, more would appear. Some more fangs rose up out of the ground, and this time they hit Dave in the leg and he fell to the floor. He looked up and saw Porkins frantically fighting off illagers with a sword; they were too close for him to use his bow. Robo-Steve was still fighting as fast and as gracefully as ever, but even he was being overwhelmed.

"Take them alive!" one of the robed illagers shouted. "They will make worthy sacrifices to the Sleeper!"

The next thing Dave saw was an illager running towards him with an axe.

He's going to kill me, Dave thought stupidly.

But then the illager twisted his axe round and used the handle to bash Dave in the face, knocking him out.

*

When Dave awoke he was inside a small cobblestone prison cell with a single iron door and no windows. He reached for his sword but it was gone. So was his backpack and his armor.

Robo-Steve, Porkins and Carl were there too, all without weapons. They were already awake. Carl was out of his iron golem suit.

"They took my suit," he said miserably. "I miss having arms."

"Can't we just bust out of here?" Dave asked. "Robo-Steve, you could punch through the cobblestone, right?"

"I could," said Robo-Steve, "but it would be unwise. There are vindicators outside and, from the faint sounds I can hear, vindicators in the room below. Even though they only have axes, we have no weapons at all. Our chance of survival would be minimal."

"What's a vindicator?" asked Carl.

"Those are the axe-wielding illagers," said Robo-Steve. "Typically in illager communities they are low status grunts who take orders from the illagers of a more senior rank, such as the evokers."

"And I'm guessing the evokers are the wizard dudes who make teeth come out of the ground and summon fairies?" said Carl.

"Correct," said Robo-Steve. "There was much about illagers in the books in the Villagertropolis libraries. For a long time, Villagertropolis was plagued by illager raids, before they built their walls."

"Ok, so we know the proper names for them now," said Dave, "but how are we going to escape?"

"Unknown," said Robo-Steve. "I'm running my processing center at one-hundred percent, but I haven't managed to come up with a solution yet."

"What do you think they're planning to do with us?" Porkins asked nervously. "These illager chaps, I mean."

"From what they were saying earlier, and from my knowledge of illager customs, I suspect they are going to sacrifice us."

"Oh that's just great," said Carl.

"I don't understand," said Robo-Steve. "How is that great?"

"He's being sarcastic," said Dave. "It's something Carl does a lot."

"I see," said Robo-Steve. "I'm aware of the fundamentals of sarcasm, but I'm not that experienced at recognizing it. Carl, please can you let me know whenever you're being sarcastic."

"Oh, I sure will," said Carl.

"The illagers mentioned something about someone called the

'Sleeper'," said Dave, "Do you know who that is?"

"It's not a name I'm familiar with," said Robo-Steve.

Suddenly the iron door creaked open. Standing in the doorway was a female evoker in a red cloak. Behind her was a crowd of vindicators with axes.

"It is time," she said, "time for you to be sacrificed to the Sleeping Queen; the One Who Waits Beneath the Bedrock. The Lady Spidroth awaits you."

"Oh *Spidroth*," Robo-Steve said to Dave. "I actually *do* know who she is. She's Herobrine's daughter."

CHAPTER SIX
Spidroth

"Wait," said Carl, "are you telling me that Herobrine has a kid?"

The four of them were being marched down the hallway, surrounded on all sides by vindicators so that they couldn't make a run for it. Dave looked wistfully out of the windows as they passed, wondering if they could make their escape through one of them, but he saw that they were at least two stories up now, high above the forest—and they probably wouldn't survive the fall.

"According to most texts, Herobrine has four children," said Robo-Steve. "Well, some say he has more, others less, and some historians doubt the existence of Herobrine as a real figure at all, saying he's merely a myth."

"That blighter is no myth," said Porkins, "we can tell you that for sure."

"So, who is this Spidroth?" Dave asked Robo-Steve.

"Well, her full name is Spidrothbrine," said Robo-Steve. "And—"

"NO!" the red-cloaked priestess roared from the front of the procession, turning back to look at them. "You will not speak the Sleeper's name! You are unworthy!"

They were led up some stairs. Dave turned round as they went up and saw that on the wall behind them was a giant illager face made from wool.

These illagers are seriously creepy, Dave thought to himself. He was anxiously wracking his brain, trying to think of an escape plan, but nothing was coming to mind. The illagers were all fairly weak, but there were so many of them, and Dave and his friends were unarmed.

The illagers led them into a long, narrow room with a window on the far side. Through the window Dave could see a lake down below.

We could break through the window and jump down into the lake, Dave thought. *If we can just find the right moment.*

In the middle of the narrow room was a cobblestone structure, with a raised platform on one end and cobblestones benches on either side. There was a line of white carpet going across it, ending at a single protruding cobblestone block, which had a piece of black carpet on top of it. There were two black banners hanging above it, one on either side.

It's some sort of altar, Dave realized.

"Make the sacrifices kneel," the red priestess commanded, and the vindicators pushed Dave and the others down onto their knees in front of the altar (apart from Carl, who had no knees).

"What do we do, Dave old bean?" Porkins whispered.

"We need to escape through that window," Dave whispered back. "As soon as they give us an opening."

"QUIET!" the priestess roared at Dave. "This is the sacred sanctum of Lady Spidroth; you will not corrupt it with your foul words." She turned to the vindicators. "Bring me the first sacrifice," she commanded. "The golden man will do."

Two vindicators grabbed Robo-Steve under the arms and dragged him to the altar.

It's now or never, Dave realized.

"Everyone, head for the window!" Dave yelled.

Dave jumped up and grabbed an axe off a vindicator, swinging it wildly to keep the others away from him.

"Get on my back!" he said to Carl.

Carl reluctantly climbed up onto Dave's shoulders.

"I miss my iron suit," the creeper moaned.

Porkins and Robo-Steve were fighting against the vindicators too. Robo-Steve had grabbed two axes, and was fighting off three of them, as Porkins was doing his best with his fists, trying to avoid getting hit. Around the room, black-cloaked evokers were raising their arms, summoning armies of their little gray-blue fairies.

"ENOUGH!" roared the red priestess, raising her hands. Suddenly Dave felt something wrapping round his legs. He looked down and saw that bony claws had risen up from the floor, and were wrapping themselves around his lower half.

"Waa!" said Carl, as he fell from Dave's shoulders. He fell to the ground, and instantly bony claws rose up and wrapped around him too.

They're not claws, Dave realized to his horror. *They're spider legs.*

Porkins and Robo-Steve were caught in the bone spider legs too. Both were pinned to the ground, trying in vain to get back to their feet.

"You are making a mockery of this sanctum," the priestess

said to the vindicators and evokers. "Keep the prisoners still, or I shall have your heads. Now, it's time for the first sacrifice."

She reached down and grabbed Robo-Steve by the arm, but suddenly a look of surprise crossed her face.

"You... you're some kind of mechanized man," she said. "And you're made of gold."

"Actually, it's gold plating," said Robo-Steve. "But yes, 'mechanized man' would be an accurate term for—"

"SILENCE!" she roared. She turned to the other illagers. "This mechanized man may be what we've been looking for: A being who can contain the glory of our Queen without being destroyed."

The illagers began muttering excitedly. The priestess raised her hands and the bony spider legs lifted Robo-Steve up and pushed him face down onto the altar.

"What are you going to do to me?" Robo-Steve asked.

The priestess ignored him, and, keeping her hands raised, she addressed the illagers.

"Long ago, before time began, there was only the Void. So it is said."

"So it is said," repeated the other illagers.

"From the Void the world was born," she continued, "and the first hero was spawned. So it is said."

"So it is said," they repeated once more.

"But unbeknown to the hero, another was spawned: the hero's dark twin. Just as the hero existed to create, the twin existed to destroy, and to help him with his dark deeds the twin spawned four children. So it is said."

"So it is said."

"The greatest of these children was Spidroth, the spider queen. But such was her greatness that Herobrine, the dark twin, feared his daughter would replace him, so he cast her down, trapping her in the endless void beneath the bedrock. There she sleeps, her body trapped but her spirit free; awaiting the day when a host strong enough will appear."

"Let me guess," said Carl, "*so it is said?*"

The priestess shot him a look of pure loathing.

"Laugh while you can, creeper," she said. "For when Lady Spidroth rises, you will have nothing to laugh about. You will be begging for mercy, I promise you that."

"I'm begging for mercy now," said Carl, "please stop with the preaching. You're boring me to tears."

"KEEP QUIET!" the priestess roared. She clenched her fists and the bone spider legs wrapped even tighter around Dave and his friends. Dave felt like his legs were going to break, their grip was so tight.

"So," said Robo-Steve, who was still being held down on the altar by a bony spider leg, "you're planning on using my body as a host for Spidroth?"

"That's right," said the red priestess, grinning. "For generations we have searched for a suitable host for the mighty Spidroth's spirit. Some have volunteered, others have been forced, but none of them were powerful enough to hold her greatness. Some were driven mad, some were destroyed, but now we have you and your golden body. Maybe you will finally be the one who can contain the power of the Sleeper, and she will awake once more."

The red evoker thrust her hands forward, waving them above Robo-Steve and the altar.

"Great Spidrothbrine," she said, "I summon you from your slumber."

The illagers all began to chant in a language Dave didn't understand.

Suddenly the altar began to glow, filling the room with a deep, blood-red light. The chanting of the illagers got louder; their voices getting deeper.

"Can you hear that?" Carl whispered to Dave, a look of horror in his eyes. "C-can you hear the spiders?"

Dave was about to say that he couldn't, but suddenly he *could*. He could hear scraping and rustling coming through the walls from the rooms next door, and through the ceiling above and the floor below. It sounded like hundreds of spiders trying to break into the room. He could hear their cries too: angry hisses and slobbering sounds.

The room began to grow warm; so warm that Dave was soon sweating. The sweat ran down his face and into his eyes, making them blur.

"Awaken my queen!" the priestess screamed. "Take this weak body and fill it with your power!"

Robo-Steve began to shake, his golden limbs flailing wildly.

"Error!" he cried. "Critical error!"

Then, with a final shudder, Robo-Steve collapsed, falling off of the altar. The purple lights of his eyes flickered and then died, and smoke poured from his mouth. The altar stopped glowing red and, instantly, the spider sounds disappeared as the room returned to normal.

"No!" Porkins cried.

"A pity," said the red priestess, looking down at Robo-Steve's lifeless body. "I really thought we'd found a suitable vessel this time. Evokers, sacrifice the remaining prisoners. I will be in my chambers."

Then Robo-Steve's body began to twitch. Only slightly at first, but then his limbs were squirming, twisting this way and that. His eyes were glowing too: not their normal purple, but a deep red. Then he stopped twitching and stood up, his head darting this way and that as he looked round the room.

No, thought Dave, *that's not Robo-Steve anymore. Something else has taken over his body.*

"My queen," said the red priestess. "Is that... is that you?"

"Yes," said Robo-Steve.

Even though the golden robot in front of him still had Robo-Steve's voice, Dave knew that it wasn't Robo-Steve talking. It was Herobrine's daughter—Spidroth.

"I am reborn!" Spidroth yelled, her voice full of triumph.

The illagers all got down on one knee, their heads bowed.

The room began to shake. No, Dave realized, it wasn't just the room, it wasn't even just the mansion—the whole forest was shaking. Outside he could see water rippling across the lake as that shook too.

"My body stirs beneath the bedrock," said Spidroth. "It is trapped for all eternity, but now my mind is free. And I am free to have my revenge against my father! I am free to destroy Herobrine!"

"Actually," said Porkins nervously, "we'd quite like to destroy that cad Herobrine as well. Maybe we could team up?"

"And then I will destroy the world!" continued Spidroth.

"Oh," said Porkins. "Maybe not then."

What are we going to do? thought Dave. An evil being had taken over the mind of his friend, and he had no clue what to do about it. The bony spider legs that had been keeping him, Carl and Porkins trapped had gone now—now that the red evoker was distracted—but they were still surrounded by illagers, they still had no weapons and he had no clue how to get Spidroth out of

Robo-Steve's body.

But then he saw the lake outside, and had an idea. It was a stupid idea, he thought, but it was the only idea he had.

He leaned forward and whispered something to Porkins and Carl.

"What?" said Carl, when he heard Dave's plan. "Are you crazy?"

"Let's do it," said Porkins.

"Ok," Dave whispered. "Now!"

Carl jumped on Dave's back, then Dave and Porkins jumped to their feet and ran forward. Before the illagers had time to think and stop them, they grabbed Robo-Steve, Dave holding one arm, Porkins holding the other.

"What are you doing?!" Spidroth roared in Robo-Steve's voice. "Unhand me!"

Then Dave and Porkins ran with Robo-Steve to the back of the room and jumped through the window.

CHAPTER SEVEN
Fire and Water

SPLOOSH!!!

Dave, Porkins, Carl and Robo-Steve landed in the lake. Dave opened his eyes underwater and saw Robo-Steve in front of him. The red lights in his eyes were flickering on and off, then suddenly they turned purple.

Dave grabbed Robo-Steve and dragged him towards the surface. He realized, suddenly, that he had no idea if Robo-Steve could float, or if he'd just sink to the bottom like Carl's iron golem suit. Thankfully it was the former, and Dave managed to pull him upwards.

Dave broke the surface of the water, spluttering and gasping, holding Robo-Steve with one arm. He looked around and saw Carl and Porkins treading water nearby.

"Where am I?" Robo-Steve asked. "What happened to me? The last thing I remember was being held down on that altar."

"You did it, Dave old chap!" said Porkins happily. "You got that monster out of his brain!"

"Thank Carl," said Dave, "he's the one who gave me the idea by throwing that bucket of water over me. I thought jumping suddenly into water might help Robo-Steve to take back control."

"Yep," said Carl, "I'm a real hero. Now, let's get out of here before those illagers swim out and get us."

Dave looked up at the mansion. The illagers were looking down at them from the broken third-floor window. They were in shock, but that wouldn't last long.

For the first time Dave could get an idea of how massive the mansion actually was. The mansion sat on the edge of the lake, three stories high and so wide that it was even bigger than the lake; its sides hidden in the forest.

The lake was surrounded by the thick, dark forest. If they could get to the far bank before the illagers caught up with them, they could lose them in the trees, Dave thought.

"Come on," he said, "let's swim to the other side."

But then the water of the lake began to shake. They could see the forest shaking too, and the mansion was shaking so much that two of the illagers fell out of the window, landing in the lake.

Seeing that their friends had survived the fall into the water, the other illagers gained confidence, and started jumping into the lake as well.

"Swim!" Dave yelled. And he Porkins, Carl and Robo-Steve began to swim for shore as the illagers tried to swim and catch up to them.

The forest continued to shake, and a mighty roar rang out, sounding like it was coming from deep, deep underground.

"*RRRRRRRAAAAAAAUGGGGGGHHHH!!!!*"

"I don't think Herobrine's daughter is happy about being trapped again," said Carl.

The sky filled with thick, swirling gray clouds, and lightning flashed above them. One bolt of lightning hit a tree on the bank of the lake and it caught fire.

The fire spread quickly, and soon all the trees around the lake were burning. The mansion was burning too, Dave saw as he turned round. There were strange groans coming from it, like the mansion itself had been alive.

Dave and the others stopped and trod water. Escaping to shore was no longer an option because of the burning trees, but twenty-or-so illagers were swimming towards them. There was nowhere to escape to.

"Weapons ready!" said Dave.

"We have no weapons, you idiot!" said Carl.

This is bad, thought Dave. *This is very bad.*

CHAPTER EIGHT
More Illagers

Dave and his friends were trapped. They were in the middle of a lake surrounded by fire, they had no weapons, no blocks and a hoard of axe-wielding illagers were swimming towards them.

What were they going to do?

Dave dived underwater. The lake was so deep that he couldn't see the bottom of it. He looked around, trying to see anything they could turn into a weapon or anywhere they could hide. But there was nothing.

Dave came back to the surface. The illagers weren't great swimmers, but they had almost reached them now.

"Anyone got any ideas?" said Dave.

"Over there!" said Carl. "There's a bit of shore that isn't on fire."

Dave turned to see where Carl was looking. He had to squint, but he could just make it out—a patch of shore where the trees had burned down completely, leaving some empty space.

"Good spot, Carl," said Dave. "Come on everyone!"

They swam as fast as they could towards the shore.

"Come on," Dave said to Carl, who was struggling. "Climb on my back."

"This is so humiliating," said Carl. But he climbed onto Dave's back all the same.

"Hey, I rode on your shoulders in Villagertropolis," said Dave.

"I know," said Carl. "But your life is one big humiliation. You're used to it."

They swam up onto the tiny patch of shore. Dave had hoped there would be some wood that they could turn into swords, but all the trees around them were ablaze, leaving nothing behind.

The tiny bit of shore was just big enough for the four of them to stand on, but there was no way they could escape through the forest: the trees were so close together that there was nothing but fire all around them, with no safe place to walk through.

Dave turned and saw the illagers splashing towards them across the lake.

"Looks like we're gonna have to fight," Dave told the others. "I know we don't have weapons, but let's give it our best shot. If this is the end, let's go down fighting."

"Before we die, I just want to let you all know that I hate you," said Carl.

"We hate you too, Carl," said Dave, grinning.

"Wait," said Robo-Steve, "was that sarcasm? Or an attempt to let your friends know that you care for them without breaking your cynical facade?"

"Here they come," said Dave, as an illager ran out of the water. "Let's give them all we've got!"

The illager ran straight at Porkins, who raised his arm up to defend himself as the illager swung down his axe.

"Oh crumbs!" said Porkins, closing his eyes and preparing for the worse.

CLANG!

Porkins opened his eyes cautiously. The illager's axe had hit his fake arm, and had barely made a dent in the metal.

"Oh my," said Porkins.

"Of course," said Robo-Steve. "Your arm is made from iron, with a diamond core inside for strength. It should work quite effectively as both a shield and a weapon."

The illager swung his axe again, and again Porkins blocked it with his arm. More illagers were running out of the water now, coming right for them with their own axes.

"Come on, Porkins!" Carl yelled. "Use that stupid arm of yours to beat them up!"

"Oh right," said Porkins. "Jolly good."

He punched the illager who'd swung the axe at him right in the face—POW! The illager went flying backwards, falling into two other illagers, the three of them all falling on the floor in a pile.

"Right," said Porkins, "who wants some?!"

He ran towards the illagers coming up from the water and POW POW POW! He blocked their axe swings and punched them in their faces.

"Grab the axes!" Dave yelled to Robo-Steve and Carl. They ran forward and picked up the axes that the injured illagers had dropped, then joined in the fight. Carl wasn't much help, holding the axe awkwardly in one of his legs, but Dave and Robo-Steve soon had two axes each, and were swinging them wildly at the illagers.

"Retreat!" one of the illagers yelled, seeing that the battle was lost.

The remaining illagers jumped into the water, and swam away, back to the middle of the lake.

"Should we follow them and continue the battle?" Robo-Steve asked Dave.

"No," said Dave. He saw that enough of the trees around them had burnt down, giving them a safe path through the forest. "Come on, this way."

They ran through the gap in the forest, trees burning on either side of them. The heat was intense.

"Everyone still with us?" yelled Dave. He looked back to check the others were still following him. Thankfully they were—Carl was riding on Robo-Steve's back.

Suddenly something burst up from beneath Dave's feet and he fell to the ground, dropping one of his axes.

Dave saw that Porkins, Robo-Steve and Carl were on the ground too.

What was that? he wondered. But he didn't have to wait long to find out the answer. A ring of bony fangs burst from the ground, surrounding them, and illagers in long black cloaks walked through the gaps in the burning trees.

"Evokers!" gasped Porkins.

Then the red priestess walked out behind them. Her red cloak was singed and her face was covered in filth and ash.

"My lady Spidroth, have they harmed you?" she asked Robo-Steve. "We will make them suffer for what they have done to you."

"Pretend you're Spidroth," Carl whispered.

"Oh, um, hello," said Robo-Steve to the red priestess. "I am Spidroth. Pleased to meet you."

"If I had fists, I'd punch you in the face," said Carl.

The red priestess' eyes went wide with horror.

"What have you done with our queen?" she hissed. "What have you done?!"

The ground began to shake, and more lightning bolts blasted down from the sky.

"I think your queen's still underground," said Carl. "And it sounds like she's very unhappy with you."

"Lady Spidroth," the red priestess said, leaning down and stroking the ground. "Please don't worry. You will have this golden man's body once more, I promise you."

She looked up at the evokers.

"Kill them all apart from the gold man!" she roared.

The evokers raised their hands and a hoard of tiny gray fairy creatures appeared in mid air.

"I hate those little things," said Carl.

"They're called vexes," said Robo-Steve.

"Thanks," said Carl. "You're always so helpful."

The vexes flew towards them, hissing and swinging their tiny swords. Dave was about to attack one with his axe when another bony fang smashed up from underneath him, sending him flying up into the air. He landed on the ground with a thump, and then the vexes surrounded him, slashing away at him.

"Ow!" he yelled. The vexes only had tiny swords, but they were cutting him all the same. He tried to swat them away with his arms and with his axe, but they moved too quickly and were too small.

Then *SWOOSH,* an axe sliced through the air, cutting the vexes to pieces.

The axe belonged to Robo-Steve. He reached out his hand.

"Come with me if you wish to increase your life expectancy," he said.

Dave took his hand and Robo-Steve pulled him to his feet. Porkins and Carl were on their feet too. The four of them stood back-to-back, axes at the ready.

"What are you doing?" the priestess yelled at the evokers. "Just kill them!"

The vexes came for them, and at the same time the evokers launched rows of fangs at them from under the ground.

Dave and the others jumped out of the way of the fangs, and at the same time swung their axes, taking out as many of the little vexes as they could.

"We need to attack the evokers," Robo-Steve said. "Or they'll keep on summoning more vexes and fangs."

He was right, Dave knew. From the looks of it, the evokers could throw as many vexes as they liked at them, all without breaking a sweat.

"Robo-Steve is right," Dave said, "go for the evokers! Charge!!"

They all ran forward with their axes. The evoker Dave was running towards had panic in his eyes. He raised his hands and suddenly he was surrounded by a protective circle of fangs, but it was too late—Dave jumped over the fangs and swung the axe at him: *SWOOSH! SWOOSH!* Then *poof,* the evoker disappeared, leaving behind a small little stone thing with green eyes. Dave would have picked it up, but he didn't have a backpack.

Another evoker sent a row of fangs at Dave, and he dived out of the way just in time. Then he ran at the evoker, dodging the vexes swarming towards him, and buried his axe in him. There was a *poof* and the evoker was gone, leaving behind another of the strange green-eyed totem things.

Dave turned and saw Porkins and Robo-Steve finishing off the last of the evokers. Carl was cheering them on from behind.

"Come on, you can do it," said Carl. "I'm giving you moral support."

Dave felt the ground rumble underneath him. He tried to jump out of the way, but he was too slow: a bony spider leg burst from the ground, grabbing him around the waist and pinning him to the floor. Other spider legs burst up, grabbing Porkins, Robo-Steve and Carl and pinning them to the ground as well.

The red priestess walked towards them, silhouetted against the flames of the burning forest in the distance. All the evokers were gone, leaving only her.

"You fought well," she said. "But now you will pay for your sins. And you, golden man, you will be the vessel for our queen, whether you wish it or not. Her superior mind will take over your body. Perhaps your own mind will survive: trapped inside your own body, silently screaming. Who knows?"

Dave was struggling, trying to push free of the bony leg

holding him down—but it was just too strong.

"But first," said the red priestess, "it's time to kill your friends."

She raised her hands in the air, but instead of summoning vexes she summoned spiders: hundreds and hundreds of tiny red spiders, each half the size of a normal one.

"Arrrgghhh!!" said Carl. He began to struggle, trying desperately to escape, fear in his eyes.

The red priestess knelt down. The spiders all turned and looked up at her, like soldiers waiting for their orders.

"Eat them," she whispered to the spiders. "Eat them *slowly.*"

CHAPTER NINE
Tiny Spiders

Dave looked on helplessly as the army of tiny spiders scurried towards him and his friends across the ground.

"Keep away!" Carl screamed. "Keep away from me!"

Dave's arms were pinned to his sides, but he still had his axe. He tried to shift it in his hand so that he could use the axe blade to cut away at the bony spider leg holding him down. He almost managed it, but then he dropped the axe and it rolled away, too far for him to reach.

The spiders were almost upon them now. Carl was screaming, Porkins had his eyes shut, preparing for the worst, and Robo-Steve was just looking at the spiders with a blank expression. It was hard to know what he was thinking.

"Wait!" Robo-Steve suddenly shouted.

The red priestess lowered her hands and the spiders stood still.

"What is it?" she said. "If you're going to beg for the lives of your friends, you're wasting your breath."

"No," said Robo-Steve. "I'm not going to beg—I'm going to make a deal. If you let my companions go free I'll submit completely to Spidroth. I won't try and fight her at all, I'll let her take over my body completely. I'll even delete my consciousness from my hard drive, leaving her a completely blank mind to takeover. But only if you let Dave, Porkins and Carl go. For you, it's the most logical choice. Your queen gets a blank mind to inhabit. What could be better than that?"

The red priestess thought for a moment. Then she said:

"No."

"No?" said Robo-Steve, sounding confused. "But from your point of view it's the most logical solution."

"That may be so," said the red priestess, "but you and your friends have destroyed my temple, killed my acolytes and burnt down my forest. So you'll have to forgive me if I'm not feeling very *logical*. The Lady Spidroth will have your body, don't you worry about that, but she'll also have the pleasure of knowing that the villager, the creeper and the pig who wronged her all died in screaming agony. Spiders... *attack!!*"

The spiders rushed forward once more. Dave frantically searched in his pockets for anything that might be useful: any spare block that he may have left in there. But all he could find was some round object, and he had no idea what it was.

But then he felt a little button on the round object, and he realized what he was holding.

The emergency teleport! he thought excitedly. *The one that was inside Robo-Steve's chest.*

Dave realized he should have given the purple ender pearl back to Robo-Steve, but he'd completely forgotten that he had it. Anyway, he thought, that was something he could worry about later. *If we all survive.*

He pressed the button.

CHAPTER TEN
Dave's Excellent Adventure

"Waaaaa!!!!"

Dave was falling. He had teleported into an underground cavern and was falling towards a lake of lava. He quickly pressed the button on the teleporter again.

ZZAP!

Now he was falling through the sky. Far below he could see the remains of the huge dark forest, most of it either on fire or gone. He could see the lake too, but he was too far up to spot the red priestess and his friends.

"Come on," he said to the teleporter. "Bring me somewhere useful. Put me back on the ground.

He pressed the button again.

ZZAP!

Now he was surrounded by darkness. At first he thought he was in some underground lake, because he was floating, but then he realized that couldn't be true, because he could breathe.

Or at least he didn't *need* to breathe.

There was something weird about the dark place he was in. It was almost like being in a dream. He could feel his mind starting to go blank, and it was becoming harder by the second to remember why he'd come here.

He headed up, kicking his legs to swim through the darkness. He found a solid barrier above him. He swung his axe at it but it didn't even budge. He looked around and saw that the hard ceiling spread out in every direction. He let go of his axe and it floated gently downwards, disappearing into the darkness below.

It's bedrock, he realized. *I'm below bedrock.*

He was about to press the button on the teleporter once more when he became aware that he wasn't alone. There was something else down here. Something huge.

He turned and saw something gigantic and terrible in the darkness. It was so dark that he couldn't really make out its shape, but he could see its eyes: thousands of tiny red eyes, staring right at him. The creature was clinging to the underside of the bedrock with what looked like legs or tentacles, Dave couldn't really tell properly.

Getting a grasp of the creature's size was difficult too. It could have been the size of a house, it could have been the size of a mountain; it was hard to tell.

I see you, worm, Dave heard a voice say. It seemed to be broadcasting directly into his brain. *How did you get down here, to Spidroth's layer?*

Dave realized with a start that the huge creature was Spidroth, Herobrine's daughter. She didn't look much like Herobrine, but then again Dave had always thought that Herobrine didn't really look like he looked like. He'd always suspected that Herobrine was wearing some sort of disguise, or was hiding his true form in some way.

I asked you a question, worm, the voice said. *How did you get here, to the Void? If you have magic that can breach the bedrock, then I demand that you tell me!*

Dave quickly tried to press the button on his teleporter. He'd been down here too long, and his friends would be spider food if he took much longer. However, when he tried to press down on the button his finger wouldn't move, like it was held in place by some invisible force.

Why are you in such a rush to press that button? the voice demanded. *Is that the magic device you used to travel down here?*

"I... er... I was sent down here by Herobrine," said Dave, saying the first thing that popped into his head. From what the red priestess had said, he'd gathered that Spidroth herself had been cast down here by her father.

So he teleported you down here too? the voice hissed. The huge creature began to shake with anger, and it let out a terrible scream.

"RRRAAAARRRGGHHH!!!!"

Dave thought of Carl, Porkins and Robo-Steve up on the surface, about to get eaten by spiders. He had to do something to save them.

Why so anxious? the voice asked. *There's no need to rush down here, worm. Time works differently in the Void. A minute is a million years, a million years is an hour. It makes no difference.*

Dave tried to press the button again, but the invisible force was still stopping him. Then suddenly he found himself moving forward towards the creature.

He was so close now that he was right in front of the creature's face. He could see no nose, no mouth, just legs and tentacles and endless eyes, all looking at him.

Dave thought again about his friends, and realized what he had to do.

"I'll make you a deal," he told the creature. "I know how you can get out of here. But you have to agree to let my friends go."

CHAPTER ELEVEN
Dave Strikes Back

Your friends are insignificant to me, worm, said the creature, its voice projecting into Dave's head. *But if you can free me from this prison you will be handsomely rewarded. I will bring you the heads of your enemies. I will lay cities to waste in your name.*

"All I want is for you to let my friends go free," said Dave. "That priestess illager who works for you was about to feed them to spiders when I teleported down here. If we don't hurry, there'll be nothing left of them."

Worm, have you not listened to a word I've said? said the creature. *Below the bedrock time works differently than it does on the surface world.*

"So time here runs slower?" said Dave. "Like, an hour down here is a minute on the surface?"

Fool! roared the creature, its eyes flickering in the darkness. *It is far more complicated than that. Your feeble brain could never comprehend it, so don't even try.*

"O-k," said Dave. While the creature was angry and distracted he tried again to press the button on the teleportation pearl, but again an invisible force was stopping him. He had no choice: if he was going to get out of here and save his friends, he was going to have to bring Spidroth with him.

I have lived under here for years beyond measure, said the creature, *but you are testing my patience, worm. Why do you keep trying to press that button? That is your teleportation device, isn't it? Give it to me, or I will inflict pain on you so terrible that you'll wish you were never spawned.*

"It is a teleportation device," said Dave, "but it... it only works with my finger. It's programmed to only work for me. So if you kill me, it won't work."

Do not lie to me, worm, said the creature.

"I'm not lying," lied Dave. "It only works for me, but I can take you with me. I just have to be touching you when I press the button."

The creature stirred in the darkness, looking at him with its thousands of red eyes.

How do I know that when you press the button you won't just teleport out of here by yourself? the creature demanded. *How do I know this isn't a trick?*

"It isn't," Dave said, trying to make his face look as trustworthy as possible.

The creature studied him, then it reached out with hundreds of huge tree-trunk sized legs, two of them wrapping round Dave.

Now we are touching, said the creature. *So if you are telling the truth, your device should teleport us both to the surface.*

"That's right," said Dave.

Just remember this, said the creature, *if you are lying to me, and you leave me here in my prison, I will get out eventually and have my revenge. If you are gone, then I will take my vengeance on your heirs, and everyone you ever loved. Do I make myself clear? Spidroth does not like to repeat herself.*

"As clear as a glass block," said Dave. "If you let me press the button on my teleporter I can get us both out of here now."

Then do it, said the creature.

Dave placed his finger on the purple ender pearl's button, ready to press down. But then he looked up at Spidroth. Could he really unleash this gigantic monster on the world? Wouldn't he then be responsible for all the death and destruction it caused?

Dave knew what he had to do.

"Ok," he said to the creature. "Here we go. In three... two... one..."

He pushed his feet against the creature and pushed away, slipping through its legs until he was free, floating alone in the void. The creature screamed with rage, reaching its legs out to grab him, but before it could, Dave pressed the button on the teleporter...

... and found himself back in the forest. All around him trees were burning, and he could hear Carl screaming nearby.

Dave ran towards the sound of Carl's screams, but suddenly the ground shook and he fell over. From deep underground he heard a terrible yell:

"YIIIAAARRRRGGGGHHH!!!!"

Spidroth is not happy, he thought. The ground was shaking and lightning was flashing across the sky, but he got to his feet and kept running.

He ran through the burning trees and found himself in the large expanse of empty ground where the trees had burnt down. In the distance he could see the red priestess and her spiders. He could see Robo-Steve, lying on the ground held down by one of the bony spider legs, but no sign of Porkins and Carl.

"Heeeelp!" he heard Carl yell.

Then he realized, to his horror, that Porkins and Carl were covered in the tiny spiders.

Dave rushed forward towards the red priestess. He'd lost his own axe somewhere in the void, but there were other axes littered across the ground from the slain vindicators. He picked one up and ran at the red priestess. She turned round, but before she could say anything Dave launched his attack—*swoosh! swoosh!*—and then *poof*, she was gone, leaving behind nothing but one of the little totems that the other evokers had left.

As soon as the red priestess was slain, the bony spider leg holding Robo-Steve disappeared, and so did all the little spiders attacking Porkins and Carl. Dave ran over to Robo-Steve, who was nearest.

"Are you alright?" Dave asked him.

"Affirmative..." said Robo-Steve weakly. "I'm running at over seventy percent efficiency. I'll soon be back to one-hundred."

Dave ran over to Carl and Porkins. Both were covered in tiny spider bites and looked very weak.

"Where did... you go..." Carl croaked, looking up at Dave. "Thought you... abandoned us."

"Never," grinned Dave. "How could I ever live without your sarcastic quips, Carl? You doing ok, Porkins?"

"Yes, thank you, old bean," gasped Porkins, sitting up. "Nothing that a bit of healing potion won't fix."

"If only we had some," said Dave, looking at the ruins of the forest around them. On the far side of the lake he could see the remains of the mansion. "I'm guessing that our stuff must have got destroyed in the fire, wherever the illagers were keeping it."

"My iron suit!" said Carl sadly.

Suddenly the ground began to shake again, and more lightning flashed across the sky.

"Herobrine's daughter doesn't know when she's defeated, does she?" said Carl. "Looks like she's still mad."

"Funny story," said Dave, "I actually met her."

"Wait, what?" said Carl.

"I used the teleporter thing to escape the red priestess, and it brought me under the bedrock," said Dave.

"What was it like?" asked Robo-Steve.

"Very dark," said Dave. "And as for Herobrine's daughter... well, she doesn't look much like her father, let's put it that way."

Dave held out the purple pearl to Robo-Steve.

"Here, this is yours," he said, "we took this from you back on Cool Island. It's your emergency teleport."

"You keep it," said Robo-Steve. "My father never got it to work properly. His original plan was that it would allow me to teleport anywhere I liked, but he couldn't figure out how to do it. So he left it inside me as an emergency teleport that would teleport me to a random place if I was in danger."

"Ok I'll keep it for now," said Dave, "but only if you're sure."

He slipped it back into his pocket.

"We need to figure out how to use it for time travel like Future Dave," said Carl. "That would be pretty cool."

"Yeah it would be," agreed Dave.

"Chaps, shall we go to the mansion and see if any of our stuff survived?" asked Porkins.

They all agreed that this was a good idea, and headed off towards the ruins of the mansion. The fire had burnt out now, leaving nothing but empty plains of dirt where thick forest had once been.

All that was left of the mansion was a few wooden walls and a few wool blocks—everything else had been destroyed. Dave held out hope that maybe their belongings had been kept in a secret basement or something, but then he saw the burnt remains of his rucksack, and the burnt-out husk of Carl's iron golem suit.

"My suit!" wailed Carl, running over to it. The suit was burnt to a crisp, and when he touched it it collapsed into dust. Dave knew that the suit was more than just a piece of armor to fight in: for Carl it had been the freedom to run around and do everything that everyone else could. Dave had never seen the creeper look so upset.

Dave looked inside his burnt backpack and saw some crispy pieces of paper: the last remains of his three books. There had been the crafting book that the old man had given him when he'd first started his adventure, all that time ago, the potion brewing book he'd bought a few days earlier from a wandering trader, and the ancient book that he'd found in the stronghold under his village: the one that had told him how to get to the End. He felt a sudden sadness. He hadn't thought about it much before, but the crafting book and the book about how the get to the End had been his oldest companions on his journey. They'd been with him before he'd even met Carl and Porkins, and they were the last pieces of his home that he had.

"It looks like we're going to have to start from scratch," Dave told the others. "We're going to need more blaze rods, ender pearls, material for weapons and armor, everything."

Porkins and Carl looked exactly like Dave felt: miserable. It felt like they were back to square one.

"Put your hands in the air!" said a voice.

"Oh great, what now?" moaned Carl.

They all turned and saw a red metal robot standing on top of a broken bit of mansion wall, aiming a bow and arrow at them. He was wearing a diamond crown.

"Charles?" said Robo-Steve, sounding confused. "What are you doing here?"

CHAPTER TWELVE
Old Friends

Charles the robot, Robo-Steve's former assistant, was aiming his bow at his former leader's face.

"I'm here to fight you," he said. "For the title of Robot King."

"You can have it," said Robo-Steve. "I'm calling myself Robo-Steve again now."

"No!" snapped Charles. "I must win it from you, to prove that I'm worthy!"

"Charles, you are worthy," said Robo-Steve. "I know you, you're a good person. You're more worthy of the Robot King title than I ever was. Build yourself some robots, make your own kingdom. You'd be a fine ruler."

"You're not listening!" said Charles. "I'm going to beat you, to prove I'm better than you. You were a king and you threw it all away! We're better than the villagers, we're smarter than them and we should rule over them. Once I've defeated you I'm going to continue what you started."

"I was wrong," said Robo-Steve. "Why don't you come with us? Dave, Carl and Porkins are good people. You can see first hand why it's not right for us to rule over people without their consent. I thought logic was the answer to everything, but life is much more complicated than that."

Charles threw his bow and arrow to one side, then jumped down, landing in front of Robo-Steve.

"That's enough talking," he said, raising his fists. "Now it's time to fight."

"Oh shut up!" yelled someone. Dave turned and was surprised to see it was Porkins. The pigman ran forward, then *POW*—he socked Charles right in the face with his metal arm. Charles went flying, landing against a broken bit of wall. He was knocked out.

"Wow, Porkins," said Carl. "What got into you?!"

"I'm dreadfully sorry," said Porkins, his cheeks glowing red. "I just lost my temper a bit. After all we went through today—losing all our stuff, nearly being sacrificed and eaten by spiders—I couldn't take anyone else trying to ruin things."

He walked over to Charles.

"Do you think the poor chap will be ok?" he asked the others.

Robo-Steve knelt down and put his hand on Charles's head.

"Yes," said Robo-Steve. "He's just unconscious. You must have caused a temporary displacement to his battery core. He should reboot successfully within an hour or so."

"What should we do with him?" Dave asked. "Should we take him with us? If we leave him here he might try and find us again. And this time he might do a better job at trying to kill us."

Robo-Steve thought for a moment. Then he said: "I've got it. I know how he found us."

"Well go on," said Carl. "Stop showing off and just tell us."

"I gave all the robots I built back in Villagertropolis a tracker chip," said Robo-Steve, "so I could know where they were at all times. Charles obviously used his chip to track me. A clever trick."

Suddenly Robo-Steve's eyes began to flicker.

"Um, are you ok?" asked Dave.

"All done," said Robo-Steve, his purple eyes returning to normal. "I've deactivated my tracker chip. Now Charles won't be able to find us when he wakes up."

He looked sadly at the red robot.

"I just hope he finds some companions who show him the error of his ways, like I have," said Robo-Steve. "I would let him come with us, but I think seeing me every day would make him angry. He thinks I've betrayed my fellow robots, and perhaps he's right."

They had a final look round to see if there was anything to salvage in the burnt out mansion, but there was nothing of any use.

Even if there was, I don't have a backpack to keep anything in, thought Dave sadly.

So the four of them headed off once more. They didn't have an ender eye to check their route, but the last time they'd used one it had told them to go north, so that was the direction they started walking.

They walked and walked, trying to put as much distance between them and Charles as they could, to make sure he didn't find them again.

"I guess we should get some wood," said Dave as they passed some trees. "We ought to make some basic weapons at least, and we need enough to build ourselves a shelter for when the sun goes down."

"Uh oh," said Carl, "I think we should have got those weapons a bit earlier."

Two riders in full diamond armor were riding diamond-armored horses towards them.

"Get that super arm of yours ready," said Carl, "we don't know if these guys are friendly."

The riders rode up to them and pulled to a stop. Their faces were hidden in the shadow of their helmets.

"Well met," said Dave to the riders. "We're just friendly travelers on the road. We mean you no harm."

One of the riders removed his helmet and Dave got the surprise of his life.

"Steve?!" he gasped.

Then the other rider removed his helmet, and Dave got an even *bigger* surprise.

"S-steve?" he said.

He looked from one rider to the other, then back again, his brain unable to take in what he was seeing.

Both riders were Steves.

"Hello, bros," said one of the Steves. "How's it going?"

EPILOGUE

Under the world, Spidroth was raging.

She slammed her legs into the bedrock again and again, screaming into the endless void.

"*YIAAARRRGGGHHH!!!!*"

That little worm tricked me, she thought angrily. *He made a fool of me!*

After being down here so long she had finally had a chance to escape, but that chance had been snatched cruelly away.

If I ever escape, that worm will pay, she thought angrily. *Once I have had my vengeance on my father, the worm will be next.*

Her acolytes had been as useless as ever. For years they had been trying to find her a suitable body to transfer her consciousness into, but they had failed over and over again. Of course, ideally she would have liked to have brought her whole body back to the surface, but transferring her mind into someone else's body had been the next best option.

Sometimes the acolytes had volunteered themselves for the mind transfer, and sometimes they had brought unwilling sacrifices, but it had never made any difference: Spidroth's mind was so huge that trying to transfer it into a mortal body had been futile.

Until the golden man.

Spidroth didn't know exactly what the golden man was, but for some reason his body *had* been able to contain her vast mind. For a moment she had seen through his eyes; she had seen the surface world once more, for the first time in hundreds—maybe thousands—of years.

But then something had happened. Someone had grabbed her and thrown her into cold water. Her mind had still been adjusting to being in a new body, and the sudden coldness had ruined everything. The shock had thrown her out of the golden man's body, and she had been trapped beneath the world once more.

Spidroth continued to rage, but then—suddenly—she became aware of a new presence in the world above.

It's another golden man!

She could *feel* the new golden man; she could sense his presence. Normally she needed her acolytes to prepare a subject before she could take control of its mind, but this new golden man was weak. He was either unconscious or nearly unconscious, his body injured from a trauma to the head, so would offer her no resistance.

Spidroth reached out with her mind, projecting it upwards through the bedrock, through the stone and dirt and the lava, and finally into the unconscious body of this new golden man.

She opened her eyes and saw the sun and the clouds above her. She was so happy that she could have cried, but this golden man had no tear ducts. She could hear the golden man inside her head, yelling to be let out, but she ignored his voice.

Your body is mine now, she told him.

She saw a lake in the distance, the sunlight glistening off the water. She walked towards it and looked into the calm, still water to get a look at her new body.

The body she was in wasn't gold after all—it was red. Some sort of red metal. It didn't feel that strong, but she was sure that in time she could make it stronger.

I'm free, she thought happily. *And now, after so many years, I will finally have my revenge!*

Dave the Villager

Dave the Villager

BOOK 8

Steveageddon

Dave the Villager

CHAPTER ONE
Seeing Double

Dave looked from one Steve to the other, but he couldn't tell the difference.

"You're... you're both Steve?" he said, feeling confused.

The Steves looked at each other.

"Wow, it happened again!" they both said at the same time.

"What happened again?" asked Robo-Steve.

Suddenly the two Steves began to glow with bright white light; it was so bright that Dave had to shield his eyes. When the light stopped and he could look again, Dave couldn't believe what he was seeing.

There were now *four* Steves. All four of them were clad in diamond armor and riding on diamond armored horses.

"Good gosh!" said Porkins.

"I've seen some weird stuff on this adventure," said Carl, "but this is definitely up there."

"Do you... do you recognize us?" Dave asked the Steves. "Do you all have Steve's memory as well?"

"Of course we recognize you, bro," said one of the Steves. "You're Dan the villager!"

Carl snorted with laughter.

"That's right," said Carl. "He's the legendary Dan the villager."

"And how could I forget you, bro?" said a different Steve to Carl. "Colin the creeper."

The smile disappeared from Carl's face.

"It's *Carl*," he muttered.

"What about me, Steve old bean?" asked Porkins. "Do you remember me?"

"Of course," said all the Steves in unison. "You're Pork Chop!"

Porkins smiled happily. Dave and Carl frowned at him.

Robo-Steve stepped forward.

"You probably don't recognize me," he said to the Steves, "as I've changed my appearance a great deal since we last met. I am Robo-Steve, the robot version of you that you fought in Snow Town. My creator Ripley made me to frame you for crimes you hadn't committed, and I apologize for all the wrong I did you. Please be rest assured that I have changed a great deal since we last met, and I am deeply sorry for the hurt my actions caused. Thanks to Dave and his friends, I am learning to be a better person and I hope to eventually understand what it means to be good."

"Cool story, bro," said one of the Steves. "Now who wants some cake?"

"Cake! Cake! Cake!" chanted the other Steves.

So the four Steves led Dave and the others across the grass until they came to a cobblestone road.

"This is the way to Steve town," one of the Steves told them. "You're gonna love it. What could be cooler than a town full of Steves?"

"Wait," said Dave, "are you telling me there's a whole town of Steves?"

"Yeah bro," said the Steve. "It's the Steviest place on Earth."

"But how did that happen?" Dave asked, as they all walked down the cobblestone road. "I always thought there was only one of you? Or have there always been loads of Steves, and no-one knew about it?"

"Nah," said the Steve, "this is a new thing. The Prof has this cool machine and when I saw it I just had to try it out, and then BLAM! Suddenly there are two of me. Then there were four, then eight, then more and more, until there was a whole town of Steves! How cool is that?"

Dave had always thought Steve was a bit hyper, but these new Steves seemed even more hyper than usual.

"Can you take us to the Prof?" Dave asked. He suspected he wasn't going to get a sensible explanation of what was going on from Steve, so this professor, whoever he was, seemed like a good person to speak to.

"Of course, bro," said the Steve. "The Prof is so cool, you're gonna love her. I mean, obviously she's not as cool as me."

"Or me," said one of the other Steves.

"Hey bro, I'm cooler than you," said another Steve.

"Bro, you're talking crazy!" said the fourth Steve. "I'm the coolest!"

"Don't listen to them, bro," said the first Steve, reaching down from his horse and putting a hand on Dave's shoulder. "Everyone knows I'm the coolest."

Suddenly the Steves began to glow white again.

"Uh oh," said Carl. "Here we go again."

When the glowing finished there were eight Steves, all on horses.

But there was someone else as well.

Dave's mouth dropped open. Standing in front of him was a villager who looked very familiar.

It was a second Dave.

CHAPTER TWO
Steve Town

"Oops," said the Steve who'd put his hand on Dave's shoulder. "I shouldn't have touched you when the glowy thing happened. Sorry bro."

Dave still couldn't believe what he was seeing. An identical copy of him standing there, looking as surprised as he was.

"What's going on?" Dave and the copy said at the same time.

"I think we ought to take you to see the Prof," said one of the Steves.

"Good idea," the two Daves said together.

It was awkward for Dave walking along the cobblestone road alongside his double. He didn't really know what to say to the other Dave—if they really were identical copies then Dave 2 (as Dave had started referring to the other Dave as in his head) would be thinking the exact same things as him.

"So, are you two identical then?" Carl asked. "Let's test it out—say the first color that comes into your head."

"Purple," said both the Daves.

"That is freaky," said Carl.

Dave decided he ought to try and make conversation with Dave 2.

"So," he said.

"So," said Dave 2. "This is a bit weird, isn't it?"

"Yeah," said Dave. "It sure is."

"So," said Carl, walking in between the two of them, "which one of you is Dave 1 and which one is Dave 2?"

"I'm Dave 1," Dave and the other Dave said in unison. They shot each other angry looks.

"I'm Dave 1!" said the other Dave.

"No you're not," said Dave, "I'm the original! Porkins, tell him that I'm the original."

"I must say chaps, it is rather hard to tell you apart," said Porkins. "Maybe you both can be Dave 1."

Dave was about to say exactly what he thought about that, but then they came over a hill and he forgot all about his squabbles with the other Dave.

In front of them was a town. Or rather, a town was being built. Builders were busy putting up new wooden houses and apartment blocks, while others chopped down trees and others were digging to level out the ground. There was a large hole that was obviously a mine near the town too, and diggers with pickaxes were going back and forth, loading materials onto minecarts.

Normally there would have been nothing too spectacular about a new town being built, but this town was unique.

Because all the people were Steves.

Steves were building the houses, Steves were going down the mine, Steves were bringing the workers cake. All of them wore blue t-shirts and pants, had a little beard and had brown hair. They were all exactly alike.

"Welcome to Steve Town, little bros," one of the Steves riding with them said.

"Crikey," said Porkins. "That's a lot of Steves."

"Our town motto is *Stevus Never Enuficus*," said another of the Steves.

"What does that mean?" Dave and his double asked at the same time.

"*You can never have enough Steves,*" said the Steve.

Suddenly the Steves all started glowing again. The Steves in the town were glowing too.

"Uh oh," said one of the Steves riding with them, "don't touch us little bros."

Dave quickly backed away, not wanting to create another clone of himself. When the glowing stopped there were sixteen Steves riding on sixteen horses in front of them, and Steve Town was packed with more Steves.

"So every time that happens, all of you Steves double?" said Robo-Steve. "How is that sustainable?"

"I don't know if it's *sustainable*," said one of the Steves with a grin, "but it's definitely *Steveainable!*"

He put his hand in the air and all the other Steves rode over on their horses to hi-five him.

"Nice one, bro!" said one of the Steves.

"Top laughs, bro," said another.

"Bro, I was just about to make that same joke!" said a third.

Carl crawled over to Dave and his double.

"You know," the creeper whispered, "I'm starting to realize why you used to find Steve so annoying."

Porkins came over and joined them.

"These Steve chaps are terrific fun, aren't they?" he grinned. "They're real jokers in the pack."

The Steves led them through the town. Dave couldn't believe how many Steves there were, all of them hard at work building the town or taking a break and eating cake. Dave also couldn't believe how much cake there was: there were redstone-powered rail tracks running through the town, and minecarts packed high with cakes would instantly whizz past.

Around the buildings under construction was some kind of wooden frame made from tubes. It allowed the Steves to reach the higher areas of the buildings with ease—which was good, because some of the new apartments they were creating were very high, some at least five stories tall.

"What is that stuff around the buildings?" Dave wondered

aloud.

"Scaffolding," said Robo-Steve. "It's a fairly new invention, made from bamboo. Apparently it can make creating tall buildings much quicker and easier."

Most of the Steves looked exactly alike, with the same facial hair and clothes, but there were a few anomalies. He spotted a Steve with a red t-shirt instead of a blue one; a chubby Steve, who was sitting on the floor stuffing his face with cake; a Steve with sunglasses; and he even thought he glimpsed a Steve made of something that looked like cake.

At the center of the town was a small cobblestone bungalow. The cobblestone was covered in moss and it looked very old. In fact, it was the only building in the village that didn't look brand new.

"This is the Prof's lab," said one of the Steves.

Dave looked at the sign by the wooden door. It said: *The Quigley Family. Guests welcome!*

"It doesn't look much like a laboratory," said Carl, looking at the mossy cobblestone. "I was expecting lots of glass and smooth metal surfaces."

Dave and his double walked inside. It was a quaint little home, with a wooden table and chairs, a fireplace, bookshelves and a couple of beds. On the wall was a sign that said: *Home Sweet Home!*

Carl, Porkins and Robo-Steve followed the two Daves inside.

"Are you sure we're not in the wrong location?" Robo-Steve asked one of the sixteen Steves, who had all followed them into the bungalow and were squeezed up against the walls.

"Nah bro," said one of the Steves, "watch this."

The Steve grabbed one of the books on the book shelf and pulled it. There was a *thunk* from within the walls and a square of the cobblestone floor slid away, revealing a secret staircase.

"How fun!" said Porkins.

"Come on, this way," said another Steve, then the sixteen Steves all started walking down the cobblestone stairs.

"Wait," said Dave and Dave 2 at the same time, "will you all fit down there?"

But the Steves were already gone.

"Right," said Carl, "let's have a look at this laboratory."

And he followed the Steves down the stairs, with Robo-Steve and Porkins following behind him.

Dave and Dave 2 looked at each other, both rolling their eyes, then they walked down the stairs too.

They walked down and down the winding stairs, until suddenly the cobblestone walls around the stairs ended, and Dave found himself looking down at a gigantic underground room.

"Wow," said Dave and Dave 2 together. "Now *this* is a laboratory."

CHAPTER THREE
Professor Quigley

The huge room was so big that Dave could only just make out the far side of it. The walls, floor and ceiling were made from iron blocks, and the room was divided into sections, separated by glass walls.

Dave and Dave 2 reached the bottom of the cobblestone stairs, joining Carl, Porkins, Robo-Steve and the sixteen Steves. They were in a long glass corridor with lots of rooms leading off from it. All the walls in the lab had glass walls, so they could see what was going on in all the rooms. There were people working away at machines and performing experiments; strange-looking people with long, thin arms and legs.

No, not people, thought Dave, as he looked closer. *They're endermen!*

A door opened and an old female villager with frizzy gray hair marched up to them. She was wearing a huge lab coat and goggles that made her eyes look huge.

"Steve!" she said to the Steves. "You know you shouldn't be down here—you need to be outside in case you double again!"

"We were just bringing these little bros to meet you," said one of the Steves, looking at Dave and his friends. "One of us was touching that villager bro when we doubled, and now there are two villager bros."

"Ah, I see," said the villager, looking from Dave to Dave 2 then back again. "Of course, one of you will have to die so that the other can live. Which one of you wants to sacrifice themselves?"

"What?!" said Dave and Dave 2.

The villager began to laugh.

"Sorry," she chuckled, "that was in bad taste. Don't worry, I can fix you. I'm Professor Quigley. To whom do I have the pleasure of speaking?"

"I'm Dave," said Dave 2.

"Er, and I'm Dave as well," said Dave.

"I'm Carl," said Carl.

"I'm Porkins," said Porkins. "Pleased to make your acquaintance, my lady."

"And I'm Robo-Steve," said Robo-Steve.

"Extraordinary," said Professor Quigley, looking Robo-Steve up and down. "You're an android version of Steve, yes? Who built you?"

"My father was a villager named Ripley," said Robo-Steve. "He lived in Snow Town."

"He must have been extraordinarily talented," said Professor Quigley, running her hand across Robo-Steve's gold chest. "I've experimented with robotics before, but I've never come close to creating anything as sophisticated as you."

"Can you show us around your lab?" Carl asked. "Have you got any weird stuff?"

Professor Quigley grinned.

"It depends on your definition of weird, little creeper," she said. "But sure, I'll show you around."

Suddenly there was a ROAR and something huge and white lumbered its way towards them across the iron block floor.

A polar bear! Dave realized, to his shock.

"Weapons ready!!" Dave and Dave 2 yelled together.

"We don't have any weapons!" said Porkins.

Dave and his friends all tried to run out of the way as the polar bear lumbered towards them.

There was another ROAR and then Dave felt something huge and heavy jump up on him from behind. He fell to the floor, the polar bear's huge weight pinning him down. He closed his eyes and prepared for the worst.

And then he felt something wet and sloppy rubbing against the back of his bald head.

The polar bear was *licking* him.

"Dean, get off him," he heard Professor Quigley laugh.

The polar bear climbed off of him. Dave nervously turned round. The polar bear was sitting down like a dog, its tongue hanging from its mouth.

Professor Quigley scratched the bear on the back of its neck and it began to purr.

"Sorry about that, Dave," Professor Quigley said. "Little Dean here can be a bit over-friendly. But he's perfectly harmless."

Carl crawled out from behind a flower pot.

"Are you sure?" Carl asked Professor Quigley. "I've been through a lot in the past few days—I don't want it all to be for nothing when I get gobbled up by a polar bear."

"You won't eat the little creeper, will you?" said Professor Quigley, rubbing the polar bear's cheek. "You're a good bear, aren't you?"

"Ruff! Ruff!" said the bear.

Professor Quigley pressed a button on the wall and a hatch opened, a large bowl full of raw meat sliding out across the floor. The polar bear cheerfully bounded over and started gobbling down the meat.

"Right," said Professor Quigley, "let's continue the tour."

"Prof, can we see the cake machine again?" one of the Steves asked.

"Cake! Cake! Cake!" the other Steves chanted.

"Yeah bro, CAKE!" one of them added.

"No," said Professor Quigley sternly. "In fact, I want you to go back to the surface. How many of you are there, sixteen? If you double again I'll have thirty-two Steves clogging up my lab."

"But what about the cake?" said one of the Steves.

Professor Quigley rolled her eyes.

"Ok," she said.

"YES!!!!" yelled all the Steves.

"Eden!" yelled Professor Quigley.

There was a *ZAP* and suddenly an enderman teleported in front of the Professor.

"Y-es, pro-fess-or?" The enderman said. Rather than the usual black, this endermen was blue with red eyes.

"A talking enderman," said Carl. "Now I really have seen everything."

"Eden, go and fetch a minecart full of cake for these Steves."

"O-k," said the enderman, it's voice strange and stilted. Then *ZAP* it teleported away.

"I didn't even know endermen could speak," Dave 2 said.

"Yes, they have the capacity for basic speech," said Professor Quigley, "but they're too stupid to say much more than nonsense phrases. However, the endermen in my lab have had their brains enhanced and I've taught them to talk. You wouldn't be able to have much of a conversation with them, but they can obey basic orders."

"What made you want to mess around with endermen brains in the first place?" asked Carl. "Couldn't you just hire some villagers to work in your lab? Or use some of the Steves?"

"I didn't enhance the endermen's brains," said Professor Quigley, "That was done at the laboratory I was working at. I merely freed them, and brought them back here to my home."

There was another *ZAP* and Eden the enderman reappeared, holding a minecart full of cakes.

"CAKES!!'" the Steves yelled, then they rushed forward as Eden placed the minecart on the ground, and they began gobbling down the cake, shoving it into their mouths as fast as they could.

"Gosh, those chaps are rather hungry, aren't they?" said Porkins.

"It's a side effect of the duplication process," said Professor Quigley. "Creating an exact copy of yourself every few minutes means you need a lot of sustenance. My endermen are duplicating cakes around the clock to feed the Steves, but it's reaching the point where we can't make cakes fast enough."

"Why are you making all these Steves anyway?" asked Carl.

"It was an accident," said Professor Quigley. "But I'll tell you more about that once we've fixed your villager friend and his clone problem."

Professor Quigley turned to the Steves.

"Once you've eaten that cake, I want you lot back on the surface," she told them. "No excuses."

"Ok, ok," said one of the Steves, his mouth full of cake.

The professor turned to the blue enderman.

"And Eden, I want you to go to the surface and record the latest Steve count. Wait until they next duplicate, then quickly count them."

"Yes, pro-fes-sor," said the enderman, then *ZAP*, it disappeared.

"Fascinating," said Robo-Steve, "so that enderman can teleport wherever he wants, rather than to a random location?"

"Wherever *she* wants," said Professor Quigley. "Eden is a girl. But yes, that's correct. As well as enhancing their brain function, Laboratory 303 enhanced their teleportation functions as well."

Dave thought about the purple teleportation pearl in his pocket, and made a mental note to ask Professor Quigley to take a look at it later. She might know how they could get it working properly.

Dave looked over at his double, who was looking back at him, and realized that Dave 2 was thinking the exact same thing.

Wait, wondered Dave, *does he have a copy of the purple teleportation pearl as well?*

"Come along!" yelled Professor Quigley at Dave and Dave 2. "Let's get your double problem sorted out."

She began to march down the corridor, and Dave and the others quickly followed behind.

"Good gracious," said Porkins, looking through a glass wall as they walked past. "What's going on in there?"

Three endermen with spears were trying to force a hideous monster into a cage. The creature had several heads, and kept lunging and hissing at them.

"Oh that's just a mutant zombie-skeleton-spider," said Professor Quigley. "The scientists at 303 made them to be soldiers to sell to the highest bidder. Unfortunately a load of them broke out and... well, let's just say they caused a bit of a mess. I found this one roaming the countryside a few days ago and took it in."

Professor Quigley kept on walking, so Dave only got a brief glimpse of the creature. Its legs seemed to be spider legs but its top half was a bit harder to figure out: it looked like a skeleton, but had green, moldy flesh sticking to its bones in places. It wasn't a creature he would have liked to have come across in the wild.

"AH WOW!!!"

Dave looked round. Carl had his face pressed up against the glass wall of one of the rooms. Through the glass Dave could see a huge browny-orange thing, with endermen walking around it, taking notes.

"What is that thing?" Dave asked Carl.

"It's... it's... a baked potato!" the creeper gasped.

Dave realized that Carl was right. It was a baked potato as big as a house.

"Probably the biggest baked potato in the world," Professor Quigley grinned, walking over to them. "The endermen are testing out my new enlarger gun. We're hoping to do tests on sentient lifeforms soon."

"Baked potato..." said Carl, unable to take his eyes off it. "So big..."

"I'm afraid I can't let you eat it," said Professor Quigley. "We need to run more tests to check that enlarged food is safe."

Professor Quigley walked up to the glass.

"How's it going, JT?" she shouted at one of the enderman. This enderman was red with pink eyes. In fact, Dave noticed, none of the endermen in the professor's lab were normal enderman color. Something about the brain enhancing must have changed their color somehow, he guessed.

"Ex-per-iment go-ing as planned," the enderman named JT replied, his voice stilted like the other enderman's had been. "Po-ta-to is stable."

Suddenly there was a rumbling; the potato began to shake.

"Uh-oh," said JT.

Then BOOM! The potato exploded, covering the glass with yellow gunk.

Professor Quigley ran over and opened the door.

"Are you all ok?" she asked.

JT and three other endermen staggered out, all of them covered in potato mush.

"We are o-k," said JT, wiping the potato from his eyes. "Ex-per-i-ment needs... more work."

"Go and get yourselves cleaned up," Professor Quigley told them, "and take the rest of the afternoon off."

She turned back to Dave and the others and gave them a grin.

"Sometimes my experiments don't go exactly as planned," she said. "Which is how this Steve situation began. Come on, I'll show you."

Finally they came to a room with a huge white cube. There was a round hole on one side, with a swirling blue portal inside.

"This is my duplication machine," Professor Quigley told them. "Here, watch."

She reached into her pocket and took an apple out. Then she threw the apple into the portal. For a second nothing happened, but then two apples shot out, rolling across the floor.

"You see," said Professor Quigley, "it duplicates things. Simple. And if you don't want the thing to be duplicated anymore..."

She picked up both apples and threw them both into the

portal. After a moment, one apple shot out.

"... you can merge them together again," she finished.

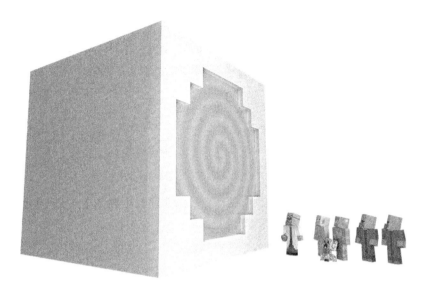

"So what's the issue with the Steve duplicating problem?" asked Robo-Steve. "Why do the Steves keep duplicating every few minutes? And why did Dave duplicate when Steve was touching him?"

"And why do they love cake so much?" asked Carl. "I mean, cake is fine, but it's nowhere near as nice as baked potatoes."

Professor Quigley sighed.

"First of all, let me just say that I think Steve's great," she said. "Years ago, when I was a little girl, this was a farmhouse. Well, not the underground lab, this wasn't there back then, but the house above. My parents were farmers. Then one day, illagers started raiding our land. They were some sort of religious fanatics or something, they kept talking about a *spider queen*. My parents tried to fight them off, buying themselves some swords and building some iron golems, but it was no good, the illagers kept coming, stealing our crops and our animals.

"Then one day, Steve was passing through on his horse and my father stopped him and asked for help. Steve was a bit different back then, a bit less goofy. Plus he didn't say *bro* all the time. Anyway, he agreed to help us. My father tried to give him payment, but Steve refused. He said helping people was what heroes did, and he didn't need a reward.

"So the next time the illagers came, Steve was waiting for them. He fought them all by himself and sent them running. And they never came back."

Professor Quigley smiled, lost in her memories.

"Over the years, Steve would always visit us when he passed by," she continued. "I grew up, my parents got old, but Steve never changed. He always looked the same age.

"Then I went off to Diamond City, trained to be a doctor, got a job at Lab 303, and I would only come back here occasionally to see my parents. When they were gone I inherited the farm, but I never came back here often. When I eventually left 303 I decided to build my own lab under the farmhouse, so I could work on my own experiments. Then, a couple of weeks ago, Steve came to visit. It was the first time I'd seen him in decades, but he still looked the same. He said he was on a quest to find a dragon."

So Steve's still looking for the ender dragon, thought Dave. He had hoped that Steve would have forgotten about the dragon by now, but it appeared that he hadn't.

"Anyway," said Professor Quigley, "Steve acted a little differently—as I said, he's a bit goofier now than he used to be—but he was still the same old Steve. I showed him my lab and he offered to help me with my experiments. We were having a good time, hanging out, trying out my inventions, but then disaster struck."

"What happened?" asked Porkins.

"Steve went into the duplicator with a cake," said Professor Quigley.

Carl snorted with laughter.

"Wait, what?" he said.

"Steve put a cake in the duplicator," said Professor Quigley, "as he wanted two cakes, and could only be bothered to make one."

"O-k," said Carl.

"He put the cake in," she continued, "but he got frustrated when two cakes didn't come out straight away. Sometimes the machine can take a bit of time. So... he climbed into the portal to see what was wrong."

"Why would he do that?" asked Porkins.

"Because he's a moron," said Professor Quigley. "I'm very fond of him, really I am, but he's not the sharpest sword in the chest. Anyway, the duplicator is only designed to handle one object or mob at once, so having Steve and the cake in there at the same time caused some sort of malfunction. At first when Steve came out of the duplicator it seemed like everything was fine. There was just one Steve and one cake. But then he duplicated. I made both the Steve's go back in the machine, to merge them together again, but it didn't work. Not only that, but now both Steves were always hungry for cake. They wouldn't eat anything else, just cake."

"Not even baked potatoes?" asked Carl.

"Nope," said Professor Quigley.

"My gosh," said Carl.

"Ever since then, the Steves have kept on duplicating," said Professor Quigley. "Every few minutes it happens. Oh, and anything they touch while duplicating is duplicated too," she added, looking at Dave and Dave 2.

She ushered the two of them over.

"Come on," she said to the Daves, "into the machine. It'll merge the two of you together again."

"You want us to go into that portal?" Dave 2 asked. "After what you just told us about what happened to Steve?"

"Yeah," said Dave, "Dave 2 is right, it doesn't sound very safe."

"Hey," said Dave 2, "*you're* Dave 2."

"Neither of you are Dave 2!" snapped Professor Quigley. "The original Dave split into two bits, that's all. So neither of you is the original and neither is the copy. You're both the same. Now come on, go into the portal and the machine will fix you back together again."

Dave and his double cautiously walked up to the duplicator. The swirling round liquid reminded Dave a bit of a nether portal.

"After you," Dave said to Dave 2.

"No, I insist, after you," said Dave 2.

"Both of you just go in!" yelled Carl. "We haven't got all day!"

Dave took a deep breath, then he and Dave 2 stepped into the portal together.

Dave found himself inside a swirling blue vortex. Dave 2 was there too, the two of them swirling round and round.

"What's going ooooon?" the two of them said at the same time.

Then the vortex swept the two of them together. Dave watched helplessly as Dave 2 crashed into him...

And then there was no Dave 2. It was the strangest sensation, but suddenly all of Dave 2's memories were in Dave's head. It was like two different minds and memories had combined into one.

The two me's have merged back together, he realized. He had two sets of memories in his head now, going back to when he'd split into two.

Then there was a bright light and Dave found himself lying back on the floor of the lab, his friends and Professor Quigley looking down at him.

"So which one are you," Carl asked him, "Dave 1 or Dave 2?"

"Both," said Dave, getting gingerly to his feet.

"The duplicates have merged back into one being," said Professor Quigley.

"Can't you just do that with the Steves?" Robo-Steve asked. "If they all went back into the duplicator, wouldn't they merge together again?"

"As I said, I've tried," said Professor Quigley. "But when Steve went in at the same time as the cake, something went wrong, and the duplicates just won't go back together again. Not only that, but sometimes there are malfunctions and the duplicates aren't exact duplicates. That shouldn't be happening."

"I saw a Steve chap with a red t-shirt," said Porkins.

"That's a minor malfunction," said Professor Quigley, "but there have been more severe ones. I've even seen some Cake Steves."

"Um, what's a Cake Steve?" asked Carl.

"A Steve made out of cake," said Professor Quigley.

"Oh," said Carl, "I guess that makes sense."

"I've kept one of the Steve malfunctions in stasis so I can study her," said the professor.

"Wait," said Dave, "what do you mean *her?*"

Professor Quigley pressed a button on the wall and a panel slide open. Inside was a glass box, and inside the box was a girl, floating asleep in some sort of pale liquid. Her clothes and hair were exactly the same color as Steve's, but her hair was longer.

"That's weird," said Carl. "What do you call her, Stevina?"

"Actually," said Professor Quigley, "I call her—"

Suddenly there was some commotion behind them. Dave looked round and saw a load of Steve's falling down the cobblestone steps. They all ended up in a heap on the floor, moaning and groaning in pain. "Ow, my head bro," Dave heard one of them say.

"Oh dear, they must have duplicated again," said Professor Quigley. "If I don't come up with a solution soon, it could be the end of everything."

"What do you mean, *everything?*" asked Carl.

"I believe the meaning is clear," said Robo-Steve. "If the Steves keep duplicating at the rate they're going, soon they will cover the entire world. The whole planet will be drowned in a sea of Steves."

Professor Quigley nodded in agreement.

"Oh my gosh," said Porkins. "It'll be Steveaggedon!"

CHAPTER FOUR
The Steve's Head

Professor Quigley brought them up out of the lab and back into her cottage, where an enderman poured them some warm milk.

"So what do you plan to do about all these Steves?" Dave asked. Out of the window he could see more construction work going on, as the Steves continued to build up the town.

"Do any other chaps and chapettes live in this town?" Porkins asked. "It must be tough for them to have to live alongside all the Steves."

"This isn't a town," said Professor Quigley. "Before a few days ago this cottage was the only building for miles around, but when the Steves started duplicating, they had to build houses for them to live in. Because they keep duplicating, they keep having to build more houses.

"And to answer your question, Dave," she said, "I'm trying to figure out a way to merge all the Steves back together, but nothing I've tried so far has worked."

"Perhaps I can assist you," said Robo-Steve. "I don't wish to cause offense, but it is a statement of fact that my robotic brain is superior to your own."

"Er, ok," said Professor Quigley. "Yeah, go on then—I could do with as much help as I can get. Oh, and just in case any of you accidentally touch a Steve when they're duplicating, drink some of this."

She reached into her lab coat and pulled out a bottle of glowing blue liquid.

"Each of you take a sip," she said, passing the bottle to Porkins. "Even you, robot man."

"What is it?" asked Porkins, studying the glowing liquid through the bottle.

"Anti-duplication matter," said Professor Quigley. "It will stop the residual duplication energy from the Steves from affecting you."

Porkins took a sip, then passed the bottle to Carl.

"It tastes very peculiar," said Porkins.

"Is there anything me, Porkins and Carl can do to help while you and Robo-Steve work in the lab?" Dave asked Professor Quigley.

"No I don't think so," she said. "Unless any of you have a degree in theoretical physics."

"Not as far as I know," said Carl. He took a sip from the bottle of glowing liquid, pulled a face, then passed the bottle to Dave.

"It's sooo tasty," Carl told Dave. "You're going to love it."

"Hmm, why don't I believe you," said Dave.

"There's a bar nearby you could hang out at if you want," Professor Quigley told them. "The research we're doing will probably take a while, so you'll have some time to kill. If you head out my front door it's on the third path to the left. It's called the Steve's Head."

"Of course it is," said Carl.

So Dave, Carl and Porkins left Professor Quigley and Robo-Steve and walked through the town towards the bar. The streets were packed full of Steves, all hard at work carrying materials back and forth or eating cake. Dave spotted another of the Cake Steves, who was also eating cake. It made Dave feel a bit weird watching a man made out of cake eating a cake.

The bar was a quaint wooden building nestled between two apartment blocks. There was a sign hanging above the door with painting of a disembodied Steve head, with the words "The Steve's Head" below it.

They walked through the door.

"STEVE!" all the Steves in the bar yelled, raising their glasses to greet them.

"Wait a minute," said one of the Steves. "You're not Steves."

It was a difficult thing for Dave to get his head round, that all the Steves were duplicates of the original, with the same memories. Of course, it didn't help that Steve had a notoriously bad memory anyway. Dave had met Steve a few times now, and he never seemed to remember their previous encounters.

Dave, Carl and Porkins walked up to the bar. The bartender was a Steve with a white apron.

"What can I get for you, Steve?" the bartender asked.

"My name's Dave, not Steve," said Dave. "Do you not remember me at all? You blew up my town and found the end portal underneath. Then you saved me and my friends from a giant zombie pigman, and we fought together in Snow Town, defeating a crazy robot."

He thought he'd leave out that the *crazy robot* was now one of his traveling companions, as that would just complicate things.

"None of that rings a bell, bro," said Bartender Steve. "But I am searching for an end portal. Once the Prof sorts out this clone thing, I'm heading off to look for one again."

"But I was the one who gave you that idea!" said Dave, exasperated. "I told you how to find end portals, and then you set off to find one. The last time we met we had a friendly rivalry to see who could get to the End first."

"Sorry little bro," said Bartender Steve, "Maybe you're thinking of a different Steve. Actually, you can't be, as I'm the only Steve there is!"

All the other Steves looked at him.

"I mean, at least I was," said Bartender Steve sheepishly.

Dave, Carl and Porkins paid for their milk, then sat down at a table. All around them were tables full of Steves, all chatting away.

"What do you think they're talking about?" Porkins asked, looking at one of the tables of Steves.

"Let's have a listen," said Carl.

They all shifted round in their seats a bit, getting as close as they could to the other table. Sitting around the table were three Steves.

"You should have seen it, bro," said one of the Steves. "I fought off five ravagers with just a torch! It was so epic."

"I know bro," said another Steve. "I was there. Anyway, did I tell you about the time I fought the Red Creeper King? I had no armor and only a wooden sword, but I kicked his butt!"

"Bro," said the third Steve, "I remember that! I must have been there too."

Then a Steve in a waitress dress came over and put a cake on their table.

"Here you go, sugars," the Steve waitress said to the three Steves.

"CAKE!" the three Steves yelled, and they all started stuffing the cake into their mouths.

"You know," said Carl, watching the Steves gobbling down the cake, "I used to think Steve was pretty cool. But... he's just an idiot, isn't he?"

"Thank you!" said Dave. "That's what I've been telling everyone for years. Everyone in my village used to talk about him like he was the greatest person who ever lived."

"How old do you reckon he is?" said Porkins. "I mean, the chap looks young enough, but there was a pretty old-looking statue of him back in Villagertropolis. And the professor said he looked the same as he does now when she was a little girl."

"Maybe that's why his memory's so bad," said Carl. "He's just old. Old people forget stuff. Or so I hear—there aren't really any old creepers."

Suddenly all the Steves began to glow white.

"Uh-oh," said Dave, "we ought to get out of here!"

But it was too late: a flood of Steves rushed towards them, knocking over their table and chairs and landing on top of them. The bright light stopped and Dave, Carl and Porkins found themselves buried under a pile of Steves.

"Bro, not cool!" said one of the Steves.

The bar was now stuffed full of Steves, from the floor to the ceiling. Dave could barely move, and the Steves kept kicking and elbowing him as they struggled to get free.

"Are you alright?" Dave asked Porkins and Carl, both of whom he could just make out through gaps in the Steves.

"Just about," said Carl. "Ow!" The creeper added, as a Steve foot kicked him in the face.

"Well," said Porkins, "at least it can't—"

"NO!" said Carl.

"What?" said Porkins.

"You were about to say that at least it can't get any worse," said Carl. "Haven't you learned by now that every time someone says that *it gets even worse!*"

"But how can it?" said Porkins. "It can't get worse than this."

And then the Steves began to glow.

"PORKINS!!!!" yelled Carl.

THAK-KRAM!!!!

The bar exploded, Steves pouring out onto the street. Dave found himself washed through the town on a river of Steves, all of them yelling "bro!" and "no way bro!" and "not cool bro!" and other similar things.

Other buildings around the town had exploded too, sending more Steves flowing down the streets.

"Waaaaaa!!!" yelled Dave, as the Steve river carried him along. He was tossing and rolling around, Steve arms and legs smashing into him over and over again.

Up ahead he saw Carl clinging to the top of a lamppost above the torrent of Steves.

"Help me!" Dave yelled, holding out his hand as he passed the lamppost.

"Sorry," said Carl, "I've got no hands."

Dave washed past the lamppost, the Steve river carrying him along.

"Good luck!" Carl yelled after him.

Finally the Steve river began to slow down. Dave kicked and pushed as hard as he could to make sure he wasn't trapped beneath the Steves. When it eventually came to a stop he was lying on top of a huge pile of Steves. Remarkably, all of them seemed to be fine.

Dave sat up as best as he could. In every direction was nothing but Steves. He could see the buildings of Steve Town in the distance; only the tops of the tallest buildings could be seen, the rest were buried under Steves.

"Porkins! Carl!" Dave yelled, looking desperately for signs of his friends. But the chatter from the thousands of Steves was so loud that there was no way they would be able to hear him.

CHAPTER FIVE
Robo-Steve vs Steves

Robo-Steve was fascinated by the professor's lab. Professor Quigley was clearly highly intelligent, and her inventions were pushing the boundaries of science in exciting new directions. He did question the logic of taming a polar bear, which, to him, seemed a pointless endeavor, but he had learned by now that organic creatures were not always entirely logical.

"You were saying before that you'd dabbled in the field of robotics, professor," he said to Professor Quigley as she fiddled with a device in the lab on her knees.

"Only a little bit," said Professor Quigley. "Some of the scientists at my old lab created some robots to help them with their experiments, but in the end they gave up. The scientist who created you must have been one smart cookie."

"I believe he was," said Robo-Steve. "I never got to know him well, and he committed some terrible crimes, but he was definitely smart. No-one could deny that."

"That's the trouble with smart people," said Professor Quigley, flicking some redstone switches, "sometimes we think we know what's best for everyone else, and we do some pretty bad things."

Robo-Steve thought back to when he'd planned to take over the world. At the time he'd thought that he was helping people, that him ruling over them would benefit them, because he was so much smarter than they were.

"Right," said Quigley, closing a panel on the device and pushing herself to her feet. "Let's see if you can help me with this duplication problem. Because if we can't work out a solution, it's going to end very badly for everyone."

The two of them went over to the big white cube with the blue circular portal in the middle.

"So normally when two duplicates go back inside that portal, they reform into one," said Robo-Steve.

"That's right," said Professor Quigley. "But for some reason that no longer works with the Steves. I've tried over and over again to put them back into the machine, but the same number of Steves always come out."

Robo-Steve studied the machine.

"And you said that the error occurred because Steve brought a cake in with him?" he asked.

"Yes," said Professor Quigley. "The machine was only designed to duplicate one thing at a time, so Steve going in with that cake must have fried the circuits somehow."

"When you put the Steves back in the machine to merge them back together, did you put the cakes back in as well?" Robo-Steve asked.

"What? No," said Professor Quigley.

"I think I know what the problem may be," said Robo-Steve. "I need a cake."

"O-k," said Professor Quigley. "Thankfully that's one thing that we have plenty of. Ever since Steve got duplicated, his clones have eaten nothing but cake."

She asked a pink enderman to get them a cake, and soon the enderman came back holding one.

"Here you go, pro-fes-or," the enderman said.

"Thank you," said Robo-Steve, taking the cake. "Now I am going to bring this cake into the portal."

"No!" Professor Quigley yelled, but Robo-Steve was already walking towards the portal.

She'll understand soon enough, he thought.

He stepped into the swirling portal. Suddenly he was being swept round and round, surrounded by blue light, but he kept hold of the cake. Then he found himself being pushed forward, towards a bright white light...

Robo-Steve walked out of the portal. He looked to his right and saw an identical copy of himself, holding an identical cake.

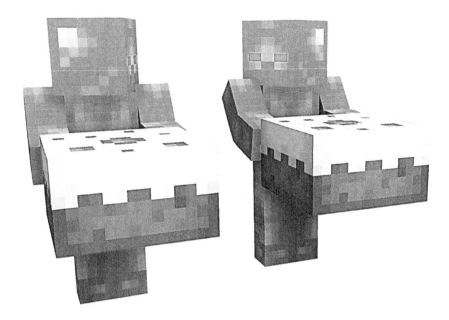

"What did you do that for?" Professor Quigley demanded. "Now we're going to have you duplicating every few minutes as well!"

"I don't think so," said Robo-Steve and his double at the same time.

Fascinating, thought Robo-Steve, as he and his double stared at each other. *He's an exact copy of me, thinking the exact same thoughts.*

"Now please observe," said Robo-Steve and his double. The two of them stepped back into the portal with their cakes.

Robo-Steve found himself swirling around in the blue void once more, but this time his double was swirling around with him. The two of them were being carried closer and closer together...

When Robo-Steve stepped out of the duplicator once more, he was alone.

"Where's your double?" Professor Quigley asked. "Did you two merge back together?"

"Yes,'"said Robo-Steve. "I believe that the reason the duplicate Steves didn't merge back together was because they didn't go back in with their cakes. The duplicator wouldn't merge them because they weren't re-entering the duplicator in the exact same way that they went in."

"So you're saying that we have to get all the Steves to go back into the duplicator holding a cake?" said Professor Quigley,

"Precisely," said Robo-Steve.

Suddenly there was some commotion from over by the cobblestone staircase. An enderman was running down the stairs yelling "dan-ger! Dan-ger!"

Then suddenly something started pouring down the cobblestone stairs.

What is that? wondered Robo-Steve. *Some kind of lumpy liquid?*

But then he realized was it was: it was Steves; a river of Steves flooding down the stairs.

"Heeelp!" The enderman yelled, as the Steve river began to catch up with him.

"Teleport, you fool!" Professor Quigley yelled.

ZAAAP!

The enderman teleported off the stairs and appeared in front of them. Robo-Steve,

Professor Quigley and all the endermen looked on as the river of Steves reached the bottom of the cobblestone stairs and flowed through the lab towards them.

"Oh dear," said Robo-Steve.

There weren't many times in his life that Robo-Steve had been unsure about how to proceed in any given situation. Normally his robotic brain would either follow its programming or come up with the most logical solution to any problem. But now, with hundreds of Steves rushing towards him, he had no idea what to do.

"If they destroy the duplicator, we'll have no way of ever fixing this!" yelled Professor Quigley.

How can I protect the duplicator? Robo-Steve wondered. Then he had a brainwave.

"Endermen!" he yelled. "Grab the duplicator and teleport it out of here."

"That won't work," said Professor Quigley, "the molecular structure of the portal will be damaged if it's teleported. I could create another one, but it might not work with the things that the first one duplicated."

Robo-Steve was at a loss once more. The river of Steves was almost upon them now. The Steves were moving so fast that there was little chance that the duplicator would survive the impact. The Steve flood was smashing through the glass block walls of Professor Quigley's laboratory, and had already destroyed a load of the experiment rooms.

Dean the polar bear was desperately running down the corridor trying to escape the Steve river, but it looked to Robo-Steve like the bear's days were numbered. The bear was big and sturdy, but not big enough to survive being hit by a solid wall of Steves.

Big, thought Robo-Steve. *That's it!*

He ran to the room with the enlarger gun. A yellow enderman was cleaning the baked potato mush from the walls with a sponge block.

"I need to be enlarged," Robo-Steve told the enderman. "Make me as big as you can—now!"

Professor Quigley ran in behind him.

"What's going on?" she asked.

"No time to explain," said Robo-Steve, "just make me as big as you can!"

"You heard him, Chloe," Professor Quigley told the yellow enderman, "do it now!"

The enderman—or rather *endergirl,* Robo-Steve realized— dropped her sponge block and teleported over to the gun, then aimed it at Robo-Steve.

"As big as you can!" said Robo-Steve.

The yellow endergirl pressed a button, the ray gun began to glow, and then a beam of green light blasted from the tip of it, hitting Robo-Steve.

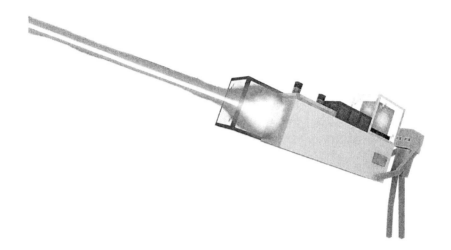

Robo-Steve felt his metal body growing warm, but he was more surprised to see Professor Quigley and the endermen shrinking.

No, they're not shrinking, he thought, *I'm growing.*

He was so tall now that he was towering over the glass walls of the enlarger room. The flood of Steves was rushing towards them, smashing through room after room.

Robo-Steve knelt down, holding his arms out, so he was creating a wall in front of the river of Steves. The Steves smashed into him, almost pushing him backwards, but he held his ground, digging his heels in and shielding Professor Quigley and the endermen from the Steves.

But more Steves were coming. There seemed to be an endless supply of them pouring down the stairs.

"I need to be bigger!" Robo-Steve yelled at the yellow endergirl. "Hit me with the beam again!"

Chloe the endergirl powered up the gun once more and Robo-Steve was blasted with the green beam. He grew and grew, using his arms and torso as a dam to stop the flow of Steves from reaching the rest of the lab. He was so tall now that his head was pressing against the high iron block ceiling.

Finally the flow of Steves came to a stop. Robo-Steve had successfully held the Steves back; the pile of Steves reached almost to the ceiling, but it had finally stopped moving.

The noise from all the chattering Steves was so loud that Robo-Steve could barely hear himself think. He looked round and saw that Professor Quigley and the endermen were ok. Even Dean the polar bear had made it. Professor Quigley gave Robo-Steve a thumbs up.

I did it, thought Robo-Steve. He was still a bit unfamiliar with emotions, but he guessed this must be what being relieved felt like.

He could see the duplicator cube, still safe in its room at the end of the hall. Now they just had to find a way to get all the Steves back inside it with each of them holding a cake.

"Listen to me," he said to the Steves, his voice booming across the lab, "you need to do as I say, and we can merge you all back together."

The Steves all started talking, so many voices that Robo-Steve couldn't understand what any of them were saying.

"You need to each hold a cake," Robo-Steve told them, "and then—"

"CAKE!" all the Steves started saying. "CAKE! CAKE! CAKE!"

And then, suddenly, the Steves started to glow with white light.

Oh no, thought Robo-Steve. *Oh no, oh no, oh no!*

CHAPTER SIX
Steveaggedon

Dave was wading through the Steves, looking for Porkins and Carl.

He'd given up on yelling their names, as the noise from all the talking Steves was too loud for his voice to be heard.

Finally up ahead he could see Carl, still clinging to the top of his lamp post.

At least he's ok, thought Dave. *But where's Porkins?*

Dave pushed his way through the Steves until he reached Carl's lamppost.

"Hey, you didn't die," said Carl, "that's good."

"Thanks," said Dave, sarcastically. "Have you seen any sign of Porkins?"

"Afraid not," said Carl. "So what do we do now? The next time the Steves duplicate... well, it's not gonna be good, let's put it that way."

Carl was right, Dave knew. They were already sitting on a mountain of Steves, with Steves as far as the eye could see. They were so high up that Dave could see different biomes in the distance, and he could even seen the remains of the forest that the lightning had burnt down back when he and the others were escaping the illager mansion.

He hoped that Robo-Steve and Professor Quigley were ok, but he assumed they must be—being underground in the lab they'd probably be safe from the river of Steves, he thought.

Suddenly, among all the thousands of Steve voices, he heard a familiar voice.

"I say chaps, do watch out!"

Porkins! Dave thought excitedly.

He followed the sound of the pigman's voice, and could just about make out Porkins's pink body underneath several layers of Steves below them.

"Porkins!" he yelled. "Can you hear me?"

Porkins smiled a huge smile.

"Dave, old bean!" he yelled back. "It's so good to see you!"

"Can you push your way up here?" Dave asked.

"I'll give it a go," said Porkins, and he started forcing his way through the Steves towards the surface.

"Hey, watch it!" a Steve said, as Porkins' foot pushed against his face.

"Dreadfully sorry," said Porkins.

Porkins was almost at the surface, when suddenly all the Steves around them began to glow. Dave looked around in horror as the whole mountain of Steves glowed with white light.

"They're duplicating again!" he yelled.

"Oh crumbs!" Porkins said.

"Oh great," sighed Carl.

BA-KOOSH!!!!

Suddenly Dave found himself thrust upwards in an explosion

of Steves. He flew up into the air, surrounded by cries of "bro!" and "not cool, bro!"

All around him he could see Steves flying upwards through the air. It was like a volcano had erupted, but instead of spewing out lava it was spewing out Steves.

This truly is Steveaggedon, thought Dave.

Then, finally, he found himself falling, alongside all the Steves. He landed on the gigantic pile of Steves, then put his hands over his head to protect himself as Steves rained down from the sky.

Finally the Steve rain ended, but now Dave could see nothing but Steves in every direction. All the other biomes he'd seen earlier were completely covered in mountains of Steves. And the *noise!* The sound of all the Steves chattering away had been loud before, but now it was so loud that it was hurting Dave's ears.

There was no sign of Porkins and Carl either, and Dave didn't have much hope that he'd be able to find them. It would be like finding a needle in a haystack, with all the thousands—maybe millions—of Steves.

What do I do now? wondered Dave.

But he had no idea.

*

Robo-Steve felt like he couldn't keep going much longer.

He was crouched over, using his body to protect Professor Quigley, the endermen, Dean the polar bear and the duplicator cube from the mountain of Steves above them. Even though his body was about as big as a five story building, Robo-Steve was still struggling to hold up the weight of all the Steves.

"Wow!" he heard one of the Steves say. "That is one big, gold Steve!"

The yellow endergirl was still holding the enlarger ray.

I need to be bigger, thought Robo-Steve, *or my body is going to break under the pressure from all these Steves.* He could feel the gold plates of his outer casing starting to bend.

"Hit me... with the... ray again," he told the yellow endergirl.

221

"Wait!" said Professor Quigley.

"It's the... only way," said Robo-Steve.

"I know," said Professor Quigley, "but there's something else you need to do as well. I know how we can win this!"

*

Porkins pushed his way to the surface, gasping for breath.

He was stranded in an ocean of Steves. It was hard to keep his balance as the Steves were all moving and jostling to get to the surface, all of them pushing and shoving.

Porkins found himself being dragged under again as Steves clambered over him.

I used to be fond of that chap Steve, he thought, *but now I wouldn't mind if I never see the blighter again!*

Using all his strength he pushed his way back to the surface, but he was getting tired now, and wouldn't be able to keep this up much longer.

What a unfortunate way to go out, after all we've been through, he thought sadly. *Squashed by millions of Steves.*

ZAAAAP!

Suddenly a blue endergirl appeared next to him, standing on the Steves. Her name was Eden, Porkins remembered.

"An enderman!" yelled one of the Steves. "Where's my sword, bro?"

The endergirl reached down and put her hands on Porkins' shoulders.

"Hello, my dear," Porkins said, confused. "What can I do for you?"

And then *ZAP!* Porkins found himself being teleported away.

*

Carl was so deep under the Steves that he could barely even see daylight. Without arms, there was no way he could push his way back up, so he'd fallen further and further down as the Steves had all clambered to get to the surface.

This would never have happened if I still had my iron body, he thought bitterly.

Ever since his iron golem suit had been destroyed in the forest fire, Carl had been feeling useless. The suit had given him agency; allowing him to fight alongside his friends as an equal. But now he was just a short creeper who couldn't even explode. What use was he? He'd even been debating the idea of leaving. What use was he to Dave and Porkins if he couldn't even fight? Plus, they had Robo-Steve now, who could fight better than Carl ever could, even with the iron suit.

Maybe this is the way I deserve to go out, thought Carl, *squashed by a zillion Steves.*

But then something inside of him said *no*-—why should it end like this, after all he'd been through. He'd been through so much with Dave and Porkins, he'd escaped from near-death situations so many times, so why should he stop fighting now?

I may have no arms, he thought, *but I've got four legs.* He began to wriggle his way upwards, using his small size to slither through the gaps in the Steves.

The more he moved upwards, the more daylight he could see, until, finally, he burst through to the surface. The sun on his face had never felt so good.

But what now? thought Carl, looking around. In every direction there was nothing but Steves.

Maybe the whole world is nothing but Steves now, he thought sadly. *Maybe this is all there is.*

ZAAAAP!

Suddenly a red enderman appeared next to him. It was the one they'd seen earlier in the lab.

"You're the enderman who had the baked potato, aren't you?" said Carl. "I don't suppose you've got any left?"

"Come with me, pl-ease," the endermen said, reaching out its arms.

*

Dave was wading through the Steves as best he could, trying to find any sign of Carl or Porkins.

"Watch it, bro!" a Steve said, as Dave accidentally put a foot on the Steve's head.

I hope Robo-Steve and Professor Quigley come up with a bright idea soon, he thought, *or this will be the end of the world.*

There were already mountains of Steves in every direction; it would only take a few more duplications for the Steves to cover the entire world, Dave thought.

ZAAAAAAP!

A pink enderman teleported out of nowhere.

"Hey!" said Dave. "Did Professor Quigley send you? Has she come up with an invention to solve all this?"

But the enderman said nothing. It just put its hands on Dave's shoulders.

CHAPTER SEVEN
Operation Bucket

ZAP!

The enderman teleported Dave to a grassy hillside. To his surprise he saw that Carl and Porkins were already there, along with Professor Quigley and the rest of her endermen.

"Good, you're all safe," said the professor when she saw Dave. She turned to a yellow endergirl.

"Tell Robo-Steve that his friends are safe," Quigley told the endergirl, "and tell him that it's time for *operation bucket.*"

The yellow endergirl nodded, then *ZAAAAP* she teleported away.

"What the heck is 'operation bucket'?" asked Carl.

"Wait and see," said Professor Quigley. "Robo-Steve and I have a plan to fix all this and... well, just keep your fingers crossed that it works."

"I have no fingers," said Carl,

Dave suddenly noticed that the grassy hill they were standing on was in the middle of an ocean of Steves. The Steve ocean stretched out in every direction, all the way to the horizon.

We're not standing on a hill, he realized, *we're standing on the top of a mountain!*

Suddenly there was a huge rumbling sound, then, in the distance, something huge and golden burst out from underneath the Steves, glowing with green light.

It's Robo-Steve! Dave realized. The robot was gigantic, and growing bigger by the second. When the green glow eventually stopped he was so tall that his golden head was above the clouds.

"As if things weren't bad enough, now we've got giant robots as well," Dave heard Carl say behind him.

Robo-Steve was holding something, Dave saw. Actually he was holding *two* somethings, one in each hand. Dave couldn't make out what Robo-Steve was holding in his left hand, but in his right hand he had the enlargement gun, which he was holding between two fingers. It looked tiny compared to Robo-Steve's gigantic hand.

ZAP!

The yellow endergirl reappeared on the grassy hill next to them.

"Good work, Chloe," said Professor Quigley. "Now it's up to Robo-Steve."

Robo-Steve pointed the enlarger gun down at the Steves. He pressed something with his huge fingers and suddenly a ray of red light blasted out of it, hitting the Steve ocean. Robo-Steve swept the ray across the Steves, blasting them all with the red light beam like a gardener watering plants.

"What's he doing?" asked Porkins.

At first Dave couldn't work out what Robo-Steve was up to, but then he saw the Steve ocean start to go down.

"He's shrinking the Steves!" said Dave.

As the red beam of light swept across the Steves, they each got smaller and smaller, and the ocean got lower and lower.

Dave looked down from the mountaintop and could see that each of the Steves was only about the size of a cat now, and they were getting smaller by the second.

In a few minutes, the Steves were so small that Dave couldn't see them anymore. In the distance Robo-Steve was still aiming the ray gun at something near his feet, which Dave assumed must be the tiny Steves.

Dave could see the ground again, now that the ocean of Steves was gone. As he'd suspected, they were standing on the top of a mountain, and Robo-Steve was standing in the middle of the farmland where Professor Quigley's cottage had been, but now it was just a crater where Robo-Steve had burst out of the laboratory when he grew big.

"Come on," said Professor Quigley, "let's go and rejoin your robot friend. Endermen, teleport us down there!"

Dave felt an enderman's hands on his shoulders and suddenly he was teleported down into the valley, along with Porkins, Carl and the professor. Towering about them was Robo-Steve.

"HELLO!" Robo-Steve said, his voice so loud that Dave had to clutch his ears.

"Shrink yourself back down!" Professor Quigley yelled up at him.

"OH, SORRY," said Robo-Steve. He knelt down and opened his left hand, revealing the duplicator portal cube. It was the same size it had always been, and looked tiny in his hand. He gently placed it down on the ground in front of Professor Quigley.

Next Robo-Steve placed the enlarger gun down on the ground in front of the yellow endergirl, then stood back up.

"I'M READY," he said.

"Just shrink him, already," Carl said to the yellow endergirl, "Before his voice destroys my ear drums."

The yellow endergirl lifted up the ray gun and aimed it at Robo-Steve. A beam of green light shot out, hitting Robo-Steve in the leg, but instead of getting smaller, he began to grow.

"Run!" yelled Dave. He picked up Carl and ran out of the way as Robo-Steve's leg got thicker and thicker.

"You're making him bigger, you idiot!" Professor Quigley yelled at the endergirl.

The yellow endergirl pressed a button on the ray gun and the beam of light changed from green to red. Robo-Steve began to shrink.

"Sorry I called you an idiot," Professor Quigley said to the yellow endergirl. "I always get a bit tetchy when I'm about to be crushed to death by a 10,000 foot robot."

Soon Robo-Steve was back to his usual size.

"Thank you, Chloe," he said to the yellow endergirl. "It's nice to be back to normal."

"What happened to all the Steves?" asked Carl. "Did you shrink them so small that they all died?"

"No!" said Robo-Steve. "Look, they're down there."

He pointed at a small pile of blue sand. Or at least that's what it first looked like to Dave, until he came closer and saw that the sand was moving and wriggling. He knelt down and looked at it, and realized—to his shock—that it wasn't sand after all. It was millions of microscopic Steves.

"Good gravy!" said Porkins. "They're so small!!"

"Are you going to keep them like that forever then?" Carl

asked.

Suddenly the pile began to glow white, and then it doubled in size.

"They're still duplicating," said Dave.

"Yes," said Professor Quigley, "but Robo-Steve and I have worked out a solution. Robo-Steve realized that since Steve went into the duplicator originally with a cake, all the Steves have to return to the portal with a cake, so they can be properly merged back together.

"Ok," said Carl, "but how do you get all of those millions of tiny Steves to all hold a cake?"

"That's the clever bit," said Robo-Steve, "they don't need to be *holding* the cake, there just needs to be roughly the same ratio of cake to Steve as there was when Steve first went in."

"I'm not sure I follow," said Porkins.

"Eden, please can I have those buckets," Robo-Steve asked.

The blue endergirl walked over, holding a bucket in each hand.

"Thank you," said Robo-Steve, taking the buckets. He placed both buckets on the floor, then gently scooped up all the Steves, placing them into one of the buckets. When all the Steves were in the bucket, it was roughly full.

"Are you sure you've got all of them?" asked Professor Quigley.

"Affirmative," said Robo-Steve, "my robotic eyes can detect objects as small as one micron. All of the Steves are safely in the bucket."

"Right," said Professor Quigley. "Let's get this sorted before they duplicate again. JT, bring me that cake!"

JT the red enderman walked over holding a cake.

"Um, what's going on?" asked Dave.

Professor Quigley dropped the cake into the empty bucket, then squished it down with her hands.

"I hope you don't expect us to eat that," said Carl. "That's pretty gross."

But Quigley was concentrating too hard to hear him.

"No, that's too much," she muttered to herself, and she scooped out some of the cake with her hands and dropped it onto the grass.

"Ok, this is getting really weird now," said Carl.

"We have to make sure there's the same amount of cake as Steves," Robo-Steve told him. "Or rather, there must be slightly less cake. One normal sized cake is about a quarter of the size of one Steve, so we need there to be quarter the amount of cake than there is of Steves."

"I guess that makes sense," said Dave. "So then you're going to put them back into the duplicator together and hope that it merges them back into one Steve and one cake?"

"Precisely," said Robo-Steve.

Carl shook his head.

"Of all the weird things we've seen on our adventures, I think a professor scooping cake out of a bucket with her hands is the weirdest," said the creeper, as he watched Professor Quigley. "I mean, I thought multiple Steves was weird, but this really takes the cake. Literally."

"I think that's it now," said Professor Quigley, standing up and looking at the two buckets. There's a full bucket of Steves and a quarter bucket of cake. They should be able to merge successfully."

"Then let's do it now," said Robo-Steve, "before the Steves duplicate again."

Robo-Steve picked up one bucket and Professor Quigley picked up the other, then they both walked over to the duplicator. The round portal was still swirling with its usual blue light.

"Right," said Professor Quigley, "we do it together on three. One... two... THREE!"

The two of them thrust their buckets forward, the Steves and the cake flying forwards out of the buckets into the portal. Quigley and Robo-Steve both took a step back.

The duplicator cube began to vibrate, the blue portal liquid swirling round faster and faster.

"What's it doing?" Porkins asked. "It didn't wobble about like that before."

"It never had millions of things to re-merge before," said Professor Quigley. "I just hope the machine can take it."

The white surface of the machine began to crack, steam pouring out of it.

"Oh no," said Professor Quigley. "This should not be happening!"

Then the cube began to break apart, the blue light inside the portal fizzing and bubbling and the cracks on the white surface sparking with electricity.

"Everyone run, it's gonna blow!" yelled Professor Quigley.
BOOOM!!!!!

They all jumped out of the way just in time as the duplicator cube exploded in a ball of blue flames. Dave fell to the floor. When he looked round there was nothing but broken bits of white plastic and a burnt patch where the cube had been.

"Oh no," he heard Porkins say, "poor Steve!"

"Wait," said Robo-Steve, "give me the enlarger."

The yellow endergirl handed him the ray gun and Robo-Steve aimed it at the patch of burnt grass.

"What are you doing?" Carl said.

"I can see something down there," said Robo-Steve. He pressed the button on the gun and a beam of green light shot out, hitting the grass. For a second nothing happened, but then a tiny figure appeared, growing bigger and bigger by the second.

"I don't believe it," said Dave.

"It worked!" Professor Quigley said happily.

Robo-Steve turned off the enlarger. Sitting on the grass, holding a cake, was Steve. Just the one, normal-sized Steve.

"Ooo, cake," said Steve, looking down at the cake.

And then he fainted.

CHAPTER EIGHT
A is for...

"Is he alright?" Porkins asked, as they all gathered around the unconscious Steve.

"He'll be fine," said Professor Quigley, putting her hand on Steve's neck to check his pulse. "His brain is probably just a bit overwhelmed. He's just had millions of different memories and thoughts merged together inside his head."

"But aren't they all his memories?" asked Carl. "If all the Steves were duplicates of him, wouldn't they all think the same?"

"Well they would have started the same, but then they all would have had slightly different experiences," said Professor Quigley. "Now all those millions of slightly different minds are back in one brain again. It'll take Steve a while to adjust."

Dave could understand what she meant. He had only been split into two people, and only for an hour or so, but it had still felt weird when his two selves had been merged back together again. He couldn't even fathom what it must feel like for Steve.

"Take care of Steve," Professor Quigley said to the endermen. "Build a house and a bed, and fill some chests with food for when he wakes up. But no cake!"

The endermen nodded, then picked up Steve and carried him away.

Professor Quigley walked over to the crater where her cottage had once been. At the bottom of the crater some of her laboratory had survived—but most of it had been destroyed.

"Sorry about your lab," said Dave, walking over to her.

"It's only a lab," she said with a smile. "I built it once, I can build it again. I'm just glad everyone is safe."

Then suddenly her face fell and her mouth dropped open.

"Oh no," she gasped. "Alex!"

"Who's Alex?" asked Carl.

But Professor Quigley was too busy rushing down into the crater to reply.

"Come on," said Dave to Porkins and Carl, and they all ran down after her.

Professor Quigley stopped in the remains of the room where the duplicator had been and pressed a button on the wall. A panel slid open, revealing the Steve girl she'd shown them earlier. She was still fast asleep in the glass tank.

"Thank goodness," said Professor Quigley. She pressed another button and the glass panel slowly opened with a *hiss* as the air pressure changed, the cloudy liquid spilling out. The Steve girl fell forward, but Professor Quigley caught her. She was breathing, Dave saw, but her skin was very pale.

"I think the life support must have broken when the lab got destroyed," said Professor Quigley. "Thank goodness we got to her when we did."

She gently laid the Steve girl down on the ground.

"Can you hear me, Alex?" she whispered. "Are you ok?"

"Why are you calling her Alex?" asked Carl. "Isn't she just another Steve clone?"

"She is," said Professor Quigley, "but it didn't feel right calling her Steve, so I named her Alex, after my mother."

She started stroking Alex's hair.

"Poor thing," said Professor Quigley, "I think her hair's changing color too. The damaged life support system messed her up."

"Will she be ok without being merged back into Steve, though?" asked Dave.

"I hope so," said Professor Quigley. "I guess there were so many Steves that having only one missing didn't seem to mess things up. Steve looks like he's going to be ok, and I think Alex is going to be fine as well. Although she may be quite different, after being in the broken life support chamber for so long. It may have messed up her mind and her memories a bit."

"To be fair," said Carl, "Steve was already pretty messed up anyway, so a clone of his was never going to be normal."

Suddenly Alex began to cough.

"Alex!" said Professor Quigley. "Are you ok?"

"Wh-where am I?" Alex asked. Her voice sounded a bit like Steve's, Dave thought, but slightly more higher pitched.

"You're in my lab," said Professor Quigley, cradling Alex's head in her lap. "What's the last thing you remember?"

"I... I remember cake," said Alex, grinning, "I had a totally awesome cake."

And then she fainted.

CHAPTER NINE
Five Go On An Adventure

Dave was amazed at how quickly the endermen were rebuilding the lab.

They'd already finished rebuilding Professor Quigley's cottage. It was an exact replica, as far as Dave could see. The only difference was that the new cobblestone they'd used wasn't mossy.

Now the endermen were hard at work putting the underground lab back together. Because they could teleport, they could fetch blocks and move them around at an incredible speed. They'd already almost finished building the iron block walls, and were now starting to rebuild the experiment rooms, with their glass walls.

Professor Quigley was directing them, every so often yelling "Not there, you idiots!" or "That's not how it's supposed to look!"

Dave had come down to the lab to see how the professor was doing, but he decided that she looked like she was too busy to be disturbed, so he climbed the winding cobblestone staircase back up to the cottage.

Dave, Porkins, Carl and Robo-Steve had been staying with Professor Quigley for three days now. Her cottage only had two beds, and Alex had taken the second one, so Dave and his friends had built a small wooden house nearby with four beds.

Steve was in another house, being looked after by the endermen. Dave had been to visit him a few times, but Steve didn't seem to be able to do much at the moment apart from ramble on about cake.

Alex was doing better: she'd spent a lot of time in bed recovering, but had gradually got her strength back. As Dave walked out of the cottage he saw her practicing sword fighting with

Robo-Steve and Porkins, while Carl sat down on a tree stump and watched.

After studying her and asking her questions, Professor Quigley had concluded that Alex had none of Steve's memories, but apart from that her mind seemed fine. To Dave's relief, Alex never said Steve's favorite word—"bro"—which immediately made him like her more than Steve.

However, even though she didn't have his memories, Alex seemed to remember how to fight like Steve. As Dave watched her parrying Robo-Steve's sword blows in the yard, Dave thought that she might be as good a fighter as the robot, if not *better*.

When Alex spotted Dave, she immediately stopped fighting and waved.

"Hi Dave!!" she yelled happily.

Robo-Steve had been aiming a sword strike against her when

she started waving, and he had to quickly move his blade mid-swipe to stop his sword taking Alex's head off.

"Careful, Alex!" Robo-Steve said.

"Careful about what?" Alex said, looking confused.

Alex's hair had completely changed color now. Rather than the dark brown of Steve's hair, hers was now orange, and her skin had become much paler than Steve's as well. Because Steve's clothes had been a bit baggy for Alex, Professor Quigley had given her some of her own spare clothes, so now Alex was dressed in a green shirt, brown pants and gray boots.

Dave decided to go and see Steve. He'd had his disagreements with Steve in the past, but he still hoped that he was going to be ok. Dave walked over to the bungalow the endermen had built for Steve and knocked on the door. The red enderman, JT, opened the door.

"Hel-lo," said JT.

"Can I see your patient?" Dave asked.

JT nodded. He led Dave inside to the bedroom. To Dave's surprise, Steve was awake. His eyes were red and his skin was coated in sweat but he smiled at Dave all the same.

"Hey..." said Steve weakly. "Good to see you."

Does he know who I am? Dave wondered. Steve barely remembered who Dave was at the best of times, so it seemed unlikely that he'd know who Dave was now, after all he'd been through.

"Bro..." said Steve, "I just wanted to say... I wanted to say..."

"Let me guess," said Dave, "you want more cake?"

"No..." said Steve, "I wanted to... thank you and your friends for putting me back to normal. That golden robot bro... he saved me."

Dave was surprised. It was unlike Steve to say anything nice about anyone apart from himself.

"Er, ok," said Dave. "I'll tell him you said thanks."

"Thank you... Dave," said Steve.

He knows my name, Dave thought, with a jolt of surprise. *He actually remembers my name.*

Dave left the bungalow and sat down on the grass, lost in his thoughts. His encounters with Steve always left him feeling confused. Even though he seemed like an idiot most of the time, Steve would often do or say things that Dave found surprising. He was also an amazing fighter, he could build things, and Dave had seen Steve do some quite complicated maths in his head, back when he'd worked out how many rabbits Porkins would have to slay in order to make himself a full set of leather armor.

And Steve was *old* too. Old enough that he had been an adult when Professor Quigley had been a girl. Old enough that there was an ancient-looking statue of him in Villagertropolis. No, Dave would have liked to have believed that Steve was an idiot and that was all there was to it—but he knew there was more to Steve than that.

Dave stood up and started walking towards Porkins, Carl and Alex, but Professor Quigley appeared from out of the cottage and walked up to him.

"Dave," she said, "can I have a word?"

Quigley led Dave back into the cottage, then the two of them sat down at the kitchen table. She poured them both a glass of warm milk.

"I want to talk to you about Alex," said Professor Quigley.

"She's doing very well," said Dave. "And she never says 'bro', which is a real plus."

"I want you to take her with you on your journey," said Professor Quigley.

Dave was taken aback.

"Are you sure?" he asked. "I know she's doing better, but I don't think she's fully recovered yet. Robo-Steve almost took her head off with a sword just now because she wasn't paying attention."

"I know," said the professor. "Her mind is in a delicate state, which is why I think it would be good for her to go with you. She has no memories. She needs to get out in the world and make new ones. New experiences and sights will stimulate her mind far more than staying at the farmhouse with me."

"We get into a lot of dangerous situations," said Dave.

"Isn't she a good fighter?" asked Professor Quigley. "I've seen her with a sword. That girl knows what she's doing."

Dave had to admit that the professor was right.

"Ok," he said, "we'll take her with us."

"That's brilliant," said Professor Quigley, smiling.

"What about Steve?" Dave asked. "Do you think he's going to be ok?"

"I think so," said Professor Quigley. "But I think he'll need a bit more time with me and my endermen before he's ready to go adventuring again. But he can stay here as long as he likes—it's the least I can do, after all he's done for my family over the years."

Dave was about to make his excuses and go back outside, but then he remembered something he'd been meaning to ask the professor for a while.

"Professor," he said, "could you take a look at this?"

He pulled out the purple ender purple from his pocket—the one that had originally been in Robo-Steve's chest—and handed it to Professor Quigley.

"Fascinating," she said. "Is it some kind of modified ender pearl?"

"Oh, don't press the button," said Dave, quickly remembering that the last time he'd used the pearl he'd ended up trapped under bedrock with a huge spider monster. "It was created by a scientist named Ripley. The same guy who created Robo-Steve. At the moment if you press the button it teleports you somewhere random, but... and this is going to sound weird... but a future version of me came back to the past using this same pearl. Somehow scientists in the future had modified it so that it could be used to *travel through time.*"

"Let me guess," said Professor Quigley, studying the pearl, "you want me to see if I can turn it into a time machine?"

"I mean, it would be useful," said Dave. "Think about if you'd had a time machine a week ago—you could have stopped Steve from bringing that cake into the duplicator in the first place."

Professor Quigley grinned.

"I have to agree, that would have been useful," she said. "Ok, I'll take a look at it."

*

Dave went back outside and watched Porkins and Alex practice their sword fighting. Robo-Steve was yelling advice, and Carl was yelling insults.

"Watch your undefended side," said Robo-Steve. "Keep your sword arm in front of you."

"You both suck," said Carl. "You should give up and go and live in the snow with the rabbits."

Dave grinned. He had a good group of friends here, and he was sure Alex would make a great addition to their team. They had lost all their materials and weapons in the forest fire, but between the five of them they would soon be able to replenish their supplies.

And then it's on to the ender dragon, he thought. *We'll get there. No matter how long it takes...*

EPILOGUE

Professor Quigley was enjoying some alone time in her new laboratory. After all the chaos with the Steves, she was relishing the chance to get back to inventing. Two days ago Dave and his friends had left, along with Alex, and Steve was still recovering in bed, so she finally had a chance to get some work done.

Her new project was something she had nicknamed 'morph gel'. It was a gel that would turn the user into someone else. She didn't know what the use for it would be yet, but she had always been of the opinion that scientists should push boundaries for the sake of it, not always to make something that would make them money or famous.

That was what had attracted her to Lab 303 all those years ago. The scientists there were committed to pushing the boundaries of science to their limits and exploring new frontiers. Unfortunately, as she eventually found out, some of them had taken it too far. That was what had led to the Entity Project, and all the horrible things that had followed.

Anyway, that was over now, and so was the Steve crisis, so she could finally get back to her own work. She had built the lab under her family home so that she could carry out experiments in privacy, and that was exactly what she intended to do from now on.

"Pro-fes-sor?"

It was Eden the endergirl.

"What is it?" Professor Quigley said. "I thought I told you that I wanted to be left alone this afternoon?"

"It is vi-si-tor," said Eden. "Vi-si-tor up-stairs, wants to see you."

A visitor? Professor Quigley wasn't expecting any visitors, and not many people knew she even lived here. The Quigley family

243

home was in the middle of nowhere, a long way from any villages and towns.

"Ok, I'll come up," she told Eden. "But I want you and the other endermen to come with me for protection. All of you."

"Yes pro-fes-sor," said Eden.

It was probably just a wandering trader or a lost traveler, Professor Quigley thought, but she knew that it never did any harm to be too careful. So when she finally climbed the cobblestone stairs to meet her guest, she was accompanied by fifteen endermen.

If the visitor was fazed by the endermen, it didn't show on his face. He was an ordinary villager, and was sitting at the wooden table, waiting for her.

"Ah, Professor Quigley," he said, standing up to greet her. "Pleased to meet you."

There was something about the villager that Quigley didn't trust, but she couldn't quite put her finger on it. She shook his hand then sat down on the chair opposite him.

"I've heard you have a machine that can create copies of things," said the man. "I'm from a village with bad soil. We struggle to produce enough food, so a machine like yours would really help. We're willing to offer a good price—we may have bad ground, but we have a lot of emeralds."

Quigley had always prided herself on being a good judge of character. The man sounded genuine enough, but she still didn't trust him.

"I'm afraid I don't know what you're talking about," she said. "If I had a machine like that, do you really think I'd be living in a run-down farmhouse?"

"I heard a strange tale in a nearby town," said the man. "They told me that the other day the town was overrun by Steves. Thousands of them; so many that they flowed through the town like water."

"Steves?" said Quigley. "I'm afraid I'm not sure what you mean."

"They were clones of the hero known as Steve," said the man.

"All exactly alike."

"How strange," said Quigley, "but I'm afraid I don't know anything about that."

"Please," said the man. "You'd be helping a lot of people. And, like I said, we'd be willing to offer a very good price. Any price you desire."

"I'm sorry that you've come all this way for nothing," Quigley told him. "I really can't help you."

"That's a pity," said the man, his smile not quite reaching his eyes. "A great pity indeed."

He looked up at the endermen.

"I must say, these endermen are remarkable," he said. "How do you get them to obey you like that?"

"Oh, I just trained them," said Professor Quigley. "If you can train a dog you can train an enderman, that's what I always say."

The man smiled. Then he noticed that one of the endermen was holding big potato—it was about the size of a wolf.

"Is that a giant baked potato?" he asked. "I've never seen one so big. Do you have a device that can make things larger as well?"

"No," said Quigley.

"That is strange," smiled the man, "as I heard another tale recently as well. I heard that a giant golden Steve appeared in the sky—a Steve so tall he could be seen for miles around."

"That is odd," said Professor Quigley. "But I'm afraid I don't know anything about that either. We've just had a very good crop of potatoes this year, and they grew bigger than usual."

She was tempted to tell the endermen to kick the villager out of her house. She was sure now that she *definitely* didn't trust him.

"That does smell nice," said the man, looking at the baked potato. "I do like a baked potato."

Quigley smiled. "You sound just like Carl," she said. She spoke without thinking, and as soon as she said the word *Carl*, and saw the reaction on the villager's face, she realized she'd made a mistake.

"Carl was here?" asked the villager, his eyes lighting up. "Carl the creeper? Was he with Dave and Porkins as well? They're all old friends of mine. Could you tell me which direction they went."

"I'm afraid I can't," said Quigley, trying her best to smile. "They stayed one night here as my guests, then they left in the morning before I woke up. I didn't see which way they went. Sorry. I'd never seen the four of them before, they just offered me some emeralds for a room. I get a lot of travelers coming through here."

"I'm sure," said the man. "And who can blame them, this is a lovely cottage."

He stood up. The endermen were all staring right at him.

They're waiting for my order, Quigley knew. *All I need to do is say the word and they'll attack him.*

But as suspicious as she was of this this stranger, she knew that he hadn't actually done anything wrong yet. Yes, he clearly wanted some of her equipment for some nefarious purpose, and he had some strange interest in Dave and his friends, but he hadn't committed any crime.

"I must be on my way," said the stranger. "Thank you for inviting me into your home."

"My pleasure," said Professor Quigley. "It's always nice to meet new people, living all the way out here."

The villager smiled and then walked towards the door.

"I'm afraid I didn't catch your name," Professor Quigley said. "Very rude of me not to ask."

The villager turned round.

"Not at all," he said with a smile. "It was rude of me not to tell you. My name is Adam."

Dave the Villager

Dave the Villager

BOOK 9

Teaching Alex

CHAPTER ONE
Teaching Alex

"Wait a minute," said Alex, "why do I have to punch a tree?"

"That's just the way it is," said Dave. "You have to punch a tree so you can get some wood. That's the first step to crafting."

"Ok," said Alex. "But that is very random."

She punched the tree—BAM! BAM! BAM!—and a small block of wood appeared.

"Ooo, it's so tiny," said Alex, picking the block up.

"Now," said Dave. "just split the wood into plank blocks."

"Oh wow," said Alex. "How do I do that?"

"Um, I dunno," said Dave, "it's hard to explain. Just pull the wood apart."

"How?" asked Alex.

"Um, just do it," said Dave. "I can't really explain how, just... grab the wood and pull it apart."

"Ok," said Alex," here goes.

She took hold of the tiny block of wood in her hands then *clunk*—she pulled it apart. In each hand she now had two tiny blocks of wooden planks.

"Awesome!" said Alex.

"Now," said Dave, "take those four wooden plank blocks and merge them together."

"Ok," said Alex uncertainly. She pressed the four blocks together in her hands.

Thonk! She opened her hands and saw that where the four blocks had been there was now only one block—a tiny crafting table.

"Sooooo cooool," said Alex, holding the tiny crafting table up to study it.

"Now put it down on the ground," said Dave.

Alex took the tiny crafting table and *thunk*—slammed it onto the grass, where it immediately turned into a full-sized crafting table.

"Oh wow," she said, "what do I craft now?"

"Anything you want," said Dave, with a grin.

"No, I need specifics," said Alex. "I literally have no idea what I should be crafting."

They were in the middle of a large plains biome. Dave and his friends had lost all their supplies in the forest fire a few days ago, so they were going to have to build up their resources from scratch. Since Alex had lost all of her memories, Dave thought this would be the perfect chance to teach her about crafting and mining. He'd built a two-story house for them, with five rooms so they could have one each. They'd probably be here a while, Dave thought, especially if they were going to get enough diamonds to replace all their armor and weapons, and blaze rods and ender pearls to replace their eyes of ender.

As Dave taught Alex about crafting, Porkins was cooking them some dinner on a stove and Carl and Robo-Steve were lying on the grass looking up at the clouds.

"That one looks like a cow," said Carl, pointing at a cloud. "And that one looks a bit like a pickaxe."

"I still find it difficult to understand this notion of clouds looking like things," said Robo-Steve. "To me, they all just look like clouds."

"And that one there looks like your butt," said Carl.

"I can't see the resemblance," said Robo-Steve.

"Lunch time!" Porkins yelled.

They all rushed over and Porkins handed them all a piece of cooked rabbit.

"Careful," Porkins told them, "it's hot."

Dave sat down on the grass and took a big bite out of his rabbit.

"This is good," said Alex, sitting down next to Dave and biting into her own rabbit. "Should we give some to those little hoppers over there? They must be hungry."

"Hoppers?" said Dave, unsure what she meant.

"Those little hoppers," said Alex, pointing at a group of rabbits nearby. "Those little creatures that jump about—*hop hop hop*. They must be hungry from all that hopping. Maybe they'd like to eat some rabbit."

"Um, Alex," said Dave, "Those *are* rabbits."

"No," said Alex, holding up her cooked rabbit, "*this* is rabbit."

"Well, yes," said Dave, "but they're rabbits too."

"I don't get it," said Alex.

"Porkins slew a load of those hoppers with arrows and now you're eating one," said Carl.

Alex's mouth fell open in horror.

"Carl," said Porkins, looking embarrassed, "did you have to put it so horribly?"

"I'm... I'm eating a hopper?" Alex said, her lip trembling. "I'm eating a cute little hopper??"

"You're eating a *delicious* little hopper," said Carl. "Although most people call them *rabbits.*"

"Carl!" said Dave. "Stop being mean. But, er, he is right, Alex. Sorry."

Alex put her cooked rabbit down on the floor.

"I can't eat that, sorry Porkins," she said. "Eating hoppers is not cool."

"No worries," said Carl, "that means there's more for me."

And he grabbed Alex's cooked rabbit and started munching down on it.

"Maybe Alex has a point," Porkins said, looking at his own piece of cooked rabbit, "Maybe eating those poor rabbit chaps is a bit of a rotten thing to do."

"Well, give it here then," said Carl, taking Porkins's rabbit. "I'll eat it for you."

After they'd eaten, Dave started teaching Alex how to make tools. Once she had all the basic wooden weapons and tools, he showed her how to dig down into the ground to get better materials.

"Remember," Dave told her, "never dig straight down, or you could end up falling into lava. Trust me."

"Right, got it," said Alex. "Lava is the blue one, right? And water is the orange one?"

"No!" said Dave. "Water is blue, lava is orange."

"Ok," said Alex, "I think I've got it now. And... water is the bad one?"

"No!" said Dave. He was trying not to get too annoyed with Alex, but her brain was a bit like Steve's—all over the place.

"Anyone for a drink?" Porkins called from the front door of the house.

"Can I have a glass of lava please?" Alex shouted back. "I'm feeling a bit thirsty."

Dave put his head in his hands.

Over the next few hours, Dave showed Alex how to dig for materials—showing her what was useful and what was not. Robo-Steve had made all five of them new backpacks, out of the leather from a herd of nearby cows, so they had plenty of room to store the useful blocks that they found.

Soon Alex's wood pickaxe broke, so Dave showed her how to make a stone one out of cobblestone. She kept on digging, and soon dug up some coal and iron ore.

"Ooo, is this iron?" Alex asked, holding up a tiny block full of shiny chunks. "Let's make an iron sword! Swoosh, swoosh, swoosh!"

"You need to smelt it first," Dave told her.

Alex gave the block a sniff.

"It doesn't smell like anything," she said.

"Not smell it," said Dave, "smelt it."

Dave showed Alex how to craft eight cobblestone blocks into a furnace, then showed her how to light it with coal.

"You can use wood as fuel too," he told her, "but it doesn't last as long as coal."

Soon Alex had a full set of iron weapons and armor. Dave, who'd been digging alongside her, made himself iron weapons and armor too.

"You need to protect yourself down in the caves," he told her. "You never know when a monster might pop out."

"But didn't you say the light from our torches would keep them away?" asked Alex.

"Yes," said Dave, "but a zombie or a spider or whatever might come from one of the darker parts of the cave. Or you might dig through a wall and come face-to-face with a creeper."

"Wait," said Alex, "aren't creepers good? Carl's a creeper, isn't he?"

"He is," Dave agreed, "but most creepers aren't as nice as him. Some can't even speak. It's a bit confusing, but some zombies and creepers can speak, but others don't seem to be able to. The way Carl puts it is that they've reverted back to being no more smart than animals. They're just mindless monsters."

"Endermen can speak too," said Alex, "like the ones in the Prof's lab."

"I think those were a unique case," said Dave. "Professor Quigley said those endermen had had their brains messed around with by scientists. Besides, even though they can speak, I don't think they're that intelligent."

"Wow," said Alex, "I've got a lot to learn."

Over the next few days, Dave, Alex, Porkins and Robo-Steve all started digging for materials. They filled their mine with torches, to keep hostile mobs away, and plenty of chests so they could dump all the treasure they found in them. It took a while, but eventually they had diamond pickaxes, and started building up their diamond supplies so they could eventually all have some diamond armor.

Because his lack of arms stopped him from being that great at digging, Carl was on food duty: cooking them meals and bringing them drinks. Alex and Porkins had both made the decision that they didn't want to eat meat anymore. Since Carl was too small to be any good at hunting anyway, he started just making them meals with vegetables. Carl didn't mind—as long as he had potatoes, he was fine—and Robo-Steve didn't need to eat anyway (although he often pretended to eat, to fit in with the others), but Dave did miss eating meat a bit. Still, Carl made them a great selection of foods, so Dave couldn't really complain.

"I think I'm starting to enjoy cooking," Carl said to Dave one night as they sat outside and looked up at the stars. "I used to hate it, but it's actually quite fun."

The one thing Dave *didn't* have to teach Alex was how to fight. How to use weapons was one of the only Steve memories that Alex had kept, and when mobs sneaked up on them in the caves, she quickly sliced them to bits.

Eventually they dug through a wall that led to a lava lake.

"Excellent," said Robo-Steve, "now we can create that obsidian you need for that nether portal."

The others didn't understand what he meant, so Robo-Steve explained to them that when water reacts with lava it turns into obsidian. They'd dug past a waterfall that led into an underground lake a few days earlier, so Robo-Steve redirected the water with a cobblestone trough, leading it to the lava. When the lava and water met, it was exactly like Robo-Steve had said—there was a hiss and some smoke and then there was obsidian. All the obsidian that they needed. Dave and the others dug it all up with their diamond pickaxes.

Dave was unsure if Herobrine and his forces still had a presence in the Nether, so he wanted to make sure they all had a set of diamond armor before they went back there. Well, apart from Carl, who decided to stay back at the cottage, and Porkins, who preferred leather armor as it allowed him to move more freely when firing his bow.

It took a few more days, but finally Dave, Robo-Steve and Alex all had a set of diamond armor and a diamond sword.

"Diamond is awesome," said Alex, examining her sword as it glistened in the sunlight. "It's so pretty."

"Diamond is indeed an attractive-looking material," said Robo-Steve, "though it is mostly prized for its hardness and durability, rather than its beauty."

They were all sitting on the grass outside their cottage, having one last meal before they left. Carl had cooked them all mushroom stew.

"I thought I'd use up the last of the mushrooms we picked the other day," said Carl. "As when you guys are gone I'm just going to eat baked potatoes for every meal."

"We shouldn't be that long," said Dave. "It depends how long it takes us to find a fortress. Once we find one we just need to find a blaze spawner, then we can get all the blaze rods we need. It should be pretty easy."

"Well whatever," said Carl. "I'll stay here and guard the cottage anyway. It's a tough job, but someone's gotta do it."

Carl was trying to make a joke of things, but Dave could tell that the creeper was feeling down. He'd seen such a transformation in Carl when he'd got his iron suit, but now it seemed like Carl had given up. He seemed to have no interest in their quest or in being a hero. Dave made a mental note to speak to Carl more when they came back from the Nether; Carl was his friend, and it was Dave's duty to cheer him up.

Once they'd eaten, Dave built a nether portal on the grass out of obsidian.

"Make sure you use the right blocks!" Carl yelled at him.

Dave smiled, remembering the time when he, Porkins and Carl had been escaping from Trotter, a giant zombie pigman, and Dave had been panicking so much that he'd built a portal out of nether brick.

When Dave finished the portal he lit it with flint and steel, the purple light barrier shimmering into existence.

"Wooow," said Alex.

Alex, Porkins and Robo-Steve walked up to the portal to join Dave. All four of them were clad head to toe in armor.

"You gonna be ok by yourself?" Dave asked Carl, who had walked over to see them off. "One of us can stay behind, it's no bother."

"I'll be fine," said Carl. "The more of you there are, the quicker you'll be able to find the blaze rods."

"Just make sure you stay inside when the sun begins to go down," said Dave.

"Yes, Mom," said Carl, rolling his eyes.

"Ok," Dave said to Alex, Porkins and Robo-Steve, "are you all ready?"

"Oh yeah," said Alex, grinning.

"I'm ready, old bean," said Porkins.

"Affirmative," said Robo-Steve.

"Ok then," said Dave, "let's get going. Porkins, you're the only other one who's been to the Nether, so you first."

"Roger," said Porkins, and he stepped through the purple barrier, disappearing from sight.

"Robo-Steve, you next," said Dave.

Robo-Steve nodded and then followed Porkins.

"Alex, you next," said Dave.

"Awesome!" said Alex, and she jumped through the portal.

Dave turned round to face Carl.

"We'll be back before you know it," he told the creeper.

"Just go," said Carl. "The sooner you leave, the sooner I can start cooking up some potatoes."

Dave smiled, then stepped into the portal.

CHAPTER TWO
Carl Alone

As Carl watched Dave disappear through the nether portal, he felt a deep feeling of emptiness. He went back to the cottage and put a potato in the smelter, but even the smell of cooking potato wasn't enough to cheer him up. The cottage seemed empty without his friends.

I couldn't even go with them to the Nether, he thought bitterly. *I'm no use to anyone.*

Dave had asked Carl if he wanted to go with them, but he was only being nice, Carl knew. Without his iron golem suit he was nothing but dead weight, slowing them all down. Porkins was a great shot with a bow, Robo-Steve was super clever *and* a terrific fighter, and Alex seemed to be the best fighter of all of them. What use was a pint-sized creeper who couldn't even explode?

I've got to get another golem suit, Carl thought to himself. Without one, he was useless.

Carl knew that villager settlements often had iron golems to guard them, but it had been a long time since they'd been through any towns or villages.

I could build a golem, thought Carl. He didn't know much about crafting, but he'd flicked through Dave's crafting book a few times when he'd been bored—before the book had been destroyed in the forest fire. He vaguely recalled that to make an iron golem you needed to place down some iron blocks in a t-shape and then put a pumpkin on top for the head.

Getting the iron blocks was the easy part. Over the past few days Dave, Porkins, Alex and Robo-Steve had done so much digging that the chests in the cottage were stuffed full of iron ore.

Carl took out the ore, smelted it down in the furnace, then

combined the iron bars it made into blocks using the crafting table. Then he took the iron blocks outside, placed one on the ground—*thunk*—one on top of it—*thunk*—and then two on either side—*thunk thunk*—creating a t-shape.

"Right," said Carl, "now for the pumpkin."

He'd seen a few pumpkins growing near a tiny pond the other day, when he'd been looking for mushrooms. It was only a short walk away from the cottage.

But the sun is starting to go down, he thought.

He considered waiting until morning, but then a tiny voice in his head said: *come on, are you a hero or are you just a coward?*

It would still be a little while before hostile mobs started spawning, he thought, so he'd be fine if he was quick. Just to be safe, he took an iron sword from one of the chests in the cottage. Carl wasn't great with a sword, since he only had his tiny legs to hold one with, but it might offer him some protection, or maybe scare the mobs off.

Besides, he thought, *I'm a creeper—who's going to attack a creeper?*

Carl's fuse was broken, so he couldn't explode, but the other mobs wouldn't know that. Back when he'd lived in the caves, before he'd met Dave and Porkins, Carl and his creeper friends had never had much trouble with hostile mobs. Most of them were scared of creepers, and stayed well away.

Carl's mind was made up. He was going pumpkin hunting.

CHAPTER THREE
Back in the Nether

The first thing Porkins noticed about the Nether was that all of Herobrine's iron corridors were gone. He didn't know if Herobrine's network of portals had reached this far, but even in the distance he could see no sign of any iron buildings.

The second thing he noticed was that there were no zombie pigmen. Their nether portal had spawned at the top of a high hill so they had a good view of the surrounding hills and cliffs and the lava that flowed around them, but there was not even one solitary zombie pigman to be seen.

"So this is where your people come from, Porkins?" asked Robo-Steve. "What do your people do for sustenance? What do they eat and drink? This doesn't look like a great environment for farming."

"Well the poor chaps don't eat or drink much of anything anymore," said Porkins sadly. "But we ate mushrooms. Pigmen don't need much water, so the moisture in the mushrooms was enough for us."

"Couldn't you just drink that orange water?" asked Alex.

"Alex, how many times!" said Dave. "That's lava! If you try and drink it you'll boil to bits."

"Oh yeah, sorry," said Alex. "Orange is lava, blue is water."

Dave walked over to Porkins.

"Where do you think all the pigmen went?" Dave asked him.

"I'm not sure," Porkins replied. "Herobrine lost that staff thingie that let him control them, but he could have built another one. That blighter might be evil, but he's as smart as a cookie."

"Are cookies intelligent?" asked Robo-Steve. "I was under the impression that they were just wheat and cocoa beans baked together."

"It's just a pigman phrase," Porkins told him. "I don't know where it comes from."

In a way, Porkins was glad that there were no zombie pigmen around. Every time he saw one it made him sad, to see his people reduced to being mindless zombies. The pigmen had been a proud people once, with a history that stretched back for thousands of years, but now there were barely a handful of them left. As far as Porkins knew, the only non-zombie pigmen left in the world were the pigmen who lived in the jungle tree-top village of Little Bacon, and him. All the others had been transformed into zombies by Herobrine.

"Right-ho," said Porkins, trying to sound jollier than he felt, "let's go and find a fortress."

"How does one find a fortress?" Robo-Steve asked.

"You just keep walking until you find one of the blighters," said Porkins, "unfortunately there's no other way."

"Ooo," said Alex, "what are those big floating things in the sky?"

Porkins looked up and saw four huge ghasts floating down towards them.

"Ghasts!" Dave yelled. "Everyone run!"

"Run where?" asked Alex.

"Just follow me!" yelled Dave.

The ghasts screamed, firing their flaming skulls at them. Porkins had to jump out of the way to avoid the blast as one of the skulls exploded against the ground.

They ran round a corner, but up ahead of them, in the sky, were *more* ghasts.

What the Dickens? thought Porkins. He'd never seen so many ghasts together in one place. The ghasts ahead of them and the ghasts behind them were all screaming and firing exploding skulls.

"Just get to cover!" Dave was yelling. "Hide anywhere you can!"

It's because there are no pigmen, Porkins realized. Back before they became zombies, Porkins and his people had fought off the ghasts, keeping their numbers under control. Even when the pigmen had been zombified the ghasts had remembered to keep away from them, even though the zombie pigmen no longer hunted them. But now, with the pigmen completely gone, the ghasts had become fearless—and were going wherever they pleased.

Porkins was blasted forward by an explosion. He fell down a hill, rolling over and over, unable to stop himself. And at the bottom of the hill, Porkins saw to his horror, was lava.

Oh crumbs, he thought. *I'm going to be one crispy chap if I don't stop in time!*

He tried to grab something to slow his fall, but there was nothing to hold on to. He tried to push his legs against the rocks to stop himself from tumbling, but it didn't work.

Looks like it's the end for this pigman, he thought sadly.

But then, suddenly, he came to a stop, just before he hit the lava. He looked up and saw Robo-Steve holding on to his ankle.

"You saved me!" said Porkins happily.

"Yes," said Robo-Steve. "That is factually correct."

Then Porkins saw a flaming skull hurtling towards them from above. He was about to yell out a warning to Robo-Steve, but he was too late—the skull hit Robo-Steve directly in the back, exploding on impact.

KA-DOOM!!!!

CHAPTER FOUR
The Pumpkin Pond

The sun was really starting to go down now, but Carl was almost at the pumpkins.

"Just grab one pumpkin, then get back to the cottage," Carl told himself. "You only need one."

Finally he reached the small pond. It was exactly as he remembered: it was in the middle of a small clearing in the trees, with the pond at the bottom of a small dip. There were a few different flowers and mushrooms scattered around, and, most importantly—*pumpkins.*

Carl ran down the slope towards the pond and then started hacking one of the pumpkins with his iron sword.

I should have brought an axe, he thought to himself. *It would have been quicker.*

Finally there was a *pop* and the pumpkin broke free from the ground, turning into a tiny pumpkin. Carl picked it up and popped it into his backpack.

"Job done," he said happily.

Then he heard a rattle of bones behind him.

Carl had never had the best reactions, but his instincts kicked in and he jumped out of the way—just in time to avoid getting hit by an arrow.

He turned round and saw a skeleton aiming its bow at him.

Just my luck, he thought. Skeletons weren't normally afraid of creepers, in Carl's experience. Unlike zombies or spiders, skeletons could attack from afar, so had no reason to fear a creeper's explosion.

The skeleton was standing on the top of the slope, looking down at Carl. It began to string its bow, aiming another arrow at him.

What do I do? thought Carl desperately. There was no way he could get up the slope and escape into the trees in time.

The skeleton fired another arrow. Carl quickly placed the tiny pumpkin down on the ground and it became full-sized once more, blocking the arrow. Carl took shelter behind the pumpkin as the skeleton prepared its bow for another shot.

Thunk! The skeleton fired another arrow into the pumpkin. It made a frustrated noise, then Carl heard it stringing its bow once more.

I've got to act while it's stringing its bow, thought Carl. After each shot it took the skeleton a few seconds to prepare the next one, so that was when Carl had to make his move.

But should he try to escape, or try to attack the skeleton? He could probably run up the slope and escape into the trees if he tried, but he wasn't a very fast runner, so might not get far.

No, thought Carl, *I have to fight it.*

He gripped his iron sword tightly in one of his feet. Sweat was pouring down his forehead.

What did I ever do to deserve this? he thought bitterly. *All I ever wanted was an easy life, relaxing and eating potatoes. Is that too much to ask?*

Thunk! Another arrow flew from the skeleton's bow, slicing into the soft flesh of the pumpkin.

It was now or never, Carl knew. He jumped over the pumpkin and ran up the slope towards the skeleton.

"Rrraaggggh!!!" Carl yelled.

The skeleton was so surprised that it almost tripped over. But it just about managed to keep its footing, and strung its bow once more, aiming an arrow directly at Carl.

This was a bad idea, thought Carl.

The skeleton pulled back the arrow, ready to fire. At the same time Carl jumped up, swinging his sword—aiming for the skeleton's neck.

Carl landed back on the ground. At first he wasn't sure if he'd even hit the skeleton with his sword. It was still for a moment, just standing there, but then its skull fell to the ground, and the rest of its body collapsed in a pile of bones.

"I did it!" Carl thought happily. "I did it!"

Then he heard the clattering of more bones, and his heart fell.

Carl looked round and saw other skeletons emerging from the trees, all aiming their bows at him. There must have been at least ten of them. There was no escape.

Just my luck, thought Carl. *Just my rotten luck.*

CHAPTER FIVE
Dave and Alex

Dave and Alex were hiding in a cave.

"I think they're gone," Dave said, peering cautiously out of the cave mouth to check for ghasts.

"What are those things?" Alex asked.

"Ghasts," Dave told her. "They live here in the Nether."

"I don't think I like ghasts very much," said Alex.

"I don't think they like us much either," said Dave. "We'll leave it a couple of minutes, to make sure the ghasts are really gone, then we'll go and look for Porkins and Robo-Steve."

Dave had no idea how intelligent ghasts were. Were they mindless beasts, or were they smart enough to pretend to be gone so that he and Alex would come out of hiding? He simply didn't know.

Dave couldn't help feeling angry with himself. He'd expected that their trip to the Nether would be a simple matter of fighting off a few zombie pigmen, finding a fortress, grabbing some blaze rods and then leaving. He certainly hadn't expected any trouble— at least nothing *this* bad.

"So," said Alex, "you want to slay a nether dragon. That's cool."

"An ender dragon," said Dave, "I don't think there's such thing as a nether dragon."

"Oh yeah," said Alex. "Not sure why I thought it was a nether dragon. I'm sure I've heard of nether dragons somewhere though. Maybe it's one of my old Steve memories."

Steve memories were what Alex called the faint memories she had from before she'd split off from Steve. It was all a bit confusing, but Alex had, in a way, once *been* Steve. She still knew how to fight like Steve, and every so often she'd pluck a piece of information or a memory out of the air that must have been from her time as Steve.

"It's a shame we don't have any wool for beds," said Dave. "We could be in the Nether longer than we thought."

"Can't use beds in the Nether," said Alex.

"Why not?" Dave asked.

"I'm not sure," said Alex. "I can't remember."

Dave sat down on the ground, leaning against the wall of the cave. Alex came over and sat next to him. Despite their situation, Alex still looked as jolly as ever. She always seemed to be smiling.

"So why do you wanna beat up that dragon then?" Alex asked.

"It's hard to explain," said Dave, "it's just... I've always wanted to be a hero, and heroes slay dragons."

"Ah cool," said Alex, "then I want to slay a dragon too. How many dragons are there?"

"I think there's only one," said Dave. "Although, to be honest, I'm not even sure about that. I had a book about the End and ender dragons once. A really old book. But it got destroyed in a fire."

Not for the first time, Dave wished he'd read the whole of the ancient book he'd found in the stronghold beneath his hometown. He'd always meant to, but the book had been so *long* and so boring. Every time he'd started reading it he had fallen asleep.

But as boring as the book had been, it had been useful. Without it Dave wouldn't have found out how to create eyes of ender, which were vital for finding ender portals. Strangely enough, no-one else he'd met had known about eyes of ender: not Robo-Steve, who'd read the whole of the Villagertropolis library, and not Herobrine, who desperately wanted to find his way to the End.

There had been something magical about the book too. When one of Herobrine's witches had tried to read it, the page about creating eyes of ender had faded, leaving nothing but empty paper. When Dave had got the book back the text had returned. Somehow the book had been protecting its contents.

"I'm going to check if the coast is clear," Dave said, standing up. He peered out of the cave again. There was still no sign of any ghasts. The only mobs he could see were some strange orange cube things in the distance, but they didn't look very dangerous. Apart from that it was just lava and netherrack in every direction, with a few clumps of glowstone hanging from the ceiling. Whenever Dave visited the Nether he was always struck by how boring it looked: there were no different biomes, no variety and it was very easy to get lost, because everything looked exactly the same.

"It looks safe," Dave told Alex, "but be on your guard."

The two of them left the cave, walking across the netherrack plains.

When he was positive that there were no ghasts above them, Dave started calling for the others.

"Porkins!" He yelled. "Robo-Steve!"

But there was no reply from either of them.

"Pooorkins!!" Dave yelled again. "Where are you?"

"Maybe they went back to the portal," Alex said.

"Good point," said Dave. It made sense that Porkins and Robo-Steve would wait for them by the portal.

I should have come up with a plan for what we should do if we get separated, thought Dave.

"So," said Alex, "which way to the portal?"

Dave looked around. Which way had they come from? He realized that he had no idea; everything looked the same.

"I don't know," he said. "Don't suppose you have any idea?"

"Nope," said Alex happily.

"Great," said Dave. "Well, let's just keep walking and hope for the best."

He had some obsidian in his bag, but he wasn't keen on leaving the Nether before they'd found Porkins and Robo-Steve. Also, they might end up somewhere completely different in the overworld and lose Carl. Dave always found the connection between the Nether and the overworld a bit confusing, so he wanted to make sure they used the same portal to get back, if possible.

They walked. And walked. And walked and walked and walked. It was hard to tell how long they'd been going, since there was no day and night in the Nether and the landscape never changed.

"Porkins!" Dave kept calling. "Robo-Steve!"

But there was no answer.

Occasionally they'd see a ghast floating nearby, and whenever they did they crept along quietly, trying to keep out of sight. There were far more ghasts floating around than Dave remembered from his previous visits to the Nether.

They came across more of the weird dark red cube mobs as well. Dave didn't know anything about them, but Alex seemed to remember them from somewhere.

"They're called magma cubes," she told Dave. "Dunno how I know that, but I do."

Once Dave and Alex got ambushed by a couple of magma cubes as they came around a corner. Up close they were bigger than Dave had thought, and he barely dodged out of the way as one tried to jump on top of him. He slashed at the cube with his sword, but then it split into three smaller cubes, each of them jumping after him. He accidentally brushed up against one and it burnt his leg.

"Ow!" Dave yelled, stumbling away before the cubes could attack him. Alex was busy fighting the other big cube, and when it split apart she made an excited noise.

"Ooo, it splits into smaller cubes!" she said happily. "That's so awesome!"

Dave didn't think it was awesome, but he was too busy fighting off his three smaller cubes to say anything. He split one open with his sword and it turned into even *smaller* cubes.

"Oh come on!" said Dave.

Thankfully these smaller cubes didn't get any smaller, and when Dave sliced one with his sword it went *poof* and disappeared.

When Dave and Alex had killed all the cubes, all that was left on the ground were a few green and red balls. Dave picked one up. It's surface was greasy and creamy.

"Do you know what this is?" Dave asked Alex.

She shook her head.

"Maybe it's food," she suggested.

Dave cautiously took a tiny nibble of the ball.

"Bluurrggh!" he said, spitting it out. "It's definitely not food."

He put the balls into his backpack, in case they did have a use. Once again he was reminded of how much he missed his crafting book.

So they kept on walking. Dave was just about to suggest that they find a safe place to sleep, as he was starting to get a bit tired, when they came over a ridge and saw a huge purple structure at the bottom of a valley in front of them. Coming out of the structure was a broken bridge that stretched across the lava sea.

"Cooool," said Alex.

"It's a fortress," said Dave.

"Shall we go and check it out?" Alex asked him. "Maybe there'll be some monsters to slay."

Dave was torn. They really should keep looking for Porkins and Robo-Steve, he knew, but since the fortress was right there... surely it wouldn't do any harm to go in and get some blaze rods?

"Let's do it," Dave said.

And the two of them began walking down the valley towards the fortress.

CHAPTER SIX
Robot Dreams

Robo-Steve knew where he was, but he didn't know how he'd got there.

He was down in his father's secret basement in Snow Town; the place where he'd been created. Standing in the middle of the room, in the arena, were four figures. The room was darker than he remembered it being, and he couldn't make out who the figures were.

As he walked towards the arena he looked around the room, remembering the time he'd spent down here. The Robo-Steve back then had been a mindless machine who only did as he was commanded, but Robo-Steve still had all his memories from that time. He remembered training in the arena with Ripley, his father; he remembered being fitted with panels that made him look like Steve; he remembered his father training him to speak like Steve; and he remembered his father giving him the order to destroy Snow Town.

I would have done anything my father commanded, Robo-Steve thought. *I would have destroyed anything... I would have slain anyone...*

It terrified Robo-Steve to remember how he'd been back then. He had obeyed Ripley without thinking, without ever considering whether the orders he was given were good or bad.

As he reached the arena, three of the four figures stepped forward out of the shadows. He was surprised to see that they were all *him.*

The first figure looked just like Steve, but with red glowing eyes. Robo-Steve knew that it wasn't Steve, it was him—him from when he'd first been created; back when he was a mindless bot who did everything Ripley had told him.

The second figure was him during the time of the Cool Dude Battle Royale. This Robo-Steve had lost its Steve colors and was now just a gray metallic shell with green glowing eyes.

The third figure looked pretty much like Robo-Steve looked now: with gold plating and purple eyes. But it was different in one way: it was wearing a diamond crown.

That's me from when I ruled Villagertropolis, Robo-Steve knew.

The three versions of Robo-Steve walked over to him. The fourth figure stayed hidden in shadow.

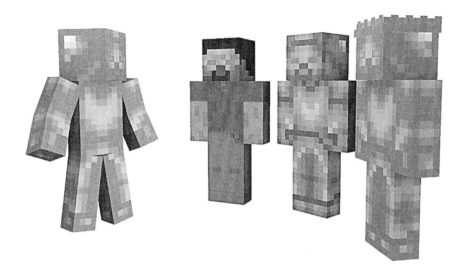

"Hello, Robo-Steve," said the Villagertropolis version of Robo-Steve, the one with a crown. "I've heard that you've abandoned your plan to rule over the villagers. That seems most illogical to me. Since you have a far superior intellect to their own, surely you owe it to them to make their decisions for them? It seems like the only logical choice."

"I don't care if it's logical," said Robo-Steve, "it's not the right thing to do. I know that now."

Villagertropolis Robo-Steve looked confused.

"I'm not sure what right and wrong have to do with it," he

said. "Surely the only thing that matters is logic."

"No," said Robo-Steve, "there's more to life than logic. Logic can't explain everything."

"That is a... most illogical idea," said Villagertropolis Robo-Steve.

"I don't know why you are making decisions like this anyway," said the Snow Town Robo-Steve, the one who looked like Steve with red eyes. "Your purpose is to obey Ripley's commands. You should not be making decisions on your own. Perhaps your programming is faulty."

"There's nothing faulty about my programming," said Robo-Steve, "I'm just evolving. I'm having new experiences and they're changing my outlook. I'm learning new thoughts and ideas every day. I'm even starting to understand emotions. And this—I assume this must be a dream of some kind. I've never had a dream before, so this is a new experience too."

"*Error,*" said the gray metal Robo-Steve, the one with green eyes. "*Error! Error! Destroy! Destroy!*"

It lunged at Robo-Steve, trying to grab him. Suddenly Robo-Steve found he had a diamond sword in his hand. He slashed at the gray-metal version of himself, cutting it in two. Then *poof,* it disappeared.

The other two Robo-Steves—the gold Villagertropolis one and the one who looked like Steve with red eyes—rushed forward to attack him as well. Robo-Steve slashed his sword at them—*swoosh swoosh*—and they both disappeared.

Now it was just Robo-Steve and the fourth figure: the one hidden in shadow. The figure slowly walked forward into the light.

It was Ripley.

"Father?" said Robo-Steve in shock.

Ripley laughed. It was a cruel laugh.

"I'm not your father," he said. "I *made* you in my lab. You're nothing more than a tool. You're no different from a redstone switch or a powered rail."

"That's not true," said Robo-Steve "I... I'm more than that. I'm learning to be more than just a robot."

278

He was feeling an emotion. At first he was unsure which emotion it was, but then it came to him:

I'm feeling sadness, he realized. But there was something else there as well. *Is this anger?* He wondered.

Robo-Steve had little experience of emotions, and suddenly feeling two at once was overwhelming. He fell to his knees, his head swimming.

"You have more in common with a shovel than you do a villager," Ripley told him. "You can pretend to be something you're not all you like, but it will never change what you really are. You're a mindless robot, created to obey. And now that your creator is gone, you have no reason to exist at all."

Suddenly Robo-Steve could hear a churning of gears and pistons, and the arena floor below him began to shake.

It's the trapdoor! he realized. There was a giant lava lake under Snow Town, and Ripley had made a trapdoor in the middle of his arena that could open up to reveal the lava below.

The blocks at the center of the arena began to slide away. Robo-Steve got up and tried to run, but he was too slow and fell down, just managing to cling on to the edge of the pit, hanging on for dear life to stop himself falling into the lava.

Ripley stood over him, grinning.

"With me gone, you have no reason to exist," Ripley told him. "Your purpose has been fulfilled."

And he stomped down on Robo-Steve's hand.

Robo-Steve yelled in pain and let go of the ledge, only holding on with one hand now. Ripley stomped on the other hand, then Robo-Steve found himself falling down, down to the lava below...

Then suddenly he wasn't in Snow Town anymore, he was back in the Nether.

"Oh crumbs!" he heard Porkins yell. "There's more coming!"

Robo-Steve tried to turn his head, but for some reason he couldn't move. He tried to move his arms and legs, but he couldn't seem to feel them.

"What's going on?" he asked.

"Oh, thank goodness you're awake!" he heard Porkins say. "I thought you might have kicked the bucket."

Robo-Steve was stuck looking at a blank piece of netherrack wall, but suddenly he found himself being lifted up into the air.

"Don't worry," said Porkins, "I've got you."

Robo-Steve then realized why he was unable to move—he was only a head! His body was nowhere to be seen. Porkins was now carrying his head under one arm.

"Where's my body?" Robo-Steve asked, feeling himself start to panic with fear: another new emotion for him.

"Don't worry, old chap, I'll explain in a bit," said Porkins. "Everything's fine. Or at least I hope it will be."

Robo-Steve saw that he and Porkins were in a netherrack cave. There were a few objects scattered on the ground: bones, coal, stone swords and a few black skulls.

"What happened here?" Robo-Steve asked.

"Just a little skeleton problem," said Porkins. "Oh gosh, here they come now!"

And Robo-Steve looked on helplessly as a hoard of black wither skeletons poured into the cave.

CHAPTER SEVEN
Bones

If I'm about to become a pin cushion, I may as well go out fighting, thought Carl. He was surrounded by skeletons and there was surely no way out, but he could at least try and take some of them with him.

"Rrrraghhh!!!!" Carl yelled.

He charged at the nearest skeleton with his sword, expecting at any moment to hear the sound of bows twanging as the skeletons all fired at him. But instead he heard a different noise...

He heard *barking.*

From nowhere a pack of wolves burst from the trees around the pond. The skeletons all tried to run, but the wolves were too quick for them, pinning them to the ground and tearing them bone from bone.

It's time for this little creeper to make his exit, thought Carl. The wolves were concentrating on the skeletons for the moment, but Carl didn't want to be around when the skeletons were all gone and the wolves were looking for their next meal. He sneaked away through the trees, heading back in the direction of the cottage as quickly as his little legs would take him.

I can't believe I made it out of that alive, he thought happily. *I guess my bad luck had to change at some point.*

"GRRRR!!!"

He turned around and saw a wolf walking slowly towards him, its teeth bared.

"Good doggy," said Carl, trying not to look as terrified as he felt. "Good doggy..."

The wolf continued to approach him, looking as if it was going to pounce on him at any moment. Carl nervously held his sword out in front of him, preparing to fight the wolf off. But then he spotted something on the ground.:

It was a bone from one of the skeletons.

Wolves likes bones, right? thought Carl. He was sure he'd heard that somewhere. He grabbed the bone, picking it up slowly as to not make any sudden movements, and offered it to the wolf.

"Here doggy," said Carl, "want a snack?"

The wolf cautiously approached the bone. Then, slowly, it began to gnaw on the end of it.

"That's it," said Carl, "good boy."

The wolf crunched up the bone and gobbled it down, but then looked back at Carl.

"Rrrr?" the wolf said.

"Oh," said Carl, "um, you want another one?"

The wolf nodded.

Carl looked desperately for another bone. When the wolves had attacked the skeletons bones had gone flying everywhere, it seemed, but he couldn't see any nearby.

The wolf began to growl impatiently.

"Don't worry boy," said Carl, "I'm sure there's one around here somewhere."

Carl was starting to worry about the other wolves now as well. At the moment he could hear them gnawing on bones in the distance, but once they finished those bones they'd come looking for more food.

And I reckon creeper's on the menu, Carl thought miserably.

Then, to his delight, he spotted a bone. The only trouble was that it was behind the wolf, so he'd have to walk past the wolf to get to it.

Carl slowly tiptoed forward towards the wolf. The wolf began to growl once more as Carl got closer.

Come on Carl, you idiot, Carl told himself. *You can do this.*

"Good doggie," said Carl, as he walked round the side of the wolf, "good doggie."

The wolf turned as well, so it was still facing him and growling. Finally Carl reached the bone. He grabbed it and held it up for the wolf to see.

"Here you go, boy," said Carl, "watch the bone."

The wolf looked at the bone eagerly, its tongue hanging out.

"And... fetch!" said Carl, and he threw the bone as hard as he could. It sailed through the trees and the wolf ran off after it.

Stupid mutt, thought Carl, and he began running in the other direction as fast as his creeper legs could carry him.

CHAPTER EIGHT
Porkins and Robo-Steve

Porkins was running as fast as his trotters could go.

He'd only ever seen small clusters of wither skeletons before, and most of them had been in fortresses, but now there were at least fifty chasing after him.

It's because the pigmen are gone, he thought. *All the other mobs are moving into pigman territory.*

"What's happening?" Robo-Steve asked. "Are the wither skeletons still chasing us?"

"They are," said Porkins, "but don't worry, I think I can lose the blighters in those caves up ahead."

Poor Robo-Steve was nothing but a head now, tucked under Porkins's arm. The explosive skull from the ghast had hit Robo-Steve full on, blowing him to bits. Thankfully all the bits had survived intact: Porkins had picked up Robo-Steve's arms, legs and torso and shoved them into his backpack.

At first Porkins had feared the worst when he saw that the purple lights in Robo-Steve's eyes had gone out, but he had taken Robo-Steve's head with him anyway, in case there was a way to fix him.

Porkins had escaped the ghasts, but then he'd been ambushed by some wither skeletons. He'd had to fight off the skeletons with his sword, as he had Robo-Steve's head under one arm and he needed two hands to use a bow.

A sword had never been Porkins preferred weapon, but somehow he'd fought his way past the wither skeletons. However, as soon as Porkins had fought off one group of skeletons, another had turned up. Which was how he'd ended up where he was now: desperately running for his life.

Up ahead there were a few cave entrances on the side of a netherrack hill. If he could get there before the skeletons caught up with him, Porkins thought he'd stand a good chance of losing the skeletons in the caves.

"*HRRRRIIIII!!!!!*"

Porkins looked up and saw something he really did not want to see: three ghasts floating above him, all looking down at him with angry eyes.

"Oh crumbs!" said Porkins.

The ghasts each threw a flaming skull down towards him. Porkins ran as fast as he could, narrowly escaping the huge explosion behind him. One bit of good news was that the explosion had taken out most of the wither skeletons, but with three ghasts still chasing after him, Porkins was in no mood to celebrate.

Porkins could hear three more skulls zooming through the air towards him. He was close to the cave now: he just had to keep running.

"Come on Porkins old chap!" he told himself, sweat dripping down his face as he ran. "You can do it!"

He reached the entrance to one of the caves, just as the flaming skulls exploded into the ground behind him. The force of the explosion sent him flying forward into the cave.

Porkins sat up. He was safely in the cave, with no way for the ghasts to reach him. He could hear them screaming angrily outside.

"How you doing, old bean?" he asked Robo-Steve, looking down at the robot's golden head.

"I've been better," said Robo-Steve, "but I'm glad we're both still alive. That's a positive outcome, at least. And thank you for saving me."

"It was no bother," said Porkins. "Now we're safe at last, shall I try putting you back together? I've never been very technical, I'm afraid, but I could give it a shot."

"Thank you Porkins, I would appreciate that," said Robo-Steve.

So, with Robo-Steve's guidance, Porkins started putting the

robot's golden body back together. It took a while—and once or twice Porkins put a leg or arm back to front—but eventually he had fixed both arms and legs to the torso.

"Right," said Porkins, "just your head now, old chap."

Porkins picked up Robo-Steve's head and placed it on top of his body. For a moment nothing happened, then Robo-Steve's body came to life, and he stood up.

"You did it," said Robo-Steve, "thank you."

"I hope it's ok," said Porkins. "Does everything feel alright?"

"It feels fine," said Robo-Steve. "My joints got a little damaged in the explosion so I'm not running at one-hundred per-cent, but I'm just happy to have my body back."

"Did you say you feel... happy?" asked Porkins. "I thought you couldn't have emotions?"

"I think that's changing," said Robo-Steve. "I think I'm finally starting to get a grasp on my emotions. It's a bit scary, but I'm looking forward to seeing where this emotional journey takes me."

"That's tip-top," said Porkins happily. "I'm happy for you."

"Right," said Robo-Steve. "What now?"

"I guess let's start looking for the other chaps," said Porkins. "I lost my bearings a bit when we were running from those skeletons, but I think I can find my way back to the portal. I'm sure that's where Dave and Alex will be waiting for us."

Then Porkins saw something that made his heart stop in his chest. Standing at the entrance to their cave, the way they'd come, was a crowd of wither skeletons—all standing still and watching them.

"Uh oh," said Porkins, I think we ought to go the other way."

He turned round, but there was another crowd of wither skeletons standing down that end of the cave as well. They were surrounded.

"Weapons at the ready, old bean," Porkins said to Robo-Steve. "I think we're in a bit of a pickle."

CHAPTER NINE
The Fortress

"This place is totally awesome!" said Alex.

"Shush," Dave told her, "we don't want to attract the wrong kind of attention."

"What does that mean?" Alex asked.

"We don't want to make a loud noise so all the monsters hear us," said Dave.

"Ooooooh," said Alex. "That makes sense. But aren't we looking for a monster? That beige thing."

"Not beige," said Dave, "*blaze*".

"That's the one," said Alex.

They were making their way down one of the huge nether brick corridors. There was no light source anywhere, as the corridor seemed to be buried deep inside a netherrack hillside, but they could still see where they were going. Just like the rest of the Nether, the inside of the corridor seemed to be of a consistent brightness, even though there was no light around.

"So what do these blazes look like?" Alex asked. "You know, so I know when I see one."

"Trust me, you'll know," said Dave. "It's hard to explain, but they're sort of like a floating yellow head with little floating rods around them."

"Riiiiight," said Alex.

"And they only spawn from these devices called 'spawners'," Dave told her, "which are like small cages."

"All of what you just said sounds really, really, really weird," said Alex.

It was a unique experience for Dave, being the guy who knew everything for once. The last time he'd been doing this, going to the Nether to find blaze rods, he had only just started his adventure and barely knew what he was doing. Every five minutes he'd had to look in his crafting book or ask one of his friends for advice. But now he was the one teaching Alex.

"I think I hear something up ahead," Alex whispered.

Dave could hear it too. It sounded like bones.

Do you get skeletons in the Nether? he wondered.

He soon got his answer, as a crowd of skeletons emerged from a corridor up ahead. They weren't like any skeletons Dave had ever seen: they were tall and black and held swords instead of bows, but they were definitely skeletons.

The skeletons charged towards them. Dave and Alex raised their diamond swords, ready to face off the attack.

"Here we go!" said Dave.

The skeletons rushed towards them and the battle began. The skeletons were fast with their swords, but Dave and Alex were faster. Once again Dave was amazed at how skilled a fighter Alex was. Somehow she managed to both attack and defend at the same time, dodging the skeleton's blows and returning her own blows without breaking a sweat. Dave wasn't fighting quite so gracefully, but he held his own nonetheless, slaying every skeleton who attacked him.

It wasn't long before all the skeletons were gone, leaving nothing but bones, coal and tiny skulls on the ground. Dave picked it all up and put it into his backpack.

"That was fun," said Alex.

"Yeah, I guess it was," said Dave, smiling.

That was something else Alex had in common with Steve, Dave thought: she actually enjoyed fighting.

They continued their journey into the fortress. Every so often they came across some more skeletons, or some magma cubes, but between the two of them they easily defeated any enemy. Finally, after a long time searching, they came across what they were looking for—a blaze spawner.

"Are those the beiges?" Alex asked, as two blazes appeared out of the spawner.

"Blazes," said Dave. "And yes, that's them."

"Ok," grinned Alex, "let's kick their blaze butts!"

As he and Alex fought the blazes with their diamond swords, Dave remembered how he and Porkins had fought the blazes the first time. He and Porkins had devised a plan, making sure the two of them worked together to slay as many blazes as possible before making a safe exit. But now he and Alex were just running around with their swords, cutting the blazes down like saplings.

Soon Dave's backpack was full of blaze rods, so he and Alex headed back the way they'd come.

"Now we just have to find the others," said Dave. "Which might be easier said than done."

Suddenly Dave heard a clattering of bones coming from a side corridor up ahead.

"Skeletons!" he whispered to Alex. "It sounds like they're coming this way—let's hide."

"Why?" said Alex. "Let's just fight them!"

"We don't know how many there are," said Dave, "Let's have a look, and then we can decide what to do."

They ran into a doorway and found themselves in a little room with some stairs leading up to the next level of the fortress. Behind the stairs there were rows of a strange red plant.

"What do you think this is?" said Alex, poking one of the red plants.

"It's nether wart," whispered Dave, who had bought some from a wandering traveler back when Porkins was teaching him to make potions. "It's useful stuff, but let's wait for the skeletons to go before we grab some."

He and Alex hid behind the stairs in the nether wart patch, and watched as the skeletons marched past their doorway. There were so many of them—at least a hundred, Dave reckoned.

He waited until it sounded like the skeletons were all gone, then he peered out into the corridor.

"I think the coast is clear," he whispered to Alex. "Let's pick that nether wart and then get out of here."

He and Alex plucked the nether wart from the ground. The

soil it was growing in was a strange brown sand that seemed to slow them down as they walked across it. When Dave had a closer look he was shocked to see that it had little screaming faces on its surface—or at least the sand *looked* like it had screaming faces on it. It was really spooky, and Dave was a bit creeped out.

It's soul sand, Dave realized. He'd never seen any before, but he'd read about it. He got his diamond shovel out and dig up the soul sand, putting it into his rucksack in case it was useful.

Once they'd picked the nether wart and dug up the soul sand, they went back to the corridor and continued walking the way they'd been going before. Dave kept his ears pricked, listening out for any sign of skeletons.

They came round a corridor and Dave had the shock of his life. Standing in front of them were hundreds of skeletons, all standing in complete silence.

They were waiting for us, Dave thought, shocked.

"Come on," he said to Alex, grabbing her arm and running back the other way. But as they came round the corner, back to the corridor they'd come from, he saw another crowd of skeletons waiting for them there.

They were trapped.

"Ok," said Alex, "now it's fighting time!"

But even together, Dave didn't think they stood much of a chance. They were completely outnumbered.

CHAPTER TEN
Bark

Carl was almost back at the cottage. He could just about make out the lights of the cottage windows through the trees.

I'm gonna eat so much baked potato tonight, he thought to himself. *I deserve it, after all the stuff I've been through!*

Then he heard the growling.

Not now, he thought, *not when I'm nearly home!*

A pack of wolves appeared from the trees around him, growling and baring their teeth.

"Um, good dogs," said Carl. "Afraid I'm all out of bones."

The wolves came closer. Carl could see the saliva dripping from their jaws.

"Seriously guys, creepers don't taste very nice," Carl said. "It's all the gunpowder. It leaves a bitter aftertaste."

The wolves ignored him, moving in closer.

Well, looks like this is the end, thought Carl miserably.

Then suddenly another wolf burst through the trees. It stood in front of Carl, baring its teeth and growling at the other wolves.

Is it defending me? Carl wondered, feeling confused. But then he realized who this wolf was—it was the wolf he'd fed the bones to.

The other wolves, seeing that the easy prey they'd found wasn't going to be so easy after all, all wandered off back into the trees.

"Yeah and good riddance!" Carl yelled after them.

The wolf who'd defended him gave him a big lick on the face.

"Eww," said Carl.

The wolf was looking at him with a friendly expression, its tongue hanging stupidly from its mouth.

"So," said Carl, "I give you a couple of bones and now you're my friend. Is that the way it is?"

"Ruff ruff!" said the wolf.

"I guess you're not so bad," said Carl, stroking the wolf under its chin. "Come on, I'm going home. You want to come with me?"

"Ruff!" said the wolf.

Carl walked back to the cottage. He opened the front door then turned round to face the wolf.

"Listen," said Carl, "no offense, but I don't feel comfortable letting you in the house just yet. I mean, if I hadn't given you those bones you probably would have eaten me. So you can sleep outside tonight."

"Arrruw..." said the wolf sadly.

"Don't look at me like that," said Carl. "Listen, if you're gonna be sticking around I guess you'd better have a name. How about... Dave Sucks?"

"Rrroff!!" said the wolf angrily.

"Ok," said Carl, "so you don't like that name. So what kind of name do you want?"

"Ruff ruff!" said the wolf.

"Right, how about... Bark?" said Carl.

"Ruff ruff ruff!" said the wolf.

"Good." said Carl, "I'm glad that's settled. "Now I'm going inside to stuff my face with baked potato. I'll see you in the morning."

"Ruff ruff!" said the wolf.

"Yeah," said Carl, "ruff ruff yourself."

He went inside, closing the door behind him. But then Carl felt an emotion that he didn't feel very often—guilt. He went over to one of the treasure chests in the cottage and pulled out a piece of raw beef, placing it in the smoker. When the beef was cooked he opened the door and threw it to the wolf.

"Here you go," he said, "that's some good steak, so make sure you savor it."

"Ruff!" said the wolf, and it gobbled the steak down whole.

"Some people have no manners," said Carl, shaking his head.

CHAPTER ELEVEN
Captured

Dave and Alex had fought hard against the skeletons, but eventually they had been overwhelmed. But, to Dave's surprise, the skeletons had captured them instead of slaying them, and now they were dragging them down a nether brick staircase, deep into the depths of the fortress.

How did I let this happen? Dave thought miserably. *First I got us all separated, now I've let Alex and me get captured.*

"We'll be back before you know it," Dave had told Carl before they entered the nether portal. He couldn't have been more wrong.

I was too arrogant, thought Dave bitterly. He'd thought going to the Nether to get some blaze rods would be easy, now that he was a better fighter and he had Robo-Steve, Alex and Porkins to fight alongside him. He'd been so confident that he hadn't even bothered to come up with a strategy, or a plan for what they should do if things went wrong.

And now everyone's paying the price for my mistake, thought Dave. He vowed to himself that if they made it out of the Nether alive, he'd never go into a mission or a fight without planning again.

Unfortunately it didn't look like there was much chance of him getting out of this alive. The skeletons had taken his and Alex's armor, weapons and backpacks, and there were so many skeletons marching down the stairs with them that there was no chance of making a run for it.

What do we do? thought Dave desperately.

Dave's only hope was that Porkins and Robo-Steve would come to their rescue. Porkins knew the Nether better than anyone, so if anyone could find them, it was him. But as Dave and Alex were dragged into a large nether brick chamber, Dave's heart sank and he lost all hope.

There was a cage in the center of the room made of iron bars, and inside the cage was Porkins and Robo-Steve.

"Hello, chaps," said Porkins sadly, when he saw Dave and Alex. "I wish we were meeting under better circumstances."

Porkins and Robo-Steve had had their weapons and armor confiscated as well.

The skeletons opened the iron door of the cage and roughly shoved Dave and Alex inside.

"Let us out of here, you bone heads!" Alex yelled at the skeletons.

She turned to Dave and the others.

"Don't worry," she told them, "we'll fight our way out of here. Biff boff pow! They won't know what hit them!"

Robo-Steve and Porkins didn't look quite so confident.

"Alex is right," Dave told them, "we've been in tougher scrapes than this before. We'll fight our way out of this."

Dave wasn't sure if he believed this himself, but he knew that it was what the others needed to hear right now. Dave had to make them believe he was confident: as if he wasn't confident, they wouldn't be either.

"I believe I'm feeling fear again," said Robo-Steve, sounding confused.

"The poor chap's been on a bit of a spiritual journey," Porkins told them. "Unlocking his emotions and what have you."

"It's ok to feel afraid," Dave told them. "But we need to overcome our fear if we're going to get through this."

"Right-ho," said Porkins. "You're our leader, Dave old chap. We'll follow your command."

Leader? Dave had never thought of himself that way before. Sure, he'd given commands when needed, but that had always been in the heat of battle, when someone had to step up and take charge.

"I'm not your leader," Dave told them. "I'm just... I'm just a villager."

"You are a villager, that is technically true," said Robo-Steve, "but you are also our leader. The three of us and Carl have all chosen to follow you in your quest. We weren't forced to, we *chose* to."

Dave didn't know what to say.

"Well, if I am a leader I'm not a very good one," he said. "My leadership has led us here, into this cage."

Suddenly there was a clattering of bones. The skeletons were crowded round the sides of the chamber, but they all moved to the side to let a skeleton in a golden crown through. The crowned skeleton marched right up to the cage.

"*You... are... trespassers,*" the skeleton said, his voice thin and croaky, as if every word was painful. "*The... wither... skeletons... rule... the... Nether... now.*"

"And we apologize," said Dave. "Honestly, if you let us go free we'll never come back here again."

"We're gonna kick your butt, bone boy!" Alex yelled at the skeleton.

"Shush!" Dave told her. "Please Alex, not now!"

The skeleton in the crown laughed, his laughter rough and coarse, like grinding gravel.

"*You... will... make... worthy... sacrifices,*" the skeleton croaked. "*Worthy... sacrifices... to... our... champion.*"

That doesn't sound good, thought Dave. *That doesn't sound good at all.*

Dave the Villager

CHAPTER TWELVE
Carl and Bark

Carl was trying to teach Bark to perform tricks, but it wasn't going well.

"Ok, Bark," he said, holding up a piece of cooked beef steak. "I want you to lie down. If you lie down you can have this delicious beef."

Bark looked at Carl with a confused expression, his tongue hanging stupidly out of the side of his mouth.

"Lie down like this," said Carl, lying down on the grass to show the wolf what to do. "If you lie down like this, you get the beef."

Carl stood back up.

"Ok, Bark," he said, "now... lie down!"

But Bark didn't lie down. Instead the wolf came over and grabbed the piece of beef in its teeth. It then proceeded to carry the piece of beef away, dragging Carl along the ground with it.

"Stop!" yelled Carl. "You mangy mutt, let go!"

But instead of stopping, the wolf started running with the beef still in its jaws, Carl hanging on for dear life.

"Waaaaaa!" said Carl.

Carl lost his grip and rolled across the grass. When he came to a stop he looked up to see Bark busy gobbling down the beef.

"Stupid dog," muttered Carl.

Carl made his way back to the cottage and sat down on the porch next to the front door. From where he was sitting he could see the nether portal standing in the field in front of him, its purple light shimmering and swirling as usual.

I hope the others are ok, he thought. Dave and the others had been gone almost a full day now. Dave had told Carl that he thought their quest would only taken a couple of hours, but they'd been gone a lot longer than that.

Anyway, Carl thought to himself, *even if they were in trouble, what could I do? I'm just a creeper who can't explode.*

Carl went inside and started cooking up some baked potatoes; Baked potatoes always made him feel better. He cooked some more steak for Bark as well.

But that night, as Carl and Bark sat outside the cottage looking up at the stars, Carl really started to worry.

"I can't just leave those idiots if they're in trouble," Carl said to Bark. "But what can I do?"

He noticed that Bark had something in his mouth.

"What's that you got, boy?" Carl asked the wolf. Bark turned and Carl saw that he had a bone in his mouth.

"A bone," said Carl, thinking. "A bone..."

And then Carl had an idea. He didn't like the idea, as it was dangerous and would probably lead to lots of bad things happening to him, but it was the only idea he had.

"Come on, you mangy mutt," Carl said to Bark. "We've got some work to do."

CHAPTER THIRTEEN
The Arena

The wither skeletons dragged Dave and the others down yet more corridors and stairs, bringing them deeper and deeper into the fortress.

Dave knew that they had to escape somehow, but there were so many skeletons, all armed with swords, that escape was impossible at the moment.

I've just got to keep my wits about me, Dave thought, *and hope an opportunity for escape comes up soon.*

Up ahead Dave could hear a wheezing, rattling sound: it sounded like hundreds of skeletons, all making strange noises. Then Dave understood what it was.

The skeletons are cheering, he realized.

They were pushed through a doorway and found themselves in a huge room. In the middle of the room was a pit, and all round the edges of the pit were nether brick stands.

"It's an arena," said Porkins.

The pigman was right, Dave saw. The stands were full of hundreds of skeletons, all cheering, and looking at Dave and his friends.

Without warning the skeletons shoved Dave and the others, and they fell into the pit. The walls of the pit were too high for them to climb out, but they could see the wither skeletons above them, all cheering and jeering them.

"Well, at least we're going to go out with an audience," said Porkins.

The wither skeleton with a crown—Dave had started calling him the *Skeleton King*—walked up to the edge of the pit. The other skeletons all fell silent.

"*Summon... the... champion!*" the Skeleton King hissed.

Another skeleton stepped forward and started building something. He placed four blocks in a t-shape, then took a step back. The blocks were made from the brown sand stuff that the nether wart had been growing in—soul sand.

"Uh-oh," said Dave. He recognized this recipe from his crafting book.

A wither skeleton walked up to the soul sand t-shape.

"*The... first... head... is... for... vengeance,*" the Skeleton King croaked.

The wither skeleton removed its own skull with its hands, then placed it on top of the left-hand side of the t-shape. Somehow the skeleton seemed to be fine without a head, and just walked off.

"How peculiar," said Porkins.

"*The... second... head... is... for... glory,*" the Skeleton King said.

A second wither skeleton walked over, popped off its own head and placed it on top of the right-hand side of the t-shape.

"Everyone get ready," Dave told the others. "They're creating a—"

"*Silence!*" the Skeleton King croaked down at them. "*Bring... the... final... head!*"

A third skeleton approached the t-shape.

"*The... third... head... is... for... DEATH!*" roared the Skeleton King.

The third wither skeleton grabbed the sides of its skull and pulled. With a *pop* its head came off. The headless wither skeleton staggered over to the t-shaped soul sand structure, and placed its skull in the middle of the two other heads.

For a moment the structure stayed as it was: four soul sand blocks arranged in the shape of a 'T' with three wither skeleton skulls on top, but then suddenly a *wither* appeared: a huge, three-headed beast made of black bones.

Its body was a floating spine with a rib cage, the three skull heads resting on top of its shoulders: two smaller skulls on the side and a larger skull in the middle.

The wither floated down into the arena, and began to glow blue.

"At last!" said Alex, marching towards the wither. "A proper enemy to fight!"

"No!" said Dave, putting a hand out to stop her. "Stay back."

"Let me at him!" said Alex, trying to push past Dave. "Let me at him!"

"W-what's it doing?" Porkins asked, looking at the wither. "Why's it glowing like that?"

"I don't know," said Dave, "but stay back until we can figure out a plan."

"The wither's initial attack is a massive explosion, once it's finished charging," said Robo-Steve. "Dave is correct—it would be sensible for us all to keep our distance."

But keeping their distance was easier said than done, as the wither was floating towards them, still glowing with blue light. Dave had seen a wither before, back in Snow Town, but he'd never fought one. From what he'd read in his crafting book, they were exceptionally difficult to kill. Since he and his friends didn't even have any weapons, he had no idea what they were going to do.

Suddenly the wither exploded in a blast of blue light. Dave and the others were sent flying backwards, slamming against the arena walls. The skeletons watching all cheered.

"No-one... can... escape... the... champion!" croaked the Skeleton King.

Dave missed Carl. Sometimes he got fed up with the creeper's sarcastic comments and jibes, but he would have liked to have seen Carl make fun of the Skeleton King, and bring him down a peg or two.

The wither had stopped glowing blue now, its bones as black as coal as it floated towards them. Where it had exploded it had left a huge crater in the nether brick floor of the arena, Dave noticed, revealing the netherrack underneath.

"Now the wither has finished its initial charging stage, it will proceed to fire projectiles at us," said Robo-Steve. "Exploding skulls, I believe."

"Oh crumbs," said Porkins.

As ever, Robo-Steve was right. All three of the wither's heads started spitting out skulls. Dave and the others had to jump out of the way as the skulls exploded into the ground.

It's destroying the arena, Dave thought, looking at the holes that the exploding skulls had created.

At last, he had an idea.

"Everyone stay together!" he yelled to the others. "I want to get all three of that things heads firing at the same place."

Porkins, Robo-Steve and Alex ran over to join him. All three of the wither's heads spat exploding skulls towards them.

"This way!" yelled Dave, and they all dodged to the left, just in time to avoid the explosion from the skulls. The explosion left another huge crater in the side of the arena.

"We have to get them to hit that same spot again," said Dave. He ran over to the crater, followed by the others.

The three heads once more spat skulls at them, and once more they dodged out of the way before they exploded. The crater was even bigger now, going deep into the netherrack.

"I see what you're doing now," said Robo-Steve. "Using the wither to dig an escape route. Very clever."

They stood in front of the crater once again, and the wither fired its skulls. This time the explosion blew a hole in the netherrack that revealed a tunnel underneath.

"It's a way out!" said Porkins happily.

"But I wanna beat up the monster!" moaned Alex.

"Maybe next time," said Dave. "Come on!"

The three of them jumped down through the hole into the tunnel. They could hear the angry jeers and yells of the skeletons back in the arena.

The tunnel was a small, natural tunnel that wound its way through the netherrack. They ran down it as fast as they could, getting as much distance between them and the arena as possible.

"Those skeleton braggarts should have built their arena out of something more sturdy," said Porkins happily. "Obsidian, perhaps."

"We're not safe yet," said Dave. "They've taken our stuff, so we've got no way of building another nether portal. Our only hope is finding our original one."

"Oh that's no bother," said Porkins, "I can find it easily. The Nether was my home, you know. Robo-Steve and I had almost got back there before when we were ambushed by the skeletons."

"You lead on then," said Dave.

Porkins nodded, then went ahead of them, leading the way.

They came out of the tunnel and Porkins led them across the vast netherrack plains. Some ghasts shrieked as they passed by, but the four of them kept running.

Before long they came over a hill and could see their nether portal in the distance.

"Thank goodness," said Dave.

Then the wither skeletons appeared, pouring out of some caves up ahead and surrounding them.

"Oh crumbs," said Porkins.

The wither skeletons parted and the Skeleton King stepped forward.

"*No-one... knows... this... land... better... than... us...*" he hissed. "*You... never... stood... a... chance.*"

CHAPTER FOURTEEN
The Cavalry

They were surrounded by hundreds of wither skeletons: without weapons and without a chance of escape.

Is this the end? thought Dave. He didn't see how it couldn't be.

And then he heard a sound he didn't expect to hear.

It was *barking*.

Are there wolves in the Nether? Dave wondered, confused. But if he was confused, the wither skeletons looked even more confused than him.

Then he heard *another* sound he didn't expect to hear.

"Let my friends go you bony idiots!" Dave heard someone yell. He would have recognized that voice anywhere. It was Carl!

Suddenly the skeletons starting pushing, shoving and panicking as a pack of wolves ran through their legs, snapping, growling and biting.

The Skeleton King was about to say something, but then a wolf pounced on top of him.

"I've never heard of there being wolves in the Nether," said Robo-Steve.

Dave noticed that one of the wolves had a small green thing riding on its back.

"Carl!" Dave said, amazed.

Carl burst through the skeletons on his wolf, coming to a stop next to them.

"Don't worry, the cavalry's here," said Carl. "You guys can't do anything without my help, it seems."

"Am I glad to see you, you little pest," said Dave, grinning.

The wolves were putting up a good fight against the skeletons, but the skeletons were starting to regroup, and had much greater numbers.

Dave saw the Skeleton King stagger to his feet. Or rather *foot*, as the wolf had eaten one of his legs.

"*Kill... them!*" he croaked. "*They're... only... wolves!*"

But then Dave heard a deep roar, and saw two huge shapes start smashing up the skeletons.

"Golems!" said Porkins.

Porkins was right: two huge iron golems were joining the fight, bashing the skeletons to bits with their fists.

"Oh yeah, I brought those two along as well," said Carl. "For backup. It wasn't easy training all these wolves and building those golems—you guys owe me big time!"

Dave noticed that on the floor nearby were four backpacks—their backpacks. The skeletons who had confiscated them must have been slain by the wolves, he thought.

"Come on," he said to the others, "our packs!"

They all dashed through the crowds of skeletons and wolves and grabbed their backpacks. Dave was pleased to see that his diamond armor and diamond sword had been put inside his pack. He quickly put his armor on and drew his sword. Porkins, Robo-Steve and Alex were all armed and ready too, he was pleased to see.

"Right," said Dave, "let's fight!"

The four of them joined the battle: Dave, Robo-Steve and Alex with their swords and Porkins with his bow. Meanwhile Carl was riding on the back of his wolf, biting and pounding on the skeletons. The rest of the wolf pack—there were about fifteen of them in total, Dave guessed—and the golems were all fighting the skeletons as well. It was a chaotic battle, with bits of bone flying everywhere, but soon all the wither skeletons were defeated, leaving nothing but bones, coal and skulls on the ground.

"Nice one chaps!" said Porkins happily. "We ruddy well did it!"

"All thanks to Carl," said Dave. "You saved us."

Carl was still riding on the back of his wolf.

"If I let you guys get slain, who would I have to complain to?" he said.

The other wolves were all gathered around Carl, eyeing Dave warily and bearing their teeth.

"Don't worry guys," Carl said to the wolves. "Dave's a good guy. A little dull, but a good guy."

Dave was just relieved that everything had worked out alright. If it wasn't for Carl, he, Porkins, Robo-Steve and Alex would have been finished.

"Come on," he said to them all, "let's get out of here."

KA-THOOOOOM!!!!

An explosion sent them all flying. Dave landed hard, rolling across the netherrack ground. The wolves were barking and howling and when he looked up he saw the wither floating above them.

"Oh no," said Dave.

The wither fired an explosive skull at the wolves. They darted out of the way in time, but then they all ran as fast as their legs could carry them, disappearing into the portal. Carl was just about managing to keep control of his own wolf, which was struggling, desperate to escape as well.

"Time to die, monster!" Dave heard Alex yell. He watched as she ran towards the wither, her diamond sword at the ready.

"Alex no!" Dave yelled.

The wither's three heads each fired a skull at Alex, hitting her square in the chest, exploding on impact and sending her flying. She landed on the netherrack ground, bruised and unconscious.

Thank goodness she was wearing diamond armor, thought Dave, *otherwise she would have been blown to bits.*

The iron golems both charged at the wither, but it simply rose up into the air so they couldn't reach it, and fired exploding skulls at them. One golem was blown to bits, but the other was just sent flying backwards.

Porkins and Robo-Steve were both firing arrows at the wither, but it seemed to barely notice.

Dave knew a losing battle when he saw one. Even together, they stood no chance against such a powerful foe.

"To the portal!" he shouted. "Run!"

They did as he said. Robo-Steve picked up Alex, carrying her with him.

Robo-Steve and Alex disappeared into the portal first, then Porkins, then Carl on his wolf and his golem. When he was sure all his friends had made it through safe, Dave made a run for it himself. He was almost at the portal when the wither fired three skulls into the ground in front of him, sending him flying backwards.

Dave landed hard on the ground, hitting his head. Somehow he managed to stay conscious, but his mind was swimming and he was seeing stars.

I was so sure that me and my friends were invincible, he thought bitterly. *I thought that this would be an easy mission and that nothing could go wrong. And now I'm going to get killed for my mistake.*

The wither floated above him, looking down at him with all three heads.

No, thought Dave. *I can't let it end like this.*

Finding strength from somewhere, Dave pushed himself to his feet. The wither fired three skulls down at him, but Dave ran forward as fast as he could.

The explosion blasted into the ground behind him, sending him flying forward, where he slammed into the ground.

Get up! he told himself.

Somehow he rose to his feet once more and ran towards the portal. He could hear the wither scream in frustration behind him.

Just a little further! Dave thought as he ran. *Just keep going!*

He reached the portal and jumped through, landing on the grass. The others were all gathered there, waiting for him.

"Destroy the portal!" he shouted.

Porkins already had a diamond pickaxe in hand, and immediately started hacking away at one of the obsidian blocks of the portal.

Good old, Porkins, Dave thought, his mind swimming. The bump on his head was really starting to hurt now.

Chunk! The obsidian block Porkins was attacking broke, and the portal disappeared.

Thank goodness, thought Dave.

And then he fainted.

CHAPTER FIFTEEN
Back on Track

When Dave awoke he was lying in bed. Alex was standing over him, grinning.

"He's awake!" she yelled.

Immediately the door opened and Porkins, Carl and Robo-Steve all ran in. Dave realized he was back in the cottage, in his bedroom.

"Alex..." said Dave, his voice weak. "I'm glad you're ok."

"Oh I've been up and about for three days," she said cheerily.

"I've been asleep for three days!" said Dave, amazed.

"No, old chap," said Porkins. "You've been asleep for *four* days."

Dave was shocked. He knew he'd been injured during the fight with the wither, but he didn't know it had been that bad.

"Thankfully we managed to get you to drink some healing potion in your sleep," said Robo-Steve. "So all your wounds have been fixed."

"Apart from the wound of ugliness," said Carl, walking over to the bed. "Unfortunately for you, that's a wound that can never be healed."

"I'm sorry," Dave told them all. "I led us all on that mission without a plan. I was so arrogant that I thought we didn't need one."

"Well, we all made it out of there in one piece," said Porkins. "That's the important thing."

The healing potion had done its job: that afternoon Dave felt strong enough to get out of bed, and joined the others on the grass outside, sitting in the sun. Dave was a bit scared at first when he saw that all of Carl's wolves were still hanging around the cottage, but Carl reassured him that they were friendly.

The remaining iron golem was there too, standing perfectly still and watching over them all.

"So are you going to turn that golem into your new suit?" Dave asked Carl.

"I have thought about it," said Carl, "and that was why I was planning on building a golem in the first place. But I've become quite attached to Basher now. I don't think I could bear to cut his head off."

"Basher," said Dave, grinning, "that's a good name."

"If you're still in need of a new armored suit, perhaps I can help," Robo-Steve said to Carl. "I managed to build that arm for Porkins, and that's been a success so far, I believe."

"It jolly well has," said Porkins, smiling.

"You could build me a new golem suit?" said Carl happily. "That... that would be amazing!"

"I'll try my best," said Robo-Steve. "Hopefully I can build something suitable.

"Aw man, can I have a super suit too?" Alex asked. "I want one with swords instead of hands!

Dave laughed.

"I don't think you need one!" he said. "You're good enough with a sword already."

"Yeah, but I wasn't good enough to fight that wither," said Alex sadly.

"To fight something like that we really needed to be more prepared," said Dave. "From now on I'm going to make sure we always have a plan when we go on a mission. Even if we think it'll be easy, you never know what unexpected things can happen."

"So I guess the next thing on our list is to get some more ender pearl things," said Porkins.

"Yeah," said Dave, "but this time we're gonna do it properly."

Dave and his friends sat down together and worked out a plan for how they could slay endermen as safely as possible. Robo-Steve's advice was invaluable, since he'd read accounts of endermen hunts from history in the Villagertropolis library.

In the end they built a small rectangular cobblestone walled base in a large open field. The inside of the base was lit up with torches, so no mobs would spawn in there, and around the outer walls of the base was a low overhang: it was tall enough for Dave and the others to walk underneath it, but too low for any endermen to get through. When night came and the endermen attacked, Dave and his friends could easily fight them off without getting hurt.

Alex got a little carried away sometimes, running out into the field and hacking away at all the endermen she could find, but she could run back to the base and make a quick escape when it all got too overwhelming. Plus, they'd filled chests in the middle of the base with food, so they could retreat and recover their strength when needed.

After a couple of nights of ender hunting, they had all the ender pearls they needed. Dave combined the pearls with the blaze rods he'd got from the Nether, turning them into eyes of ender.

'These things are freeeeaky," said Alex, holding one of the eyes of ender. "I swear it's looking at me."

They went to bed, and then in the morning they all gathered outside on the grass once more.

"So what do you do with the eye things anyway?" Alex asked.

"This," said Dave, and he threw an ender eye up into the air.

The eye hovered for a moment, then it sped off towards the horizon.

"And that's the direction we go to reach an end portal," Dave told Alex.

"Ooo," said Alex. "Cool."

They gathered all the items from the chests in their cottage and then destroyed the cottage, putting all the blocks and items into their rucksacks. Then Dave, Carl, Porkins, Robo-Steve, Alex, Basher the golem and the sixteen wolves all set off, following the direction the ender eye had taken.

How did we suddenly become such a big group? Dave wondered. It seemed like only yesterday it had been only him, Carl and Porkins, and now they were a small army.

"At least no blaggards will attack us on the road with this many of us," said Porkins.

Dave didn't say anything, but he wasn't quite so confident. If he'd learned anything on their adventure it was that it was always when you felt the safest that things started to go wrong.

But he didn't want to say that in front of the others, not when they were finally back on track, on their way to an end portal once more. So he just kept quiet and kept on walking.

BOOK 10

Herobrine Strikes Back

PROLOGUE

Adam was nervous. The longer he waited, the more nervous he got, and Herobrine was making him wait a very long time.

Adam was in the Nether, inside Herobrine's secret underground castle. After Dave and his friends had defeated his invasion and destroyed his old bases, Herobrine had built this new castle deep underground, beneath a netherrack hill, so that no-one would be able to find it.

Herobrine liked making people wait, Adam had come to realize. When Adam had first been recruited by Herobrine he'd expected that Herobrine would involve him in secret plots to take over the world and get revenge on Dave, but Herobrine had barely spoken to him since that day in the snow. Instead, Herobrine's witches had given Adam orders, telling him to investigate rumors of end portals or sightings of Dave and his friends.

For some reason Adam didn't understand, Herobrine was *really* keen to find an end portal. Adam had heard of the End, but he'd always been told that it was just a desolate place where dragons lived. He didn't see what Herobrine would want to go to the End for.

Suddenly the iron doors to Herobrine's chamber swung open.

"Enter," Herobrine said. He was sitting at the far end of the chamber, but Adam could hear his voice as loudly and as clearly as if Herobrine was standing right next to him. Hearing Herobrine's voice always made Adam feel a bit ill. He didn't understand why.

Adam walked into the chamber. It was a long, thin room with cobblestone walls. There were only two torches—one on either side of the door—and when the doors swung shut behind him, Adam was plunged into near darkness. Herobrine was at the end of the room, sitting on a cobblestone throne. It was so dark that Adam could barely see him.

"You did well, bringing that woman here," said Herobrine. "She has already proved to be of value, and I'm sure she will be for many years to come."

Adam felt a pang of guilt. He tried not to think of what Professor Quigley was going through, held in Herobrine's dungeons against her will.

I had to bring her here, Adam reassured himself. *I need to win Herobrine's favor so he'll spare Sally.*

Adam had convinced himself that Herobrine was going to take over the world no matter what, so he wanted to make sure that he was in a position of power when it happened. The more he pleased Herobrine now, the higher his position would be in the new world.

"Thank you, Lord Herobrine," Adam said. "I'm glad she's being of use."

"How did you find her?" Herobrine asked.

"A stroke of luck," Adam replied. "I was following a lead that I thought might lead to the villager named Dave. A wandering trader had told me he'd sold goods to a villager, a pigman, a tiny creeper and a robot, so I followed the path he'd said they'd taken. I didn't find them, but I heard stories of strange goings on— thousands of clones of Steve appearing from nowhere and a giant golden man. I followed the trail and found Professor Quigley."

"And Dave the villager?" asked Herobrine. "Did you hear any more news of him?"

"I'm afraid not," said Adam.

He felt a trickle of sweat run down his neck.

Does he know I'm lying? Adam wondered. Sometimes it felt as if Herobrine could read his thoughts.

"A pity," said Herobrine. "But we have the professor and we have Steve. That is something, at least. My witches have tried questioning Steve, but he seems half mad. Whatever the professor did to him really seems to have made a mess of his brain. I always thought when Steve and I came face to face it would be more dramatic, but instead he just babbled like a fool, talking about golden giants and cake."

"What have you done with him?" asked Adam, dreading the

answer. All his childhood he'd heard stories of Steve and his heroics. Adam's grandmother had been saved by Steve in her youth. He didn't want to be the person responsible for delivering Steve to his death.

I had no idea Professor Quigley had Steve with her, Adam thought miserably. *I never would have brought Herobrine's forces to her cottage if I had known.*

"He is in the dungeons," Herobrine said.

Adam breathed a sigh of relief.

"I would have killed him," said Herobrine, "but he's not going anywhere, and I may find a use for him in time."

Herobrine fell silent. Adam knew better than to speak if he hadn't been spoken to, so he just stayed quiet. He could see Herobrine's white eyes watching him in the darkness.

Does he know? Adam wondered. *Maybe I should just tell him the truth?*

"You may go," Herobrine said finally.

"Thank you, Lord Herobrine," said Adam, trying not to look too relieved.

He turned around and walked towards the doors, his legs wobbling like jelly. As he reached the doors they swung open, and after he'd gone through they slammed shut behind him.

The witch on guard duty outside the door looked at him in surprise.

"I thought you were done for," she said to Adam. "Dunno why Lord Herobrine keeps a little runt like you around."

"Lord Herobrine can see how useful I am," snapped Adam. "I brought him that professor, didn't I?"

The witch just sneered at him, but Adam ignored her, making his way down the cobblestone stairs. As he walked through the castle, all the witches gave him disapproving looks.

They think I'm not worthy to be here, Adam thought. *Just because I can't brew potions or do magic. But I'll show them. I'll prove to Herobrine that I'm his most faithful servant of all.*

The truth was, Adam *had* lied to Herobrine. Or, at least, he'd not told him the whole truth. Adam *did* know where Dave the villager was, because Professor Quigley had told him. Well, he knew which direction Dave had been heading at least. Adam knew that he really should have given Herobrine this information, but he also knew that if the information turned out to be false, Herobrine would be very angry with him.

So Adam had decided to find Dave himself, and either capture him or follow him until he revealed how to find end portals.

Adam left the castle and walked through the Nether until he found the portal he'd originally come from. He walked through, emerging in an endless plains biome, then checked his compass.

I'm coming for you, Dave, he thought bitterly. *I'm going to get revenge on you for ruining my life and turning my Sally against me.*

Adam knew from the maps the witches had given him that if Dave was traveling in the direction that Professor Quigley had said then there was only one place he could be headed....

Diamond City.

CHAPTER ONE
Dragon Dreams

Dave threw an eye of ender into the air. It hovered for a moment, the sunlight glistening off its surface, then it sped off towards the horizon.

"Still north," Dave said, checking the compass that Robo-Steve had built him. "I told you it would be."

"I know, but it's always good to check," said Carl, taking a bite out of his baked potato. Carl was wearing his new golem suit that Robo-Steve had built him—it was the same shape and size as his old iron golem suit, but this one was made of diamond. They hadn't been in any battles since Carl had got the suit, but Dave knew that Carl was itching to try it out in combat.

They were all walking along in the sunshine, through another seemingly-endless plains biome. There were twenty two of them now, by Dave's count: Dave, Porkins, Carl, Robo-Steve, Alex, Basher the iron golem and sixteen wolves. Thankfully the wolves fed themselves—they would often go off hunting for hours at a time, coming back with full bellies. At the moment, however, all the wolves were here, and Dave was struck once again by how big his group had become.

Suddenly the wolves started growling at something up ahead. Dave squinted and in the distance he could make out a herd of horses.

The wolves began to dash forward, obviously thinking they'd found their next meal.

"No!" Dave yelled at them. To his surprise, the wolves all stopped and looked round at him.

"Don't harm the horses," Dave told the wolves. He had no idea if the wolves could understand him or not, but they seemed to be behaving themselves for now.

"What's the story, old chap?" Porkins asked Dave. "Are we going to get ourselves some steeds?"

"That's exactly what we're going to do," said Dave. "Robo-Steve, I assume you know how to tame wild horses?"

"Affirmative," said Robo-Steve. "You walk slowly up to them, making sure not to scare them, then you jump on their back. If they throw you off, you jump back on, and keep jumping back on until they don't throw you off anymore."

"Is that it?" said Dave. "I thought it would be more complicated than that."

"Oh, there is one thing," said Robo-Steve, "to control a horse you need to put a saddle on them. Otherwise they won't go where you want them to go."

"Ah," said Dave. "How do we craft saddles? Out of leather, I suppose?"

"Unfortunately they can't be crafted," said Robo-Steve.

"Oh dear," said Dave. "That's a shame."

He'd had images of them all riding through the plains on horseback, but now that plan was over before it had started.

"We could go to that village over there and see if they've got any for sale," said Carl.

"What village?" asked Dave. He looked around but all he could see was endless grass.

"Oh sorry," said Carl, "I always forget that you lot have such rubbish eyesight. There's a little village up ahead on the left."

Robo-Steve squinted.

"Carl is correct," he said. "With my magnification sights equipped I can see it clearly. A small farming village. There appears to be a market taking place."

"Show off," said Carl.

So they headed off towards the village. When they got there, the traders ran over to them, trying to sell them stuff.

"You can't get many customers all the way out here?" Dave said to one of the traders, just trying to make conversation.

"Oh you'd be surprised," said one of the traders. "We get quite a few people coming through on their way to Diamond City. We've got ender pearls if you're looking for some—we got a shipment of them from some of those Ender Hunters a few weeks back."

"We've got plenty of ender pearls, thanks," said Dave. "We're after saddles, if you've got them."

One of the traders did have saddles in stock, so Dave bought four. He also bought some ingredients for potions and some more obscure crafting materials, such as sponge and some glowstone.

Once they had the saddles, the next step was taming the horses. So they left the village and headed back to the horses out on the plain. There were six of them, munching on grass without a care in the world.

"Ok," Dave told the others, "you heard what Robo-Steve said. You jump on a horse's back and keep jumping back on until you've tamed it."

"I want the brown one!" said Alex, excitedly.

"They're all brown," says Dave. "Well, apart from one that's brown with white spots."

"I want the one that's brown with white spots!" said Alex.

Dave rolled his eyes.

"Come on," he said, "let's saddle up."

Alex ran forward, jumped up, span around in the air a few times then landed on the back of the horse with the white spots. Immediately little red hearts appeared above the horse's head.

"Ah, she's tamed it," said Robo-Steve.

"First try?!" said Dave, unable to believe it.

"Are you jealous?" asked Carl, grinning. Carl didn't need a horse, so he was sitting on the grass in his diamond golem suit, ready to watch the others make fools of themselves. Basher was sat next to him. Carl had tied the wolves up to a tree nearby so they wouldn't try to attack the horses.

As Alex happily rode her horse around the field, Porkins stepped up to the remaining horses.

"Right, chaps," he said to the horses, "please be gentle with me."

Porkins climbed up onto a horse, swinging his legs across it. For a second it looked like the horse was going to let him stay there, but then it rose up onto its hind legs, throwing him off. Porkins hit the grass hard, and Carl burst out laughing.

"Bad luck, Pork Chop," said Carl.

"If at first you don't succeed, try and try again!" said Porkins, standing back up. "Us pigmen don't give up easily."

Porkins got back onto the horse. It neighed loudly, and it looked to Dave like it was about to rear up again, but then hearts appeared above its head.

"I did it!" said Porkins happily. "I ruddy well did it!"

"You got lucky," said Carl.

Porkins rode off, joining Alex as she galloped across the field.

"Would you like to go next, Dave?" Robo-Steve asked.

"No, you go," said Dave. Dave knew that he'd probably be kicked off of his horse a few times, so he wanted to put it off as long as possible. He wasn't looking forward to having Carl laughing at him.

"Very well," said Robo-Steve. He took a step forward, his golden metal body glistening in the sun.

Robo-Steve climbed neatly onto a horse's back, swinging his golden legs over it. For a moment the horse stayed still, but then it reared up. Robo-Steve was sent flying, but instead of falling onto the grass as Porkins had, he flipped gracefully into the air and landed on his feet.

"I'll attempt it again," said Robo-Steve, walking back towards the horse.

It took four attempts, but Robo-Steve eventually tamed his horse.

"Just you left now," he said to Dave.

"Yes, I know," said Dave irritably. He walked slowly towards one of the horses.

"Don't approach it directly from behind," Robo-Steve advised. "Or the horse might kick you."

"Ok, ok," said Dave. Dave had ridden tamed horses before during his adventure, but he'd never felt entirely comfortable on horseback. And the idea of taming a new horse from scratch filled him with dread.

He approached the horse from the side, but then the horse turned round, putting its back to him again.

"Don't approach it from behind," said Robo-Steve.

"Yes I know!" snapped Dave.

He again moved round so he was approaching the horse from the side, walking as slowly as he could so as not to startle the horse.

"Easy there, girl," said Dave. He placed a hand on the horse's side. "It is a girl, isn't it?" Dave asked Robo-Steve.

"Affirmative," said Robo-Steve.

When the horse didn't run off or turn away from him, Dave took that as a good sign. He reached up and pulled himself up onto the horse's back, then swung his left leg over, so he was sitting on it properly: one leg on either side of the horse.

"I did it!" Dave said happily.

And then the horse reared up onto its hind legs and Dave went flying. Unlike Robo-Steve he didn't land gracefully on the grass: he landed with a THUD on the hard ground.

"Ow!" said Dave.

"Bad luck, Dave!" laughed Carl.

"Humph!" said Dave.

It took Dave five more attempts, but eventually little hearts appeared above the horse's head and she accepted Dave as her rider. He was battered and bruised from being thrown off so many times, but he was happy that he'd finally managed to tame her.

"Ok, so now you've all got horses," said Carl. "Hip-hip hooray. Can we get going again now? Basher is eager for adventure."

Basher the golem said nothing. He had the same blank expression on his face that he always had, as far as Dave could see.

They rode on (or ran on, in the case of Carl, Basher and the wolves) until the sun started to go down, then Robo-Steve built them all a house to stop the night in. Unlike the simple houses that Dave built when it was his turn, Robo-Steve built complicated houses with separate kitchens, bedrooms, balconies, the works.

Dave always felt a bit jealous, as it would have taken him forever to build something like that, but Robo-Steve could do it in five minutes.

The house Robo-Steve had built them tonight was even more impressive than usual. It even had a fireplace, with a flaming netherrack block in it to keep them warm.

Since everyone was used to the wolves now, Dave let Carl keep them inside, rather than tying them up outside.

"Have you given them all names yet?" Dave asked Carl.

"Well," said Carl, "the first wolf I tamed was called Bark, so I thought I'd give them all names along a similar theme. So there's Bark 2, Bark 3, Bark 4, Bark 5, Bark 6, Bark 7, Bark 8, Bark 9, Bark 10, Bark 11, Bark 12, Bark 13, Bark 14 and Alan."

"Alan?" said Dave.

"Named after my uncle," said Carl. "He blew himself up when he was frightened by a sheep. He was a bit of an idiot."

That night in bed, Dave dreamed of dragons again. He hadn't had his weird dragon dreams in a while, so it took him by surprise when he suddenly found himself underneath an empty black sky without a star in sight. The land he was standing on was made of bleak yellow rock, and stretched out in all directions: an endless bleak landscape.

"*Don't let him take it,*" said a voice.

Dave turned and was terrified to see hundreds of endermen behind him. He reached for his sword, but found that he didn't have one.

"*Don't let him take it!*" said one of the endermen.

"Who?" Dave asked.

"*You know who,*" said another endermen.

"Herobrine?" said Dave.

"*The traitor!*" the endermen all said. "*The betrayer!*"

"I don't understand," said Dave. "What is Herobrine trying to take?"

"*The egg,*" said the first endermen. "*That's all he wants.*"

That's all he's ever wanted."

The endermen all began to scream. The noise was so horrible that Dave dropped to the floor, clutching his ears.

"*He betrayed us!*" the endermen wailed. "*He cursed us!*"

Then Dave felt a huge blast of air. It was so powerful that it almost sent him flying. He looked up and saw a huge black shape above him, flapping its heavy wings.

The ender dragon, Dave thought.

The screaming of the endermen was so loud that Dave felt like his ears were going to explode.

"*Don't let him come here!*" one of the endermen shouted at Dave. "*Don't let him get the egg!*"

Dave heard a roar from above. He looked up to see the dragon opening its mouth, then Dave was engulfed in purple fire...

He woke up, covered in sweat.

What was that all about? Dave wondered. He got up and went outside, sitting on the dew-covered grass and watching the sun as it began to rise over the treetops.

That was the End, Dave knew. Was it just a dream, or something more? He didn't know.

"Can't sleep, Dave?"

It was Robo-Steve. He was leaning against the wall of the house. Dave wasn't too surprised to see him: Robo-Steve didn't need sleep, so he would often spend time outside while the rest of them were tucked up in bed.

"I was having a nightmare," said Dave. "Or at least I think it was a nightmare. Do you... I don't suppose you know anything about whether or not dreams can be warnings? I keep having these same dreams about Herobrine and the End."

"There are plenty of recorded cases of dreams being premonitions of the future," said Robo-Steve. "Some scholars think that it's to do with magic. Others think that significant events in history create ripples through space time that can be felt both before and after the events happen. Our minds are not sophisticated enough to make sense of these warnings from the future, so our brains try to make sense of them in our dreams."

"Right," said Dave, feeling more confused than ever.

The next day, Carl cooked them all some breakfast. Porkins and Alex had given up eating meat, so they had mushroom stew, and Dave, Carl and the wolves all had steak. Robo-Steve and Basher didn't need to eat.

"Come on," said Dave, after they'd eaten, let's dismantle the house and then get going.

Dave was lost in thought as they rode along through the plains on their horses, thinking about Herobrine, the End and his strange dreams.

Maybe I'm making a mistake trying to find the End in the first place, he thought. If the End was somewhere that Herobrine desperately wanted to get to, maybe finding it wasn't such a good idea.

"What's that in the distance?" Porkins said, waking Dave from his daydreaming.

Dave squinted. On the horizon he could see something glistening in the sun.

"I think those are buildings," Robo-Steve said. "Buildings made of diamond blocks."

"Diamond City," said Dave, remembering what the villagers back at the trading village had said.

"Just try to resist taking over it," Carl said to Robo-Steve. "We all know what you're like with cities."

"Is that a joke?" Robo-Steve asked. "I still find it difficult to tell sometimes."

Dave laughed. He was in high spirits: the sun was shining, he was with his friends, and tonight he'd be spending the night in a nice inn in a big city. Things were looking up.

"Ruff ruff!"

It was one of the wolves. It was barking at a cluster of trees to the left of them.

"What's it barking at?" Dave asked Carl.

"*She,*" said Carl, "not *it.*"

The wolf barked again, then started prowling towards the trees.

"She probably smells a rabbit or something," said Carl. "Come on Bark 3, come here! Good girl! You can go hunting later."

The wolf reluctantly turned away from the trees and came back to join them.

"Those wolves are always hungry," Dave said to Carl. "Make sure you bring enough meat for them when we enter the city. We don't want to have to buy more meat when we get inside—they'll probably charge a fortune."

"Yes, Mum," said Carl, rolling his eyes.

*

Adam brought his horse to a stop behind some trees. He climbed off the horse, then peered through the trees, trying to remain hidden.

It's them! he thought happily. A short distance in front of him he could see Dave and his friends. They were all looking out at Diamond City.

Since the last time Adam had seen him, Dave had acquired some new traveling companions. There was a golden robot, a thing that looked a bit like Steve with long orange hair, an iron golem and more wolves than Adam could count. The little creeper, Carl, had upgraded his golem armor as well, and was now wearing something made of diamond.

I don't care if you're wearing iron, diamond or obsidian, Adam thought. *Herobrine will defeat you either way.*

Seeing Dave again filled Adam with rage. Dave had been the one who had turned Adam's wife Sally against him; filling her head full of ideas of being a hero.

Suddenly one of the wolves began growling and barking in his direction, so Adam quickly hid behind a tree.

"What's it barking at?" Adam heard Dave say.

Thankfully the little creeper soon called the wolf away, then

Dave and his friends all rode off towards Diamond City, taking the wolves with them.

"I'm on your trail, Dave," said Adam. "I'm going to deliver you to Herobrine, and this time there'll be no escape."

CHAPTER TWO
Diamond City

As they got closer to the city, Dave and his friends joined a wide cobblestone road which ran through wheat fields and farmlands. There were other travelers on the road too, both heading towards the city and leaving it. Most of them were wandering traders who kept trying to sell them things. Some of them had llamas.

"They're sooooo cute," said Alex, stroking a llama. "I want one!"

Dave just about convinced Alex that spending all her emeralds on a llama wasn't the best idea, and then they continued on to the city.

The city was surrounded by high walls made of diamond blocks. Dave had learned from one of the traders that long ago Diamond City had had the biggest diamond mine in the world. The founders of the mine built a town for their workers, but as more workers came to make their fortune, the town turned into a city. They'd found so many diamonds that eventually all the old wooden buildings had been replaced by diamond ones. The diamond mine has dried out years ago, but the diamond walls and buildings remained.

The cobblestone road led them to a large open gate where they could pass through the wall. Guarding the gate were five iron golems and a bored-looking villager in diamond armor, who was sitting down on a wooden bench, enjoying the sun.

As they approached the guard hastily got to his feet, trying to look professional.

"Who goes there?" the guard called out.

"We're adventurers," said Dave. "My name's Dave and this is Carl the creeper, Porkins the pigman, Robo-Steve the robot and Alex the... Alex."

"Wait," said the guard. "You're Dave! Dave, Porky and Barl!"

"It's Carl," said Carl. "He literally just told you!"

"We've heard all about you, of course," said the guard. "About how you defeated Herobrine and his witches. Come in, come in—I'm sure the mayor will be pleased to hear that such big heroes have come to visit our city!"

"Please, we really don't want any fuss," said Dave. But it was too late: as soon as they'd walked through the gate, the guard ran off to go and speak to the mayor.

"Come on," said Carl, "let's have a bit of a look round before that idiot gets back."

The first thing that struck Dave about Diamond City was how traditional the buildings were. Unlike the skyscrapers of Cool City and Villagertropolis, the diamond buildings had columns, spires and domed roofs. They all looked like they'd been built a long time ago. The roads were made from stone bricks, much to Carl's disappointment.

"They spent all that time making everything out of diamond, and then they don't even bother with the roads?" Carl said, shaking his head. "That's just lazy."

Practically everything else *was* made of diamond, though. Dave actually found it a bit confusing to look at, as there was so much blue everywhere.

They passed a large stable—which was also made of diamond—and paid the stable keeper some emeralds to take care of their horses, then continued into town on foot.

The city was busy, with crowds of people walking back and forth, and they soon found themselves in a market district. There were wooden stalls everywhere selling all sorts of goods. As Dave had suspected, all the goods—especially the food—were really overpriced.

As they walked through the market all the other villagers gave them a wide berth, and Dave couldn't really blame them—they did have sixteen wolves and an iron golem trailing behind them.

"Maybe we should have left the wolves outside," said Dave.

"Nah, they're fine," said Carl. "And look, some of the villagers have pet wolves of their own."

Carl was right: there were other wolves. But they were the only ones with this many wolves with them. He could understand why the other villagers were a bit scared.

One of the stalls that caught Dave's eye was a potion stall. He walked over and the woman behind the counter greeted him with a toothless smile.

"Hello dearie," she said, "welcome to Madame Misty's potion emporium. The finest ready-mixed potions in Diamond City. What you in the market for? We've got potions, splash potions, ingredients, books, everything potion-related you could ask for."

"Can I see your books?" asked Dave. The last potion-making book he'd had had been destroyed when the woodland mansion had burnt down, and he was eager to get a new one so he could start learning to craft potions again.

Madame Misty pulled out a pile of dusty old books from underneath her stall and slammed them onto the counter. Dave flicked through them, but they all seemed overly complicated.

"Do you have anything simpler?" Dave asked.

Madame Misty rolled her eyes, then pulled out another book. This one was a lot newer looking.

It was called *Potions for Noobs: The Noob's Guide to Brewing Potions.*

"I originally bought this for my grandson," said Madame Misty, "but even he thought it was a bit too simple. Plus, all he reads are those Seth the Elf comics these days."

"I'll take it," said Dave, picking up *Potions for Noobs.*

Carl laughed and laughed when he saw the book.

"Well," he said, wiping the tears of laughter from his eyes with his diamond golem fist, "you are a noob, so I guess it makes sense. It's the perfect book for you."

Porkins came up to them holding a strange-looking bow.

"It's a crossbow," he said happily. "Apparently they take longer to load than normal bows, but they're more powerful and can shoot further. Plus, I got some ruddy cool arrows."

He pulled out a bunch of new arrows from his quiver; each of them with different color tips.

"I've got all sorts of fun arrows now," said Porkins. "They're all tipped with different potions. This one is poison, this one is slowness, and this one is health regeneration!"

"Why would you want to help enemies to regenerate their health?" Carl asked.

"They're not for bad chaps," said Porkins, "they're for chums! Say you're injured in a battle and feeling weak, I could shoot you with this arrow and heal you!"

"Please don't shoot me with an arrow," said Carl. "Under any circumstance."

Robo-Steve had bought himself a load of redstone and redstone devices, such as switches, rails and repeaters. Dave thought to himself that he ought to learn to use redstone at some point, but it just looked so complicated.

Alex had bought herself a few more diamond swords and a custom shield with a picture of her face painted on it.

"It's me!" she said happily, holding up the shield. "How awesome is that?!"

"It's um... very nice, Alex," said Dave.

"It's very weird," said Carl.

"It's so the last thing my enemies will see will be my face," said Alex.

"But Alex," said Dave, "surely the last thing they would see would be your face anyway. When they see your actual face."

Alex looked confused.

Suddenly a horn was blown somewhere nearby. The villagers in the market quickly stood to the side as a procession of horses rode down the road towards them. The riders came to a stop right in front of Dave and his friends.

"You must be Dave the villager!" said the lead rider. He was a slim villager wearing a trendy-looking suit. The top two buttons on his shirt were undone, and he was constantly grinning.

The lead rider swung down from his horse gracefully, then held out his hand for Dave to shake.

"Hi, I'm Mayor Birchwood," he said, shaking Dave's hand. "But please, call me Birchy. Everyone else does. It's so great to have you guys here. Dave, right?"

"Um, yes," said Dave.

"Great, great," said Mayor Birchwood. "I'm a big fan. Huge. And you must be Carl the creeper."

"Well, at least you got my name right," said Carl, shaking Mayor Birchwood's hand with his diamond golem hand.

"Fantastic diamond armor that," said the mayor, looking at Carl's diamond golem suit. "We are partial to diamonds here ourselves, you may have noticed. Ha ha ha!"

"HA HA HA HA HA!!!" said Robo-Steve loudly. Everyone looked at him.

"Sorry" said Robo-Steve. "I saw you were making a joke and I wanted to join in."

"Not to worry," said the mayor, flashing Robo-Steve a big grin and shaking his hand. "I'm afraid I'm not sure who you are, but it's very nice to meet you."

"I'm Robo-Steve," said Robo-Steve. "I'm a robotic version of the hero Steve."

"Interesting," said Mayor Birchwood, looking a bit confused, but still managing to keep grinning. "We're all big fans of Steve, of course. Big fans. He helped to found this city."

The mayor turned to Porkins.

"And you must be Porkins, the heroic pigman," he said, shaking Porkins by the hands.

"Well, I don't know if I'd use the word *heroic*," smiled Porkins, "but that's very kind of you, my dear boy."

"We heard about the loss of your arm, of course," said Mayor Birchwood, pointing at Porkins's iron arm. "Glad to see you got a new one."

Finally he turned to Alex.

"I'm Alex!" said Alex, grabbing Mayor Birchwood by the hand and shaking it. "I'm a clone of Steve, but I was left in a cryogenic tube for too long and I lost all my memories and my hair turned orange."

"Riiiight," said Mayor Birchwood. "That's a bit of a confusing backstory. Maybe my public relations guy can help you out. Simon!"

A villager in glasses jumped down from one of the other horses. He looked very nervous.

"Y-yes, Mayor Birchwood?" he said. "I mean, Mayor Birchy. I mean Birchy."

"You'll have to forgive Simon," the mayor said. "He's a bit nervous, but he's a ruddy good PR guy. Simon, this little lady has an overly complicated backstory. Can you help?"

"Um, w-what's your backstory?" Simon asked Alex.

"I'm a clone of Steve who was kept in a vat so long that my hair went orange," said Alex. "Oh, and my skin went a bit paler and I lost all of my memories."

"O-k," said Simon. "Um, how about... *Alex: The female Steve.*"

"Ooo, that's cool," said Alex.

"I don't know," said Mayor Birchwood, "it implies that she should only be judged by her relationship to Steve; that she's nothing but a copy of the original. We need something that says who Alex is, what her personality is like."

"Um, ok," said Simon, "A-Alex, what word or phrase would you use to describe yourself?"

"Alex," said Alex.

"Right," said Simon, "but that's just your name."

"Let's put that on the back burner for now," grinned Mayor Birchwood. "Simon will put his thinking cap on and come up with something for you, Alex. He came up with this for me: *Mayor Birchwood—the diamond of Diamond City*. A bit cheesy, but it helped get me elected three terms in a row. Ha ha ha!"

"Right," said Dave, who was getting a bit bored of Mayor Birchwood and his endless grinning, "we'd better be heading off."

"Where are you staying tonight?"

said Mayor Birchwood, clasping his hands together.

"Probably just an inn," said Dave.

"Nonsense!" said Mayor Birchwood, "I can't let heroes like you stay in some crummy old inn. Tonight you'll be guests of mine at City Hall. We've got plenty of spare rooms, all with nice double beds, and we've got hot baths. I'm sure you'd all like a hot bath after your long journey."

"That sounds awesome!" said Alex.

"Awesome, I like that word," said Mayor Birchwood thoughtfully. "Simon, how about... *Awesome Alex!*"

"That's totally awesome!" said Alex.

"How about... *Totally Awesome Alex,*" suggested Simon.

"I like it... no, I LOVE it!" said Mayor Birchwood. "So, after you've spent the day shopping and exploring the city, come to City Hall. You can't miss it—it's a big diamond building. Ha ha, just a joke of course—all our buildings are diamond! Just ask anyone where City Hall is and they'll give you directions. It's right in the center of town: a diamond building with emerald pillars."

"Right," said Dave, "that's very generous of you."

"And don't worry about your wolves," said the mayor, "they're welcome too. We've got plenty of room in our kennels."

Mayor Birchwood and Simon got back on their horses and the group of riders all rode off down the road.

"He was a bit much, wasn't he," said Dave.

"Who cares," said Carl. "We're gonna get to have a hot bath! You would not believe how sweaty and clammy it gets in this suit."

"That's far, far too much information," said Dave.

They spent another hour or so walking round the market, then they found a little café with a balcony that overlooked the city. As Dave ate his pumpkin pie he was overwhelmed at how big Diamond City was.

"Blimey," said Porkins, looking out at the view. "Imagine how many diamonds it must have taken to build all those buildings. Thousands, maybe millions!"

"It does seem a bit of a waste," said Robo-Steve, "when wood and stone are perfectly good building materials that can be found in abundance, and diamonds are far more useful for building tools and weapons."

"Plus it hurts my eyes," said Carl. "The sun reflects right off of it."

"I think it looks cool," said Alex. "Diamonds are awesome."

After they'd finished eating they walked round the city a bit more, taking in the beautiful traditional architecture and the fountains and statues. Dave wasn't surprised to see a Steve statue in one of the squares, but he was surprised to see it was made of smooth stone rather than diamond. The stone Steve was holding a pickaxe, and looked very old.

"This statue predates the building of Diamond City," Robo-Steve read from a plaque at the base of the statue. "It depicts Steve the Builder, one of the four founders of the mining town that originally stood on this spot."

"Steve the Builder," said Dave, rolling his eyes. "He was probably trying to blow the town up, knowing him."

The sun was starting to go down, so they asked some villagers for directions, then made their way towards City Hall. The City Hall building was nestled in the heart of the city. As Mayor Birchwood had told them, it had pillars made of emerald, but the rest of the building was diamond.

The doors were open, with an iron golem stood on either side, standing guard. Dave and his friends walked through, finding themselves in a huge lobby. The walls were made of diamond, but the floor was made from white quartz.

A villager woman in a diamond-blue dress came up to greet them.

"Dave, it's so good to meet you," she said, shaking Dave's hand. "Mayor Birchwood told me you were coming. Our kennel master will take care of your wolves, if that's ok, and then we'll show you to your quarters."

A villager in leather overalls came over to fetch the wolves.

"It's ok," Carl told the wolves, "you go with him, and I'll see you soon."

After the wolves were gone, Dave and the others were brought up a quartz staircase to a huge lounge, with plush sofas and walls made from shiny blocks with a unique blue yellow and white pattern.

"Glazed terracotta," said Robo-Steve in awe, stroking the smooth surface of the patterned walls. "The unique patterns come from smelting dyed terracotta blocks."

"It's jolly pretty," said Porkins.

"Anything you want, just ring this little bell here," said the female villager, pointing to a bell on a table. There are five bedrooms. Does your, um, golem need a room too?"

"Nah, Basher doesn't sleep really,"'said Carl. "He'll just sit on the couch."

"Well, the hot baths are through those double doors there," said the female villager, pointing. "You all freshen up for an hour or so, then we'll bring you down for the feast."

"A feast?" said Dave. "I'm afraid we've already eaten."

"Oh no," said the villager. "Our chefs will be so disappointed. Mayor Birchwood hired the greatest chefs in the city to prepare a feast in your honor. You should see the amazing things they were going to do with baked potatoes."

"We'll be there!" said Carl.

Once the villager and her aides had gone, Dave and the others went to check out the baths. The bath room had walls with a shiny red swirl pattern ("more glazed terracotta," said Robo-Steve, "how fantastic") and there were three large rectangular pools. A sign above the first pool said 'Cold Pool', the sign above the second pool said 'Warm Pool' and the sign above the third said 'Warning: Very Hot Pool!'. There was steam coming off of this pool.

Having spent most of his life in the Nether, Porkins had no doubt about which pool he wanted to try out. He ran over and jumped into the Very Hot Pool without a moment's hesitation.

"It's actually a bit cold for my tastes," the pigman said as he floated in the water. "But it's jolly nice all the same."

Robo-Steve was a bit worried about what the pools might do to his circuits.

"My body is meant to be waterproof," he told Dave as he sat down on one of the wooden deckchairs, "but there's no point tempting fate."

Carl and Dave both climbed in to the Warm Pool. The warm water felt amazing on Dave's skin after being on the road for so long.

Alex couldn't decide which pool she wanted to use, so she kept jumping from one to the other.

"Ooo that's too cool!" she said. Then, "Ooo, that's too hot," then "Ooo I want to try a different pool now."

Eventually she settled upon the Very Hot Pool with Porkins.

After they'd relaxed for a while, Dave thought they ought to get ready for the feast. While they'd been in the baths, someone had laid them all out some fancy clothes. All the clothes were diamond-blue. Even Carl, Porkins and Robo-Steve, who never normally wore clothes, had blue three-piece suits to wear.

"This is too uncomfortable," said Carl, as Dave tightened his blue bow tie. "Can't I just go naked? Or wear my diamond armor?"

"At least you don't have to wear one of these horrible things," said Alex, looking at herself in the mirror. She'd been given a diamond-blue dress to wear.

Dave was actually quite pleased with his blue suit. As he looked at himself in the mirror he felt really smart and well dressed, for once in his life.

Robo-Steve was pleased with his three-piece suit as well.

"My understanding of fashion is very limited," he told the others, "but I believe the blue of the suit really brings out the shine in my gold plating."

"Bah," said Carl.

Soon some villagers came to take them downstairs to a huge banqueting hall. There were five long tables running down the length of the hall, with benches on either side which were packed with villagers. Dave and his friends were brought to a table at the top of the room. The top table was packed with important-looking people, all wearing fancy robes, dresses and suits. In the middle of the table was Mayor Birchwood, wearing a white shirt and trousers with no tie.

"My friends!" the mayor said to Dave and the others. "Please sit, please sit! You're our honored guests this evening."

Dave hadn't been that hungry, but once the food arrived he couldn't resist. The food the Diamond City chefs had prepared was spectacular: delicious pies, meats, puddings and more. They brought a platter of baked potatoes over for the table, but Carl grabbed it for himself.

"These... are... the... most... delicious... potatoes... EVER!" Carl said, his mouth stuffed full.

"Carl, old chap," said Porkins, "could I try one of those potatoes?"

"NO!" said Carl.

After they'd eaten, the mayor stood up and made a big speech, telling everyone what an honor it was to have Dave, Porkins and Carl in his city.

"Your legend grows stronger every day, Dave," said the mayor, grinning away. "We can't wait to see what you do next!"

The audience all chuckled.

"Everyone raise a glass," said the mayor, raising his own. "To Dave the hero!"

"Dave the hero!" everyone repeated, standing up and raising their glasses high.

Dave felt his cheeks glow red. He was blushing.

"Don't worry, Dave," Carl whispered to him, "I still think you're a loser."

The meals were cleared away and the waiters and waitresses moved the tables to the side of the room so everyone could stand up and chat. For the rest of the evening, Dave, Porkins and Carl answered questions from villagers, who were eager to hear about their adventures. Dave noticed that Carl's stories got more fantastic each time he told them.

"So there were actually *ten* blue creeper queens," said Carl, "and I had to fight off all ten by myself. Not only that, but I only had a wooden sword. And it was broken."

"So," a posh villager with a monocle said to Dave, "why exactly are you and your friends traveling from place to place, defeating monsters and what-have-you? On some sort of epic quest, I suppose?"

"No, we just like traveling," said Dave.

Before they'd gone down to the feast, Dave had told his friends that they should keep quiet about their quest to reach the End. In a city this big they didn't know who might be listening, and Dave was concerned that he'd already told too many people about the eyes of ender. Herobrine desperately wanted to find the End for his own evil purposes, Dave knew, so he should be keeping a lower profile.

Eventually the night came to an end and Dave and the others were allowed to head off to bed.

"That was terrific fun," said Alex, as they walked back into the lounge of their apartment.

"I guess so," said Dave. He was feeling uneasy. He knew that he and the others should stop attracting so much attention to themselves, but tonight there had been a huge banquet in their honor. If Herobrine had any spies in Diamond City, they would definitely know where to find them now.

Maybe we should start using fake names, Dave thought. But they were a villager, a pigman, a creeper, a robot and a female clone of Steve—it would be difficult for them to blend in, no matter what names they used.

Dave retired to his bedroom. The bed was so plush and comfortable that even with all his worries he soon found himself drifting off to sleep.

For the second time in two days he had nightmares about the End. He was surrounded by endermen, all of them screaming at him.

"He's coming!" one of the endermen moaned.

"You must protect it!" another one said.

"Do whatever it takes!" said a third. "The betrayer must be stopped!"

Dave woke up screaming. His door opened and Porkins ran into the room.

"Are you ok, dear boy?" Porkins asked. "I heard screaming."

"Just a nightmare," said Dave. "It's nothing."

The next morning the mayor's staff brought breakfast up to their apartment. Dave was still pretty full from the night before, but he still managed to finish off a couple of loaves of bread. The bread was delicious and freshly made: still warm from the oven.

"Right," said Dave, when they'd all finished eating, "I guess we should get going."

"Aw, can't we just stay here forever?" said Carl, taking a bite out of a baked potato.

"You can if you want," said Dave, "but the rest of us have an adventure to get back to."

"Fiiiiine," said Carl, rolling his eyes.

They got their backpacks on then headed down to the lobby. When they got there the mayor ran up to them.

"Come on, Dave," he grinned, "do you have to leave so soon? Stay a few more days. Everyone loves having you here. And having a hero staying in our city is doing wonders for my approval ratings!"

"Sorry," said Dave, "we need to get going. But thanks so much for putting us up and for all the lovely food."

"It was our pleasure," said Mayor Birchwood. "Please do come visit us if you're ever passing this way again. Everyone loves you! And Carl, we'd love to hear more of your stories next time. I can't believe you defeated the Kraken single handed!"

"It was actually two krakens," said Carl. "And they both breathed fire."

"Fantastic," grinned Mayor Birchwood. "Simply fantastic!"

A lot of other villagers had come to say goodbye to them, so it was well past midday when Dave and the others finally managed to pick the wolf pack up from the kennels and then leave City Hall.

They made their way down the cobblestone streets until they reached one of the gates that led through the city wall. It was a different gate from the one they'd entered, but this one also has a solitary villager guarding it, along with two iron golems.

"They don't guard the city very well, do they?" Robo-Steve said. "I think that guard's asleep."

After they'd walked for a bit, Carl asked Dave if he was going to throw an eye of ender up to see which way they should go.

"I don't need to," said Dave. "We know we're meant to be heading north, and we left the city through the north gate, so we're going in the right direction."

"How can you tell?" said Carl, looking up at the sky. "It's all cloudy. You can't see where the sun is. And if you can't see where the sun is, how do you know we're going north?"

"Because we left through the north gate!" said Dave, getting annoyed. "There was a big sign above the gate that said 'North Gate'."

"Maybe that's just the name of the gate," said Carl. "Maybe it was named after a guy named North."

Dave sighed. "Ok, ok," he said. "If it'll shut you up, let's use an eye of ender."

He reached into his rucksack and pulled out a smooth green disk.

"Those things are creepy," said Alex, "I swear it's looking at me."

Dave had to agree. The eyes of ender *did* always seem like they were looking at you. There was something sinister about them, and they always made Dave feel a bit uneasy.

"Ok," said Dave. "Here goes."

He threw the disk up into the sky. It hovered for a moment, then—to Dave's surprise—it sped back towards Diamond City.

"I told you," said Carl. "You've brought us the wrong way."

Dave was confused, but there was no denying it—they were going the wrong way.

"Ok," he said, "let's head back into the city and see where the eyes take us."

As they walked through the gate the guard was still fast asleep and the golems didn't pay them any attention. Dave looked back as they passed through the gate and saw that he hadn't been mistaken: it did say *North Gate*.

Maybe it <u>was</u> named after someone named North, thought Dave. *Although that would be very confusing.*

They kept on walking until they reached the market district, near the center of the city. The market was closed and the streets were fairly empty.

"Come on," said Carl, "throw another one up."

Dave took another ender eye from his bag. This one went off to their right, in a completely different direction to where the first one had headed.

"Maybe they're faulty," said Porkins. "You didn't bring them into the baths with you, did you?"

They followed the route the second eye of ender had taken, and soon found themselves next to the secluded square with the ancient statue of Steve. They were at a crossroads, where a few different streets led off in various different directions, so Dave decided to throw another eye up. It hovered for a moment, then it slowly drifted over the statue of Steve, before disappearing into thin air.

Dave felt his heart beating rapidly in his chest. He walked over to the statue and took out another ender eye. His hand was sweaty.

"What's going on?" Alex asked, sounding confused.

Dave threw the ender eye into the air. It hovered over the statue, then *POOF*, it disappeared.

"Good gravy," said Porkins. "Does that mean..."

"Aw yeah," said Carl. "Finally!"

Dave fell to his knees. He tried to speak, but couldn't get any words to come out. Then he realized he was *crying:* huge tears of happiness rolling down his cheeks.

"What is it, Dave?" asked Alex. "Why are you all acting like weirdos?"

"Because we've finally made it," Robo-Steve told her. "Underneath our feet is a portal to the End."

CHAPTER THREE
The End?

Adam was furious with himself. He'd followed Dave all the way to Diamond City, but once Dave and his friends had entered the city he'd lost them in the busy market district. That had been yesterday, and he'd still seen no sign of Dave or any of his idiot friends.

It's a good job I didn't tell Herobrine I'd found Dave, thought Adam. *If he found out that I'd lost him then I'd be in serious trouble.*

Adam had stayed the night in an alleyway. He had enough emeralds for an inn, but he didn't want to waste his money on unnecessary purchases. Herobrine's witches had given him a bag of emeralds for expenses, and he didn't want to have to go back to them and ask for more.

It'll all be worth it once Herobrine takes over the world, thought Adam. *He'll probably give me my own palace if I help find Dave. Maybe even servants! Then Sally will definitely take me back.*

But thinking about Sally made him sad, so he concentrated on looking for Dave.

"Have you seen a villager, a pigman, a creeper and a load of wolves?" he kept asking people. Most people *had* seen Dave and his friends—they'd been very hard to miss—but they weren't sure where they'd gone after the market. Apparently the mayor had rode out to meet them, but when Adam tried to get into City Hall, the guards had blocked his way.

"City Hall isn't open to the public," he'd been told. "Especially for smelly people like you."

Adam sniffed his clothes. He *did* smell. He couldn't remember the last time he'd washed.

I used to have a nice house, baths every day and a loving wife, Adam thought bitterly. *But now I have nothing. All because of Dave.*

*

Dave still couldn't believe it. Could he finally be at the end of his journey? It didn't seem possible.

"Throw another eye up," said Porkins excitedly. "Just to make sure that one wasn't faulty."

Dave reached into his rucksack and pulled out another eye. He threw it up and it hovered above the statue before disappearing.

There's no doubt about it, Dave thought. *We're above an End portal! We've finally made it!*

"Right," said Carl, reaching into his rucksack and pulling out a shovel, "let's get digging."

"I say old bean," said Porkins, "we can't just dig up the street. We'll get arrested."

"Fine," said Carl, rolling his eyes. "Let's go outside the city and then start digging from there. That'll take forever though."

"No, Porkins is right," said Dave, "if we're going to dig underneath the city we ought to ask permission, whichever way we do it. It's only fair, especially after they treated us so well. Let's go and speak to the mayor."

"Listen," said Carl, "I get it. You want to do things the right way. But what if the mayor says no? Have you thought about that?"

"We'll... we'll cross that bridge when we come to it," said Dave.

"You're making a mistake," said Carl. "We should just do this secretly."

"I have to agree with Carl," said Robo-Steve. "You've stated before that it was of the utmost importance that the villain Herobrine doesn't find an end portal, but if you tell the mayor that there's one under Diamond City, there's no telling how far the news will spread."

"We'll tell the mayor to keep it quiet," said Dave.

"You have met Mayor Birchwood, haven't you?" said Carl. "He couldn't keep anything quiet."

Dave was torn. He knew Carl and Robo-Steve were right, but he also knew that they really should tell Mayor Birchwood. They had no idea what might happen when they went through the portal. Could the ender dragon possibly escape and cause havoc in the city once they activated the portal? Could there be some other danger? They simply didn't know.

"What about you, Alex?" asked Dave. "What do you think we should do?"

"Maybe we should just blow up the city?" she suggested. "Then we won't have to worry about it."

"Right," sighed Dave. "Thanks for that."

Dave's joy at finally finding an end portal had gone, and was replaced with the frustration of not knowing what to do next.

"I think... we have to tell the mayor," he said. "I don't think we have a choice."

"Alright," said Carl, "but don't blame me when this all goes horribly wrong."

"You lot stay here," said Dave. "I'll go and speak to the mayor."

So Dave left his friends and walked through the streets towards the City Hall. The market district had opened now and the city was starting to get busy, so it took him a little while to push through the crowds.

Finally he reached City Hall and asked for the mayor at reception. Before long the mayor came bounding happily down the stairs.

"Davey boy!" he said happily. "I'm so glad you changed your mind. I'll get the servants to get the apartment ready for you."

"Actually," said Dave, "I came to talk to you about something else. Is there anywhere private we can go?"

"Of course, of course," said Mayor Birchwood, with a big grin. "Come through to my office."

The mayor's office was a cosy room with plush sofas, a thick carpet and walls made from dark oak planks.

"I prefer wood to all that glazed terracotta," said the mayor. "Wood's a more classic look."

The mayor sat down behind a big oak desk. Dave sat down opposite him.

"Ok, Dave," grinned the mayor, "how can I help?"

"Right," said Dave, figuring out where to start. "To be honest, me and my friends weren't entirely honest with you when we said that we weren't on a specific quest. We've actually been looking for an end portal."

"An end portal?" said the mayor. "As in a portal that leads to the End? I remember learning at school that those were all destroyed by the Old People."

"That's what everyone thought," said Dave. "But then we found one underneath my village."

"Ah wow," said the mayor, "that's fantastic. What village do you come from?"

"My village was called Grass Hill," said Dave. "Although it's not there anymore. It got blown up, and the end portal was damaged beyond repair."

"Oh dear," said Mayor Birchwood. "I'm sorry to hear that."

"Since then I've been trying to find another end portal," said Dave. He was still reluctant to reveal how he'd been tracking the end portal, so he just said: "there's a secret method I use to find end portals, and I've discovered that there's one underneath this city."

"Good heavens," said Mayor Birchwood, his eyes lighting up. "A real life end portal, under my city! Are you sure?"

"One hundred percent sure," said Dave. "That's why I came to see you. We'd like to dig under the city to find the portal. With your blessing, of course."

"Why of course you have my blessing!" exclaimed Mayor Birchwood. "This is fantastic news! Think of the money this will bring in! Tourists will flock from miles around to see the world's last end portal. Of course, you and your friends will have a cut of the profits. We do business properly here in Diamond City!"

"No," said Dave, "you don't understand. We have to keep the portal a secret. Herobrine can't find out about it."

"Herobrine?" said Mayor Birchwood, looking confused. "What's he got to do with it?"

"Herobrine wants to find an end portal," Dave told him.

"Why?" asked the mayor.

"To get a dragon egg," said Dave. The words came to him without thinking, but as soon as he said them he knew it was true.

That's what my dreams have been warming me about, he thought. *Herobrine mustn't get to the End because he mustn't get his hands on an ender dragon egg.*

"Right," said the mayor. "I admit that's a pretty terrifying thought—Herobrine with his own dragon. These are strange times we live in: a few months ago I thought Herobrine was just a fairy story, made up to scare children."

"He's definitely real," said Dave. "I've met him."

The mayor stood up and took out a glass bottle of milk from a chest.

"Milk?" he asked Dave.

"No thank you," said Dave.

Mayor Birchwood poured himself a cup of milk and then sat back down again.

"Listen, Dave," he said, "Diamond City may have been spared from Herobrine's zombie pigmen invasion, but once we heard about it we doubled our defenses. Our diamond walls are a third higher than they were, and we have guards and golems positioned at all four of our gates."

Dave couldn't help thinking of the sleeping guard he'd seen at the North Gate. That gate didn't look very well defended to him.

"Herobrine could also attack from the Nether," said Dave. "A nether portal could just appear one day in the middle of your city and pigmen would come pouring out. The last time I was in the Nether, all the pigmen were gone. I think Herobrine's keeping them somewhere: his own private army, ready and waiting. That's why we can't risk letting Herobrine know that an end portal is here. He'd attack with his full strength: pigmen, witches and goodness knows what else."

"Aha," said Mayor Birchwood, grinning, "that's where you're wrong. We may not be great warriors or adventurers here in Diamond City, but we're no dummies. We also heard that Herobrine likes to invade from the Nether, so we came up with a plan.

"The Nether is, most of our scientists agree, eight times smaller than our world. So we've built a base in the Nether that's an eighth the size of Diamond City. The only way Herobrine could get into the city via the Nether would be to break into our Nether base first, and it's guarded by high walls, iron golems and villagers with crossbows. Plus we have ten well-guarded nether portals inside the city, so even if Herobrine's forces managed to take out our Nether base, the portals they built would link to our portals inside the city, and our iron golems would be ready for them."

Dave was impressed. Thinking about the difference in distance between the Nether and the overworld and how portals linked still gave him a headache, but it seemed like Mayor Birchwood's scientists had thought of everything.

"Still," said Dave, "it won't be enough. Herobrine won't stop until he captures that portal. We have to keep it a secret."

"I do understand your concerns, really I do," said Mayor Birchwood, "but I can't pass up an opportunity like this. Diamond City has been suffering since our diamond mines dried up, and this could really help put us back on the map and create new jobs."

"There won't be any jobs at all if your city is destroyed," said Dave.

"It won't be," said the mayor. "When you defeated Herobrine you wiped his army out and defeated his castle, from the reports I've heard. Have you even heard any reports of Herobrine since you stopped his invasion? Because I haven't. For all we know he's gone away and given up."

Dave didn't think Herobrine had given up, but he had to admit that there was some truth to what the mayor was saying. Since Dave and the others had defeated the witches and the pigmen in the Nether, they hadn't heard a peep out of Herobrine at all.

But Dave still didn't want to take that risk.

"Please," he said to Mayor Birchwood. "I'm asking you one last time... please keep the end portal a secret."

"I'm sorry, Dave," said the mayor, his usual grin gone, "but I can't. This is an opportunity to improve the lives of my citizens, and I can't pass it up."

＊

Adam had finally managed to find out what had happened to Dave.

"He left," a random villager told him. "I saw him, the creeper, that pigman, that gold thing, the woman, the golem and all them dogs. They were heading out of the north gate."

Adam kept asking around, but the story he heard was always the same:

Dave had left Diamond City.

I need to catch up with him, thought Adam, desperately. He knew that Dave had left via the North Gate, so he had to head there. But as he was making his way through the city he ended up swept up in a crowd, all moving in the same direction.

"What's going on?" he asked a villager.

"Apparently the mayor's making a big announcement," said the villager. "He's probably made a new trade deal or something. That man will make an announcement about anything."

Adam has no time to listen to some politician waffle on about trade deals, but the crowd was so thick that he couldn't do anything but join it.

Every moment I waste here, Dave gets further and further away, thought Adam bitterly.

Finally the crowd stopped. But there were so many people crammed together that there was no way that Adam could push his way through.

They were all crammed into a square and the surrounding side streets. In the middle of the square was an ancient-looking statue of Steve, and that made Adam feel guilty, remembering that the real Steve was currently a prisoner of Herobrine.

It's not my fault, thought Adam. *I didn't know Steve was there. I didn't want that to happen.*

Next to the statue a stage has been set up. The mayor walked out onto the stage, waving and grinning like an idiot.

"Hello!" shouted the mayor. "So good to see you all! Hello!"

The mayor lifted his hands up and the crowd fell quiet.

"Right-ho," said the mayor, "you're probably wondering why I've called you here today, so I'll get straight to the point. First of all, I'm sure you know this fellow and his friends. Come on Dave, come on Dave's friends, up you come!"

Adam's mouth dropped open in shock. Dave walked up onto the stage, followed by his idiot friends.

He's still here! Adam thought happily. *He didn't leave the city!*

The villagers around Adam all cheered for Dave, which just made Adam angry.

"Of course, you all know Dave the Hero," the mayor continued. "But what you may not know is that Dave and his friends are explorers as well, and they've made an astonishing discovery about Diamond City."

The mayor paused for dramatic effect, grinning stupidly.

"You see," said the mayor, "Dave has discovered that under our city... under our very *feet*... is one of the legendary end portals. A gateway to the End itself!"

The crowd began to talk excitedly all around him, but Adam could barely hear them. He was grinning now too. For the first time in a long time he felt happy. Ridiculously happy.

An end portal! he thought. *If I tell Herobrine where an end portal is he'll make me into a king!*

The mayor started blabbing on about starting a digging project, but Adam wasn't listening; He was thinking about what he should do next.

His first instinct was to go immediately back to Herobrine and tell him about the end portal, but he knew that if this all turned out to be a mistake, Herobrine would be furious with Adam for wasting his time.

No, Adam realized that he needed to see the portal with his own eyes first.

I'll stay here until they've found the portal, he thought, *and then, when I've seen it myself, I'll go and tell Herobrine.*

When the mayor eventually finished his speech and the crowd started to disperse, Adam went to the nearest milk bar and ordered a pumpkin-flavored milkshake. Back in his old life, he and Sally had always made pumpkin milkshakes when they had something to celebrate. And today Adam had a *lot* to celebrate.

CHAPTER FOUR
The Dig Site

The digging began almost immediately.

The builders set up scaffolding and then began digging up the square. The only thing they left intact was the statue of Steve, digging a pit in front of it as they descended down into the earth.

"We really don't need all this fuss," Dave told Mayor Birchwood, as the two of them watched the digging. "Me and my friends could have just dug down."

"To be honest, these men needed the work," said Mayor Birchwood, looking at the builders. "They all used to be miners, but since the mines ran low on diamonds there hasn't been much for them to do."

Instead of digging straight down, the builders were removing the ground layer by layer, creating a deep pit where the square had been. As they dug down they continued to build more scaffolding, so they could easily get in and out of the pit.

"There's no need for you to stay here, Dave," said Mayor Birchwood. "We'll send word to you as soon as we find something, I promise. I think your friends went to visit Diamond City Park, you should go join them."

So Dave reluctantly left the digging site and followed the mayor's directions to get to the park. However, when he got there he realized there would have been no way he could have missed it, even without instructions. The park was *huge:* a massive expanse of green in the middle of the city. There were trees of all different types, and grass and flowers everywhere he looked.

As Dave walked through the park he passed villagers relaxing on the grass. Some had picnic baskets and some were just lying down and enjoying the sun. With all the trees, Dave soon could no longer see the diamond buildings of the city, and it was like being out in the countryside again.

I wish we were on the road again, he thought. He much preferred being out on the open road in the fresh air than he did being cooped up in a city.

Soon he came across a building that looked strangely out of place in the park. It was a square stone building with no windows and a pair of iron doors. Outside the doors were two iron golems and a villager in diamond armor with a crossbow.

"I know you!" said the villager, "you're Dave! I saw you at the mayor's speech yesterday. Well done on finding that end portal!"

"Er, thanks," said Dave. "What is this building?"

"Oh, there's a nether portal inside here," said the villager. "There are ten of these bases around the city, each with a nether portal—so if anyone tries to get into the city via the nether, we'll be able to sort them out. There are two more iron golems and another guard inside, all watching the portal."

"Right," said Dave, "well, keep up the good work."

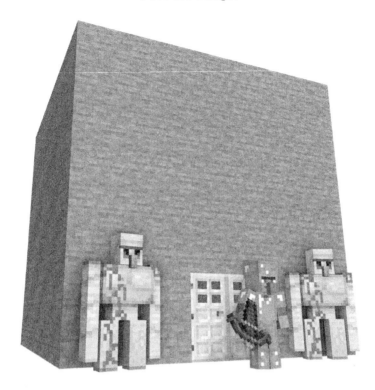

"Thank you, Dave!" the guard said happily.

Dave couldn't help but be impressed at how well Diamond City was guarded, but he still had doubts that it would be any use against Herobrine.

He kept walking, eventually coming to a huge lake. On the lake villagers were relaxing in small wooden boats. It was so peaceful and tranquil, until he suddenly heard the sound of a load of yapping wolves.

The wolves ran out from some nearby trees, barking and yapping and growling. All the villagers relaxing by the side of the lake ran for cover, screaming and yelling "Hellllp!!!"

Dave was about to pull out his sword, but then he noticed the little green thing riding on the back of one of the wolves.

It was Carl.

Carl was riding on the back of the head wolf, leading all the others. He looked like he was having the time of his life, running around and scaring villagers.

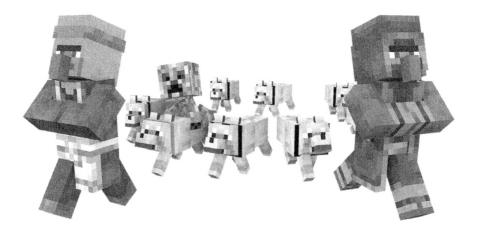

"Heeeelp me!!!" a fat woman villager yelled as she ran from the wolves. "I don't want to be eaten!!!"

"Carl!" Dave yelled.

Carl looked at him in surprise. He whistled, and suddenly all the wolves came to a stop.

"What are you doing?" Dave said to Carl, walking over to him. "Why are you scaring people?"

"Because it's fun," shrugged Carl. "Besides, the wolves needed some exercise."

"Can't you put them on leads at least?" said Dave.

"They're wild animals, they need to run free," said Carl. "And if they eat a few villagers, that's a small price to pay."

Dave's blood went cold.

"T-they haven't?" he asked Carl. "They haven't e-eaten anyone have they?"

Carl started laughing.

"Got ya!" he said.

Dave was furious.

"Put your diamond suit back on and walk them on leads," said Dave. "Or I'll make them all into a wolf pie."

"Wolves don't drop any meat, so you wouldn't be able to," said Carl.

"Just do it!" said Dave.

"O-k," said Carl. "Come on boys and girls, let's go."

And with that, all the wolves ran off.

"That creeper," Dave muttered to himself.

"HI DAVE!"

Dave jumped with shock. He turned around and saw Alex standing right behind him. She was holding a crossbow.

"Watch this!" she said. She threw an apple up into the sky, then—moving faster than Dave would have thought possible—she fired an arrow at the apple, blowing it to bits.

"What was that for?" said Dave, wiping the bits of apple off of his bald head.

"Fun," said Alex, shrugging. "Isn't this bow cool? It's called a crossbow, I don't know why. Instead of taking forever to fire one arrow, it can fire arrows quickly. Pew pew pew! Think of how many bad guys you could slay—pew pew pew pew pew!"

"You know, there's more to adventuring than slaying bad

guys," said Dave.

"Like what?" said Alex, looking confused. "Blowing things up?"

"No!" said Dave. "Stuff like building, making food, making potions. Things like that."

Suddenly Dave has a brainwave. He rummaged around in his bag and pulled out the potion making book he'd bought from the market: *Potions for Noobs*.

"Here you go," he said, handing the book to Alex. "Why don't you try learning some potion recipes?"

"That sounds a bit boring," said Alex.

"It's not," said Dave, "you can make all sorts of potions. Swiftness to make you faster, night vision to let you see in the dark, invisibility to make you, well, invisible. And you can make splash potions to use on your enemies."

Alex took the book and had a flick through it.

"Ooo, fire resistance," she said. "I could go around wearing a suit of lava armor. And I could have a lava sword!"

"Er, yeah," said Dave. "I'm not sure if you could craft a sword out of lava though."

"Oh nice, there's stories in here too," said Alex. "Stories about how witches used potions to defeat their enemies! *We blew up his house, we chopped off his head, but the big bedrock monster just wouldn't stay dead. So we brewed up some potions, and what do you know, the big bedrock monster did crumble to snow.* Wait, why would a monster made of bedrock crumble into snow?"

"I suspect because it rhymes with 'know'," said Dave. "The woman at the potion store did say the book was a bit childish, but hopefully there's still some useful stuff in there."

"Thanks Dave," said Alex. "This book is cool."

"Ok then," said Dave, "I'll leave that with you then. I don't suppose you know where Porkins and Robo-Steve are?"

Porkins and Robo-Steve were, it turned out, both sailing on row boats on the lake. A villager was hiring out wooden boats and oars from a small shack, so Dave paid for a boat and then rowed across the water to see his friends.

"Ahoy there, Dave old bean!" said Porkins as Dave approached. "It's a lovely day for some sailing isn't it?"

"It is," Dave admitted. "But I'm a bit confused... all of you are relaxing and having a good time. Aren't you excited about the end portal?"

"We are," said Robo-Steve. "But we've been on the road a long time—we need some time to recuperate."

"Besides we're at the end of our journey now!" said Porkins excitedly. "Once those builder chaps find the portal, all we need to do is go through and give the ender dragon a ruddy good thrashing."

"You say that like it'll be easy," grinned Dave. "Remember that wither? We almost never made it out of the Nether alive."

"None of us underestimates the challenge of fighting a dragon," said Robo-Steve, "but we know that with you as our leader and a solid battle plan, we can defeat it. You should take a day off to relax. There'll be plenty of time for training and figuring out how to defeat dragons in the days to come. But until they find that portal, there's nothing we can do but wait."

"I guess you're right," said Dave. He pulled his oars into the boat, then lay on his back, enjoying the sun. For the first time in a long time he felt completely relaxed. He wasn't worried about the End or Herobrine or whether they had enough supplies, he was just thinking about nothing. And when he drifted off to sleep he dreamed of home.

*

That evening Dave and his friends ate dinner in their apartment in City Hall. Servants brought them up plates of meat and vegetable and pies and desserts, and Dave ate so much that he thought his stomach might burst.

After dinner they all lay on the sofas and talked. Carl told the others funny stories about his childhood, about how he and his brothers would always play tricks on each other and how they'd constantly played pranks on all the other mobs who lived in their cave.

Porkins told them about his life in the Nether; about picking mushrooms and running from ghasts. It sounded to Dave like Porkins had lived a very tough life in the Nether, but the pigman seemed to remember it fondly.

Robo-Steve and Alex had fewer stories to tell, since both of them had only been created fairly recently, but Robo-Steve told them all stories from history that he'd read in the Villagertropolis library. He told them about the Mushroom Wars, the Nether Crusades and the tale of the Cowman Exiles. All the stories seemed to involve Steve in some way, which annoyed Dave.

After hours of good stories and good food, they were all about ready to head off to their bedrooms when a villager messenger came running in.

"Mr Dave!" said the messenger. "They've found it! They've found the portal!"

Dave had been ready to go to sleep, but suddenly he was wide awake. He jumped off the sofa.

"Come on!" he said to others. "Let's go!"

They all ran down the stairs (Carl jumped into his diamond suit first) and then ran across the city towards the dig site. When they got there the mayor and his assistants were there to greet them.

"Hello, hello!" the mayor said happily. "What a joyous day this is! You were right Dave—there was an end portal under our fine city!"

It was the middle of the night, but the dig sight was lit up by some redstone lamps. The scaffolding was still up, but the mayor instead led them down some cobblestone steps that had been built into the pit, going down and down in a spiral.

When they reached the bottom of the pit the ground had all been flattened out.

"This way," said Mayor Birchwood.

Dave and the others followed the mayor and his assistants through a torch-lit corridor that had been dug into the stone, but soon they found themselves in an area with stone brick walls.

Dave's heart jumped with excitement as he remembered how the stronghold underneath his home village had been made of stone brick.

Eventually they came to an iron door with a button next to it.

"Why did your builders put a door in?" Carl asked.

"They didn't," said the mayor excitedly. "The only things they added were the torches. The rest of it was already here."

The mayor pressed the button and the iron door swung open. Dave walked through and found himself in another stone brick corridor, lit by torches on the walls. Some of the stone brick was mossy or cracked, and all of it looked so *old*.

"If this place was really built by the Old People, then it must be thousands of years old," said Robo-Steve. "It's remarkable any of it has survived."

"Come and check this out!" said the mayor. He led them through a wooden door to a huge room crammed full of bookshelves. There was a balcony above them with even more bookshelves, and a wooden chandelier overhead.

"When the builders found this library, the torches on the chandelier were still lit," said the mayor. "They were burning all these years."

"Ok, I have to admit this place is pretty cool," said Carl.

"Think about all the lost knowledge in these books," said Robo-Steve. "The Old People had technology far more sophisticated than us—we could learn so much."

"Come on then," Carl said to the mayor, "show us this famous end portal, or Robo-Steve's going to start reading to us."

"This way," said the mayor.

He led them through more doors and down staircase after staircase.

"It's very big this stronghold," said the mayor. "But I guess that just means there's more room for tourists! There was a bit of a silverfish infestation, but the builders managed to clear them all out. There was even a spawner next to the end portal."

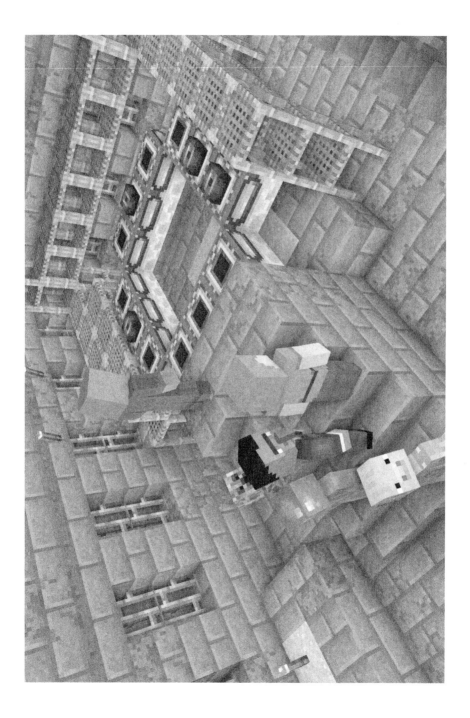

Dave was getting impatient. It had taken him so long to get here that it barely seemed real. After all the troubles he and his friends had gone through, they were finally here: at the end of their journey. It was getting him quite emotional, and it was all he could do not to burst into tears.

Keep it together, Dave, he told himself.

"Right," said Mayor Birchwood finally. "Here we are."

They walked down a short set of stairs, and then in front of him was the thing Dave had been searching for for so long...

An end portal.

The end portal room was identical to the one that had been underneath Dave's village. It was a small rectangular room with stone brick walls and windows covered in iron bars (though the windows weren't looking out on anything but stone), and in the center of the room was a stone brick staircase that led up to a square made of strange green and yellow blocks: the end portal itself.

"So that's an end portal?" said Porkins. "How do you activate the blighter?"

"We've been trying to work it out, but with no luck," said the mayor.

Dave walked up the stone steps. As he suspected, some of the end portal frame blocks had ender eyes in them and some didn't.

All I have to do is put eyes of ender into the empty frame blocks, he thought excitedly, *and then the portal will activate!*

"Come on, Dave," said Carl, "activate that thing so we can go and beat up the dragon."

Dave took off his rucksack and reached inside for an ender eye. He was so excited that his hand was shaking.

"Now you're just drawing it out," said Carl, "stop keeping us waiting!"

Dave turned round and was about to say something to Carl when he noticed someone standing on the staircase behind them. It was a villager, who was clearly trying to hide in the shadows to avoid being seen. Dave recognised the villager, but he couldn't place where from. His face was so familiar...

"Who are you?" Dave asked.

Everyone else turned. The villager looked terrified.

"Good gosh!" said Porkins, smiling. "It's Adam! Hello Adam old chap!"

Then Adam turned and ran.

CHAPTER FIVE
The Chase

"Get him!" yelled Dave. "Don't let him get away!"

Dave had no idea what Adam was up to, but the last time Dave had seen him, Adam had betrayed his own village to Herobrine. Dave knew that whatever Adam was up to, it couldn't be good.

Dave and his friends ran up the staircase then followed Adam as he fled through the stone brick corridors.

"You can't get away, Adam!" Dave yelled at him. "You might as well give up now!"

"Yeah, give up so we can kick your butt, whoever you are!" said Alex.

"No chance!" yelled Adam. He reached into his bag and pulled out a blue egg.

"A spawn egg!" yelled Dave. "Watch out!"

Adam threw the blue egg on the ground and a blue creeper appeared.

"Take this, monster!" yelled Alex, rushing towards the blue creeper with her sword.

"Alex... NO!" yelled Dave.

KA-BOOOOM!!!!!

Dave dived into Alex, pushing her through a doorway just in time to avoid being vaporized by the blast.

"You ok?" he asked Alex.

"Y-yeah, I think so," she said, sounding dazed.

Dave got to his feet and staggered back into the corridor. Thankfully the others had avoided the blast as well, but now the corridor was swarming with silverfish. Porkins, Robo-Steve and Carl were fighting them off.

"These ruddy things must have been living in the bricks," said Porkins. "We'll deal with them, Dave—you go and catch that rapscallion Adam!"

"Ok," said Dave. "Carl, you're the fastest—run on ahead and see if you can catch him."

"Got it," said Carl, and he disappeared down the corridor in his iron suit. Dave ran after him as fast as he could, following the sound of Carl's heavy footsteps.

"Arrgh!" Dave heard Carl yell from somewhere up ahead.

Dave came round a corner and saw Carl covered in spiders. They were crawling all over his diamond suit.

"Spiders!" said Carl, terror in his eyes. "Why did it have to be spiders?!"

Dave started hacking at the spiders with his diamond sword.

"No," said Carl, "I can handle them—you keep going!"

"Are you sure?" Dave asked. He knew that Carl hated spiders.

"Just go!" said Carl. "Don't let that idiot get away."

So Dave ran on, leaving Carl to fight off the spiders. He ran through stone brick corridor after stone brick corridor, and began to fear that he'd lost Adam, when finally he saw him up ahead.

Adam stopped and turned around to face Dave.

"You like spiders, Dave?" Adam said. "Here, have some!"

Adam reached into his bag and pulled out a black egg with red spots. He threw the egg onto the ground and it turned into a spider. Then he threw another one down and another, until the corridor was full of spiders.

"Have fun!" said Adam, then he turned and started running again.

I haven't got time for this, thought Dave. He would easily be able to defeat the spiders with his diamond sword, he knew, but by the time he'd done it, Adam would be long gone. So instead he ran forward and jumped on the spiders' backs—*boing boing boing*—to get past them.

Dave ran down the corridor and found himself at the bottom of the pit that the builders had dug. Far above him he could see the moon and the night sky.

Adam was already climbing up the scaffolding, so Dave started climbing up after him.

"Give up, Dave!" Adam yelled down at him. "You can't catch me!"

"We'll see about that!" Dave yelled back.

Adam reached the top of the scaffolding and climbed out of the pit, but Dave wasn't far behind him. As Adam fled through the streets, Dave was right on his tail, running as fast as he could.

Finally Dave chased Adam down an alleyway with a dead end.

"There's no way out," Dave told Adam. "Just give up now. I'm not going to hurt you, I just want to know what you're up to."

Adam grinned.

"I'm working for Lord Herobrine," he said. "He's been looking for an end portal for so long, as you well know, and now I've found him one."

"It's a shame you're going to be too busy locked in a jail cell to tell him the good news," said Dave.

"Oh, I don't think so," Adam laughed. "I'll see you around, Dave."

Adam took out a shiny green ball from his bag.

An ender pearl! Dave realized.

With one swift flick of the wrist, Adam threw the ender pearl into the air. It landed on the roof of one of the surrounding buildings, and then *ZAP*, Adam teleported onto the roof.

"See you around, Dave," Adam said.

And then he ran off across the rooftops.

But Dave wasn't defeated yet. He reached into his own bag and pulled out an ender pearl. He'd never teleported via ender pearl before, but as far as he knew all you had to do was throw the ender pearl somewhere and you'd instantly teleport to that location.

Dave pulled his arm back and threw the pearl. He wasn't much of a thrower, but thankfully he managed to get it onto the roof. The next thing he knew he'd teleported onto the roof himself, and he could see Adam running off into the distance.

Dave gave chase, running as fast as he could to catch up with Adam. Adam was jumping from roof to roof, dodging around the diamond spires and domes of the buildings, but eventually he came to a gap between roofs that was far too big to jump, and he came to a sudden stop.

I have you now, thought Dave. There was nowhere for Adam to run to.

Adam reached into his bag and pulled out another ender pearl, then he lobbed the pearl through the air. It landed on the roof on the far side of the street, and Adam teleported over.

Two can play at that game, thought Dave. He pulled out another pearl from his back and threw it...

... and missed.

Instead of landing on one of the rooftops across the street, Dave's pearl landed *on* the street, and he teleported there too.

"Darn it," said Dave, quickly rummaging in his bag for another pearl. He found one and managed to throw it up onto a rooftop, but by the time he teleported up there, Adam was gone. Dave looked all around, but could see no sign of him.

I've lost him, Dave thought miserably.

CHAPTER SIX
What Now?

"We have to evacuate the city," Dave said.

Mayor Birchwood looked astounded.

"What are you talking about?" he said.

Dave had rejoined the mayor and his aides outside the dig sight, underneath the statue of Steve. His friends were there too, and thankfully they were all alright. Alex was still slightly dazed and Porkins, Robo-Steve and Carl were a bit tired from fighting monsters, but other than that they were fine.

"Adam was working for Herobrine," Dave said, "he admitted as much. Herobrine wants to find an end portal more than anything, and once he knows that there's one underneath this city he'll come here with all the forces he has."

"But his pigman army was defeated!" said the mayor. "That's

what we heard."

"Most of the pigmen survived the battle in the Nether," Dave said. "We just broke the magic staff that let the witches control them. It was built by Herobrine, so I'm sure he could build another one."

"Plus the blighter is strong enough without an army," said Porkins. "We saw him transform into a giant lava chap once. A giant lava chap!"

"Listen," said Mayor Birchwood, "I appreciate your concern, really I do, but Diamond City is well defended. You've seen how high our walls are, and Dave, I told you about our base in the Nether. Whatever Herobrine throws at us, we can defeat him."

"Maybe," said Dave, "but it would be safer to evacuate."

"But If we evacuate, who will defend the portal from Herobrine?" said Carl.

They all went silent, no-one sure what they should do.

"M-maybe... we should, um... destroy it?" said Simon, the mayor's adviser.

"WHAT?!" said Dave and Mayor Birchwood at the same time.

"Maybe this dear chap is right," said Porkins sadly. "If it will save lives, maybe we should destroy the end portal."

With a heavy heart, Dave realized that Porkins was right. As much as it pained him, it looked like there was no other choice.

"But we can't just destroy it!" said Mayor Birchwood. "This portal could be the only one of its kind in the whole world. It will put Diamond City on the map!"

"Diamond City's already on the map, you doofus," said Carl.

"What do you think, Dave old bean?" Porkins asked.

Dave realized that everyone was looking at him.

"I want to reach the End more than anyone," said Dave, "but if people are in danger because of this portal... then we ought to destroy it."

"No!" said Mayor Birchwood. "This is my city, I won't let you!"

"We can use TNT!" said Alex excitedly.

Dave put his hand on the hilt of his sword, just in case things started to get nasty. But then Robo-Steve stepped forward.

"Actually, I'm not sure destroying the portal at this time will do any good," said Robo-Steve. "If we tell Herobrine that we've destroyed it he probably won't believe us. He'll probably still attack the city anyway, just so he can check with his own eyes."

"Then what should we do?" asked Dave.

"When Herobrine comes we defend the city," said Robo-Steve. "If all looks lost then we destroy the portal and evacuate to the Nether."

"If we can," said Carl. "For all we know, Herobrine will attack from the Nether as well."

"Chances are he probably will," said Dave. "We should at least evacuate people from the city first. Anyone who wants to fight can stay, but everyone else needs to get as far away from here as possible. What do you think, Mayor Birchwood?"

The mayor sighed.

"Fine," he said. "I suppose you're right."

"I'm sorry we brought this problem to your city," said Dave. "This is all our fault."

"Nah, it's his fault as well," said Carl. "We wanted to keep the portal a secret, but Mayor Blabbermouth wanted to tell the whole world about it."

"Arguing about who's to blame isn't going to do us any good," said Robo-Steve. "It's completely illogical. Instead we need to come up with a defense plan. As the only one who has defended a city from invasion before, I would like to volunteer myself to take charge of preparations."

"You've defended a city?" said Simon.

"He defended Villagertropolis from the pigman invasion," said Carl. "Although he did have an army of robots to help him."

"Ok, ok, you're in charge, robot boy," Mayor Birchwood said to Robo-Steve. "What do you need?"

"First of all," said Robo-Steve, "how many soldiers do you have?"

"Um... I'm going to say none," said Mayor Birchwood.

"You don't have any soldiers to defend your city?" said Dave in disbelief. "What about the villagers who guard the gates? And the ones I saw guarding the nether portals?"

"They're just volunteers," said Mayor Birchwood. "They can't really fight, they just keep a lookout. We use iron golems for defense, and we've got plenty of those."

"Any archers?" asked Dave.

"Afraid not," said the mayor. "We're villagers—our job is trading, not fighting."

"Porkins," said Robo-Steve, "If we found some volunteers, would you be able to train them to use bows?"

"Of course," said Porkins. "And it might be even easier with those crossbow things. They look a lot simpler to use."

"Good," said Robo-Steve. "Mayor Birchwood, I need you to arrange the evacuation of the city, and see if you can recruit some volunteers for Porkins."

"I will," said the mayor.

"Carl," said Robo-Steve, "Herobrine may launch an attack from underground, so I need you to defend the end portal. Take your wolves and your iron golem and build some basic defenses. When Porkins has trained his volunteers we'll send some down to aid you. Is that ok?"

"Sounds good to me," said Carl, "I like being underground. And I must say, this is a new side to you, Robo-Steve. Dave, if you're not careful he's going to take your job as leader!"

"I meant no offense," said Robo-Steve, turning to Dave. "Dave I hope you don't think I'm trying to usurp you as leader. I merely thought that because of my previous city-defending experience—"

"Honestly, Robo-Steve, it's fine," said Dave.

In truth, Dave was happy that someone else was taking over as leader for once. Normally it was something the others always left to him, but at the moment he was still shell-shocked from the double blow of finding an end portal and then realizing he may need to destroy it. It was like having a delicious birthday cake and then someone snatching it away before you'd had a chance to have a bite.

"Alex," continued Robo-Steve, "while Porkins, his volunteers and the golems defend the city walls and Carl and his wolves defend underneath the city, you and I will help defend the base in the Nether. Does that sound good to you?"

"It sounds awesome," grinned Alex.

"Um, what about me?" said Dave.

"From the sounds of it, there are very few villagers in Diamond City with fighting experience," said Robo-Steve. "Dave, if it's ok with you I'd like you to bring us more allies. Professor Quigley and her endermen would be invaluable in the battle. And with any luck she may still have Steve with her."

"Ok," said Dave, "but by the time I've gone to get her the battle might be over. We've traveled a long way since then."

"That's why I will give you my latest invention," said Robo-Steve. "Since I don't need to sleep, I've been working on it late at night while you've all been in bed. The kennel master let me use one of his sheds as a workshop. It is a robot steed—it can travel incredibly fast."

"A robot horse?" asked Dave.

"Close," said Robo-Steve. "It's a robot pig."

"Ha ha!" said Carl. "Dave, you're going to have to ride a pig!"

"I call him Robo-Pig," said Robo-Steve.

"Robo-Pig!" snorted Carl. "That is too funny!"

"Robo-Pig will chart your journey across the overworld," said Robo-Steve, "and then on the way back he can use that information to plot you a course through the Nether. His tracking technology is groundbreaking—even if I do say so myself."

"Ok," said Dave, "so I ride the super-fast pig across the overworld, then lead Professor Quigley and the others back through the Nether."

"Precisely," said Robo-Steve. "Traveling through the Nether will save you a lot of time, but at the moment Robo-Pig doesn't know the route, so he can only go via the Nether on your way back."

"You make it all sound so simple," said Carl.

"Right," said Dave, "we've all got our instructions. Does all of that sound ok to you, Mayor Birchwood?"

"I guess so," said the mayor. "I may look amazing in a dapper suit, but I'm afraid battle strategy isn't one of my many strengths—so I'll have to leave that to you fine people."

"There is one thing though," said Simon, the mayor's assistant. "We don't even know if Herobrine is definitely going to attack. And if he is, he might not even attack for ages."

"Simon, stay in your lane!" said Mayor Birchwood. "Just worry about coming up with a snappy name for this battle, so I can use it in my election campaign next year."

"Y-yes, Mr Mayor," said Simon. "I mean Birchy."

"He's got a point though," said Carl. "We might be waiting ages before Herobrine shows up."

"Maybe," said Dave, "but I doubt it. Herobrine has been wanting to find one of these portals for years, as far as I can tell. I don't think he'll waste any time."

They discussed their plan of attack a bit longer, then they all went off to do their respective tasks. Robo-Steve brought Dave to the stables, to show him *Robo-Pig*.

The pig was the same size as a normal pig, apart from it was made from shiny iron metal and had red light bulbs for eyes.

"I'm afraid I haven't had time to add the pink outer casing," said Robo-Steve, "but a saddle should still fit on her back."

He took a saddle and some reigns down from a rack and placed them on the metal pig's back.

"Saddle and reigns detected," said Robo-Pig. "Ride-on mode initiated."

"When you're ready, just get on its back and use the reigns to guide him," said Robo-Steve. "Just like a horse. If you need an extra blast of speed, say 'turbo blasters activated'. Although I warn you that he may go extremely fast. I haven't really tested the turbo blaster function properly yet."

"Right," said Dave. He thought he'd probably avoid using the 'turbo blasters' if he could—they didn't sound particularly safe.

"Good luck, Dave," said Robo-Steve, shaking his hand. "We'll defend the city until you return."

"Good luck to you too," said Dave. "I'll try to return as quickly as I can with the professor. Hopefully we'll get back here before Herobrine's forces and we can use her inventions to turn ourselves into giants or duplicate millions of soldiers or something."

There was no more time to lose, so Dave climbed aboard Robo-Pig and pulled at his reigns. Just as Robo-Steve has said, he started galloping along like a horse, his little legs moving at super-quick speed.

As Dave left the kennels he met Carl and Basher the golem, who were about to go and fetch the wolves. When Carl saw Dave on Robo-Pig, he burst into laughter.

"Oh wow," said Carl, wiping tears of laughter from his eyes, "you look like such a dork."

"Yeah, yeah, laugh it up," said Dave. "Carl, I'm going now, so I just wanna say... good luck. I hope Herobrine doesn't attack before I get back, but if he does I know you guys will do a great job defending the city."

"Yeah, good luck to you too, Dave," said Carl. "Out of all the idiots in the world, you're one of my favorites."

Dave rode out of the kennels and found Porkins and Alex outside of City Hall. Porkins had a load of crossbows that he was checking out and Alex was using a potion stand to make potions.

"Hey Dave!" said Alex. "That's a cool pig you've got."

She pressed her finger against Robo-Pig's metal nose.

"Good piggy," said Alex.

"False statement detected," said Robo-Pig. "I have no programmed morals or ethics, so I am neither good nor bad."

"Can you say 'oink'?" asked Alex.

"I have a full vocabulary and can speak in six different languages," said Robo-Pig. "Oink is one of the many words that I can say."

Alex put her finger on her own nose, pushing it back like a pig's.

"Oink oink!" said Alex. "I'm a pig too!"

Dave decided to look away before things got any stranger.

"How are those bows?" he asked Porkins.

"They're amazing," said Porkins, "so much easier to use than regular bows. I just hope Mayor Birchwood can find enough volunteers."

"I'm sure he will," said Dave. "I know us villagers can seem a bit like boring traders, but given the chance we can do great things."

Porkins grinned.

"Yes Dave," he said. "I think you're proof of that."

Dave blushed.

"I was thinking more about the villagers at Greenleaf we trained," said Dave. "I wasn't trying to show off."

"I know, old bean," said Porkins. "And I know that whatever Herobrine throws at us, we'll prevail."

"I hope you're right," said Dave.

"I am," said Porkins, "mark my words."

Dave turned back to Alex. She was playing with Robo-Pig's nose.

"It's not squishy like a normal pig's nose," she said.

"Alex, you take care of yourself too," said Dave.

"Thanks, Dave, I will," said Alex cheerily.

Dave tugged on Robo-Pig's reigns.

"I'll hopefully see you both soon," he said to Alex and Porkins. He gave a sharp tug on the reigns and Robo-Pig rushed forward at incredible speed—running much faster than any horse Dave had ever ridden.

"Waaaaaa!" yelled Dave, as he sped down the Diamond City streets. Before he knew it, he had gone through the gate and was riding through the countryside. He gave Robo-Pig's reigns another sharp tug, bringing him to a sudden stop.

Dave turned and looked at Diamond City; its blue walls and buildings glistening in the moonlight. The walls were huge, but Dave knew that they'd never keep out Herobrine.

I'll be back soon, he thought. *I promise.*

And then he rode off into the night.

CHAPTER SEVEN
Preparations Begin

In morning Mayor Birchwood brought Porkins out to meet the volunteers, who had gathered in the street outside City Hall.

"Good gravy!" said Porkins when he saw them. He couldn't believe how many there were.

"Some of the children wanted to volunteer as well," said the mayor. "But we wouldn't let them."

Porkins and the mayor were looking down at the volunteers from the steps that led into the building.

They're all looking at me like they're expecting me to say something, thought Porkins, feeling a little nervous. He'd never been much of a public speaker.

"Right-ho, chaps" he said. "Once more into the breach, what-what and tally-ho!"

The volunteers all looked at him like he'd grown an extra head.

"Right, um, let's see," he continued. "There's an old pigman saying—you can't make mushroom stew without cooking some mushrooms. And in that same spirit, you can't defend a city without some ruddy brave soldiers. I'm going to train you up as best I can, teaching you archery and all that. And by the end of it you'll all be ready to boot old Herobrine in the behind and send him home crying for mummy!"

This time the villagers all cheered.

What-ho, thought Porkins happily. *That speech was actually quite ruddy good!*

So Porkins got to work training his volunteer soldiers. Diamond City had plenty of supplies, so they were able to build all the extra crossbows they needed. There were also enough diamonds to build them each a suit of armor. Porkins primarily wanted his troops to be archers, so they could defend the city from the walls, but he knew that if things went wrong they might need to be involved in close-quarter combat, so he made all the volunteers build diamond swords for themselves as well, and trained them in basic sword fighting techniques.

By the end of the day the volunteers were really starting to get both the archery and the sword fighting, but Porkins knew that they'd need a lot more time if they were going to get good enough.

Unfortunately time may be something we don't have much of, thought Porkins sadly. Porkins knew from bitter experience how ruthless Herobrine could be: he'd turned all the pigmen into zombies, destroying their entire culture and their thousands of years of history in one fell swoop—all so he could have them as his own personal army if he needed them.

But you won't win this time, Herobrine old chap, thought Porkins, as he watched his volunteers firing arrows at targets as the sun began to go down. *This time we're going to beat you for good!*

*

Carl, Basher and the ten other iron golems that Mayor Birchwood had given him had spent the morning expanding the area around the end portal. Occasionally one of the stone brick blocks they'd dug up had been full of silverfish, but Carl and the golems had made short work of them.

When they finished the end portal was now at the center of a big open underground space (they'd destroyed the stone brick stairs that led up to it). Robo-Steve had told Carl that they needed to make sure they were defending the portal from all sides, and now they had plenty of room to do it.

There was also the danger that Herobrine's forces might dig from above or below to get to the portal, so they dug a moat around the portal and the stairs and filled it full of lava. Anyone digging from below would get a face full of lava, and anyone digging from above would fall into the lava.

Next Carl and the golems built a low diamond block wall, creating a small base that they could defend, with the portal and its lava moat in the middle. Carl filled some chests with plenty of food for him and the wolves, since he had no idea how long they'd be down there.

Once the base was complete, Carl ordered the iron golems to stand around the outside of the walls, guarding it from all sides. The golems didn't need rest or food, so they would just stay where they were until an attack came.

Carl kept his wolves inside the base for now. He wanted them well-rested for when the attack came.

Eventually, when all the preparations were made, Carl climbed out of his diamond suit and lay down on the stone ground, utterly exhausted. The wolves all came over and lay down around him.

"Good dogs," said Carl.

Carl had ordered Basher to guard him at all times during the battle, so the golem was standing next to them, looking down at Carl and the wolves.

If Carl had been a bit less exhausted he might have been scared about the attack to come, but he was so tired that all he wanted to do was sleep. He knew that Basher would wake him if there was an attack, so he let himself fall into a deep slumber.

His dreams were full of confusing flashes of dragons and endermen and white eyes glowing in the darkness.

"Don't let him in!" the endermen were screaming at him. *"Don't let the deceiver in! Destroy it! DESTROY IT!"*

Carl woke up covered in sweat. All the wolves were still fast asleep, but Basher was awake and watching over him. There was a faint hum in the air, and Carl realized it as coming from the portal. The portal was still inactive, but it seemed to be *alive* in some way that Carl didn't understand.

The portal gave me those visions in my dream, Carl realized. *It wants me to destroy it so that Herobrine can't use it.*

He couldn't say how, but he knew that it was true.

"Maybe I should just destroy it," Carl muttered to himself. It wouldn't take much: all he'd have to do was put on his diamond suit and smash one of the green and yellow blocks, then the portal would be useless. Herobrine would be unable to use it.

But we wouldn't be able to use it either.

Carl knew that going to the End was Dave's dream. He didn't care much about going and slaying the ender dragon himself, but Dave did—and Carl cared about Dave. He couldn't rob Dave of the chance to finally achieve his goal.

Carl checked the gold clock that Robo-Steve had given him. It was still the middle of the night, so he rested his head against one of the wolves and tried to get back to sleep.

*

Alex was excited. Not only was an awesome battle coming up, but she'd now mastered all the potions in Dave's potion book.

"Potion of swiftness," she told Robo-Steve, "that's the last one!"

Alex took a swig from the bottle of light-blue liquid and suddenly she felt hyper charged. She dashed forward, doing lap after lap around the base: *zoom zoom zoom!*

"Very impressive," said Robo-Steve with a smile, as Alex came to a stop next to him.

The two of them were inside Diamond City's base in the Nether. The base was an eighth the size of the city, and Alex saw it as a miniature version of the city above. It had diamond block walls, just as the city did, but they weren't quite as high. There were stone brick staircases up to the top of the wall in several places, and the wall was two blocks wide, with the outer blocks one block higher so you could stand on the wall and look out into the Nether without accidentally falling off.

Most of the area inside the walls had been left empty, but in the middle of the base were some wooden buildings: two dormitories with beds for them to sleep in, a kitchen with cooking equipment and chests full of food, an armor full of weapons and a supply room, full of every type of material and block imaginable.

Scattered around the base were ten nether portals, each guarded at all times by two iron golems. These each led to one of the ten nether portals in Diamond City. One of the nether portals was by the wooden buildings, right outside the kitchen.

The whole base had been flattened out, and the netherrack ground had been covered with a floor of stone brick blocks. Alex had set up her brewing stand on the stone brick ground outside the dormitory, and had been brewing potions all afternoon while Robo-Steve went back and forth making preparations for the battle ahead.

"When is Herobrine getting here?" Alex asked Robo-Steve. "I'm bored."

"We've sent out patrols to look for signs of him and his forces," said Robo-Steve. "They haven't seen anything yet."

Alex liked talking to Robo-Steve. He didn't use weird words that she didn't understand like Porkins did, or say things that were mean like Carl. She liked Dave too, but sometimes he got frustrated with her when she said something wrong or got too excited. Robo-Steve never got frustrated: he was always calm and nice, and that was why Alex liked him the best.

"What made you take up potion making?" Robo-Steve asked.

"Dave said that there's more to adventuring than battling," Alex replied, "so I thought I'd try some other stuff out."

Robo-Steve opened the chest that Alex had stored her potions in and leaned over to have a look.

"Well, you've certainly picked up potion making exceptionally quickly," said Robo-Steve. "It's a difficult skill to master, and you look like you've mastered it."

"Maybe I knew how to make potions already from my Steve memory thingies," said Alex.

Alex was a clone of Steve, who was some sort of legendary hero. Alex had never met Steve properly, but from what she'd heard he seemed to be a fantastic adventurer who'd done lots of awesome stuff. He was also really, really old, apparently, even though he didn't look it. Alex had asked about that a few times, but no-one seemed to have a good answer.

Occasionally Alex would have flashbacks to events she had no memory of, or would suddenly remember a random fact or piece of information. As far as she could tell, these were *Steve's* memories. Alex had forgotten nearly all her time as Steve, but occasionally these little snippets would come back to her.

The Steve memories surfaced in different ways. Sometimes Alex would find she was really good at something, even though she couldn't remember ever having done it before. One of these things was *fighting*. Alex has been told that Steve was a legendary warrior, and she seemed to have inherited his fighting skills. She knew exactly how to use a sword, a bow and all kinds of weapons, and when she fought she always seemed to know the best way to parry a blow or deliver a devastating attack.

This was the reason Alex loved fighting so much. There was so much stuff she didn't understand or didn't know, but when she was fighting everything just made sense. Normally Dave and the others knew so much more than her, making her feel a bit stupid in comparison, but when she fought she had no doubts and no fear of looking stupid; she could just lose herself in the excitement of battle.

Alex followed Robo-Steve up one of the staircases that led to the top of the base wall, and they both looked out across the Nether. There was nothing but netherrack and lava in every direction. In the distance they could just make out some ghasts as well.

"Still no sign of Herobrine," said Robo-Steve. "I'm going to go back to the overworld to see how the preparations are going. Are you ok looking after the base on your own for a bit?"

"Of course," said Alex, eager to prove herself.

So Robo-Steve left, going back to the overworld via one of the nether portals, leaving Alex on her own with the golems. As she looked out over the Nether she couldn't help but think what a lonely place it was.

Come on Herobrine, she thought, *hurry up so we can kick your butt.*

*

"Waaaaaaaaa!!!!" yelled Dave.

Against his better judgment he'd decided to try out Robo-Pig's turbo boosters, to attempt to get to Professor Quigley's house as quickly as possible. He'd said the words "Robo-Pig, activate turbo boosters," but he hadn't been prepared for what happened next. A jet of fire had shot out of the back of the pig, and now it was running at a ridiculous speed: so fast that all Dave could see was a blur of green all around him. He kept worrying they were going to crash into a tree, but somehow Robo-Pig was always able to dodge and weave past any obstacles in their path.

"I think I'm gonna be sick," said Dave. "Can you slow down a bit?!"

"I can't hear you over the sound of my turbo blaster," said Robo-Pig. "Please repeat the question."

"SLOW DOWN!" yelled Dave.

Robo-Pig came to a sudden stop and Dave went flying off of his back, rolling across the grass.

"Oof oof oof!!"

He came to a stop lying face-down on the ground.

"Ow..." said Dave.

Dave pushed himself to his feet. He was in a large plains biome, with trees and grass and all the usual plains biome things, but it all looked very familiar.

"I think we're near Professor Quigley's," he said to Robo-Pig. "I think it's just through these trees..."

He walked through a patch of trees, expecting to see the professor's house and the farmland around it in the distance, but instead all he could see was a blackened ruin.

"Oh no," said Dave.

He ran across the fields as fast as he could. When he got to Professor Quigley's house it was nothing but a pile of burnt-up cobblestone. He looked over and saw that the house the endermen had built for Steve was destroyed too. There were ender pearls scattered across the ground.

The endermen must have been slain defending the professor, thought Dave.

"Professor!" He yelled. "Professor Quigley! Steve!"

But there was no answer.

Dave walked through the burnt ruins of Professor Quigley's house. The secret panel in the floor that led to the lab was already open, so he walked down the cobblestone stairs.

The huge laboratory was in almost complete darkness. Only two of the redstone lamps that normally lit it were still working, and they were flickering.

"Hello?" Dave called from the stairs. "Is there anyone down there?"

There was no answer.

He didn't really want to walk down into the dark lab, but he had to check to make sure Professor Quigley wasn't down there. She might be hurt and unable to speak.

When Dave reached the bottom of the spiral staircase he put a torch down. The tiny torch did little to illuminate the huge room, but he could at least get an idea of what had happened down there.

Professor Quigley's enormous iron block-walled lab had been divided into different rooms by glass panels, but now most of the panels were broken, and ender pearls were scattered across the floor.

Dave walked through the darkness, placing torches as he went. He checked each room in turn, but there was no sign of life. All Professor Quigley's equipment was either destroyed or gone.

When he'd checked everywhere and was absolutely sure there was no-one down there, Dave left the laboratory and walked back outside to rejoin Robo-Pig, who was standing there waiting for him.

"Something bad happened here," Dave said. "I don't know if one of the professor's inventions went wrong, or maybe one of the monsters she had got out, or… something else."

Robo-Pig said nothing.

The sun was starting to go down, but Dave thought he ought to head back to Diamond City. With the help of Robo-Pig's turbo boosters he knew they could probably get back before nightfall. And if they took a route back through the Nether, as Robo-Steve had suggested, it wouldn't take much time at all.

"So if we go to the Nether, you'll know the way back to Diamond City?" Dave asked the pig.

"Affirmative," said Robo-Pig. "During our journey I tracked our route through my internal mapping system. I am always mapping my location, so I can always find my way back to any location I have visited before—either via the overworld or via the Nether."

Dave was about to climb onto Robo-Pig's back, but then he thought of Diamond City and how ill-prepared its people were to defend it. He was sure Porkins would do a good job at training his volunteers, but that was no match for having experienced fighters who had seen battle before.

"A change of plan," said Dave. "We're not going back to Diamond City just yet. We're going south."

"Affirmative," said Robo-Pig.

CHAPTER EIGHT
Pink Spiders

So far all the scouting parties had returned saying that they'd seen no sign of Herobrine.

"Maybe he really isn't coming?" said Mayor Birchwood hopefully.

Robo-Steve was meeting with the mayor and his advisors in City Hall to discuss the progress of the battle preparations.

"I've never met Herobrine," said Robo-Steve, "but from what I've been told of him, and all the stories I've read about him, I believe he'll come. Finding an end portal is very important to him. Possibly the most important thing in the world to him."

"In happier news, the evacuation of the city has now been completed," said Simon, the mayor's adviser. "All those who can't fight or don't want to fight have now left the city. T-they should be reaching Bumbletown by tonight."

"And the Bumbletown Mayor has agreed to take them all in?" asked Robo-Steve.

"She has," said Simon. "They've built some houses for them."

"Good," said Mayor Birchwood. "Robo-Steve, how's the training of the recruits coming along?"

"It's going well," said Robo-Steve. "Porkins has trained them all to use crossbows, and now he's helping them to get better with their swords. Once they're trained I'm going to move some of the volunteers down to the Nether, as we could do with archers down there too."

"Very good," said the mayor. "So, what do we want to do about the patrol situation? Do we want to send anyone else out to look for Herobrine, or shall we just wait for him to come to us?"

"No more patrols, I don't think," said Robo-Steve, "we need all our volunteers to spend the rest of the time we've got left training. But I want to go out myself to look for Herobrine."

"Just you?" asked Simon. "By yourself?"

"My eyes can see much further than a villagers eyes, so I should be able to avoid running into danger," said Robo-Steve, "and I'll be more likely to spot any signs of Herobrine. I won't be gone for long, just a few hours. I just want to do a walk around the whole city. I'll be near enough that I can get back quickly if the battle kicks off."

"Ok, I guess," said Mayor Birchwood. "But be careful. You're the one who's meant to be organizing our defense plan—we can't afford to lose you!"

"Understood," said Robo-Steve.

After the meeting Robo-Steve put on his diamond armor and found his diamond sword and then set out through one of the city gates on horseback. He rode through the farmland that surrounded the city, then out to the woods beyond that, scanning the land for any sign of Herobrine's forces.

He was riding alongside the bank of a small river when he did spot something unusual: gathered around a cave entrance in some distant hills was a large cluster of spiders. But unlike any spiders that Robo-Steve had ever seen, these spiders were *pink.*

It's probably nothing, he thought to himself, *but I ought to check it out.*

In the historical accounts that Robo-Steve had read, Herobrine had often used modified versions of mobs in his army, so pink spiders seemed like exactly the kind of troops he might have.

Robo-Steve tied his horse to a tree and then snuck forward, using trees for cover. Eventually he was close enough to the cave entrance to get a proper look at it. He could see torchlight inside, and there were around ten spiders, who all looked like they were standing guard.

Something's definitely going on here, thought Robo-Steve.

Then he heard a rustle behind him.

Robo-Steve span around and drew his sword. On the ground behind him and on the trees above were *hundreds* of spiders, all staring right at him.

Why didn't I hear them? he wondered. Robo-Steve normally had hearing that was second to none, but the spiders had managed to catch him completely unawares.

The spiders dashed towards him, screaming and baring their fangs. Robo-Steve tried to slash at them with his sword, but there were too many of them, and soon he was pinned to the ground. He thought he was done for, but instead of finishing him off the spiders lifted him up and began carrying him towards the cave. There were so many of them, all clinging to him with their pink hairy legs, that he was unable to struggle free.

He was carried down a narrow torch-lit passageway, the red eyes of spiders watching him from every corner. There were so many spiders that the walls themselves seemed to be moving.

Finally Robo-Steve was brought into a small chamber and dumped in front of a cobblestone throne. Sitting on the throne, surrounded by spiders, was the last person he expected to see.

"*Charles?*" said Robo-Steve, amazed. Sitting in front of him was the red chrome robot that he himself had created: Charles. Robo-Steve had created Charles to be his personal assistant, although the last time Robo-Steve had seen Charles, the red robot had turned against him, declaring himself the new Robot King.

"No," said the red robot, his voice different than Robo-Steve remembered. "I'm not Charles. Not anymore."

Charles's new voice was more female than male, and Robo-Steve recognised it immediately.

"Spidroth," said Robo-Steve. "You've taken over Charles's body."

"Very observant, golden man," grinned Spidroth. "Or should I call you the *Robot King?* That's what Charles remembers you as, and all his memories are mine now."

"I don't use that name anymore," said Robo-Steve. "I realized that ruling over the villagers was wrong, so I abandoned my crown."

"Then you are a fool," hissed Spidroth. "The strong rule over the weak. That is the way it has always been."

"Maybe that *is* the way it has always been," said Robo-Steve, "but that doesn't mean that's the way it *should* be."

Spidroth frowned at him.

"I tire of this conversation," she said. "Once I had need of you and your metal body, *Robo-Steve,* but now I have a new body, so you are of no more use to me. Your death shall not be quick, however—you defied me before, so now you shall suffer."

"Wait," said Robo-Steve. "I know you must hate me and my friends for defying you, but I know of someone you hate more: Herobrine—your father. He is on his way here, and me and my friends are preparing to fight him. Join us, and you can get your revenge on him."

According to the legends that Robo-Steve had read, Herobrine's children had rose up against him hundreds, maybe thousands, of years ago. Herobrine had defeated them, and punished them for their treachery. Spidroth, who had been the ringleader of the group, had been cast beneath the bedrock, where she had remained ever since. Until a few weeks ago, when some illagers had tried to transfer Spidroth's spirit into Robo-Steve's body. They had failed, but it looked like Spidroth has found her way into Charles's body instead.

"If you are lying to me, your punishment will be terrible," hissed Spidroth.

"I'm telling the truth," said Robo-Steve. "Herobrine is on his way to Diamond City with all his forces. Join us in our fight and I'll make sure that you alone get to fight Herobrine himself. You can finally get your vengeance."

Spidroth studied Robo-Steve with Charles's glowing yellow eyes. Robo-Steve could hear the pink spiders all around them rustling and hissing

"There is one more thing," said Robo-Steve. "After the battle, you must leave my friend Charles's body. I will build you a new robot body of your own, but you must give Charles his freedom."

Spidroth grinned.

"You care for this Charles, don't you?" she grinned. "Even though the last time he saw you he was trying to slay you."

"I believe that people can change," said Robo-Steve. "I've done bad things in my past, but I've been taught the error of my ways."

Spidroth laughed.

"There is no good and bad or right and wrong," she said, "only power. You will find this out in time, golden man. But I do agree to your deal. I will help you fight my father, and once he has been defeated I will grant your friend his body back."

"Thank you, Lady Spidroth," said Robo-Steve.

"Now begone," said Spidroth.

"Actually," said Robo-Steve, "if you come back with me to the city we can discuss battle strategy and where your spiders would be most useful—"

"SILENCE!" Spidroth roared. "You test my patience, golden man. No mortal gives commands to Spidrothbrine, daughter of Herobrine. I will decide when, and if, I involve myself in your battle."

"Of course," said Robo-Steve. "I apologize."

"You are lucky I'm in a generous mood," she hissed. "Or I would order my spiders to strip the gold from your body. Now go, before I change my mind!"

So Robo-Steve left.

CHAPTER NINE
The Bells

"Jolly good show, chaps and chapettes!" said Porkins happily. "You're all a bunch of crack shots if ever I saw some!"

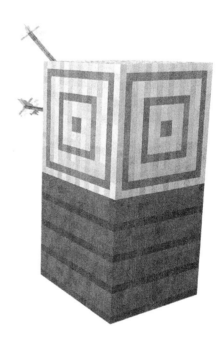

Porkins was in a good mood. All his recruits had come on fantastically in the last week, and they'd just finished a very successful training session in their training yard next to the city wall. All the targets were full of arrows, and Porkins and the recruits were going around collecting all the arrows up. They had a lot of arrows, but Porkins knew that they shouldn't waste them—they didn't know how many arrows they might need in the battle ahead.

Although when that battle would come, Porkins had no idea. It had been just over a week since Adam had escaped and Dave had left to find Professor Quigley, and there had been no sign of either of them since, or of Herobrine. Robo-Steve had told them that Spidroth, Herobrine's so-called daughter, would be joining them in the battle as well, but there had been no sign of her either. Porkins still found the whole Spidroth thing very confusing: he didn't really get who she was and kept forgetting her name. To make things even more confusing, Robo-Steve said that Spidroth was now using the body of Charles, a red robot who Robo-Steve himself had created.

"Thanks for another amazing training session," one of the villagers said to Porkins. "A week ago I'd never even held a bow, and now I'm shooting bullseyes!"

"You've done fantastically well, Daisy," Porkins told her. "But remember to practice with your sword as well."

"I will," she grinned, and she ran off to join her friends.

The recruits were splitting their time between training with Porkins, standing guard with Carl in his underground base and standing guard in the Nether with Alex and Robo-Steve, spending two days at a time with each before moving on. That meant there were always enough villagers to guard each of the three locations, in case a surprise attack came.

Porkins put all the crossbows back on the rack and then headed over to the barracks. The villagers had built some wooden homes next to the city wall, so they wouldn't have to travel far when an attack came. Porkins opened the door to the small wooden house he'd built himself, turned on the fireplace, took off his metal arm and rested in his favorite chair with a slice of pumpkin pie. It had been a long day and he was looking forward to a nice sleep. Through the window he could see the sun beginning to go down.

I hope you're ok, Dave old chap, Porkins thought. Dave had been gone far too long; according to Robo-Steve it should have taken him less than a day to get to Professor Quigley's on Robo-

Pig, and since the plan had been for Dave to bring Professor Quigley to Diamond City via the Nether, it shouldn't have taken them more than a day or so to get back.

Porkins supposed that they may have got lost, but even then it wouldn't have taken them *this* long. He'd wanted to go looking for his friend, but Robo-Steve had said that it was more important that he stay in Diamond City to train the volunteers; and Porkins had reluctantly conceded that he was right.

Still, it didn't stop Porkins from worrying, and he was constantly hoping that the bells of the city walls would ring, announcing that Dave had returned.

Suddenly there was a knock on the door.

"Dave!" said Porkins excitedly.

"Afraid not," said Carl, opening the door with a grin. He was wearing his diamond armor.

"Sorry old boy," said Porkins, "I was daydreaming. It's good to see you. How are things underground?"

"Noisy," said Carl. "Your volunteers never stop talking. I miss when it was just me, the golems and the wolves."

Porkins chuckled.

"I know it's bad, but I wish Herobrine would just jolly well hurry up and attack," he said. "All this waiting around is putting me on edge."

"Agreed," said Carl. "Though it would be nice if Dave could come back first. We could do with Professor Quigley's inventions."

"Do you think he's ok?" asked Porkins. "Dave, I mean. I am a tad worried for the chap."

Carl crouched down, crawled out of his diamond suit and waddled over to sit by the fire.

"I wouldn't say this to his face, but Dave's the toughest of the lot of us," said Carl. "Think of all the sticky situations he's saved us from since we started this journey. Whatever's happened to him, I'm sure he'll be fine."

"I hope so," said Porkins. "You and Dave were the first friends I made after I escaped the Nether. I couldn't bear it if anything happened to either of you."

"Come on," said Carl, rolling his eyes, "don't get all soppy."

KLANG! KLANG!

It was one of the bells on the city wall. Porkins jumped up out of his seat.

"Dave!" he said happily. "It must be Dave!"

"Maybe," said Carl, climbing back into his diamond suit. "Or it could be something worse."

Porkins and Carl ran out of the house. All the other villagers had come out of their houses in the barracks too, eager to see what was going on.

"I say, what's the situation?" Porkins yelled up at the top of the wall. "Is it Dave?"

A villager in diamond armor stuck his head over to look down at them.

"No," he shouted back, looking terrified. "I... I think it's Herobrine."

Porkins and Carl ran up the cobblestone steps that ran along the diamond block wall, the villager recruits running along behind them. When they reached the top, Porkins looked out across the fields that surrounded Diamond City.

"Where?" said Porkins, looking for signs of an army, "I can't see anything."

The villager in diamond armor pointed. Porkins could just make out a small cluster of figures: he squinted and saw that it was a few witches, some illagers and two of the ravager beasts that the illagers sometimes rode.

"There's only about ten of them," said Porkins, feeling confused. "Maybe twenty at most. Where's the rest of their army?"

The witches, illagers and ravagers were alone in the middle of a wheat field. The villager guard had done well to spot them, as with the sun going down they were barely visible.

"Ok, armor up and get your weapons," Porkins told the villagers who had come up to join them on the wall. "There may be other blighters on their way. And send word to Robo-Steve and Alex in the Nether."

"I'll go back underground to the end portal base," said Carl. "They might try and attack on multiple fronts."

As everyone went about their business, Porkins ran down and grabbed his own armor and weapons, then he and his recruits spread across the city walls, guarding the city from every direction.

Porkins looked out at the witches and illagers, trying to work out what they were up to.

"Crossbows at the ready," he yelled to the villagers near him. They all picked their crossbows up and laid them on top of the wall, aiming out at the fields.

Then something began to glow green in the middle of the witches and illagers.

"What's that glowing thing?" one of the villagers asked nervously. "Have the witches got a magic weapon?"

"Look!" yelled another villager. "Look what's happening to that ravager!"

"Oh no," said Porkins. He knew exactly what was happening to the ravager; and he knew what the green glow was as well.

The ravager was *growing.*

"I don't know how, but they've got Professor Quigley's enlarger Ray!" yelled Porkins. "Load your crossbows, we're going to be facing some very big chaps!"

The ravager kept growing and growing. First it was as big as a tree, then bigger and bigger until it was as tall as Diamond City's wall. Only then did the witch holding the enlarger ray aim it at the other ravager, which also started growing.

Porkins had never seen a ravager in person before, but he'd always heard they were jolly tough to defeat. And now there were two *gigantic* ravagers, both snorting and scraping the ground angrily with their hooves.

"We're doomed!" yelled one of the villagers on the wall, and he started running towards the cobblestone steps. "We need to get out of here!"

"He's right!" said another villager. "We don't stand a chance against those things!"

All the villagers were starting to panic now. Porkins was terrified himself by the huge ravagers, but he knew that he had to show the villagers that he was brave.

If I'm brave, they'll be brave, he thought. He wondered if this was how Dave had thought all those times he'd led them into battle.

"Steady on, chaps!" shouted Porkins. All the villagers stopped and looked at him—even the one who'd been half way down the cobblestone steps.

"Remember, we have a wall made of solid ruddy diamond," said Porkins. "And you chaps and chapettes are some of the best shots I've ever seen. Those ravager blighters may be a bit overgrown, but stick them full of arrows and they'll fall, I promise you that!"

A mild cheer went up from some of the villagers.

"So come on, let's return to our positions," said Porkins. "And when those ravagers come at us, we'll give them a darn good thrashing!"

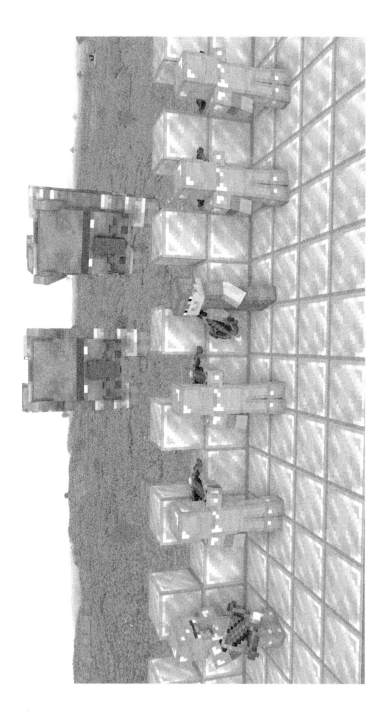

There was a louder cheer this time, and the villagers returned to their positions on the wall. Even the one on the cobblestone steps.

"Sorry, Porkins," the villager said, looking embarrassed.

"Not to worry, old bean," said Porkins, putting a reassuring hand on the villager's shoulder. "It's natural to be afraid. The key is overcoming that fear."

The villager nodded, and returned to his position.

Porkins took his own position on the wall, aiming his crossbow at the ravagers. They were much too far to hit yet, but as soon as they got near to the city he would order his troops to fill them full of arrows.

The sun had gone down now. Porkins could no longer see the witches and illagers, but he could still make out the two gigantic ravagers by the light of the moon.

Then from somewhere in the darkness a horn blew: a deep, long note that made the hairs on Porkins's chin stand on end.

And the ravagers charged.

"Hold your fire until I say!" yelled Porkins, as the ravagers ran towards them, churning up fields of wheat and flattening farmhouses. Each huge-hoofed footstep shook the ground, and it was all Porkins could do to hold on to his bow. Two of the villagers weren't able to keep hold of theirs, and their bows fell out of their fingers, tumbling down into the darkness outside the city.

"Run and get new bows!" Porkins yelled.

The ravagers were almost at the city now; they were so close that Porkins could *smell* them.

"Hold it!" Porkins screamed. "Hold it.... and FIRE!!!"

The villagers let loose with their crossbows, sending a hail of arrows at the ravagers. At the same time the ravagers smashed into the diamond wall, ramming it with their heads. For a moment Porkins was scared they were going to barge right through, but the wall held.

"FIRE!" Porkins yelled again, and another flood of arrows rained down on the ravagers.

The arrows were sticking into the ravagers' backs, but Porkins wasn't sure how much damage they were doing.

"Man the TNT cannons!" Porkins yelled.

Robo-Steve had set up some TNT-launching cannons for them in case they needed them: but he'd warned Porkins to only use them if they were really necessary, as the TNT might accidentally damage the city walls. Also there was no way of turning them, as they were made from cobblestone troughs filled with water, so it was impossible to aim. However, it looked to Porkins that TNT might be the only way of harming the giant ravagers.

"Fire TNT!" yelled Porkins.

There were two TNT cannons near Porkins, and both began firing. *KADOOM KADOOM!*

One of the cannons was aiming too high, and the TNT blocks sailed over the ravagers, exploding into the fields in the distance. But the other cannon was right on target: the TNT blocks exploding against one of the ravager's backs.

The ravager roared in pain and started thrashing around, crashing into the other ravager.

"Keep firing!" Porkins yelled at the cannon-operators and the archers. "Give those ruddy cad blighters everything you've got!"

CHAPTER TEN
Kick their Butts!

"I'm boooooored," said Alex.

She wasn't the only one. As Robo-Steve looked around the courtyard of the Nether base, all the villagers looked like they were fed up. As usual, Alex had put them all through a long day of fighting training and Robo-Steve had talked them through tactics and strategy, but in the evenings there was never much to do, down here in the Nether.

Of course *evening* was a relative term in the Nether: down here it was always the same—no night, no day, no change. It was enough to drive you mad.

I should have put Porkins down here instead of Alex, thought Robo-Steve. Porkins was used to the Nether; he wouldn't have minded seeing the same orangey rocks day in and day out. For him this was home. But for someone like Alex, who got bored easily, the Nether was not a fun place to be.

What do I say to them? Robo-Steve wondered, looking at the bored faces all around him. *Dave would know what to do.*

Once Robo-Steve had thought of himself as a leader, but he now knew that it wasn't true. A leader wasn't just someone who was smart, they also had to be able to inspire others. Dave was able to do that, but Robo-Steve had come to realize that this wasn't a skill that he possessed. His robot brain made him excellent at preparing battle plans and devising strategies, but he couldn't inspire people with a rousing speech like Dave could, or make them believe in themselves.

Dave should have stayed here and I should I have gone to get Professor Quigley, thought Robo-Steve. *I realize that now.*

Suddenly there was a *bloop* from the nether portal next to the barracks, and a villager in diamond armor ran through it, sweat dripping from his face.

"The city's under attack!" he said.

KLANG KLANG KLANG!

The guards on the base walls were ringing the bells.

"Everyone arm yourself and get to your positions on the wall!" shouted Robo-Steve.

Robo-Steve and Alex ran towards the sound of the bell, but then they heard other bells coming from all around the base. They reached the base wall, ran up the steps...

And looked out at a sea of zombie pigmen.

"How are there so many of them?" Alex gasped. For once she actually sounded a bit scared.

The base was completely surrounded by zombie pigmen; more zombie pigmen than Robo-Steve would have thought possible. He was reminded of all the Steves that had surrounded Professor Quigley's house—and then he realized what must have happened.

"Herobrine must have Professor Quigley," said Robo-Steve. "Only her duplicator could have created so many zombie pigmen."

"What are we gonna do?" one of the villagers asked, sounding terrified. All the villagers had put on their diamond armor and were aiming their crossbows out at the infinite army of pigmen.

"We're going to fight as long as we can" said Robo-Steve. "We have walls, we have arrows and we have TNT. All they have are swords."

"I guess," said the villager.

"The villagers need someone to inspire them," Robo-Steve whispered to Alex, "or they're going to start running away as soon as the battle begins. They need Dave!"

"But we don't have Dave," said Alex.

"I know," said Robo-Steve. "And it's my fault: I sent him away when we needed him the most. He would have given them a rousing speech and stopped them from being afraid."

"Don't worry," Alex said, giving him a wink, "let me try."

"Um, I'm not sure about that," said Robo-Steve—but it was too late, Alex had already placed a cobblestone block down and was standing on top of it, addressing the villagers.

"Alright you lot," she said, "I know that this looks like a lot of zombie pigmen, but zombie pigmen are rubbish! They use gold swords like noobs, and they don't even enchant them! We've got awesome crossbows and a wall made of diamond—we're gonna kick their butts! What are we gonna do?"

The villagers looked at her like she'd grown two heads.

"Er... kick their butts?" said a villager.

"Louder!" yelled Alex.

"Kick their butts."

"LOUDER!"

"KICK THEIR BUTTS!"

To Robo-Steve's astonishment, the chant began to spread across the wall like wildfire, and soon all the villagers were chanting together:

"KICK THEIR BUTTS! KICK THEIR BUTTS!"

Then the zombie pigmen started running towards the base; hundreds, maybe thousands of them all rushing forward.

"Oh yeah!" Alex yelled. "Some butts are about to get KICKED!"

"Fire everything!" Robo-Steve yelled. "Fire everything and keep firing!"

All his careful planning suddenly seemed pointless: there were so many zombie pigmen that it was impossible *not* to hit one. The crossbow villagers rained arrows down on the pigmen and the cannon-operators fired TNT block after TNT block into them. It was utter chaos.

The pigmen ran at the wall, climbing over each other like the mindless zombies that they were. The base walls were high, but soon the pile of pigmen was so high that they could reach the top of the wall and pull themselves up.

"Swordsmen, draw your blades!" yelled Robo-Steve.

Robo-Steve had prepared for this: half of the villager recruits had been assigned as *swordsmen,* and it was their job to defend the archers once the base walls were breached. The swordsmen put down their crossbows and pulled out their diamond swords, fighting the pigmen off as the other villagers continued firing arrows and TNT.

Alex was running across the wall, slashing at every zombie pigman who she came across, sending them falling back down.

"Wahoo!" she yelled. "This is fun!"

That's one word for it, thought Robo-Steve, but he was worried. All the villagers were doing a fantastic job, but for every pigman they slew, there were many, many more waiting to take their place.

How can we possibly win this? he thought. *It's impossible!*

CHAPTER ELEVEN
The Battle Under the City

"Fire!" Carl yelled. "Fire, fire fire!"

The villagers fired their crossbows, but the illagers kept charging. However, the iron golems and wolves were waiting for them, attacking the illagers before they could reach the wall.

"Retreat!" the illager leader yelled, "fall back!"

As soon as the attack in the city above had begun, Carl had run down to the end portal base to check on it: and when he got there he found it already under attack by illagers.

The illagers had attacked with crossbow-wielding pillagers and axe-wielding vindicators, and their leader—a pillager with a crossbow and an eyepatch—was riding on the back of a ravager. There were other illagers riding on ravagers too, maybe about five in total.

"Golems and wolves fall back to the base!" Carl yelled. When the battle had broken out, the wolves and golems had rushed forward to attack the illagers, but if they stayed out there they might get hit by Carl's archers.

"In you come, boys!" Carl said to the wolves as he opened one of the iron doors for them.

"Rrruff!" growled one of the wolves.

"Don't worry, Bark 3," said Carl, "I'm sure you'll get another taste of battle soon enough. I don't know how long these walls will keep those illager idiots out."

Once all his forces were safely inside the walls of the base, Carl climbed up onto the wall to join the villager archers. His diamond golem hands were too big to hold a bow, so he just gave orders.

I never thought I'd end up being a military commander, thought Carl. *All I ever wanted to do was eat baked potatoes, and now I'm leading a battle!*

"Right," Carl told the archers, "I don't have a super brain like Robo-Steve, so I've got no fancy tactics. And I can't give you an uplifting speech like Dave would. All I want you to do is fire arrows at every illager and ravager who comes near this wall. Take the ravagers out first, if you can, but other than that—just keep firing."

The illagers has regrouped now, lining up behind their leader on his ravager.

Come on, thought Carl. *Come over here so we can fill you full of arrows.*

The illager leader raised his crossbow in the air.

"Charge!" the leader yelled, and the illagers rushed towards the wall. The vindicators ran forward first with their axes, then the pillagers with their crossbows behind them. The pillagers fired arrows at Carl's archers, while the vindicators pulled out iron pickaxes and started hacking away at the wall.

The villagers on the wall didn't know what to do: They had to avoid the arrows from the pillagers, but at the same time they had to shoot at the vindicators, to stop them breaking through the wall.

"They're breaking through!" a villager yelled.

Carl looked down over the wall and saw that she was right: some of the vindicators had already broken a few diamond blocks. Not enough for them to get through, but it was only a matter of time.

What do I do? thought Carl. *I blame Robo-Steve. He's the idiot who put me in charge!*

"Ruff ruff!"

It was one of the wolves. Carl looked around and saw the wolves and golems all gathered in the courtyard.

I need to use them now, thought Carl. It was useless having such good troops stuck inside the base. But at the same time, if he just opened the door and let the wolves and golems join the battle, they'd probably get accidentally shot full of arrows by the villagers on the walls.

Then, suddenly, Carl realized what he had to do: He needed to open one of the gates. If he opened one of the gates, the vindicators would pour through it, instead of trying to break through the wall in multiple places. Then when they entered the courtyard the golems and wolves could attack them. Meanwhile, the villager archers on the walls could keep on shooting the illagers outside of the wall, so they'd be fighting the illagers on two fronts.

When Carl told the villagers his plan they thought he was mad.

"The illagers will chop us to pieces!" said one villager archer.

"My wolves and golems won't let them get to you, I promise," said Carl. "Well, they'll try their best at least."

"That's not very reassuring," said the villager.

So with the villagers' reluctant consent, Carl ran down to one of the iron doors.

"I hope this isn't the stupidest plan ever," he muttered to himself. And then pressed the switch and the door swung open.

"The door's open!" Carl heard one of the vindicators yell, and they started pouring through. But before they could switch their pickaxes for axes again, the wolves and golems fell upon them, a huge battle breaking out in the courtyard. Carl ran down and joined in, smashing the vindicators with his huge diamond fists.

At first it looked like the wolves and golems were going to have an easy victory, but more and more vindicators kept pouring in through the door, swinging their axes wildly.

"Rrrroww!!"

Carl looked over and saw one of the wolves go *poof.*

"Bark 4!" he yelled.

There were two deep groans, and two of the iron golems fell too, leaving behind nothing but a few iron ingots.

Carl was so distracted that he didn't notice the vindicators running around behind him. Three of them jumped up on his back, hacking away at his diamond suit with their iron axes.

"Get off!" Carl yelled. Other vindicators were hacking at his armor now: *clink clink clink!*

I think opening that door was a big mistake, Carl thought, as the weight of the vindicators clinging on to his suit made him fall to his knees. *I've really made a right idiot of myself.*

"*Rrrow rrrow rrrow!!!*"

From out of nowhere the wolves appeared, jumping on the

villagers and pulling them off of Carl. With the vindicators off of his back, Carl stood up.

"Thanks boys," he said to the wolves. "You saved me."

But they were too busy chasing the vindicators away to hear him. Carl grinned—he'd really grown attached to those wolves.

As the golems and wolves continued their fight in the courtyard, Carl ran over to check the end portal was ok. Thankfully the illagers hadn't managed to reach it yet, and the four golems he'd ordered to wait by the corners of the lava moat they'd build around the portal were still standing guard.

"Good boys," Carl said to the golems. One of them was Basher, and Carl put a hand on his shoulder. "Don't worry Basher," he said, "we're gonna get through this. Trust me."

The golem said nothing, just looking at him with its blank eyes.

Next Carl ran back to the wall, climbing the stairs to check on the archers. The villagers were still firing arrow after arrow at the illagers below.

"There are so many of them," said one of the villagers. "How can we defeat them?"

"Just keep firing," said Carl. "Keep firing until we beat them."

In the distance Carl could see the illager leader with the eyepatch, sitting aside his ravager. The other ravager riders were waiting in the distance as well.

They're waiting until our walls fall, Carl realized. *Then they'll charge in and destroy us all.*

"Keep fighting!" Carl yelled at the villagers. "We can win this!"

He hoped he was right, but looking at the huge number of illagers remaining, he wasn't so sure.

CHAPTER TWELVE
Defending the Wall

One giant ravager had been slain. That was the good news.

The bad news? The other one was still alive, and had broken through the city wall.

"Shoot it!" Porkins yelled. "Keep shooting the blighter!"

The giant ravager was thrashing down the city streets, destroying buildings left right and center. The ground was littered with diamonds; with more raining from the sky with every building that the beast destroyed.

Porkins and about twenty of his villager recruits were running down the street after the ravager, shooting it with their crossbows. He'd left the rest of the villagers back on the wall, in case the illagers and witches launched another attack.

"Come back here, you oversized cow!" Porkins shouted at the ravager. "Come back and face me like a man!"

Suddenly the ravager came to a stop, then it shuffled round, smashing an apartment building to smithereens as it turned.

"Oh dear," said Porkins meekly as the ravager turned to face them. "I may have made a big mistake."

With a mighty *ROAR* the ravager charged down the street towards them.

"Run!" shouted one of the villagers.

The villagers all dashed out of the way, hiding down side streets or in the ruins of buildings, but Porkins stood his ground, holding his crossbow up and aiming at the ravager.

"What are you doing?" one of the villagers yelled at him from behind a broken wall.

"I think I've got an opening," said Porkins. "The next time the blighter opens its mouth…"

The ravager opened its mouth and roared, and Porkins fired his crossbow.

Gosh I hope this works, he thought.

The arrow sailed through the air, flying through the ravager's open mouth and down its throat. For a second it looked like the arrow hadn't done anything, but then the ravager made a choking sound and collapsed on its belly. It had been charging so fast that it kept moving for a few seconds, sliding along the ground towards Porkins. He closed his eyes, expecting to get flattened at any moment, but nothing happened. He opened his eyes to see the ravager had come to a stop right in front of him.

With an almighty *POOF* the ravager disappeared—leaving behind nothing but a normal-sized saddle.

The villagers all cheered, running over and hugging Porkins. "You did it!" they said. "You did it!"

"Oh, it was nothing," said Porkins, feeling his cheeks glow red.

But their victory was short lived, as in the distance they could hear the bells ringing once more.

"Oh no," said Porkins. "Everyone back to the wall!"

They ran down the street, ruined buildings on either side of them. Finally they could see the broken section of the city wall in front of them that the ravager had destroyed. And in the distance, beyond the city, was the biggest green creeper Porkins had ever seen.

They ran forward to the gap in the wall. In the distance, crawling slowly across the fields towards the city, was the creeper. It was even bigger than Porkins had first thought: almost twice as tall as the giant ravagers had been.

Those witches are certainly getting a lot of use out of Professor Quigley's enlarging ray, he thought bitterly.

"What are our orders?" one of the villagers asked Porkins.

Porkins was about to say that they should get back on top of the wall and get ready to fire at the creeper, but then he realized that would be the worst idea possible. As soon as the giant creeper got near enough to the city wall for them to fire on, it would be near enough to explode and destroy half the city.

"Our only hope is the TNT cannons," said Porkins. "They have a much longer range than our bows. Go up to the wall and tell the cannon operators to fire fire fire!"

The villager nodded, then all the villagers ran towards the nearest set of stairs so they could get back on top of the wall. Porkins followed them, and once he was on top of the wall he looked at the dark fields that surrounded the city. He was thankful for the moonlight, as without it they probably wouldn't have even been able to see the giant creeper before it was too late.

DOOM DOOM DOOM DOOM!!!

Porkins watched as the cannons on top of the wall sent TNT blocks hurtling towards the giant creeper.

BOOM BOOM BOOM BOOM!

The TNT blocks exploded against the creeper's skin, but barely seemed to do any damage. Meanwhile the creeper kept slowly walking towards the city.

It we don't retreat soon, we'll be within its blast radius, thought Porkins. *What are we going to do?*

The villagers fired another round of TNT at the creeper, but these also exploded harmlessly on its skin.

It's no use, thought Porkins. *We have to retreat!*

He was about to shout an order for the villagers to fall back into the city, but suddenly he saw something strange happening: Hundreds of tiny pink things were crawling up the side of the creeper. The creeper hissed in pain, but then its hiss was drowned out as it was smothered in the tiny things.

"They're pink spiders!" one of the villagers said. "Spiders are attacking the creeper!"

"They're not just attacking it," said another villager, "they're eating it!"

They were right, Porkins realized. The creeper was now completely covered in spiders, and it was getting smaller and smaller by the second. Soon the spiders all fell to ground, the creeper completely gone.

"Gosh," said Porkins.

Next the pink spiders scurried towards the city wall, clambering on top of each other to build some kind of structure.

They're turning themselves into stairs! Porkins realized.

"Should we shoot them?" one of the archers asked Porkins.

Porkins wasn't sure. The spiders had saved them from the creeper, but did that mean they were friendly or just hungry?

The spiders finished their huge staircase—it reached all the way from the ground to the top of the city wall. Porkins saw a figure approach it from the bottom and begin to walk up it.

"Charles?" he gasped in amazement.

"You know that guy?" one of the villagers asked.

Porkins did. The red robot walking up the staircase was none other than Charles, a robot built by Robo-Steve to be his assistant. Porkins had punched Charles the last time they'd seen each other, so he wasn't expecting a warm welcome. However, Robo-Steve has told Porkins that Spidroth, Herobrine's daughter, was now living inside Charles's body. It was all jolly confusing.

"String your bows and be ready to fire on my command," Porkins told the archers.

Charles reached the top of the staircase and snarled at Porkins.

"Who is in command here, pigman?" Charles asked. His voice was different than usual, Porkins thought. It sounded more *feminine*. "Where is the golden Steve?"

"Charles," said Porkins, "I just want to say, I hope there are no hard feelings about that sucker punch. It was a bad show by me, even though you were being a real cad."

"SILENCE!" roared Charles. "The being you knew as Charles no longer controls this body. You will address me as *Lady Spidroth*."

"Oh ok, sorry Charles—I mean, Lady Spidroth," said Porkins. Spidroth/Charles sneered.

"I agreed to join Robo-Steve's fight because he promised me that Herobrine would be coming," she said. "I have been waiting and watching, but have seen no sign of him yet. So I will join my forces to your own, fighting back against Herobrine's army until he is forced to reveal himself. But be warned, Pigman, I must be the one to slay Herobrine. Any man who takes that pleasure from me shall suffer as no man has suffered before."

"Right-ho," said Porkins. "We'll bear that in mind."

Suddenly the bells rang again: *KLANG KLANG KLANG!*

Porkins looked out across the dark fields and saw a sight that chilled him to the bone.

Hundreds, maybe thousands, of zombie pigmen were marching out of the trees towards the city. There were more of them than Porkins would have thought possible.

"Repair the broken section of wall!" he shouted to the villagers. "Use cobblestone, or whatever you can find!"

Porkins looked at Spidroth and saw something in her eyes that he never would have suspected: *terror.*

"How are there so many of them?" she said. "Are those pigmen?"

"Zombie pigmen," said Porkins.

"I didn't know pigmen could become zombies," said Spidroth. "This must be some new sorcery my father has cooked up! Either way, I must leave this battle."

"What? Why?" said Porkins.

"Do you not have eyes, fool?" Spidroth spat. "Look at how many soldiers my father has. We'll never defeat him!"

"I think the red robot lady may be right," said Mayor Birchwood, coming over to join them, his assistant Simon trailing along behind him. "We'll never win against that many troops. We need to retreat."

"The only problem, old chap," said Porkins sadly, "is that we may not be able to. Look."

He pointed, showing the mayor that the pigman army was completely surrounding the city.

"There's no escape," gasped Simon. "We're doomed!"

"Maybe," said Porkins, "but let's at least go down fighting. Let's give Herobrine and these blaggards the fight of their lives."

Mayor Birchwood grinned and nodded.

"I guess we don't have much choice," he said.

"What about you, Lady Spidroth?" asked Porkins.

"Although there is no danger of me being killed, I have no desire to throw this new metal body away on a futile whim," she hissed. "My spiders and I will fight alongside you, but if it looks like the battle is lost we will abandon you without hesitation. Your pitiful lives mean nothing to me."

"Right-ho," said Porkins. "That's good enough."

He stood up to address the archers.

"Ok chaps," he said, "I know things look rather sticky at the moment, but this battle isn't lost yet. This is your city, and if Herobrine wants to take it, he's going to have the fight of his life. Who's with me?"

The villagers all cheered.

Ok, thought Porkins, looking out at the thousands of zombie pigmen surrounding them. *I've convinced them we can win. Now I just need to convince myself...*

CHAPTER THIRTEEN
A Battle on Three Fronts

The walls had broken and the illagers had flooded into the base.

"Fall back!" Carl yelled to the villagers still standing on the remaining sections of wall. "Fall back and defend the end portal!"

The villagers did as he said, retreating to form a ring around the end portal and its lava moat.

"We need to get out of here!" a villager said to Carl. "We should escape up the stairs, back into the city."

"We need to defend the end portal," said Carl.

"Why?" said the villager. "If it's so dangerous, why don't we just destroy it?"

The villager was right, Carl realized. He couldn't ask the villagers to give their lives to defend the portal.

"All of you, go back up and help defend the city," Carl told the villagers. "I'm gonna stay down here with the golems and wolves. If it looks like we're going to lose the battle, I'll destroy the portal."

"If you're staying, we're staying with you," said another villager. "We volunteered to fight."

"Don't be stupid," said Carl. "The only reason I'm protecting the portal is because my idiot friend Dave has been looking for it for so long. If I can protect it I will, but I won't let anyone else throw away their life to save it. Now go!"

Reluctantly the villagers all left, leaving Carl alone with the golems and the wolves. The illagers had all come through into the base now, and were completely surrounding them.

The illager leader marched to the front on his ravager.

"Give up the portal and we'll let you live," he told Carl.

"Afraid I can't do that," said Carl.

"Then you have sealed your own fate," said the leader.

"Maybe," said Carl. "Out of interest, how much is Herobrine paying you?"

"We fight for honor," growled the illager leader.

"Nah," said Carl, "you lot look like you're here for the pay. Have you given any thought to the fact that you're attacking a city made of diamond? The mayor of Diamond City could pay you far more than Herobrine ever could. Join us against him and you'll be swimming in diamonds."

The illager leader laughed.

"That was a good sales pitch, creeper," he said, "but we've been made a better offer. Herobrine has said we can take *all* the diamonds of Diamond City once this battle is won. We'll tear down every building and every block and will be rich beyond imagining. All he wants in return is the portal."

"Ok," said Carl, "that's fair enough."

What now? he wondered. Offering the illagers money had been his only idea.

"Last chance," said the illager leader. "Will you surrender the end portal? I won't ask again."

Carl looked at his remaining army: ten wolves and seven golems. There were more illagers than he could count surrounding them, and four ravagers. Could they possibly win? It didn't seem likely.

"Looks like you've made your choice, creeper," said the illager leader. "Attack!"

The illagers and the ravagers all rushed forward.

"Charge!" Carl yelled, and he ran forward to meet them, the wolves and iron golems running alongside him.

*

Robo-Steve, Alex and the villagers were putting up a good fight, but it was clear that the nether base was lost. The zombie pigmen has swarmed over the walls and the base had turned into a battleground. The villager archers had been forced off of the walls and were instead fighting the pigmen on the ground with their swords.

As much as he hated to do it, Robo-Steve knew he had to order a retreat.

"Everyone fall back!" Robo-Steve yelled. "Go back to the overworld and guard the nether portals from that side!"

The villagers did as he said: rushing to their nearest portals and leaving the Nether. Robo-Steve waited until he was sure all the villagers had escaped, then he grabbed Alex's hand and ran with her to the portal nearest them: the one outside the barracks.

"Aren't we going to stay and fight?" said Alex disappointedly.

"Sometimes there's more to winning a battle than just fighting," said Robo-Steve. "We've lost the Nether, but if we go to the overworld and guard the portals we can still stop the zombie pigmen coming through."

"I suppose that makes sense," said Alex. "Though fighting is more fun. I guess it's time for Plan B."

"What's Plan B?" asked Robo-Steve.

"You'll see," grinned Alex, and she ran over to a switch on the outer wall of one of the buildings and pulled it.

Nothing happened.

"It might take a minute," she said.

"Come on," said Robo-Steve, grabbing her hand again. "We haven't got time for this."

They ran through the portal and found themselves in a small stone room: one of the many guard houses that Mayor Quigley had built to protect the nether portals. A crowd of villagers and two iron golems were waiting for them.

"Aim your crossbows at the portal," Robo-Steve told the villagers. "Destroy any zombie pigmen who come through."

They didn't have long to wait: soon a horde of zombie pigmen came streaming through the portal. The villagers fired arrows at them—*thunk thunk thunk*—but there were just too many of them.

Robo-Steve and Alex started slashing at the zombie pigmen with their swords, and the two iron golems starting beating the pigmen with their huge arms, but for every one they slew, many more came through the portal.

"Get out of here!" Robo-Steve yelled to the villagers, when he realized that the battle was lost.

They all ran out of the guard house, the door slamming shut behind them. They were in the park in the middle of Diamond City, but immediately Robo-Steve could tell that the battle up here must be going badly, as in the distance he could see ruined buildings.

Robo-Steve could hear the zombie pigmen hacking at the wall of the guard house, trying to get out. They only had gold swords, but there were so many of them that Robo-Steve knew it wouldn't be long before they broke through.

"Do we retreat or do we stay here to fight them?" one of the villagers asked Robo-Steve.

"I... I don't know," Robo-Steve replied.

He could feel the fear creeping over: not fear for himself, but fear for the others. If he ordered them to stay and they all got slain, that would be on him. But if he ordered a retreat the zombie pigmen might win the battle and end up slaying them anyway.

"I can't believe Plan B didn't work," said Alex.

What do I do? wondered Robo-Steve.

Even with his superior, super-high robot IQ, he had no idea.

*

It was utter chaos outside Diamond City. Porkins and his archers were firing endless arrows and TNT blocks at the huge army of zombie pigmen swarming against the city walls, but it was barely making a dent in their numbers.

Meanwhile Spidroth's spider army were attacking the zombie pigmen on the ground, Lady Spidroth commanding them from the top of the wall. She wasn't shouting orders, just waving her hands about and hissing. Porkins supposed she was using some kind of magic. And where she had got her army of pink spiders from, he had no idea.

As he fired arrow after arrow down at the zombie pigmen, Porkins thought about how these mindless monsters had once been his people. When he'd first left the Nether he'd vowed that one day he would cure the pigmen, but he'd come to realize that there probably was no cure. Whatever Herobrine had done to them was permanent.

That cad Herobrine is nothing but a coward, thought Porkins bitterly. *He gets others to fight his battles and doesn't care who gets hurt along the way.*

"They're reaching the top of the wall!" one of the villagers yelled, shaking Porkins out of his thoughts.

"Oh my!" said Mayor Birchwood, as he and Porkins ran over to the wall to have a look.

Below them the zombie pigmen were clambering on top of each other like ants, creating a huge pile of pigmen against the wall that was getting higher by the second. The villagers kept shooting them with arrows, but more and more zombie pigmen kept joining the pile. Soon the tower of pigmen would be so high that they'd be able to climb up the top of the wall.

Porkins was about to say something, but then he looked over and saw more piles of zombie pigmen further down the wall in the distance. Soon the zombie pigmen would be coming over the wall at multiple points, and the wall would be lost.

"Spidroth!" Porkins yelled. "Get those spider chaps of yours to deal with the pigmen trying to get over the wall!"

"Do you dare to give me orders, maggot?" hissed Spidroth.

"Just ruddy well do it!" said Porkins. "Or we'll all be in the soup."

Spidroth hissed angrily, but did as Porkins said. She waved her hands and her spiders returned to the wall: attacking the zombie pigmen there. The zombie pigmen piles collapsed and Porkins breathed a sigh of relief. But the battle was far from over—the zombie pigman army still stretched out into the distance as far as the eye could see.

Then Porkins saw a sight that made him fill with fear. Towards the back of the pigman army there were some flashes of green light, and suddenly some of the pigmen started growing.

The enlarger ray of Professor Quigley's must need time to recharge, thought Porkins, *otherwise I guess they'd use it to make their entire army huge!*

Around ten gigantic zombie pigmen now towered over the rest of the army. They were slightly taller than the city wall, as far as Porkins could tell.

"Oh no, oh no, oh no!" whimpered Mayor Birchwood, dropping his crossbow. "This is not what I got into politics for!"

The ten giant zombie pigmen charged, rushing towards the city wall.

"Shoot them!" Porkins yelled. "Hold your ground—if those ravagers had trouble breaking through the wall, these chumps won't stand a chance."

A couple of the giant zombie pigmen were hit by TNT blasts from the cannons, slowing them down, but the others kept running. They reached the city wall, but instead of attacking it with their swords they leaned down and picked up handfuls of normal-sized zombie pigmen. Then they stood up and dropped the zombie pigmen on top of the wall. Porkins and the mayor had to run to avoid the pigmen falling on top of them.

Now the zombie pigmen were on top of the wall, the archers had to drop their bows and fight with their swords. Porkins stood back to back with Mayor Birchwood, both of them fighting off the zombie pigmen with their swords.

"This isn't the life I envisioned when I stood to be mayor," moaned Mayor Birchwood. "I thought I'd be kissing babies and holding parades."

"Spidroth, bring your spiders back to the wall!" yelled Porkins.

"I think not, pigman," said Spidroth, as she fought off zombie pigmen with a diamond sword. "I think it's time for me and my army to take our leave."

"You can't leave us now!" said Porkins.

"I can do whatever I choose," she hissed.

A huge column of pink spiders rose up above the battlefield, twisting and contorting themselves into the shape of a giant arm with a hand on the end. The hand reached down to the wall and opened its palm for Spidroth. She stepped onto it.

"Goodbye, pigman," she said to Porkins. "You and your villager slaves fought well, but I fear that this will be your last battle."

"Wait, Spidroth, Please!" cried Porkins.

But it was no use the huge arm was carrying Spidroth away across the battlefield.

"Some use she was," said Mayor Birchwood miserably.

For a moment it looked like Spidroth was going to make her escape, but then one of the huge pigmen spotted the giant spider-arm and drew its giant gold sword.

"Spidroth, watch out!" said Porkins.

The giant pigman swung its sword through the column of spiders, causing the entire arm to collapse.

"Eiiiiiiiieeeee!!!" yelled Spidroth as she plummeted to the ground. And then she was gone: disappearing under the endless army of pigmen.

"Well, good riddance," said Mayor Birchwood.

Porkins, the mayor and the other villagers continued to fight the endless army of zombie pigmen that the giant zombie pigmen kept dumping on top of the wall.

We can't keep this up much longer, thought Porkins desperately. He had hoped that Robo-Steve or Carl would win their battles and come to join the fight up here, but it didn't look like that was going to happen.

Then suddenly in the distance he heard a scream:

"*EIYYEEEEEE!!!!*"

It was a monstrous, inhuman scream, but Porkins thought there was something familiar about it. He was sure he'd heard it before.

The sun was beginning to rise now, the faint orange glow spreading across the battlefield and the endless army of zombie pigmen.

"*EIYYEEEEEE!!!!*"

Porkins could hear where the noise was coming from now—it was coming from behind the zombie pigmen, and there was some sort of scuffle going on. A blast of blue fire spat up into the sky.

"Oh yes," said Porkins happily. "Oh yes, oh yes, oh yes!"

"What are you so happy about?" asked Mayor Birchwood as he fought off three zombie pigmen with his diamond sword.

"I think the cavalry's here," said Porkins. "This battle's not lost yet!"

CHAPTER FOURTEEN
Reinforcements

The zombie pigmen burst out of the guardhouse, and Alex, Robo-Steve and the villagers ran forward to meet them with their swords.

We should have run, Robo-Steve thought, as hundreds and hundreds of zombie pigmen ran towards them. *There's too many of them.*

The zombie pigman had demolished the guardhouse now, leaving just the nether portal standing in the middle of the park, with more and more zombie pigmen rushing out of it every second.

KA-DOOOOOOM!!!!

Suddenly a fireball shot out from the portal, blowing all the zombie pigmen to bits. The ones who survived were quickly filled full of arrows by the villagers. Robo-Steve waited for another wave of zombie pigmen to run out of the portal, but none came.

"What happened?" said Robo-Steve.

"Plan B!" said Alex happily. "It worked!"

Alex skipped happily towards the portal.

"Wait!" said Robo-Steve, but Alex didn't listen—she just ran straight through the purple liquid back into the Nether.

"What's that all about?" asked one of the villagers.

Robo-Steve ran over to the portal and jumped through it. For the moment there was the familiar swirling purple haze, and then he found himself back in the Nether: But things had changed.

The base was gone; the zombie pigmen were gone. All that was left was a huge crater. Alex was standing in the middle of it, a big grin on her face.

"What happened?" asked Robo-Steve.

"Plan B," said Alex. "You and Dave kept telling me that you can't win every battle by fighting, so I thought I'd come up with a back-up plan in case the battle went wrong. I had all that time alone in the Nether base, so rather than just being bored out of my head, I put a load of TNT under the base."

"TNT under the base!" said Robo-Steve in disbelief. "Alex, if that had gone off when we all still in there—"

"Relax," said Alex. "It was all perfectly safe. Besides, it worked didn't it?"

Robo-Steve had to admit that Alex was right. The TNT explosion had destroyed all of the zombie pigmen, and the Nether was secure once more. In the distance he could see villagers coming through the other portals to see what was going on. They all looked very confused.

"The zombie pigmen have all been defeated by Alex," Robo-Steve told the villagers when they walked over.

"Then what now?" one of the villagers asked.

"The battle for the Nether has been won," said Robo-Steve, "but the battle in the overworld still goes on. We will leave a few troops to guard the portals, in case more zombie pigmen come, but the rest of us must go to the city walls and join the fight. The fight for Diamond City isn't over yet."

*

Of all the things Carl thought he would do in his life, wrestling with a ravager was never on the list. But somehow that was exactly what he was now doing: grabbing a ravager by the horns with his diamond golem suit and trying to wrestle it to the ground.

"You can't win, creeper!" the illager on the ravager's back shouted at him, as he fired yet another crossbow bolt at Carl's diamond armor. "There are too many of us!"

"Maybe not," said Carl, "but I can at least beat you up."

Using all his strength, Carl swung the ravager around by the horns, lifting it into the air, then he let go and the ravager and rider went flying into a crowd of illagers, squashing them flat.

Carl and his wolves and golems were fighting well, but they were so outnumbered by the illagers that it was clear they couldn't last much longer. To Carl's sorrow, almost half the wolves had been slain and most of the golems too. Basher was still alive, thankfully, but his iron body was full of so many arrows that he looked more like a cactus than a golem.

We need to end this now or none of us are getting out of here alive, Carl thought. *It's time to destroy the portal.*

Carl had built a moat of lava around the end portal, so he pulled out some sand blocks and placed them down in the lava to create a bridge. Then he walked across to the portal. It wasn't even active, but Carl could still feel a strange, ancient energy coming from it. The portal blocks with ender eyes in them seemed to be looking at him, staring right into his soul.

Sorry, Dave, thought Carl, as he lifted a diamond fist up, getting ready to smash one of the portal blocks. But as he swung his fist down, suddenly a gaggle of illagers leapt onto his back, all slashing at his armor with their axes. He had to use one arm to protect his head, and the other to try and fight them off.

Soon there were so many illagers on top of him that the weight of all of them pushed him to the floor, and he had to use both his arms to cover his head. The *clink clink clink* of their axes hitting his armor was all he could hear.

Through his iron fingers Carl watched helplessly as the illagers' arrows slayed the last of the wolves and the golems. Basher was the last one standing, fighting the illagers with everything he had, until finally he was defeated by a charging ravager, and then *poof,* he was gone.

Oh no, thought Carl, *I'm the last one left.*

With all the wolves and golems slain, the entire illager army turned on Carl. The vindicators were still hitting him with their axes, but their leader ordered them to stop.

"Push him in the lava," the illager leader said, with a grin.

The illagers all began to push Carl. He tried to push back against them, but there were so many, and he was getting closer and closer to the lava moat. His back foot was practically hanging over the lava, and it wouldn't be long before he fell in.

And even my diamond armor won't save me then, thought Carl.

"Goodbye creeper golem, or whatever you are," Carl heard the illager leader say. "You fought well. You should be proud."

Then, suddenly, Carl heard a horn blowing in the distance.

ARRRROOOOOOOOO!!!!

The illagers must be blowing that horn to declare their victory, he thought miserably. But then he noticed that the illagers were looking confused, as if they didn't know where the sound was coming from.

"What is that?" the illager leader was yelling. "Go and see what that sound is!"

But then *thunk*—an arrow hit him in the side of the head, and *poof,* he was gone.

Arrows began raining down on the illagers, who scattered and began running for their lives. Some were so desperate to run away that they accidentally went straight into the lava moat.

"The leader's been slain!" one of the illagers yelled. "Come on, we're not getting paid enough for this!"

The illagers ran as fast as they could away from the base. The illager leader's ravager ran so fast that it trampled a load of the illagers in the process. Arrows continued to rain down on them as they ran, and Carl suddenly saw where the arrows were coming from: there were pigmen standing on the walls of the base—not zombie pigmen, but actual pigmen.

"Show the brutes no mercy!" a tall pigman with a huge barrel chest was yelling. "Keep firing!"

I know that pigman, thought Carl. *I know all those pigmen...*

"When you meet your maker, tell him that Elder Crispy sent you!" the tall pigman yelled at the illagers. "Elder Crispy and the pigmen of Little Bacon!"

*

"What is that thing?" Mayor Birchwood said, looking down on the battlefield. "It's like a giant blue creeper... but with spider legs."

"And there's a villager riding on its back!" said Simon. "I think... I think it's Dave!"

Simon was right, Porkins knew. He didn't know how, but Dave had arrived in the nick of time, riding on the back of the blue creeper queen and leading an army of villagers. Among the army he could see Sally from Greenleaf, clad head-to-toe in iron armor and swinging an iron sword. It looked like she was riding on the back of a pig.

The ten giant zombie pigmen had rushed over to try and fight Dave, Sally and the villager reinforcements, but that had put them right in the sights of Porkins's TNT cannons: and the villagers on the wall had fired block after block of TNT at them, blowing them all to bits.

But even with the giant zombie pigmen gone and Dave's reinforcements, the villagers were still vastly outnumbered.

"Let's go out and help those chaps," Porkins yelled to the villagers on the wall.

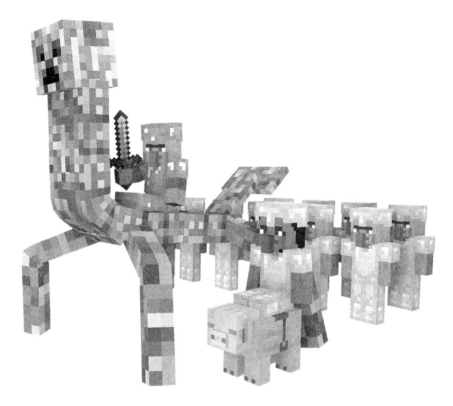

"Are you mad?" said Simon. "We'll get pulverized if we go out there."

"We're a well-trained army and they're mindless zombies," said Porkins. "We can do this. Who's with me?"

"I am," said Mayor Birchwood.

"Sir?" said Simon. "We'll never win!"

"Maybe not," said the mayor, "but if we stay up here we'll lose the city anyway. We might as well go down fighting. I'm with you Porkins."

"And me," said a villager.

"Me too," said another.

Soon all the villagers were loudly declaring that they were with Porkins—they all wanted to join the fight.

"Well, me too then, I guess," said Simon.

Porkins led them down the stairs, then they all gathered outside one of the closed city gates. He was about to order the gates to be opened when he saw an unexpected sight: an army of villagers was coming up the street to meet them, led by Robo-Steve and Alex.

"Robo-Steve!" said Porkins. "What happened? Has the Nether been lost?"

"The Nether's been won," said Robo-Steve. "They sent an army of pigmen against us, but we defeated them—thanks to Alex."

Alex was grinning.

"We've left some soldiers to guard the portals in case they send another army from the Nether," said Robo-Steve, "but I think it's safe for us to join you now."

"Jolly good," said Porkins. "Right, open the—"

But then he saw *another* unexpected sight. Another small army was running down the street towards them. But this wasn't an army of villagers: it was an army of *pigmen.*

"Good gravy!" said Porkins.

"Well met, Porkins," said Elder Crispy, picking up Porkins and hugging him against his huge barrel chest. "Bet you never thought you'd see us again!"

All the pigmen from Little Bacon were there. There was Ricco, Nathan, Pat the pig-girl and all the others.

"How did you get into the city?" Mayor Birchwood asked Elder Crispy.

"We came from underground," Elder Crispy replied. "We helped your creeper friend out of a bit of a scrape. I must say, I'm loving that diamond golem suit of his. Might try and get one of my own."

"He's still guarding the end portal, along with some of our pigmen troops," said Pat. "It's good to see you, Porkins," she added.

"It's good to see you too," said Porkins, smiling. "It's good to see all of you."

"Come on then," said Ricco. "It sounds like there's still a big battle going on outside these walls. Are we gonna fight or what?"

"Yeah," said Nathan. "I've got a quiver full of arrows that need using."

"I need to warn you, we'll be fighting our own," said Porkins. "Herobrine is using zombie pigmen."

"That's fine with us," said Pat. "As much as I hate to admit it, those things aren't pigmen anymore, and they're not changing back."

"Ok everyone," said Porkins, "get ready—this is going to be the fight of our lives. Open the gates!"

The villager at the gate controls flicked a switch and the huge diamond gates slowly swung open. As soon as they saw an opening, the zombie pigmen outside rushed towards them.

"Attack!" Porkins yelled.

*

Why aren't they coming out to join the battle? Dave wondered, looking at Diamond City. It looked like the city had sustained some considerable damage: a lot of the city's diamond walls had been damaged, and sections had been rebuilt in cobblestone. He wondered if perhaps Herobrine's forces had already got inside; maybe through the Nether or underground. He'd sent Elder Crispy and his pigmen underground to help protect the end portal, but maybe they'd been too late.

Dave looked desperately at the city gates, but there was no sign of them opening. Sally and the villagers from Greenleaf, Villagertropolis and the other settlements were fighting a good fight, but they wouldn't last forever against Herobrine's huge zombie pigmen army. Not without backup.

After finding Professor Quigley's lab in ruins and the professor gone, Dave had rode Robo-Pig to Greenleaf, to ask Sally and the other villagers to aid him in the battle. Then he'd gone to Villagertropolis and all the other towns and villages that had been taken over by Herobrine the first time, to ask for their help too. He'd even gone to Little Bacon, the village in the jungle where the pigmen lived. Elder Crispy, the leader of Little Bacon, had been glad to join in the fight.

Dave and his army had gathered at Greenleaf and were about to head back to Diamond City when suddenly they'd heard a terrible, monstrous scream. The blue creeper queen had come down from the mountains and was causing havoc: breathing blue fire and chasing the villagers.

Remembering that his future self had once ridden the creeper queen, Dave had nervously stepped forward. His logic was that maybe if the creeper queen thought he was Future Dave she wouldn't attack him. Thankfully the plan worked, and not only did the creeper queen not attack him, she lowered her head so that he could climb onto her back.

Dave had continued to ride the creeper queen, giving Robo-Pig to Sally. Then Dave and his new army had traveled back to Diamond City as fast as they could, traveling most of the way via the Nether to make faster time. Eventually, when Robo-Pig's navigation system had told them that they were just outside Diamond City, they'd built a portal back to the overworld. Seeing the city surrounded by zombie pigmen, Dave had sent the Little Bacon pigmen underground to make sure the end portal was safe, while he, Sally and the villagers had taken the zombie pigmen by surprise. Dave had charged through the ranks of the zombie pigmen on his creeper queen, as she breathed blasts of blue fire down on them.

Dave had expected the villagers inside the city to come out and join the battle, but so far there had been no sign of them. He could see archers on the walls firing arrows and TNT down on the zombie pigmen, but that was about it.

"Come on," he said to himself. "Porkins, if you're still in there, come out and join us."

"SKRIIIII!"

The creeper queen was stirring restlessly, eager to get back into the battle.

"Ok," said Dave, pulling at her reigns, "let's go."

He rode her over to a crowd of zombie pigmen. They all charged, but then the creeper queen opened her mouth, blasting them to dust with blue fire.

"KRIIIIII!" she screamed triumphantly.

"Nice one, Dave!"

It was Sally. She has pulled up alongside the creeper queen on Robo-Pig.

"How are you getting on?" Dave shouted down at her, struggling to be heard over the din of the battle.

"Excellent," she said. "This pig is faster than any horse I've ever ridden. I can just speed past the zombie pigmen and slice them with my sword."

"I am five times faster than the average horse," said Robo-Pig. "And faster still with turbo boost activated."

Suddenly in the distance Dave could hear a clanking noise. He looked up and saw a sight that filled his heart with joy: one of the city gates was opening.

Through the gate came Porkins, the pigmen of Little Bacon and the villagers of Diamond City.

"Looks like the reinforcements are here," grinned Sally. "Robo-Pig, ho!

Robo-Pig and Sally sped off, charging into a crowd of zombie pigmen.

"Come on, girl," Dave said to the creeper queen. "Let's win this battle!"

*

On a nearby hillside, Herobrine watched the battle unfold.

"We've lost the Nether and the illagers have abandoned the attack on the end portal," said a witch, running up to him out of breath. "Lord Herobrine, we must retreat. The Diamond City forces have opened the gates and are attacking us in the field, the enlarger rays have both overloaded and the duplicator has broken from overuse. The battle is lost."

"No," said Herobrine. "We stay."

"But Lord Herobrine—"

Herobrine raised a hand and a bolt of lightning shot down from the sky, obliterating the witch into dust. The other witches who'd been with her looked terrified.

"Now," he said, "it's time to put an end to Dave and his friends once and for all."

And he raised both hands towards the sky.

CHAPTER FIFTEEN
The Melting

"Porkins!" said Dave, jumping off the back of the creeper queen and hugging his old friend.

"It's so good to see you, dear chap," said Porkins. "You were gone so long that we feared the worst."

"Glad to have you back, Dave," said Robo-Steve. Dave came over and gave him a hug as well.

"Hi Dave!" said Alex, leaping up and hugging him too. "Everyone thought you were dead, but I knew you weren't."

"This is all very touching," said Mayor Birchwood, "but we are still in the middle of a battle!"

He was right: all around them the battle between. The villagers, pigmen and zombie pigmen was still raging. All the giant zombie pigmen had now been defeated, but there were still plenty of the normal-sized ones left.

"Come on," said Dave, jumping back onto the creeper queen's back, "let's fight!"

As he raised his sword all the villagers and pigmen around them cheered.

"You heard him, boys and girls," growled Elder Crispy. "Let them have it!"

KRAKA-DOOM!

Suddenly there was a crash of thunder overhead and lightning bolts flashed across the sky. Huge gray clouds swirled above them and it began to rain.

"Come on, it's just a bit of thunder," shouted Elder Crispy. "Keep fighting!"

"Wait!" said Mayor Birchwood. "What's happening to the zombie pigmen?"

All around them the zombie pigmen were shuddering and contorting, their bodies twisting in unnatural ways. Then they started *dripping*.

"I... I think they're melting," said Robo-Steve.

"Gross," said Alex.

The pigmen *were* melting, Dave realized. Their bodies were slowly dripping and turning into piles of mush.

"It must be Herobrine," Dave said. "But why would he destroy his own troops?"

Now the zombie pigmen were nothing but pink and green puddles on the floor. It was one of the most disgusting things Dave had ever seen, and it was all he could do not to spew his breakfast back up.

"Maybe the clones reached their expiration date or they were faulty," suggested Robo-Steve.

"Well, whatever happened, we've won!" yelled Elder Crispy. All the Little Bacon pigmen cheered, raising their bows in the air.

Have we won? wondered Dave. As he looked round at the battlefield covered in nothing but pink mush, it looked like they had, but he knew by now that a battle was never over until it was over.

And then the mush began to *move*. The pink puddles began to slop together, forming into bigger and bigger puddles.

Suddenly lightning flashed across the sky once more, and Dave saw Herobrine walking towards them through the field of pink mush.

"It's Herobrine!" Porkins yelled. "Get him!"

Some of the villagers and pigmen charged forward, but as they ran across the puddles of mush their feet got stuck.

"It's like glue!" said Elder Crispy, trying to pull his trotters free. "Wait, it's... oh no!"

Something horrible was happening to Elder Crispy and the villagers and pigmen who'd stepped into the pink goo. At first Dave thought the mush was sucking them down, but then he realized it was *melting* them, turning them into goo as well.

"Avenge me!" Elder Crispy yelled. And then he was nothing

but a puddle on the ground.

"KRIIIIIIEEEEE!!!!"

It was the creeper queen. Her feet had got stuck in the pink goo too, and she was struggling desperately to get free. She was bucking so hard that Dave was thrown off of her back onto the grass.

"KRIII! SHRIIIIII!!!" the creeper queen screamed, as she continued to try and free herself from the muck. But her body was starting to melt now; big blue gloops dripping down to the ground.

Finally there was nothing left of her but a huge blue puddle; a blue patch of goo in the middle of the pink.

"Everyone back to the city!" yelled Dave.

They all ran towards the city gates. As they ran Dave turned and saw that the goo was all moving towards Herobrine, rising into the air and swirling around him; a tornado of sticky pink muck.

What is he doing? Dave wondered.

The villagers and pigmen armies all managed to escape into the city, the gates clanging shut behind them. Together they were a big army, but what use would they be against goo, Dave wondered.

"Come on, up to the top of the wall so we can see what's going on," Dave said to the others.

The majority of the army stayed down below, but Dave, Mayor Birchwood, Simon, Robo-Steve, Alex and Porkins all ran up the stairs to the top of the city wall.

In the field outside the city, the pink goo had all merged together into a giant blob. It was still swirling and slopping and looked like it was *transforming* into something.

"Herobrine's in the middle of that thing," said Dave.

The huge pink blob began to take form, rising up on two huge pink pillars.

Legs, Dave realized.

Next two huge goo pillars sprouted out of the side of it, then two gleaming white eyes appeared.

"It's a giant zombie pigman mush Herobrine!" gasped Porkins.

Porkins was right: the pink goo had taken the form of Herobrine. The giant pink Herobrine towered over the city, almost three times the height of the city walls. It looked down at them with its evil white eyes.

"Wow," said Alex. "This makes that wither we fought look like a pushover."

"That's it!" said Dave, suddenly getting a brainwave. "It's the only chance we have."

"What is it, Dave?" Robo-Steve asked.

"Mayor Birchwood," said Dave, "did you successfully evacuate the city?"

"Er, yes," said Mayor Birchwood.

"And do I have your permission to destroy the city?" asked Dave.

"What?!" said Mayor Birchwood. "No, of course you don't!"

"It might be the only way to defeat Herobrine," said Dave. "Herobrine can't go in the end portal as a giant gloop monster. If I wait by the end portal for him to come out of that thing, I can blow him to bits."

"Do you really think TNT can harm him though?" asked Simon. "I mean, he can summon lightning and turn himself into a giant gloop monster."

"And the chap survived a bath in lava," Porkins added. "He's a tough nut to crack, old boy."

"I'm not thinking of using TNT," said Dave. "I'm gonna use withers. When a wither spawns it creates an explosion, and I read in my old crafting book that the blast is almost twice as powerful as TNT. With enough withers all exploding at once, even Herobrine wouldn't be able to survive."

"So you lure Herobrine down to the end portal, create a load of withers and then blow him and the city to bits?" asked the mayor.

"That's right," said Dave.

"But what about you?" asked Porkins.

"I'll build a nether portal and escape into it before the withers explode," said Dave. "The rest of you can escape into the Nether beforehand."

"That plan is absolutely bonkers," said Porkins. "But it might just work."

"What do you think, Simon?" Mayor Birchwood asked. "Shall we destroy the city?"

"I don't think it would be great for your re-election chances," said Simon.

"Come on, Simon!" said Mayor Birchwood. "There must be a way you could spin it."

"Um, maybe.... *Mayor Birchwood: the mayor who destroyed the city to save the city*," suggested Simon.

"Simon, you genius, you've done it again!" said Mayor Birchwood.

"Ok," said Dave, "So everyone evacuate to the Nether now. I'll join you once I've set the withers off."

"Carl and some pigmen chaps are still guarding the end portal," said Porkins.

"I'll make sure they get out safely," said Dave.

"We'll come with you, Dave," said Alex.

"No," said Dave. "It's a dangerous plan and I'll be quicker if I'm doing it on my own. Now all of you, go!"

"Good luck, old bean," said Porkins.

The others left. Dave watched as they climbed down the stairs and told the villagers and pigmen below what the plan was. Then they all ran off towards the nearest nether portal. Porkins, Alex And Robo-Steve all gave Dave a wave and a "good luck!" before they disappeared down the street.

Dave stood alone on top of the city wall. He looked up and saw the giant pink Herobrine looking down on the city. Suddenly it began to move, each huge step shaking the ground. It stepped effortlessly over the city wall, then stood in the middle of the city, looking down.

Herobrine's trying to figure out where the end portal is, Dave thought to himself.

Then the giant goo Herobrine exploded. For one brief, happy moment Dave thought that it had been defeated somehow, but then he watched as the pink goo landed on the city, flowing down the streets and around the buildings. The goo wasn't flowing like water, it was moving in a deliberate way, as if it was being controlled.

Herobrine is using the goo to search the city, Dave realized. He had to act now.

Dave ran down the steps to get down from the wall, then he ran across the city towards the end portal dig site, weaving his way down the streets between the ruined buildings and avoiding the goo. When he got to the site the scaffolding was still in place; the ancient statue of Steve still standing.

He ran down the steps that had been built into the side of the pit. When he reached the bottom he ran through the torch-lit corridors until finally he reached the end portal room. It had been made much bigger since he'd last been down here, and there were diamond walls surrounding the portal, which had been broken in a few places.

He ran through one of the gaps in the wall. In the distance he could see the end portal, which was now surrounded by a three-block wide moat of lava. Sitting next to it were around ten pigmen, and a creeper wearing the body of a diamond golem.

"Dave?" The creeper said. "Is that you?"

"Hey, Carl," said Dave, running over. "I don't have much time to explain, but I'm going to blow up the city."

"Wow," said Carl, "for the first time in your life you've just said something cool."

CHAPTER SIXTEEN
Diamond City Falls

"Blow up the city?" asked one of the pigmen. "What are you talking about?"

Dave explained—as quickly as he could—about the giant goo Herobrine and his plan to defeat him by blowing him up with withers.

"You're crazy," said a pig-girl.

"Maybe," said Dave.

"He is crazy," said Carl, "but that doesn't mean his plan won't work. What do you need us to do, Dave?"

"I could do with your help building the wither t-shapes," said Dave, reaching into his bag and handing them all some soul sand. "Two blocks up, three across. Build as many as you can."

It took a bit of explaining, but soon the pigmen got what Dave meant, and set about building the t-shapes.

"Carl," said Dave, handing the creeper some of the tiny wither skeleton skulls he'd collected the last time they were in the Nether, "put two skulls on each t-shape—but only two! I'll add the third skulls when I'm ready to activate them."

"You got it," said Carl, taking the skulls.

Right, thought Dave, *now to build the Nether portal so we can escape.*

Suddenly he heard crashing and smashing in the city above, and the ground began to shake.

"Quickly!" he yelled to Carl and the pigmen. "Herobrine's doing something up there, and whatever it is, it won't be good!"

Dave reached into his bag, pulled out some obsidian blocks and started building a nether portal. But then, to his horror, he realized he didn't have enough blocks: he only had nine. Using dirt blocks for the corners, he had two obsidian blocks on the bottom and top, three blocks along the left side but only two along the right side: he was missing one block. He rummaged around in his bag, but couldn't find any more obsidian.

"Does anyone have any obsidian?" he yelled.

No-one did.

Oh no, thought Dave. *Oh no, oh no, oh no..."*

"What's wrong?" Carl asked.

"My plan was to activate the withers and then escape into the Nether," said Dave. "But I don't have enough obsidian to build a portal! I must have used up the last of my supply on the journey from Greenleaf to Diamond City."

There was more crashing and smashing up above.

"What now?" Carl asked.

"You and the pigmen need to get out of here," said Dave. "Find one of the nether portals in the city and make your escape. I'll stay here and activate the withers."

"Er, you do realize you'll only have ten seconds before each wither explodes?" said Carl. "You'll be blown to bits."

"I don't have any choice," said Dave. "This could be our only chance to defeat Herobrine. And even if it doesn't defeat him, it'll slow him down and let everyone escape. They've all evacuated to the Nether, and you and the pigmen need to do that too."

"Can't you just activate the withers and escape through the end portal?" asked Carl. "I mean, it's right there."

They both looked at the portal. As he stared at its ancient blocks, Dave was reminded of the dreams he'd been having.

"*Don't let him come here!*" the endermen in his dream had told him. "*Don't let him get the egg!*

"It's too risky," said Dave. "If I activate the portal and the withers don't destroy it, Herobrine could use it. I need to make sure it's destroyed."

Some sand blocks had been laid across the lava moat. Dave walked across them and went over to the end portal: the thing he'd been searching for for so long.

He pulled out his diamond pickaxe.

"It needs to be destroyed," said Dave sadly, and he smashed the pickaxe down: *ching, ching, CHING!*

One of the end blocks shattered. The end portal let out a faint ghostly *hiss.*

The portal's dead now, Dave knew.

Carl sighed.

"Dave," he said, "you once saved me from sacrificing myself like an idiot, back when I was going to fire myself out of a cannon at the Kraken. Do you really think I'm going to let *you* sacrifice yourself like an idiot?"

"But this isn't for nothing," said Dave. "Think of all the evil things Herobrine has done, and all the things he might go on to do. I can't throw away this chance to finally defeat him."

"Do you really believe that?" said Carl. "That this is worth sacrificing yourself for?"

"I do," said Dave.

"Ok," said Carl. "Dave, I know I talk a lot of rubbish, but I... you're my best friend. I want you to know that."

"Thanks Carl," said Dave, smiling. "Make sure you tell everyone... just tell them I care for them."

"You can tell them yourself," said Carl.

And then he punched Dave in the face, knocking him out cold.

*

When Dave awoke he was in the Nether. The pigmen who'd been with Carl were standing over him.

"What's going on?" said Dave groggily. "Where's Carl?"

The pigmen looked at each other awkwardly.

"Where's Carl?!" shouted Dave, sitting up.

"Carl told the pigmen to carry you here."

Dave turned around. It was Robo-Steve. He, the others and all the villagers and pigmen were there too, all gathered in the Nether. Everyone was there but Carl.

"No no no!" said Dave. "We can't let him do this! We have to go back and save him!"

Dave saw a nether portal nearby. He made a run for it, but Robo-Steve tackled him to the ground. He tried to struggle free but the robot was too strong.

"Let me go!" said Dave. "I have to save Carl! He's going to activate the withers!"

"You can't go back," said Robo-Steve. "That portal leads into the middle of the city—you'll get blown to bits. All the portals in this crater lead inside the city."

"Then I'll build one outside the crater," said Dave. "Give me all the obsidian you have—now!"

Robo-Steve handed over his obsidian, then Dave grabbed a horse from one of the villagers and rode as fast as he could across the crater. When he had gone far enough he quickly built a portal, lit it, and jumped through.

The portal brought him to a hillside. He could see Diamond City in the distance—and thankfully it wasn't destroyed yet.

"Thank goodness," said Dave.

Then KA-DOOOOOOOOOOM! The city exploded. The force from the blast sent Dave flying backwards, rolling across the ground. When he lifted his head to look up, Diamond City was no more.

CHAPTER SEVENTEEN
The Lord of the Void

"Carl!" Dave yelled. "Caaaarl!"

He began to run towards the city, but something grabbed him and held him back. He looked around and saw it was Porkins and Robo-Steve, both of them holding one of his arms. They and all the others, all the villagers and pigmen, had followed him out of the portal.

"He's gone," Porkins said to Dave. The pigman has tears in his eyes. "But the dear chap saved us. He saved us all."

Where Diamond City has stood was a huge crater. There were a few lumps of ruined diamond buildings scattered about, but other than that there was no sign that a city had ever been there.

"I should have been the one to do it," said Dave sadly, falling to his knees. "It was my stupid plan."

"It wasn't a stupid plan," said Robo-Steve kindly. "It worked. Herobrine was defeated."

There were a few more explosions from the ruins, then the withers rose up into the air, floating eerily above the dead city.

"We should go before those withers spot us," said Robo-Steve.

But no-one seemed to hear him. The villagers from Diamond City were all looking on in despair at the place that had once been their home.

"What now?" one of them said. "Where will we go now?"

"We'll build a new city," Mayor Birchwood said. "One even bigger and grander than before. Obviously we'll have to use a few less diamonds though."

"At least Herobrine was defeated, I guess," said Simon.

"I'm not so sure about that," said Mayor Birchwood, pointing. "Look!"

Walking away from the burning crater was a solitary figure: a man in a blue t-shirt and pants with glowing white eyes.

"How?" exclaimed Porkins. "That blighter can't be killed!"

"Well I'm gonna kill him!" yelled Dave, pulling out his sword.

"Dave, he survived ten wither spawn explosions at once," said Robo-Steve. "Maybe Porkins is right—he can't be slain. We all need to get out of here."

"We blew up his house, we chopped off his head, but the big bedrock monster just wouldn't stay dead."

Everyone looked round. Alex was grinning.

"I think I know how we can defeat him," she said.

*

Herobrine was going to kill Dave last.

He was going to slay the villagers first, then the pigmen, and then, one by one, he was going to finish off Dave's friends. Then, and only then, he was going to kill Dave—once the villager had watched everyone he loved get destroyed.

Making Dave suffer was a small consolation for losing the portal, but it would make Herobrine feel a bit better at least. He knew he should really leave Dave alive so he could reveal his method for finding end portals, but Herobrine was too angry. He wanted Dave dead.

As he walked towards the villager and pigman army, Herobrine was surprised to see Dave walking towards him, sword in hand.

The fool is actually going to try and fight me, thought Herobrine. He smiled; this was going to be fun.

"So," said Herobrine to Dave, as they came face to face with each other. "You wish to fight me."

"No," said Dave. And then, to Herobrine's surprise, the idiot villager started to grin.

"Then you wish to plead for your life?" asked Herobrine. "Or the lives of your friends? I'm afraid neither will do you any good. I'm going to kill them all. And I will continue my search for an end portal. I thought they'd all been destroyed but you've shown me that that isn't the case. I will find another one, and then I will destroy this world, leaving nothing but the void. Now, what is it you wish to do with that weapon?"

"Oh this?" said Dave, looking at his diamond sword. "I'm not going to use this. I'm just here to distract you."

Suddenly Herobrine felt something smash against the side of his face, a sticky liquid covering his cheek.

A splash potion, he realized.

He tried to raise his arms to use some magic but they were moving slower than usual. Another potion hit him, and another, and he could barely move at all.

Splash potion of slowness!" he heard a girl say. "Booya!"

A girl with a red hair, a golden robot and Dave's pigman friend had appeared in front of him, standing next to Dave.

They were using invisibility potion, Herobrine realized, *that's how they snuck up to me.* It was of no matter though: the fools would be dead in seconds. He concentrated hard, summoning lightning down from the sky.

KRAKOOM! KRAKOOM! KRAKOOM! KRAKOOM!

Four blasts of lightning blasted into the ground in a flash of white light. When the light faded, Dave and his three friends were gone.

Too easy, thought Herobrine.

"Nice try," he heard the girl say. Then *zip zip zip zip,* Dave and his three friends reappeared in front of him.

"Potion of swiftness," said the girl, grinning. "It makes us run really fast. It's pretty awesome."

"You fools really think you can defeat me with *potions?*" Herobrine growled, feeling the anger growing inside of him.

"I don't know," said Dave, "but it's worth a try. Everyone, throw your potions!"

Herobrine felt bottle after bottle smash into him as Dave and his foolish friends pelted him with splash potions.

What's happening to me? thought Herobrine desperately. *I feel... weak.* He knew that potions worked on him, but it had been years—*centuries*—since anyone had used them on him. He'd kept himself away from battle for so long, hidden behind his witches and his armies. *I let myself become weak and foolish,* he thought bitterly.

SPLASH SPLASH SPLASH!

More potions splashed into him. Herobrine felt his eyelids

start to droop.

"No!" he hissed. "I am Herobrine, Lord of the Void! You cannot defeat me!"

*

Dave took another slowness potion from Alex's bag. Herobrine was on his hands and knees now, looking weak; but there was still fury in his eyes.

"No," Herobrine hissed. "I am Herobrine, Lord of the Void! You cannot defeat me!"

"It looks like we can," said Dave, throwing his potion. The potion splashed into Herobrine's face. Herobrine opened his mouth to say something, but then he collapsed.

Herobrine was defeated.

"Is he... you know?" asked Porkins.

"No," said Robo-Steve. "He's still breathing."

"What do we do with him?" asked Alex.

"I guess we can't keep hitting with splash potions forever," said Porkins.

"No," said Robo-Steve, "that's *exactly* what we do. In a manner of speaking."

*

It didn't take the villagers long to build a tank made from glass blocks. Then they filled it full of potion of slowness and dropped Herobrine inside.

Herobrine floated eerily in the blue-gray liquid; asleep but still alive.

"Are you sure you're alright to keep him here?" Dave asked Mayor Birchwood.

"Well, it's better to have him somewhere we can keep an eye on him," said the mayor. "We'll build our new city around him. His tank can be an ornament—like a very weird fish tank."

"Mr Mayor, we've taken some prisoners," said a villager in diamond armor.

Two other villagers in armor led forward the prisoners. There were two of Herobrine's witches and a villager who Dave recognised all too well.

"Adam," said Dave angrily. "Give me one reason why I shouldn't throw you into that tank with your master. This is all your doing."

"Adam, how could you?"

It was Sally. She walked over to them with tears in her eyes.

"Sally..." said Adam. "Everything I did, I did for you."

"Don't you dare," snapped Sally. "Don't you dare use me as an excuse for your crimes! You're nothing but a coward and a villain."

Adam couldn't even look his wife in the eye, he just looked down at his feet.

"Where's Professor Quigley?" Dave asked Adam. "And Steve?"

"Why would I tell you?"snarled Adam. "You've ruined my life and turned my wife against me."

"You did that yourself, Adam," said Sally. "You can't undo the crimes you've done, but at least help Dave to find his friends."

"Fine," said Adam. "But this is for you, not for him."

CHAPTER EIGHTEEN
The Rescue

The witches gave up Herobrine's nether castle without a fight.

"We surrender!" they said, coming out with their hands in the air.

Adam had led Dave, Sally, Robo-Steve, Porkins and Alex through the Nether to the castle. They'd all worn armor in case there was a battle.

"Aw man, I was hoping they'd give us a fight," said Alex.

"Robo-Steve and Alex, stay out here and guard the prisoners," said Dave. "The rest of us will go in and rescue the professor and Steve."

He turned to Adam.

"If this is a trick..." Dave said.

"It's not!" said Adam.

"I know he's done bad things, Dave, but I don't think he'd lie to me," said Sally sadly.

"You'd better not be," Dave said to Adam. "I've already lost one of my best friends today, so I'm not in the best mood."

Everything had happened so fast since Diamond City blew up that Dave had barely had a moment to think about Carl. But suddenly he thought of the creeper and a wave of intense sadness washed over him.

I can't believe he's gone, Dave thought. *I can't believe I'll never see him again.*

The pain was worse than any injury Dave had ever received. It hurt so much that it was all he could do to stay standing, but he knew that he had to stay strong. They still had to save the professor and Steve.

"Lead the way," he said to Adam.

505

Adam led them down to some dungeons. In the first cell they found Steve. He was asleep on the floor with a modified iron helmet on his head. There were lights flashing on it.

"They gave him that helmet to stop him waking up and breaking out," said Adam.

Dave carefully took off the helmet, and immediately Steve woke up.

"Dan!" Steve said happily. "Dan the villager! How you doing buddy?"

Porkins led Steve out of the castle as Dave, Adam and Sally continued through the dungeon. All the other cells were empty, apart from one at the end. Dave looked through the cell door window and saw a woman with gray hair lying on the floor.

"Professor Quigley?" he said.

The woman turned around, squinting.

"Dave?" she said. "Is it really you?"

"It is," said Dave, smiling. "We're here to rescue you."

*

They brought Steve, Professor Quigley and the witches they'd taken prisoner back to Diamond City. By the time they got there the villagers had already started to build new houses out of wood and stone.

"We thought there was no point delaying the building of the new city," Mayor Birchwood told Dave. "Simon came up with a slogan for my next election campaign: *Mayor Birchwood—the man who rebuilt Diamond City.*"

"I like it," said Dave.

"Also," said Mayor Birchwood, "you'll never guess what we found."

He pointed and Dave was amazed to see a red robot walking towards them.

"Spidroth!" said Porkins.

"No," said the robot, "not anymore."

"Wait," said Robo-Steve, "Charles? Is that you?"

"It is," said the robot. "I think Spidroth was pushed out of me by the shock of the impact when she fell and hit the ground. She's gone."

Robo-Steve stepped forward and gave Charles a hug.

"What are you doing?" said Charles. "This is highly illogical."

"Dave," said Professor Quigley quietly, "can I have a word?"

Dave went with Professor Quigley to a little grove in the middle of some trees. The professor sat down on a stump.

"How are you doing, Professor?" Dave asked.

"I... I'll be fine," said Professor Quigley. She seemed a shadow of her former self, Dave thought. The time she'd spent in Herobrine's dungeon had really affected her. "There's... there's something I wanted to give you back."

She reached into her pocket and pulled out a purple pearl.

"While I was alone in my cell I had a lot of time to think," she said, "and I think with some redstone I'll be able to get this working. It'll only be able to give you two trips though, I think—the trip there and the trip back. After that it'll probably break."

"What... What are you talking about?" said Dave.

"I've done what you asked me to do," she said, smiling. "I've modified the pearl so it can travel through time. I heard about what happened to Carl. You can save him!"

CHAPTER NINETEEN
The Pearl

"Are you sure about this, old bean?" said Porkins.

Dave and Porkins were standing next to the crater that had once been Diamond City. Porkins was the only one who Dave had told about the time travel pearl. Porkins had known Carl as long as Dave had, so Dave thought the pigman should have a say about what they should do. Also, as much as Dave liked Robo-Steve, Dave knew the robot would have a million reasons why going back in time was illogical or dangerous.

"I've been given this second chance to save him," said Dave. "Carl would do the same for me."

"How does it work then?" Porkins asked. "That time travel thingie."

"Well according to Professor Quigley all I have to do is press the button and think about when in time I want to travel to," said Dave. "Then I have to do the same when I want to travel back."

"Fair enough," said Porkins. "Are you sure I can't come with you?"

"Professor Quigley says the pearl only has enough energy to take two people at a time" said Dave. "So it'll only have enough energy to bring me and Carl back."

"Well, good luck, I guess," said Porkins. "Bring our chap back safely. And yourself."

"I will," said Dave. "But in case anything does happen to me, I just want you to know that you and Carl are my best friends. Meeting the two of you changed my life."

"Oh, you're going to make me start crying," smiled Porkins, and he gave Dave a hug.

When they'd finished hugging, Dave took the purple time

travel pearl from his pocket. The same pearl that Ripley had put inside Robo-Steve's chest; the same pearl that Future Dave has used to travel through time.

"Well, see you when I get back I guess," said Dave.

Just then he noticed something in the crater: among the few scraps of buildings that had survived was the statue of Steve. It was badly damaged, but most of it was still in one piece.

Wow, they really built that statue to last, thought Dave. *It was there before Diamond City was built, and it's still mostly there after it's been destroyed.*

"Ok," said Dave to Porkins. "Here goes."

And he pressed the button.

There was a swirl of purple light, then Dave found himself in the middle of a huge plains biome. There were a few trees and flowers scattered about, but no sign of Diamond City.

Had the pearl teleported him somewhere else rather than back in time? Maybe Professor Quigley hadn't fixed it as well as she'd thought she had.

Right, well I'd better figure out where I am and get back to Diamond City, thought Dave to himself.

"HIIIISSSS!!!!!"

Dave turned and saw two creepers slithering towards him. He quickly reached for his sword, but fumbled and dropped it on the ground.

The creepers began to flash white. Dave closed his eyes, preparing for the worst and hoping his diamond armor would save him.

Thunk thunk!

Dave opened his eyes. Two arrows had hit the creepers. They fell over and then *poof poof,* they were gone.

An armored man on horseback rode over to Dave, clutching a bow. Both the man and his horse were clad in diamond armor.

"Well met," said the stranger on horseback. Dave couldn't make out the man's face, but his voice sounded familiar.

"Thanks for saving me," said Dave. "Sorry, do I know you? I think I recognize your voice."

"Maybe," said the man. "I do travel around a lot."

The man took off his helmet.

It can't be, thought Dave.

"Pleased to meet you, stranger" said the man. "My name is Steve."

EPILOGUE

Finkus had been farming potatoes his entire life. His grandfather had been a potato farmer, his father had been a potato farmer, and if Finkus ever had a son, he would be a potato farmer too.

It had been a long day out in the fields and Finkus was heading back with a wheelbarrow full of potatoes when he bumped into old Mrs Boggins heading the other way. Finkus's heart fell: all he wanted to do was get home and climb into his nice warm bed, but he knew Mrs Boggins would want to talk. She was known throughout the village as the *Gossip Queen*, and she never missed the chance to share the latest rumors.

"Hello, Mrs Boggins," said Finkus.

"Hello Finkus," said Mrs Boggins. "Have you heard the news? Diamond City was destroyed! Apparently there was a huge battle and it ended with an explosion taking out the whole city."

"Oh really," said Finkus. "How unfortunate."

Finkus didn't believe a word of it. The other thing about Mrs Boggins was that she was always exaggerating and making stuff up.

Finkus brought his wheelbarrow full of potatoes back to his farm and opened his shed. The shed was full of potatoes, all waiting to be brought to market at the end of the week. He was about to dump the potatoes in his wheelbarrow onto the pile, when he heard a *voice* from somewhere inside the shed.

"Where am I?" said the voice. "Fool, I demand you tell me where I am!"

"Um, you're in my shed," said Finkus.

"And what form have I taken?"

"Um, I don't understand the question," said Finkus.

"FOOL!" said the voice. "The shock from my fall must have forced my soul from that idiot robot's body, but it seems that I

ve found a new vessel. So tell me, you small-minded peasant,
hat is this body I'm in?"

Finkus kneeled down. With a jolt of shock he realized where
the voice was coming from.

"Speak fool!" said the voice. "What body has been blessed with
he soul of Lady Spidroth? And why can't I move?"

"Um, I don't know how to say this," said Finkus. "But you're…
you're a potato."

TO BE CONTINUED…

Thanks for Reading!

Thank you so much for reading this book. I hope you enjoyed it!

Want to get three *Dave the Villager* books for free? If you sign up to the Dave the Villager monthly newsletter, you get access to these newsletter-excusive ebooks:

- *Porkins: Return from the Nether*
- *The Last Pig Girl*
- *Future Dave: Future Imperfect*

More info at: **davethevillager.com**

Printed in Great Britain
by Amazon

78268636R10292